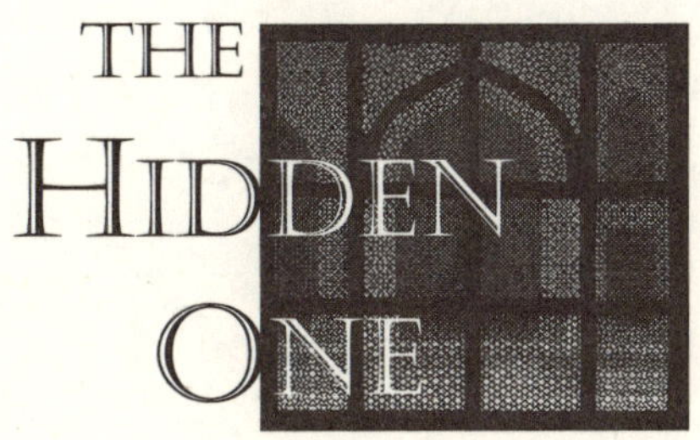
THE
HIDDEN
ONE

# The Hidden One

## The Untold Story Of Aurengzeb's Daughter

RUCHIR GUPTA

PLATINUM PRESS

ISBN 978-93-52011-40-7

Cover design: Nelson Lopes, Kitsune & Khan Bahadur M.S. Commissariat
Layout: Hitanshi Shah
Printing: Thomson Press

Published in 2019 by
PLATINUM PRESS
*An imprint of*
LEADSTART PUBLISHING PVT LTD
Unit 25/26, Building A/1, Wadala (East),
Mumbai 400037, Maharashtra, INDIA
**T** +91 96 99933000 **E** info@leadstartcorp.com
**W** www.leadstartcorp.com

To my three wonderful children,
Hema, Ishaan, and aarav

## ABOUT THE AUTHOR

RUCHIR GUPTA, a graduate of Upstate Medical University, USA, currently lives in Long Island NY, with his wife and three children. His interests include reading, blogging, travelling and history.

His debut novel, *Mistress of the Throne,* sold thousands of copies worldwide. *The Hidden One* is the second title in the same series: *The Mughal Intrigues.*

Ruchir can be reached at themughalintrigues@gmail.com

# Contents

# Preface

There was no plan to write a sequel to *Mistress of the Throne,* which focused on Jahanara, a Mughal Princess, as its inspiration. However, the emails I received from individuals across the world commending me on the book and asking for a 'second edition' were truly overwhelming. My mind immediately wandered to a little known nugget in the history of the time – the Makhfi. Though there is a transient mention of the Makhfi in *Mistress of the Throne,* I had no plan at the time of writing, to construct an entire book around this secret society. Immediately, I began researching this secret poetic society and its founder – Zebunissa. Using information from Mughal sources as well as the writings of European travellers of the era, Zebunissa's life began to come into clearer focus – the fact that she was her father's most beloved child; that it was she who decided to form the secret society; that her original suitor, Sulaimon, was executed; and that she herself was ultimately imprisoned.

*The Hidden One* is a work of fiction, but the story is based on historical facts. Unlike the story of Jahanara, for which there were ample sources available, it appeared that history had relegated Zebunissa to a minor footnote; to lie buried in the dust of those turbulent times when the Mughal Empire was in its heyday. Yet the concept of a Muslim Queen, the daughter of a sitting Emperor, personally supporting her brother's coup against her father seemed like a story worth telling.

The research seemed to point to two separate but parallel events in Zebunissa's life – the formation and functioning of her secret poetic society and her support of Akbar's rebellion. It was at this point that I decided to use poetic license and merge the two to show the secret society was in fact formed for the purpose of fomenting rebellion – a concept for which there is no factual basis. That is not to say it was not indeed the case, but there is no clear evidence to support it.

As with my first book, I tried to stay as close to the historical record as possible. However, since there was so little recorded information on Zebunissa, there was also ample room for creativity.

I used actual poems from Zebunissa's writings to support the events of the time. Again, it is unclear if her writings were influenced even in part by political events. But it would be wrong to write a book about the Makhfi without any mention of the actual writings they composed. Thus I have inserted a couplet or two at the beginning of every chapter to support the events in that chapter. In doing this, my hope is the reader will appreciate the beautiful work of Zebunissa herself. Ultimately, that is what she herself would have wanted most.

## Cast of Primary Characters

* denotes fictional character

Farouk Malik: Prince of Persia

Aurengzeb: Emperor of India

Nawab Bai: Wife of Aurengzeb and mother of Sultan, Muazzam and Badrunissa

Dilras: Wife of Aurengzeb and mother of Zebunissa

Sultan: Eldest son of Aurengzeb

Muazzam: Second son of Aurengzeb

Azam: Third son of Aurengzeb

Akbar: Fourth son of Aurengzeb

Zebunissa: Eldest daughter of Aurengzeb

Zinat: Second daughter of Aurengzeb

Badrunissa: Third daughter of Aurengzeb

Zubdat: Fourth daughter of Aurengzeb

Mihirunissa: Fifth daughter of Aurengzeb

Dara: Eldest brother of Aurengzeb

Jahanara: Eldest sister of Aurengzeb

Raushanara: Younger sister of Aurengzeb

Sulaimon: Son of Prince Dara

Jani: Daughter of Prince Dara

Zafar Khan*: Prime Minister of India

Aqil Khan: Advisor to Aurengzeb

Didar*: Zebunissa's eunuch

# MUGHAL FAMILY TREE

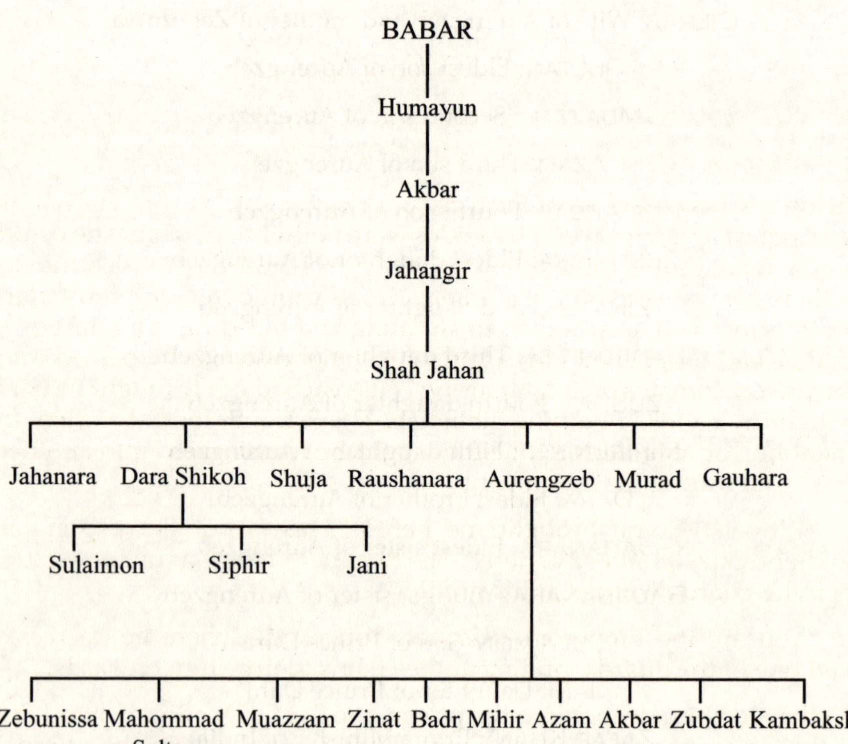

# PART I

## 1
## Her Father's Daughter

*When I behold the garden in the spring,*
*Rejoicing like a nightingale I sing.*

4 February 1659

Heavy chains crisscrossed the torso of Prisoner 721, binding his hands to his chest as if in prayer. His ankles were bound so close that he could barely manage to shuffle forward. Two prison guards prodded him to walk faster, causing him to stumble. Broad shouldered and muscular, the prisoner was accustomed to sweating and bleeding; a lifetime as a soldier had toughened him against most elements. As he passed into the prison, inmates of neighbouring cells reached out through the bars with filthy hands, mouthing gibberish. The Prisoner looked at them in silent horror, wondering if he too would be transformed into another poor soul during his internment.

"Why have you brought me here? This is not the prison for soldiers. Only lunatics live here!" The Prisoner's tone was unapologetic, as if the guards worked at his privilege.

"You are the Emperor's prisoner. You reside where he decrees," said one of the guards, pulling at the chains to urge him onwards.

As they led him deeper into the prison, the light grew dimmer and the hallways more narrow and damp. Wherever light from the guards' flaming torches fell, spiders and rats could be seen scampering into the darkness. But Prisoner 721 would not be shaken. Even though the airlessness and damp odour began to suffocate him, he refused to display distress. His stoic face belied his inner agony as he marched deeper into the abyss.

"Wait here," instructed one of the guards, continuing down the passageway. The Prisoner stood still, awaiting his destiny. As the moments passed, he felt something crawling up his leg but refused to allow himself to be affected; he would not offer such satisfaction to the solitary guard watching him.

The guard eventually returned, calling out, "Come, let's go!" Grabbing the Prisoner's elbows, the two guards escorted him further down the dark passage. A loud screech pierced the air as one of the guards kicked open a door. The Prisoner knew the cell was meant for him. The guards pushed him in causing him to fall face down onto the damp, uneven ground. Turning him onto his back, they undid his chains. There was nowhere to run.

The Prisoner examined his dwelling closely: The ceiling was of stone, with some marks, memorials of previous inhabitants no doubt. The side walls were coarser. In the corner, there was a small two-foot wide and one-foot high window, barred with metal rails. He quickly concluded that any attempt of escape from this small opening would be futile. All this aperture would provide him with is help in determining the time of day, the weather and offer some miniscule amount of fresh air, he reckoned. He would sustain himself on that much until help arrived. Closing his eyes the prisoner began murmuring to himself: *There is no God but God and Allah is his name. There is no God but God and Allah is his name. There is no God but God and Allah is his name.*

***

Saturday through Thursday, they hummed to break the monotony of their existence. On Friday, they paused for prayer. Zebunissa squinted her eyes in distress at her sisters' off-note humming. "No…no…stop!"

Her sister, Badrunissa, raised her eyebrows in bewilderment. "But this is what you taught me."

Zebunissa shook her head. "No, I most certainly did not. Try again, this time with a deeper tone at the end."

Again the sisters began their tune and again, Zebunissa interrupted the vocal symphony. "Stop!" she yelled as she looked at her other sister, Zubdat. "You must harmonize your voice to mine because your voice is higher pitched!"

Zebunissa's instructions were rarely, if ever, ignored by her four younger sisters, who respected her more than anyone in the harem, even their own mothers. There was wise Zubdat, innocent Mihir, provocative Badr, and spinster Zinat. She would go to Zubdat for advice, Mihir for comfort, Badr for entertainment, and Zinat for harem gossip. However, on this day, her sisters' humming was annoying her. Zebunissa was a perfectionist in all she did and her sisters' imperfect skills were always a source of frustration for her. The ladies continued to sit and hum, wearing long dark burqas with thin veils over their faces barely allowing them to discern each other's facial expressions.

Though their father, Mughal Emperor Aurengzeb, had forbade the practice of music and the arts, Zebunissa had succeeded in convincing her sisters that humming a tune was different from playing an instrument like the sitar, and so, was technically allowed.

"Zebo, we must be quieter now. I fear Samsher Khan will hear us." Samsher Khan was the chief eunuch of Zebunissa's stepmother, Nawab Bai. Though assigned to represent Nawab Bai to the outside world, Samsher instead became Aurengzeb's spy inside the harem. Zebunissa would not relent. "Worry not about Samsher!" she said. "I am your King and Queen right now! This is my harem and you will do as I say!"

"She may be her mother's daughter, but she has her father's temper," Zubdat whispered to the concubine seated next to her. Zebunissa had good reason to feel emboldened. Her father had just won the war of succession to become the next Mughal Emperor of India, defeating all three of his brothers in battle. With the war over, she knew she would soon marry her fiancé and true love, Sulaimon. The married daughter of a sitting Emperor could wield extraordinary power and she was already making plans for how she would exercise hers.

"Perfect! The symphony sounds wonderful! Tomorrow we will take a break from this and do our Friday prayers instead. But I want you all to practice your humming in your private quarters. And no humming in the mosque! Those backward *mullahs* will stop at nothing to get us in trouble!"

Zebunissa heard her sister, Zubdat, whisper to a concubine, "God help us. First, we feared father, then the *mullahs,* and now her. It seems there is not a question of whether we will be in trouble but rather with whom." Zebunissa grinned.

A few moments later, a thin emaciated figure walked into the room. "Why are you girls sitting here?" The maidens instantly recognized the broken and saddened voice of Nawab Bai.

Zebunissa sat up. "Uh...Ami, we are just reciting the Koran." She looked at her sisters for acquiescence. "Right?" The women hesitated to respond. "Right?" she repeated. They finally succumbed to her instigation, "Yes, yes, the Koran!" Zebunissa looked annoyed at the initial hesitation, but redoubled her own efforts to convince her stepmother. "We are preparing for tomorrow's prayer service."

Nawab Bai smiled. "You girls are so wonderful. Your father would be proud. Make sure to pack your belongings. We leave next week for Delhi for your father's coronation." Nawab Bai did not bother to look at the musical notes written on the papers that the harem women were holding, choosing to be oblivious to what was truly happening in her harem without her knowledge.

Zebunissa stared at the limping silhouette of her emaciated stepmother as she entered the passageway into her chambers. Of course, all of the harem women knew the cause of the limp: her mother had been beaten with a mace by her father when she gave birth to a daughter rather than a son. Nawab Bai had spent several months in bed recovering from her injuries, but developed a well-defined limp in her right leg for the rest of her life.

"They say she used to look just like me when she was my age," Zebunissa's step sister, Mihirunissa, remarked. "Father did this to her. I wonder if one day I too, will walk with a limp."

"I will never let that happen!" Zebunissa shot back. "If anyone ever touches any of my sisters, I will rip their testicles out and make them wear it around their necks and beg you for mercy!" The maidens erupted in laughter. Zebunissa, meanwhile, continued to remain livid, knowing that her comment was not made in levity but in earnest. Nothing Zebunissa ever said was mild. Equally ferocious in hatred as she was passionate in love, the other harem women vacillated in humor and admiration at her emotions.

Mihirunissa, a child of only twelve years of age, chuckled. "I feel sorry for Sulaimon already!"

Zebunissa began to blush. "Sulaimon knows not to cross me." She grinned. "Sulaimon knows how to please me. Sulaimon is perfect."

"Zebo," Zubdat interjected, "you are fortunate that you were engaged before Aba became Emperor, otherwise you would have had to spend your days alone, like aunt Jahanara." Zebunissa's heart sank. As the daughter of a sitting Emperor, her beloved Aunt Jahanara was not allowed to marry. Aurengzeb had been a Prince at the time of Zebunissa's engagement, so the rules did not apply.

"Zebo!" exclaimed Mihirunissa. "You don't think Aba will cancel your engagement and force you to live alone now that he is Emperor, do you?" Mihirunissa was markedly worried in her expression.

"Nonsense, little girl," Zebunissa said confidently. "Aba loves me. He promised that I will be wed to Sulaimon before he set out for Delhi. I have faith in his words."

The following morning, at sunrise, Zebunissa watched a long line of imperial servants load the elephants and caravans with the harem possessions. The burgundy robes of the servants glistened bright red in the early morning rays. From atop her palace, they appeared like a row of red ants. And like ants they moved purposefully, as a unit, slowly emptying the palace and securing as much atop the massive beasts as could be safely permitted.

Months had passed since her father had emerged victorious on the battlefield against his brothers, each contesting the throne of India. While he had already coronated himself in a hastily arranged ceremony attended by just his generals, the real coronation with all its pomp and splendour had yet to take place. To witness this event, the entire harem was to travel north to Delhi, to their new home – the Red Fort. The harem was guarded by a hierarchy of guards. First were the female slaves, then the eunuchs, who acted as messengers for the harem ladies to the outside world, and then the Tatar guards, strong burly women with gigantic arms, whose gargantuan size dwarfed the mightiest soldiers in the Mughal army. Men were strictly forbidden in the harem unless the Emperor himself made an exception, which he had for Aqil Khan.

"How is it possible for Aqil Khan to travel with us?" Zebunissa asked, disgusted at the mere notion of a man accompanying the harem on their journey to Agra.

"Your father has specifically entrusted the safety of you girls to Aqil Khan. He is to bring you to Agra for the coronation, safe and secure," Samsher Khan replied.

"Safe and secure?" Zebunissa protested. "What are we, milk drinking babies who need a man to supervise us?"

"Oh Zebo," Zinat, the spinster sister, interjected. "What does it matter? So what if we have a male escort with us during our journey? I'm tired of being here with nothing but these eunuchs and Tatar guards to look at." Zinat fanned herself with her palm as the entire harem stood, heavily veiled, in the open, sun blazing above.

"And it is not just any man," Badrunissa added, raising her draped arms in the air, exposing the damp muslin clinging to her underarms. Badrunissa had the distinction of being the most flamboyant of the sisters. Harem rumours whispered she had the same voracious sexual appetite as a man and that she engaged in promiscuous behaviour with any male escort she encountered. While Zebunissa squinted in disgust, Badrunissa continued unabashed, "It is Aqil Khan! The most handsome debonair Persian man I have ever seen! Just imagine him on horseback." Badrunissa gasped theatrically, tugging at her veil, almost tearing it off. "The hot steamy weather causing his strong, muscular body to gleam with sweat and perspiration to roll down his beautifully angled face!"

Zebunissa became enraged by the violation of harem rules. She glared at Badrunissa in disgust. Her sister's lewd gestures and provocative language about their escort disturbed her sense of propriety. Did Badrunissa forget she was the daughter of the Emperor?

Badrunissa, ignoring her sister, said, "It has been so tough lately in this terrible heat that even the Tatar women are beginning to look good!" The harem women chuckled as the hot sun scorched down on them, but Zebunissa was not amused.

Young Zinat, taking her que from her sister, clapped her hands together. "I get wet when I see the new Tatar from Uzbekistan, *Hira, oh Hira…break away your chains…*" The women's laughter grew louder while the servants continued to load supplies, seemingly oblivious to the lurid conversation of the harem women. Zebunissa noticed their step-mother, Nawab Bai, look away, embarrassed by the spectacle.

*"Oh, Hira/"* Badrunissa intoned, *"Break away your chains/ Put to rest my pains/ Visit me at night/ I have you in my sight/ Wear your tightest kurta set/ The thought of you makes me wet!"*

While the women applauded boisterously, Zebunissa, her eyes in slits, walked over to Badrunissa and slapped her viscously across the face. There was immediate silence. Badrunissa began to weep while the other women stood around, frozen.

"Zebo!" Nawab Bai exclaimed, "That is your sister. You have no right to raise your hand against her!"

Zebunissa looked at Nawab Bai, "See how she is misusing the poetic skills I taught her!" she protested.

"You did not teach your sister poetry, Zebunissa, Aqil Khan did. Never forget that you, too, can recite verses today because Aqil Khan taught you how to! Your father trusts him to watch over you more than any other man."

Still enraged, Zebunissa continued to stare at her loudly weeping sister. "Tell her she must apologize to Aqil Khan, then!" she declared imperiously.

***

Later that day, Zebunissa looked for Badrunissa as the women mounted their respective elephants for their journey to Delhi. From a distance she noticed Aqil Khan, the debonair, middle-aged heart-throb of the harem, though old enough to be her father. Lustful gazes followed his every move. As always, he looked handsome this morning, his long wavy hair oiled until it glistened back in the sun; his small moustache and thin beard perfectly trimmed; his skin clear and fair. She saw Badrunissa, heavily draped in a veil, being escorted by Nawab Bai's eunuch to Aqil Khan. Zebunissa could not hear what was being said, but saw a smile flash across Aqil Khan's handsome face as he held Badrunissa's covered head and kissed her forehead.

'Bastard!' Zebunissa thought to herself. 'He could have scolded her at least!' But Aqil Khan was already walking over to Zebunissa's elephant. He asked her eunuch, Didar, for audience with her. Zebunissa knew not what to make of this. What did he want and why had he chosen such a public place to address her?

"You have no right to slap your sister!" Aqil Khan's voice rang out loud and clear, heard by all.

Shocked at being thus publicly scolded, Zebunissa said angrily, "But she misused the poetry you taught us."

"Silence! You have no right to hit anyone! I had better not hear of any more such mischief from you during this journey, for I take the place of your father on this trip."

With that Aqil walked off towards his horse, but Zebunissa yelled after him, "You are not my father!"

Aqil Khan, enraged at first, began to laugh. He knew Zebunissa always had to have the last word.

***

The imperial procession paused at a lakeside on their journey to the capital. Zebunissa took in the undulating landscape, knowing it was soon to be transformed into a beautiful metropolis. The Mughal soldiers hurriedly created a vast platform and covered it with cloth. Sounds of mid-level supervisors yelling instructions to the labourers permeated the air as Zebunissa looked on, keenly cognizant of what was occurring before her. Before long she saw a dozen labourers hoisting a turquoise cloth edifice into the sky as if the ground below had ordered its erection. She knew this would be the harem quarters. Immediately thereafter, multiple other tents began taking shape throughout the vast area. She knew the smaller ones were for the soldiers, while the medium-sized ones would be for the imperial cooks and their supplies. As the tents were raised, narrow alleys and broad avenues began to appear in a gridlike pattern. Soon, the children of the cooks and soldiers began playing in the alleys, bringing the artificial city alive with their laughter. The Mughal lion flag was hoisted on top of the tents, demonstrating to any passerby that this was now a Mughal city.

Zebunissa noticed her belongings, along with those of her four sisters, being unloaded and taken to the tents. Zebunissa fell asleep as soon as she entered her tented home, even though the sun still shone. She knew she would need to conserve her energy for she had called for a night meeting of her secret poetic society. She dozed off into dream filled slumber. The windows of her tent were lined with *tattis,* scented kass grass, used to create screens to keep out the unforgiving rays of the sun. The maids had poured scented water on the screens to fill the space with a sweet aroma and obliterate the stench of dung from the nearby wildlife. Briefly, Zebunissa opened her eyes but soon realized she was in a tent. She felt unable to rise from her bed, such was her exhaustion. Her desire to end her nap grew but she remained on her bed, as if chained to it.

Eventually, the loud sounds of soldiers unloading trunks and supplies outside startled her awake and she sat up with a jerk. She peeked out of the tent at the sun to determine the time of day; it was early afternoon. "Didar!" she called, beckoning her eunuch. She inquired if her four sisters, wise Zubdat, promiscuous Badr, spinster Zinat and innocent Mihirunissa, had received official word of the meeting later that evening. When he told her he had delivered the messages himself, she nodded. Delicately she opened the trunk labelled 'Prayer items. Handle gently.' Carefully, she took out the elegantly embroidered *Koran,* in Persian, that her father had given her. Then she took out the prayer rug on which she kneeled to pray. Then out came a small box. Prying it open, she removed her *cholis* (brazier). What remained was a large bottle of dark red wine. Holding it up she grinned, murmuring, "We will open you tonight."

Meanwhile, Zubdat, Badr, Zinat and Mihir had gathered at Zubdat's tent to ready themselves for the festivities that night. Badr lay on Zubdat's divan as a slave girl massaged scented oil into her slightly plump, olive skinned, barely clad body.

"Must you do this in front of us?" asked Zubdat, annoyed.

"Why not?" responded Badr. "We are sisters are we not? We have all seen each other naked many times."

"As children," Zinat reminded her. "Do you really feel no shame in lying almost naked in front of others?"

"You girls need to surrender your shame and be open with your sexuality."

"Just do not do it around Zebunissa; she does not approve of your flamboyance," young Mihir admonished.

"What nonsense!" retorted Badr. "Zebunissa is more flamboyant than me, I bet! See the way she looks at Aqil Khan!"

"No, she does not," responded Zubdat as she sat facing the mirror, another slave girl applying *kajal* to her eyes. "Tell me Badr, what do you know about Zebunissa and Aqil?"

Badrunissa grinned mischievously. "Well, rumor has it that when Aqil Khan was teaching us poetry, Zebunissa was spending long hours with him, not because of poetry, but because she wished to be alone in his company."

"Nonsense," responded Zubdat dismissively. She rubbed her lips together as a red paint was applied to them. "Zebunissa merely wished to learn poetry."

Spinster Zinat could not allow herself to stay out of the conversation. "Badr may be onto something, Zubdat," she suggested without really believing her own words. "They say Zebunissa anxiously agreed to marriage with Sulaimon to deflect attention from her and Aqil."

Zubdat turned to look at her sisters. "Ladies! This stops here. We are sisters and cannot spread such rumors. If you care to dwell on this, I suggest you speak to Zebunissa before giving credence to such silly rumors." Zubdat walked over to the divan where Badr's near-naked body was being massaged and nudged her. "Get up...my turn."

***

Secretly, the heavily veiled women, *Koran* in hand, walked with their eunuchs to Zebunissa's tent. Zubdat and Zinat were elated at the thought of spending the evening with her, but Badrunissa still felt upset about the earlier events. Reluctantly she had accepted the invitation. Now, feeling both rage and fear, she walked with the others to Zebunissa's tent.

Zebunissa had designed special *Korans* for her sisters – the cover and first few pages were from the Holy Book, while the rest of the pages had famous poetry composed by Mughal, Persian and Arabic poets over the ages. Each maiden took her place. Shedding their *burqas*, they revealed their colourful and even scandalous outfits to one another. Badr was dressed in a silver *kameez* with a thin turquoise pajama that allowed the others to see the contours of her legs.

"Badr, you look beautiful." Zebunissa said admiringly.

"Thank you, Zebunissa," replied Badr, looking down at the diaphanous material over her legs.

Zebunissa continued to stare at her sister. "You are so beautiful. You cheapen your body by bathing it in sewage." Badr looked away shame faced. Zebunissa turned to the other maidens gathered. "Ladies, shall we begin?" she asked. The women nodded in acquiescence.

Only Zinat objected. "What's he doing here?" she asked, pointing to a young lad of four, seated on Zebunissa's lap.

"Little Akbar is the newest addition to our gathering," Zebunissa told them. She looked with fondness at her youngest brother, the last offspring of her biological mother, Dilras, and her most beloved child. Thus Zebunissa willingly accepted the role of surrogate mother to him.

"But he is only a child," protested Zinat. "He can't even speak in full sentences yet."

"Nonsense." Zebunissa was firm. She had expected some protest and had prepared her arguments. "This is when it begins," she said, "the love of poetry and the arts. I was Akbar's age when my aunt Jahanara balanced me on her lap and taught me to love poetry." She looked at Akbar and kissed him on the top of his head. "One day he too will recite the sweetest poems."

The women, as usual, acquiesced to Zebunissa's wishes and began their recitals. First, there was the ceremonial humming of tunes while one of the concubines played the *sitar*. The evening was then transformed into a recital of poetic compositions by the sisters. As planned, each in turn shared their verses, with Zebunissa's composition being the most impressive, as usual. Akbar remained calm and attentive during the recitations, prompting Zebunissa to conclude that he was indeed worthy of being called the youngest member of the society. Finally, after several hours, the women paused for wine, which as usual Zebunissa had smuggled in.

"Zebo," Mihir began innocently, "what do you think Aba will do to

Brother Sultan?"

Sultan, their eldest brother, had been entrusted by Aurengzeb with the task of imprisoning his uncle, Aurengzeb's brother, Prince Shuja, during the war of succession. Instead, Sultan had defected to Shuja.

"I know not what he will do," responded Zebunissa, taking a delicate sip of the red wine in her enameled glass. "But I hope he has him killed!" The women gasped, looking up in horror.

"Why so shocked?" Zebunissa protested. "He deserted his father and Emperor during a war."

Zinat leaned forward, her wine nearly sloshing from her glass. "But he is our brother and the rightful heir after Aba, Zebo!"

Zebunissa shook her head. "There is no rightful heir in the Mughal tradition. 'Throne or coffin' is the code we live by. He who fights and wins, rules. Aba defeated his three brothers – Shuja, Dara and Murad fairly for the throne, and his successor will also have to win it. A traitor like Sultan could never be considered!"

Fearful of her temper, Zinat ceased to argue. Zebunissa, with Prince Akbar still on her lap, sipped her coarse arak wine. "I hate the taste of arak!" she said, squinted her eyes at the sour taste. "Had Aba not banned wines in the kingdom, I would be sipping shirazi."

Despite prohibition, Shirazi and Canary were in high demand in the kingdom. Both were imported from Surat, and took at least forty-six days to arrive in Delhi. The high cost of such transportation prohibited its sale in the open market. Araq, the native wine made from local grapes and unrefined sugar, was what most noblemen drank when the foreign wines were unavailable.

"Rumors are circulating that Prince Sultan is in love with Shuja's daughter; that he did it for love," exclaimed Badrunissa.

"He's in love with that whore?" Zebunissa asked, her lips curled in disgust. "He betrayed Aba for her?"

"Princess Zebunissa..." Mira, a low level concubine about her mother's age, motioned to her. "Have you ever been in love?" she asked quietly.

Zebunissa stared at the concubine. "I do not see how that is any business of yours," she declared with hauteur.

"Oh but it is, Princess," Mira replied quickly. "People in love do all sorts of things, including shifting allegiance, especially when they fear losing their loved one."

Zebunissa thought about her fiancé, Sulaimon. Did she love him? She supposed she did, but she could not imagine those tepid feelings shifting her allegiances.

"Ask Badr," Zubdat suggested, hiding a smile. "She has loved many men in her life!" As the women chuckled, Zubdat added, "And many women." Badr merely grinned. It was true.

Zebunissa stared at Prince Akbar for a moment. "I love my Akbar," she observed. Rising from her seat, she walked away with him in her arms, dismissing from her mind what the concubine had said.

As night fell, the golden border of the turquoise tent began to glisten in the moonlight, as if the two were somehow connected. The burgundy of the soldier's robes changed to a brownish hue, till their presence along the perimeter of the grandiose tent was barely discernable.

# 2
# Usurper-Emperor

*O Prophet, shining like a lonely gem,*
*The fairest of Heaven's highest diadem,*
*Look on men's need and intercede for them.*

13 June 1659

As the imperial procession entered the majestic capital city of Delhi, Zebunissa gazed in awe at her new home. She had visited the city many times when her grandfather Shah Jahan had been Emperor but today, with her father on the imperial throne, she looked at the city with fresh eyes, seeing it as her own. Far grander than any place she had ever lived in, Delhi was built as a walled semicircle, enclosing over 1,500 acres. It boasted eight gates, each named after the city towards which it pointed – Lahori Gate led to the city of Lahore; the Kashmiri Gate opened north towards Kashmir; Ajmeri Gate to the western Rajput city of Ajmer, and so on. The design of the eight gates was specific, with four gates representing the four directions and the other four representing the gates of heaven.

Within the city, to the west, was another walled structure – the brand new Red Fort, built by her grandfather. West was an important direction for the Mughals and indeed all godfearing Muslims, for it faced Mecca. People prayed facing west and the doors of mosques opened in the same direction. Built of stone quarried from the abandoned city of Fatehpur Sikri, the walls of the fort formed an irregular octagon. Four large gateways, two small entrances, and twenty-one towers, were set into its walls. A deep moat surrounded it, filled with water and fish. Inside were gardens of jasmine, rose, frangipani, and violets. Mango, apple and banyan trees grew in profusion, lending their gracious shade to the red stone fort.

Zebunissa noticed a sudden heaviness in the air as they approached. The levity that had marked her previous visits had vanished. She ducked her head out of the canopy to steal a view of the townspeople. To her dismay, the people seemed to hurry past, their heads bent in fear. There were no women. She noticed the muted voices as the men stared at the procession without smiling. 'Why do all the men have beards now?' she wondered.

Even the smell of the place was different. Before, the enticing aroma of sweetmeats and incense from Hindu shops had fused with the raw smells of the butcher's shops. Now, the smell of sweetmeats and incense had disappeared, along with the Hindu shopkeepers. Zebunissa ducked back into the shelter of the canopy and shut her eyes in solemn prayer: 'Allah…give my father the wisdom to fight intolerance. Let him spread love among all his people, Hindu, Christian and Muslim. Lord of all, save him from himself.'

As the harem women dismounted from their respective elephants, Zebunissa followed Nawab Bai into their new harem along with her sisters. The concubines followed.

"Welcome my dears to your new home!" Zebunissa immediately recognized the plump tan-skinned woman standing at the harem entrance to welcome them and their entourage. "As Empress of India, I welcome you all to Delhi and the Red Fort." *Empress* Raushanara, as she would now be called, was Aurengzeb's younger sister and was the nemesis of Zebunissa's favourite aunt, Jahanara. As a result Zebunissa had disliked Raushanara from an early age.

One by one, the women of the harem hugged Raushanara, as if doing so was a prerequisite to entering the harem and failure to do so would result in exile. Zebunissa noticed that Badrunissa's face turned pale as she approached Raushanara, who said, "Come my dear, give your aunt a hug." Badr, normally affectionate to a fault, hesitated. Zebunissa noticed that Raushanara held Badr in a long embrace while her sister looked uncomfortable, almost frightened. Finally, she broke away and ran towards the other women, gasping for air.

"What's wrong Badr?" inquired Zubdat, but Badr merely shook her head from side to side and then vomited onto the marble floor. "Badr!" exclaimed Zubdat, alarmed.

Raushanara looked towards the other ladies awaiting entry into the zenana and smiled. "She is probably tired from the journey," she remarked in dulcet tones.

As Zebunissa approached the new Empress, their eyes met. Raushanara rightly interpreted the look in Zebunissa's eyes as unfriendly but nevertheless stretched out her arms. Zebunissa accepted the embrace reluctantly. "My, you have grown Zebunissa! So tall and healthy."

Zebunissa knew 'healthy' implied she was heavy. Men viewed the term as a compliment, and women with suspicion. "I am worried my skin will turn dark in the Delhi sun, Aunt," Zebunissa responded.

Raushanara looked into her niece's eyes and smiled. Unlike Jahanara and Zebunissa, Raushanara was neither fair skinned nor sharp featured. Her complexion was tan and her face round and plump. She had little of her Persian ancestry. Viewed as the least beautiful of all Aurengzeb's sisters, Raushanara had always felt neglected and maligned. Zebunissa knew this. From an early age, Aunt Jahanara and Uncle Dara were the favoured ones by their parents. Her own father, Aurengzeb, along with Raushanara, had always been left to second fiddle to their more desirable siblings. Thus, many years ago, Aurengzeb had reluctantly formed an alliance with Raushanara to wrest the throne once their father's reign ended. She had been instrumental in helping him defeat Dara and had now been rewarded with the title of Empress and recognized as one of Aurengzeb's most trusted confidantes.

"Do not concern yourself, Zebunissa," responded Raushanara with a caustic smile. "I will take good care of you here, I promise!"

***

Zebunissa was woken from a drunken stupor as dawn caressed the sky. Along with the other Princesses, she had been fetched to be bathed, dressed and bejewelled in preparation for the day's events. With little control over what was happening, Zebunissa merely moved and bent whichever way the Tatars and eunuchs instructed; one applied make-up, another placed jewellery. No one asked her what she desired for it had all been planned by Raushanara, Empress of this new India. Strands of pearls adorned their necks while precious stones dangled from their ears. Gold and silver rings with diamonds and sapphire insets were placed on their fingers. Their *lenghas* were adorned with rubies and gold embroidery. As the harem women were readied, they went like lambs, one by one, to the lattice windows from which they would observe the new Emperor's coronation. Zebunissa stood peering over her sisters' shoulders, all equally bewildered by how quickly and efficiently they had been readied, with no say about which *lengha* or what jewellery would adorn their young bodies. "Move over Zubdat," Zebunissa said, maneuvering to stand at the front.

*Alamgir zindabad! Alamgir zindabad!* The crowd in the *Diwan-i-am* (Hall of Public Audience), chanted loudly as they awaited the arrival of the new Emperor. Zebunissa too whispered the chant to herself; as a Princess it would be inappropriate for her to chant loudly. 'Allah, grant my father a long life,' she prayed with eyes closed. Zebunissa adored her father and followed his every command, even though she disagreed with most of them. In turn, she enjoyed his devoted love. When, as a child, she had learned the *Koran*, her father had given a grand feast to celebrate her accomplishment; when she learned Persian, he rewarded her with jewels. It had been clear to Zebunissa from a young age that among his daughters, Aurengzeb loved her the most. And though those who wished him ill painted him as a ruthless fanatic, she knew her father also believed in the passages from the Holy Book that spoke of forgiveness, charity and goodness. 'The *Koran* has many faces,' she told herself. As Emperor he would show everyone in the kingdom the different sides of his piety. He would forgive the brothers he had defeated and protect the weak, even if they were not Muslims. He would rule with justice.

Zebunissa could sense that her father was arriving for she noticed the first flurries of a major procession approaching in the distance. Slaves scattered rose petals and the sound of drumbeats, flutes and *sankas* rose into the air. The nobles waited in the hall, where the orthodox *mullahs* had been given a special area near the throne – a position they had long coveted but till now had remained beyond their reach. Seeing them huddled in their long robes at the foot of the marble edifice bearing the throne, Zebunissa thought, 'My father is not one of you. You are here merely for political purposes.' The Hindu Rajputs had been placed at the very back, signalling that their place in the new dispensation would be more precarious.

As the sound of drumbeats grew louder, Zebunissa saw a white stallion glittering with gold and precious stones. The saddle, bit, bridle and stirrups were of gleaming silver and atop the magnificent beast sat a pale, muscular figure sporting a neatly trimmed beard and moustache. From where she stood behind the trellis window, Zebunissa could not tell whether her father was smiling or serious. She knew he had waited for this day his whole life, so she smiled for him, ensconced in her own private world, watching the spectacle with the other women of the zenana.

As Aurengzeb, or Alamgir as he now wished to be known, dismounted from his stallion and walked towards the throne, Zebunissa thought in admiration that her father seemed made for this day. A broad shouldered muscular man whose skin was even paler than her own, he was covered with emeralds, sapphire, rubies and diamonds, the largest of which was pinned to his turban like a third eye. Her gaze fell on the gold encrusted sword he wore, weighted down with the precious metals and stones that adorned it, yet her father wore it as if it were no more than a feather. 'There is something special in a man of great physical strength who also possesses moral conviction,' Zebunissa thought in excitement. 'They are scared of no one and abide only by their own rules. Their strength raises them above the codes and laws that govern common men.' But her father was different. While knowing he had the physical strength of ten soldiers, he nevertheless feared Allah, kneeling before the *Koran* and its laws whenever he could.

As Alamgir mounted the Peacock Throne, it was a vision of pure greatness in Zebunissa's eyes. The throne he sat on was six *gaz* in length, one-and-a-half in breadth, and five in height. The base of the throne was supported by six massive feet, made of solid gold, sprinkled with rubies, emeralds and diamonds. The outer canopy had enamel work with gems, while the inner was thickly set with rubies, garnets and other jewels. The canopy was supported by twelve emerald coloured, enamelled columns. Among the jewels on the throne was a ruby worth one *lakh* rupaiya; on it was inscribed the names of the great Timur. A single large peacock sat above the quadrangular-shaped, dome-like canopy, with its outspread tail embedded with blue sapphires and other coloured stones. The body of the peacock was made of gold, inlaid with precious stones. On its breast was a large ruby, from which hung a pear-shaped pearl of 60 carats. Four richly decorated steps led to the throne.

Zebunissa's gaze fell on the two large Uzbek guards who were fanning the new Emperor with large peacock feathers as the Qazi read the proclamation in his name. Nobles approached one by one in a continuous stream, each bearing presents: crates of pearls, rubies, diamonds, slaves, tigers, elephants, exotic birds and horses. Zebunissa and her sisters knew the celebrations would continue all day and night, with feasting all over the kingdom.

As the continuous stream of nobility bearing gifts finally came to an end, the *sanka* sounded once again. The Prime Minister stepped forward to say, "Your Majesty, on the day of your coronation, all your children have been summoned, but it grieves me to say that Prince Sultan is here as a prisoner of state."

Zebunissa stared at her father, sitting motionless at the mention of her brother. She recalled how Sultan had been captured at the western border of the empire, trying to escape with Shuja and his daughter, but had been caught by Aurengzeb's forces before he could flee the kingdom. Shuja and his daughter, however, had evaded capture and were still at large.

"I suggest that we not present Prince Sultan before you today since this day is of joy and pleasure. Why visit this unpleasant subject on such a day of celebration?" the Prime Minister said, bowing low.

Much to Zebunissa's chagrin, Aurengzeb's long-bearded face remained frozen as he listened to his counsellor. There was silence in the audience hall. When Alamgir spoke, it was to say, "Present Prince Sultan before me now; I wish to see the face of my traitor son."

The crowd gave a collective gasp and muted chatter ran around the audience hall. The Emperor's wishes had to be obeyed. Moments turned to minutes as the onlookers waited, sweating in their finery. Finally, a heavily chained fair skinned young man with broad shoulders was brought before Aurengzeb. Still retaining the status of a Prince, the court barbers had trimmed his hair and beard so that he would not appear in abject condition when taken before the Emperor. Zebunissa saw the heavy chains, the heavy steps, and could scarcely believe the prisoner was her handsome brother. The harem women began to weep; Prince Sultan had always been a favourite with them – so tall, so handsome, so brave! But Zebunissa remained firm, filled with anger more than sorrow, convinced that Sultan had sealed his own fate with his actions.

Prince Sultan bowed before his father and stood at attention. Aurengzeb's face showed no emotion, neither anger nor outrage; remaining calm and frozen, his eyes surveyed his favourite child. Finally he said in a voice from which all emotion had fled, "My son, my heart grieves to see you appear before me in this manner on this day of joy."

Prince Sultan looked unwaveringly up at his father, the hint of an ironic smile on his face. "I beg forgiveness, Majesty, that I do not have jewels and garments to present to you on this day of your coronation."

"Oh?" growled Aurengzeb. "Your presents arrived some time ago, my son – the corpses of my two Generals, whom you slayed when you decided to betray me and defect to my evil brother, Shuja-the-Usurper."

Sultan bowed politely, his eyes cast downwards.

"You could have had anything, Sultan. All this, all of this vast empire, could have been yours. You were my first, most beloved son. You would have been my heir!" Alamgir's voice could no longer hide the torment in his soul as he looked at his firstborn.

"Forgive me, Majesty, but appointing one's son as heir has no basis in the Mughal dominion. Your own father, Emperor Shah Jahan, declared your brother, Prince Dara, as his heir in this very hall. What good did it do? There was still war, and you, the son Shah Jahan favoured the least, now sit on the Peacock Throne."

"My father was demented! Riches, wine and women corrupted his mind so he chose that infidel-loving Dara as his heir! I am not demented."

"So say you, Majesty. But one day your sons may make the same claim about you."

"Sultan!" Alamgir's voice rang out like a whiplash.

There was dead silence in the audience hall as everyone stood in shock, awed by the brave but foolish words of the Prince. Zebunissa knew her father's temper, once aroused, knew no bounds and anyone standing in his path would suffer from his wrath.

"Princess Zebunissa!" Alamgir raised a hand towards the screens behind which the women stood.

Zebunissa was surprised, but felt honoured to hear her name called; the first among the harem women to be addressed by the newly declared Emperor. She felt a rush of power.

"You are a beloved sister to Sultan, and a dear daughter to me. You therefore carry no bias. What say you? What punishment befits a son who betrayed me in my hour of greatest need?"

Zebunissa did not hesitate. It was almost like she had expected the question. "Majesty, there is only one answer for such an act: Death!"

Immediately there was an outcry from the harem women. 'No, Zebo!' 'What have you done?' 'He is your brother!' 'Not death!' The women tugged at her clothes, pulling and pushing at her.

"Silence!" Alamgir was pleased with his daughter's response; he had anticipated it. "Prince Sultan, I grant you one more chance," he said to his son. "Bow before me, kiss the ground and beg forgiveness for what you have done. You have my word, I will forgive you."

"Majesty," replied Sultan, standing motionless, "I believe your rule is illegal; that the real Emperor is my grandfather, Shah Jahan, whom you have illegally imprisoned; the real Empress is Aunt Jahanara, whom you have also illegally imprisoned, and after them, my uncle, Prince Dara, should rule. As long as I live I will believe this and do all I can to remove you from the Peacock Throne, bringing charges against you for your illegal acts."

Zebunissa felt enraged. She longed to lunge at Sultan. How dare he insult their father the Emperor on his coronation day? What kind of son did that? If she could she would have ordered his head severed right there in court.

"Fiend!" Alamgir's voice trembled with rage. "Traitor! You are no longer my son. Prime Minister, send this man to Salimgarh and let him view the Red Fort from there! Let him see my empire grow and prosper while he spends his days wasting away in a cold, damp cell with nothing but memories of his treachery to keep him company."

The damning words echoed in Zebunissa's ears as the guards dragged Sultan away. He continued to resist, shouting, "It is you who are the usurper! Downfall of the Usurper-Emperor!"

The spectacle shocked all those present. All except Zebunissa, who felt anger rather than outrage. Till that day no one had ever spoken ill of the Emperor to his face. Sultan deserved his fate. Zebunissa smiled as the other women stood petrified, listening to the cries of the doomed Prince. Soon, there was only thick, suffocating silence.

# 3
# Kiss The Moon

*Whether it be in Mecca's holiest shrine,*
*Or in the Temple pilgrim feet have trod,*
*Still Thou art mine,*
*Wherever God is worshipped is my God.*

20 June 1659

Prisoner 721 ran his dry calloused fingers along the edges of his thick beard, lamenting the disappearance of the perfect edges his body servant had always created when trimming it. Now it had grown upwards onto his cheeks and downwards onto his neck. His moustache drooped to his lips. His hair, once oiled and combed straight back, was now an entangled mess filled with lice and other bugs. He constantly scratched his infested head with long, jagged nails, cutting open his own scalp. He had not bathed since his imprisonment three months ago, and used a bowl in the corner of his prison cell for bodily wastes. The small window on the wall that he had once thought would give him fresh air, merely served to keep him conscious and aware of the hopelessness of his situation. Every time the wind blew, it merely amplified the putrid odour of filth and sewage that filled his cell.

"The Emperor wishes you to drink this." The prison guards visited him once a day for the sole purpose of ensuring he drank the elixir.

"I do not drink that which I do not know."

"You are the Emperor's prisoner. Do as he commands, or starve."

Defiant, Prisoner 721 chose to starve. As the days passed, his body became emaciated. His once strong biceps became flaccid and weak, like the shrivelled remnant of a once succulent fruit. His thighs shrank to the point when he could wrap his hands around them. His stomach roared with hunger.

Days went by. The guards felt increasingly frustrated by the prisoner's will power. They knew they had to feed him the elixir or they would face death themselves. Cunningly, they brought in Mughlai delights – lamb korma, grilled fish in lemon sauce, chicken biryani, mutton kebabs – and sat feasting in front of the cell. But Prisoner 721 simply sat with his head down, concentrating his will on his god.

*There is no God but God and Allah is his name!*
*There is no God but God and Allah is his name!*
*There is no God but God and Allah is his name!*

The soldiers threw scraps and bones from their meals towards the rats living in the corners of the prisoner's cell, watching them scurry towards the succulent morsels. Prisoner 721 considered scrambling for the marrow from the bones, hoping it would provide sufficient sustenance for a day. But no, he would not give the guards the satisfaction of seeing him fighting rodents for scraps of food thrown from their plates. So he continued to stare down and meditate: 'Allah, forgive the sins I have committed. Give me strength to pass this test you have placed before me. I pray to your goodness, Lord.'

The guards, frustrated by their inability to break the prisoner's resolve, walked into the cell again. "You will drink the elixir!" the Commander yelled at the mute prisoner. While two guards pinned his arms, the Commander prised open the prisoner's lips. But it was futile. The teeth remained clenched together. "Open your mouth, wretch! You will drink this tonight!" Yanking the prisoner's mouth with one hand, the Commander set his elbow in the wretched man's face, suffocating him. "Open your mouth, I say!" he shouted.

Asphyxiated, the prisoner finally succumbed and opened his mouth, gasping for air.

One of the guards stuck a wooden stick into the prisoner's mouth, preventing him from shutting it again. The other guard hurriedly passed the elixir to the Commander, who poured it down the prisoner's throat. Slowly, unwillingly, the prisoner swallowed the elixir made of unknown ingredients, coughing and choking as some of it burned down his throat. Unable to spit it out, he was forced to ingest the burning potion. Before long, all of the elixir had been poured into his mouth, half spilling out onto his face and the surrounding floor. The guards finally released their hold and walked out, locking the cell.

Prisoner 721 began to feel dizzy, then euphoric, and eventually realized he was intoxicated. The elixir must have had opium, he thought. Before the opium gained control of his mind, he fell to his knees and began to pray, facing west towards Mecca. "Forgive me, O Allah, for having sinned against you by partaking in the devil's drink. Wash me clean of my sins and let me break free from this prison of hell. Grant me absolution."

It was the last time he would be completely lucid.

***

"There will be no *darshan*. I am not God, only his humble servant." Aurengzeb's announcement to his advisors came as a surprise. No Mughal Emperor had ever refused to be present at the daily *jharoka darshan* to his subjects. Though pompous, the centuries-old tradition served to legitimize the ruler's position and glorified the sovereign's image before the masses, while assuring them of his daily wellbeing.

"I beg your indulgence, Majesty, but may I ask in all humility the reason for your decision?" Zafar Khan, the Prime Minister, asked, his voice a nice blend of servitude and authority.

"I wish to show my people how a true Muslim should be. There will be no fancy robes or jewels commissioned for me. Royal funds will no longer be frittered away on useless and vain monuments such as the Taj Mahal, or even the Peacock Throne. Humility brings one closer to Allah."

"Your devotion to the Almighty is indeed noteworthy, Majesty," continued Zafar Khan, "but do you think that denying your subjects *darshan* will help legitimize your position as the true Emperor of India? Is it wise at a time when the *Qazi* of Delhi has refused to read the sermon in your name, knowing the previous monarch still lives?"

Aurengzeb sighed. "The Qazi's refusal reflects his own confusion. He finds it sacrilegious to read the sermon in my name since my father is alive. But what he fails to see is that my father is demented. If left on the throne, he would bring the empire to its knees with his lavish, vain architectural pursuits. Worry not! The Qazi will change his mind. As for my father, he is at the sunset of his life and will not live much longer. Trust me, we have nothing to fear. I wish to retire now to the harem."

Zafar Khan looked away. "Sire, this is your first visit to the harem as Emperor. Have you any wishes you desire conveyed?"

"No," pronounced Aurengzeb coldly. "The women well know what I expect of them."

***

The doors to the harem opened for the new monarch. All the colourful decorative tapestries had been removed and the paintings had been replaced with cloth emblazoned with phrases from the *Koran* in black ink; no ornaments were on display and all semblance of opulence had vanished as if wiped clean by an unseen hand. All the women were dressed in black, their faces covered except for a small horizontal slit through which they peered fearfully.

No one was permitted to approach the Emperor; it was he who initiated action or speech. He scanned the room carefully. Finally, his gaze fixed upon a tall figure – his beloved Zebunissa. "Did you have a good journey?"

Zebunissa, usually verbose, quietly replied, "Yes, Aba."

"Aqil Khan treated you all well?" he asked, looking around the room, soliciting responses.

"Very well, Majesty, yes, yes…" One of the women replied for the others. There was a feeling of palpable fear in the room; no one dared answer in the negative.

Aurengzeb nodded, satisfied. He had not expected anything else. Looking up, he told them, "The previous Emperor's incarceration was necessary, as was that of the last Empress. You should know this."

It was Zebunissa who answered anxiously, "Yes, of course, Aba. We are all with you in whatever you decide."

Aurengzeb's aquiline face broke into a rare smile. "Zebunissa, I wish to speak to you in my private chambers later in the day."

"As you wish, Aba."

Aurengzeb's face froze once again into austere lines. "Zebunissa, you may address me as Majesty."

Beneath her *burqa* Zebunissa raised her eyebrows in surprise but did not protest, merely saying, "As you wish, Majesty."

There was a brief silence. The harem women looked on, fearful of offending and uncertain of the new ways.

Leaving the harem, Aurengzeb retreated to his quarters. He had chosen for himself the apartment his father had built for himself in the Red Fort. Initially, Aurengzeb had found the apartments appalling. The walls were gold and red and the vanity of such splendour made Aurengzeb uncomfortable. He immediately decided that if he wished to change the kingdom, he would first need to change his own living quarters. Relics of the past were thus removed – mirrors, tapestries, the centuries-old collection of fine art, and replaced with painted quotations from the Holy Book. The room was repainted in white to signify humility, and simple rugs replaced the lavish Persian carpets that had once decorated the floor like bright jewels.

"Majesty, Princess Zebunissa desires audience," a servant said, bowing low.

Aurengzeb waved a hand and Zebunissa entered, her head bent. But her eyes behind the veil took in the royal chambers in bewilderment. Why did her father, the Great Mughal, choose to live like a *fakir*? Aurengzeb rose and led his daughter to a prayer rug, indicating she should kneel with him before his personal copy of the *Koran*. Like everything else, it was a simple clothbound volume. They knelt, facing west with upraised palms. Then they faced right; then left again, uttering the ancient prayers. Zebunissa was eager to show her father that she understood the true ritual of prayer, far more than any other in the harem, which was why he was right to invite her alone to pray with him. It was a signal honour.

When they finished, father and daughter rose and went to sit on a low floor cushion. "A matter has come to my attention," said Aurengzeb. "A soldier of the enemy has been captured and I wish to hear your counsel..."

***

"What did the Emperor wish to speak to you about?" inquired Didar Khan, Zebunissa's eunuch. "Was it about Prince Sultan?"

Zebunissa looked away, disinterested in discussing the matter with her chief eunuch. "He wished for advice on a State matter."

"The Emperor trusts you, Princess. Play your hand well. Perhaps you will be made Queen in place of that witch, Raushanara."

Zebunissa hid a smile as she looked away. "We will see what happens," she said calmly.

Didar was not satisfied. He continued to implore Zebunissa for more details, but she resisted. Finally, he said with a resigned sigh, "I hope you did not advise him to execute anyone again."

Zebunissa turned her gaze towards Didar. "What if I did?"

"Who was it this time?" Didar asked with agonized foreboding.

Zebunissa heard the rebuke in his voice, but composing herself, spoke confidently, "The Emperor asked what should be done with Prisoner 721. That is his number. He was a leader in the rebel army. I told my father the prisoner should be executed like other soldiers who betray their King."

Didar shrank back in horror. "Are you crazy?"

"Didar!" shot back Zebunissa. «Know your place and watch your tongue!»

Didar looked away, suddenly fearful of the girl he had guarded from birth. He rearranged the long scarf he wore to hide the tears that filled his eyes. "I know to watch my tongue, Princess," he said softly. "In this kingdom anyone who offends the Emperor is either castrated, dismembered or executed. What protection does a eunuch like me have?"

Zebunissa looked away, unwilling to see the truth in his eyes.

"Princess, with an Emperor so bent on revenge and killing, do you really believe it right to instigate him to commit more horrors?"

"Didar..." admonished Zebunissa, this time in a lower tone, "do not forget how you got here," referring to Didar's troubled past. An orphan from Bengal in the eastern reaches of the empire, Didar had been raised by his uncle. When he reached puberty, his uncle castrated him and offered him in place of revenue to the Governor of the region. Eunuchs were always in high demand throughout the Mughal Empire, with a eunuch being worth three regular slaves. Eventually, Didar found a home in the Mughal Emperor's harem.

"You are here because my grandfather and his predecessors encouraged the castration of boys in order to staff their harems with eunuchs. My father has banned this practice."

Didar spun around, his eyes glittering. "No, Princess! The Emperor has only issued a proclamation. There is no penalty for doing this. Hyderabad, just last month, sent 20,000 eunuchs to Delhi! Why? If your father is so opposed to castration, why did he accept them?"

Zebunissa waved a hand in dismissal. "That is not true. I do not have time for this."

Infuriated, Didar grabbed Zebunissa by the hand and forced her to turn around. "Look out the window, Princess! See what you and your father are creating," he hissed through clenched teeth. "Go into the city in disguise and see the world he has made. Use your skills of deception for something other than poetry."

Zebunissa's eyes arched upward, afraid of her once docile eunuch. Didar saw the fear in her eyes and tightened his grip, bringing her closer to him. "Your brothers are all impotent. Only Prince Sultan had the ability to overthrow this monster, and now he is in prison. It is for you to stop him, my child, or he will destroy us all!"

***

Zebunissa walked along the narrow uphill path at the tail end of a line of refugees. It was mid-afternoon and the scorching sun beat down mercilessly on the bedraggled folk. Zebunissa's dark *burqa* provided little relief. Sweating profusely, she ducked into a small alley and raised her veil to allow a gush of fresh air to enter the hot oven created by her gown. Breathing deeply, she dropped the veil once again and continued through the narrow streets of Delhi, viewing the world through the small grid-shaped window over her eyes. It made her feel like a caged animal being paraded in town for the amusement of people; the world moved around her while she remained confined in her prison of cotton and silk.

Everywhere Zebunissa looked she saw men with long beards; the few women she saw were squatting on alley corners, begging for alms. 'Beggars in Delhi?' she wondered in amazement, unaware that when Aurengzeb's army ravaged the city and killed the soldiers who had remained loyal to his brother during the war of succession, he had made no provision for their widows. In a final act of humiliation, Aurengzeb had decreed that if no man existed in a household to provide for the woman, they could earn only in the manner he deemed fit for woman – begging.

Zebunissa continued into the inner city and found Hindu subjects of her father cooking their evening meals over a smoking fire while their children jumped over dung and sewage left in streets that had not been cleaned. Disguising her refined voice, she knelt beside a women cradling a young child in her arms. "Why are you out here, madam? Why do you not go inside your home?"

The woman, skinny and dehydrated, murmured, "I have no home. The Emperor destroyed it because we refuse to practice his religion."

"Forced conversion?"

The woman began to sob, her eyes dry; there was no moisture in her body for tears. "This is his realm now. We are burdens not subjects. He wants nothing more than for us to die out here in the heat."

Zebunissa shifted her gaze to the young boy on the woman's lap, his hair brown with dirt. Snot ran down from his nose to his mouth; he tried to lick it with his tongue. Zebunissa gently caressed his hot head. Feeling helpless, she continued her journey.

Suddenly, she heard screams from a distance – Mughal soldiers were shouting at some townspeople, who were screaming in protest. She hurried towards the noise and noticed people running away in the opposite direction. As she ran she wondered what could have frightened the people so much that men, women and children were all running away. She reached an open space where an edifice had been reduced to rubble; it had been a Hindu temple. A dhoti-clad Chief Priest of the ill-fated temple was being flogged by the Mughal soldiers while the lesser priests were being forced to eat beef, forbidden in Hinduism. Nearby, an elderly man lay on the ground, his head bloody. His eyes were open but he was no longer breathing; his arms still wrapped around a young child, who was crying for him to awaken.

Zebunissa realized the man had been trying to flee with his child to safety when he was struck by one of the soldiers. She began to sob inside her *burqa,* finding it hard to breath. Turning, she ran from the dastardly sight and hid in a narrow alley, raising her veil and breathing heavily between muted sobs. Feeling disillusioned, she slowly began walking back towards the palace, feeling dizzy. Her deliberate gait was that of an aged woman rather than a young lady as she traversed the Mughal capital like an unseen ghost. Was it the heat or the horror or a sickening combination of both she knew not. Everywhere she looked she saw destitution and silence; rows upon rows of houses with doors and windows shut, as if shielding themselves from an imminent storm. Nowhere could she see any evidence of joy or happiness.

***

Every day the guards returned, and each day forced the elixir down the throat of Prisoner 721, and each day it became easier as his resistance became weaker and the hallucinogenic effects lingered longer from his previous intoxications. Briefly, in a moment of clarity, he wondered if there was more than just opium in the drink, which caused him to feel increasingly disoriented even hours later.

After a week, the prisoner began muttering nonsense: "The monkey has a tail. The monkey caught his tail, a monkey live in the tail." He began shivering incessantly and started eating his own hair.

The guards kept vigil, monitoring his slow degeneration into imbecility. "Who has the tail?" one mocked.

"The monkey has the tail," the prisoner said, staring at the ground with eyes wide open as he sat in a corner in his own filth.

"Who is the monkey?" another guard laughed.

"The monkey has the tail."

The guards broke into raucous laughter. "Are you the monkey?"

"The monkey has the tail. The monkey has the tail."

"Crawl to us and drink this, you beast!"

Prisoner 721 crawled hurriedly to the guards and began devouring the elixir, neither aware of his surroundings nor what the drink was doing to him.

***

As dusk fell Zebunissa sat on the divan in her chamber, composing poetry for the next meeting of the Makhfi; a mental diversion from the horrors she had witnessed. Poetry was once again the medium she used to expressed her emotions and heal her heavy heart.

*I stand in the halls of life, a motionless statue*
*Love of my people is my home*
*Where once a bustling melody of children sang*
*Rancorous cries of agony now roam*

*I do not wish to defy my master*
*Of his goodness I still believe*
*Lift the veil of darkness from his eyes, O God*
*May only righteous decisions his heart conceive*

*Give my motionless state life again*
*Not too late, but rather soon*
*Or else lift me away from here forever*
*So far away that I can kiss the moon*

## 4
## Final Farewell

*I will not lift my veil,*
*For, if I did, who knows?*

22 June 1659

"Majesty, Didar desires audience."

Dressed in his finest turquoise silks, Didar entered Zebunissa's chamber.

"You look most elegant today, Didar. Where have you been all day? We were looking for you."

Didar bowed in acknowledgement at the compliment and then motioned for someone to enter. "Princess, this is Mansa. She washes clothes for Princess Zubdat." The mild mannered, plump woman bowed her head. "Her husband works in the Emperor's prison," Didar continued. "She knows who Prisoner 721 is."

Zebunissa's eyebrows arched upwards. "Well, Mansa," she said, "who is this ill-fated individual my father will soon have executed."

"Princess, my husband tells me Prisoner 721 is Prince Sulaimon."

Zebunissa froze, her blood running cold. In the silence that followed, she could hear her heart thudding in her chest. She felt Didar's gentle touch on her arm and heard him say, "Mansa has agreed to take you in disguise to meet the prisoner. But it must be tonight for the execution is set for tomorrow."

Zebunissa did not respond. She remained as still as a *statue*, with no more life than the divan on which she sat. Then she began to breathe heavily, her eyes glistening with the hint of tears. She began to rock back and forth, her head swaying from side to side. She did not want to believe what she heard was true. Her betrothed! Imprisoned!

"Will you go?" Didar asked.

She knew he dared not state the obvious, that her father had not only decided to execute her fiancé, but planned to do so in a cold hearted manner, and had sought her counsel in making the decision. In fact, he had ensured she made the decision, not he; that she would have only herself to blame for her fiancé's death.

"Princess, will you go?" Didar asked again.

She slowly turned her head in his direction, revealing the true nature of her sorrow. Her eyes were filled with tears and flowing in glistening streams over her cheeks. She began to whimper. Didar pursed his lips, waiting. Gently, she nodded yes.

***

In the dark of night, Zebunissa and Mansa made their way from the harem quarters like two shadows. Heavily draped and veiled to evade any recognition, they flitted past the grand courtyards of the Red Fort with their spacious pools and well-defined fountains, and slipped out of the fort through a small wooden door that Didar had heavily bribed the guard to leave open. They made their way to the river bank and stepped silently into a waiting barque. Crossing the river, they made their way to Salimgarh prison. Mansa knew her husband, Bhima, would be standing guard at the entrance. With his help they would reach Sulaimon before he was taken to his execution.

As they slowly made their way down the suffocating corridor Prisoner 721 had once walked chain-bound, the light became dim, making Zebunissa nervous. She could feel the pounding of her heart. "How much further? I can't breathe," she asked, her voice echoing through the stone passage.

"We are almost there, Princess. It will help you to take slow deep breaths," replied Bhima in a whisper.

The humidity increased as they travelled through patches of darkness. Zebunissa feared she would lose consciousness. Bhima held his candle between the ladies whenever he felt uneven ground beneath his feet. At one point Zebunissa saw rodents and ants rushing away as the candlelight reached them. "Ahhhhh!" she screeched in horror.

Bhima spun around, finger on lips. "Princess, you must be silent!" he warned her in a stern voice.

"But there are rodents everywhere," she cried.

"This is a prison, Majesty, not a palace. Here rodents live, breathe, and eat alongside us. They are our only companions. Now, if you are ready, shall we proceed?"

Zebunissa nodded and they moved on towards a hallway to the right, with several cells leading off it. Darker than the rest of the prison, these cells were meant for complete seclusion and solitary confinement.

"Are you ready, Princess?" Bhima asked, gesturing towards the gated cell on his right.

Zebunissa nodded reluctantly. Slowly, she moved closer and looked into the cell. In one corner, crouched on the floor, was Prisoner 721 – Sulaimon Shikoh. Zebunissa fell to her knees, barely recognizing him. His once muscular physique was now a thin frame of skin and bones. His once thick dark hair was thinned and tangled, as was his beard. He was naked and faeces covered his emaciated body.

"Sulaimon?" Zebunissa said in an incredulous whisper, but there was no response. It was clear he did not recognize his first love. Zebunissa had vowed she would remain calm, but nothing had prepared her for the shocking sight that confronted her. She broke down, crying, "Sulaimon! It is I, Zebunissa!"

Staring at the ground he uttered in the tones of a mad man, "Zeb… Zeb…Zebunissa." A sense of shock overcame her as he continued to repeat again and again, "Zeb…Zeb…Zebunissa. Zeb…Zeb… Zebunissa. "

"Sulaimon, come to me," she pleaded weeping, feeling as though her heart was breaking. She grabbed the bars that separated her from her love and called desperately, "Sulaimon!"

Bhima shifted uneasily, not knowing what to do to comfort her. Finally he said, "Princess, please allow me. He only responds to certain commands." Opening the door, he grabbed a filthy bucket from the corner and filled it with water from a flask he carried for himself. "Come…come and drink this!" he called out to the prisoner.

Sulaimon hesitated and then crawled hastily to the bucket, gulping from it. Zebunissa stared at him drinking, shocked to see the state he was in, secretly hoping it was not Sulaimon but an imposter the clever Sulaimon she had known had sent to dupe her father's men.

"The elixir they have been giving him for the past few weeks makes him very thirsty," Bhima told Zebunissa as they watched Sulaimon lap the water like a dog. "The guards have been ordered by the Emperor himself to give him anything but water to drink, so the guards torture him by filling the bucket with their own urine and other wastes, and then laughing when he drinks it in great haste."

"What is in this elixir?" Zebunissa enquired, her tear-stained face flushing with anger.

"It is a mixture of opium seeds and hallucinogens. They want him to become an imbecile before they kill him."

"But why?" Mansa asked as if the words had been dragged from her. She had been standing in shocked silence behind them.

"Why is an interesting word, begum. Why does the Emperor do anything? Why did he imprison his own father? Why does he continue to destroy Hindu temples and force conversions to Islam? Why does he require us to keep beards longer than four finger breadths? The Emperor is possessed with a strange madness and all of India will sink in it one day."

Zebunissa continued to stare at Sulaimon while Bhima spoke. She noticed the birthmark on his right temple, which she knew well, confirming his identity. "Sulaimon!" she wept. "It is I, Zebunissa." She reached through the bars and touched his dirty, rough hands. She saw him freeze for a moment and wondered if he had recognized her touch.

"Zeb…Zeb…Zebunissa," he muttered, looking at her with a wide eyed gaze. His mouth hung open, as if shocked. His eyebrows drew together and his lips began to quiver. He began to sob incessantly, as if releasing the heavy weight of the torture he had suffered while waiting for Zebunissa to free him.

As she continued to grip his hand, Bhima motioned for her to release her hold. "Princess, we must go or we risk being caught; the Emperor keeps tight security around Sulaimon."

"I am not leaving him," Zebunissa hissed, moving her head from side to side in agonized protest.

Bhima motioned to Mansa and together they dragged Zebunissa away as Sulaimon desperately reached out to hold onto her. "No!" he yelled, his eyes wide open in horror.

"Leave me!" cried Zebunissa, fighting to release herself.

"If you shout we will all be executed!" warned Bhima.

Sobbing profusely, Zebunissa stopped struggling, falling forward limply like a rag doll. "What have I done? Forgive me, my love," she whispered in despair, seeking forgiveness more from herself, than from Sulaimon.

As Bhima and Mansa pulled her away, all Zebunissa could focus on was the crouching skeletal figure of Sulaimon gazing at her helplessly. The image grew smaller as the distance between them increased, eventually disappearing into the darkness of eternal wretchedness. She knew she would never see him again. From that day forward, he would live only in her memories.

***

Zebunissa rocked back and forth, a suffocating, drowning sense of grief rising from deep within her bosom and increasing in intensity until it swallowed her. Though Sulaimon had another wife, and even children, she had cherished his courtship. In her own private world where no one but she was allowed to enter, she had already married him and become the premier wife of his harem. Sulaimon's other wife was Hindu, not Muslim of half-Persian descent like herself. This, Zebunissa felt, elevated her above those around her, giving her a superior status. The top spot in any Prince's harem belonged to her, should the Prince be fortunate enough to win her affection. Sulaimon was such a Prince. Proposed as a political liaison in an effort to heal old wounds between her father, Aurengzeb, and her uncle, Dara, she and Sulaimon had regardless fallen in love and hoped to marry before war broke out.

Zebunissa never ceased recounting how beautiful the sonnets he composed for her were, how gentle the feel of his beard and sensual his touch. He was not her first love, though she had told him that, but he was the first man to release emotions within her that she had not known to exist. But now, as the news of her beloved's death was brought to her, she shut her eyes as if in agonizing pain and let out a loud screech; tears rolled down her face like an untamed river after the bursting of a dam. Rolling rapidly down her cheek, the tears traversed over her lips, and fell off her chin, wetting the muslin gown she wore. Zebunissa's mouth became salty from the taste of her tears and her vision to blur.

The women of the harem stood around, afraid to comfort one who never cried. "Water! Get Zebunissa water!" one of them implored. A slave girl hurried to the pitcher in the corner and quickly sloshed some of the cool water into a tumbler and dropped in some lemon pieces. She stood holding the tumbler in a quivering hand, afraid to go back. Finally, she walked forward and set it in front of Zebunissa.

Rocking back and forth, Zebunissa's face had transformed into a visage of sadness and rage. In that moment she felt she could do anything to anyone, even herself. She picked up the porcelain water tumbler placed in front of her and hurled it against the wall. "Aghhh!" she yelled. As black rage possessed her, she began throwing whatever came within her reach. The women began to scream as shattered glass shards flew around the chamber, but Zebunissa would not relent. She picked up a brass salver and threw it against the bejewelled mirror, shattering it and injuring a slave girl, who screamed, holding her bleeding face, "My eye! My eye has glass in it!" But Zebunissa was like a woman possessed. She grabbed the golden dagger she kept for protection and began ripping open the velvet cushions of the divan on which she sat. The women cried out in horror as she stabbed cushion after cushion with the gold encrusted weapon. They trembled in fear as she turned towards them, her eyes blazing. Quickly, they all ran out, locking the door from outside. Inside, Zebunissa continued to yell and scream, destroying whatever she could lay her hands on. The concubines ran to the distant quarters of the harem where Zebunissa's step-mothers lived.

After hours of sheer horror, the cries from Zebunissa's chamber abated. Eventually, there was silence. Zubdat and Zinat unlocked the door and slowly opened it. They saw Zebunissa sitting on the floor, in the corner where the light was the dimmest, her head covered. On her face was an expression they had never before seen – withdrawal. She had stopped crying and simply sat staring straight ahead. Her hands were coated with blood and she still held a glass. Both sisters rushed in and knelt on either side to console her.

"Zebo, give me that," Zubdat said quietly, pulling the glass piece from Zebunissa's grasp and throwing it into a corner. Cupping her sister's head, she pulled it down onto her own shoulder, patting it as Zinat leaned in from the opposite side. "God is great, Zebo," she reminded her sister. "He will welcome Sulaimon to the halls of paradise."

Zebunissa sat in silence, filled with grief; rage had left her being.

"My lovely Zebo," said Zinat sorrowfully, "look what you have done to yourself."

***

Drifting off to sleep with the putrid odour of the prison still in her nostrils, Zebunissa dreamt of her mother, Dilras. Usually she thought little of her docile and timid mother, but now, to her surprise, Dilras stood before her, every aspect of her physical being visible – her sharp

Persian features, her beautiful smile, her nurturing hands. Her mother walked towards her, limping just as she had in real life. Having suffered Aurengzeb's wrath on more than one occasion, she too had never fully regained strength in her left leg after one of his beatings. Zebunissa had often heard her mother whispering verses of fine Persian poetry that she had composed, afraid to recite them aloud for fear her orthodox husband would hear. Frightened and suppressed, Dilras had never been able to express her vast hidden spirit of creativity and had slowly withered away, like a flower deprived of water. Secretly, Zebunissa had always known that her own love of poetry came from her mother. Now, in her dream, Dilras said to Zebunissa, "You have forgotten me."

"Ami, no! I could never forget you. You gave me life and the greatest gift one can bestow on a child – creativity."

"Yet you have forgotten much else, child. You have forgotten that I taught you to stand up to your father; never to allow a man to rule you the way I was ruled."

Zebunissa began to weep, tears oozing from between her closed lids. "What can I do? Everything is gone. Aunt Jahanara is in prison, with grandfather; Sulaimon is dead. Where do I go? What do I do?"

"Choke him!"

"Choke whom?"

"Your father! Choke him!"

Zebunissa stared at Dilras in bewilderment. Was this her gentle mother? What was she saying?

"Choke him the way he has choked everyone else! He wants to kill the arts. But you must give it new life! It will show him he cannot control us. He can pass one bigoted *fatwa* after another, but creativity will live on in people. We will drink, recite, sing, dance and continue to shine through the dark veils he has draped over our faces!"

Zebunissa had never heard Dilras sound so strong and determined.

"After Sulaimon's death, even a stone-hearted man like your father will feel your pain. Strike now! Ask to create a society where men and women can gather to pray and read from the *Koran*. Tell him the society will function to allow men and women of intellect to delve more deeply into the teachings of the Book. But when you meet, celebrate the arts! Recite poetry you have written. Give life to that which he desires to kill. And more, use this court to formulate how to destroy him. You will never win by attacking him from the front. You must attack him hidden from behind."

"*Hidden from behind*?" Zebunissa asked, pondering her mother's message.

"Hidden from behind, my child."

## 5
## Demoralised Prince

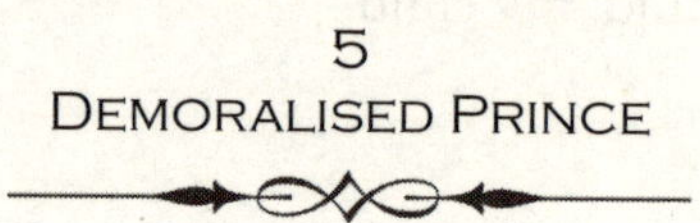

*My soul is proud*
*Though I beat my head in sorrow,*
*It has never bowed.*

9 August 1659

The colour of the sky was a beautiful, bright blue. Full fluffy clouds floated in asymmetrical patterns. The day, so full of promise, was however overshadowed by the dark silhouette of a fallen Prince. As the elephant ambled within sight of the harem windows, Zebunissa observed her once proud uncle, Prince Dara, now in a wretched state. She had heard of his capture, but what had saddened her most was learning how he had been caught. Disheartened and sorrowful, Dara had stopped running on hearing of Sulaimon's death. One of his own confidantes betrayed him in return for jewels from the royal treasury.

Zebunissa knew Dara's capture was the greatest prize for her father. With his imprisonment, the war of succession was effectively over. Her weak and ineffectual uncle, Shah Shuja, did not command the following to topple a man of Aurengzeb's stature. Aurengzeb seized the moment to humiliate Dara. Dressed in coarse, filthy rags, Dara was paraded on the main avenue of Delhi riding atop a filthy old elephant as the townspeople watched in sheer horror. Zebunissa felt tears spring to her eyes; she loved Uncle Dara and had learned fine poetic skills from him. She had assumed that her father would spare his brother's life. Instead, he was being made to endure an agonizing and humiliating end.

As a child, Dara would often grab Zebunissa by the waist and throw her up into the air and then catch her as she came down. "Fly, Zebunissa! Reach the sky!" he would call out. Her childish laughter as she was catapulted into the air by her charming uncle echoed again in her ears: "Higher, Uncle Dara! I want to reach the sky!" Her uncle would throw her higher and higher but eventually stop to catch his breath. Still gasping, her handsome, bearded uncle would smile and say gently, "You must not reach the sky, my child. You live in the world of mortals. Never reach too high." Zebunissa sat pondering the irony of his words; how he had risen too high in the world of men, trusting in people's goodness and turning his back on the reality that his own siblings were ruthless warriors.

On this day Dara looked exhausted and resigned. His face was darkened by the sun from months of running and his shoulders drooped; his once charismatic smile had vanished forever, and his once majestic form was now skeletal. Zebunissa understood her father's intention in parading Dara this way. She knew his dark spirit had assumed the townspeople would mock and laugh at the noble state prisoner, perhaps even throw waste and rotten produce at him. This was common in the kingdom. After any great battle, whether against invaders from the north or rogue states from the south, the defeated Generals were routinely imprisoned and paraded through the streets of Delhi. The townspeople would rejoice at the procession of defeated foes and subject them to further humiliation. However, to the astonishment of everyone present, wherever Dara's elephant went, the people wept, as if witnessing their own Emperor being paraded as a captive. Zebunissa too, watched in amazement as women began throwing themselves on the ground as the elephant passed, breaking their glass bangles as if their own husbands had died. The men took off their turbans and bowed before the filthy beast carrying the pure-hearted brother of their fanatical Emperor.

"Hinduism and Islam are the same," he had proudly proclaimed many years ago, when his father was Emperor and Aurengzeb a minor Prince. It was then that the orthodox *mullahs* had taken note and begun to secretly groom Aurengzeb to seize the throne, fearing their position would be threatened if Dara became Emperor.

As Zebunissa watched, she noticed Hindus gathering on the far end of the street, folding their hands and bowing their heads in prayer as Dara passed; a gesture normally reserved for deities. Surprisingly, Muslim men too, sobbed openly, allowing their vanity to evaporate as they tacitly displayed their protest against the Emperor's actions. Zebunissa also noticed Raushanara standing behind Aurengzeb in the main courtyard, overlooking the street where Dara's elephant was parading. "Why is she there?" she asked her sisters.

Zinat responded. "She hates Uncle Dara even more than she hates Aba! She probably wants to see this even more than he does!"

Zebunissa squinted her eyes at Raushanara's bejewelled figure and noticed that her face was exposed. 'How strange that the Emperor had permitted her to stand behind him with no veil,' she thought. Raushanara was smiling and laughing. Suddenly, Zebunissa saw her father rise and gesture for the parade to halt. "What is Aba doing?" she asked.

"I don't know," Zinat replied, "but I think he is instructing the elephant to be escorted to Salimgarh prison. Perhaps he has realized the march is not having its intended effect and now wishes to execute Uncle Dara sooner rather than later."

Zebunissa watched the elephant amble closer to the Red Fort, then turn west towards Salimgarh prison. She squinted again, hoping to catch a glimpse of her uncle's face. He appeared surprisingly close and she looked into his eyes. For a brief moment it seemed that he was staring back at her, his eyes asking her: *How could* you *support this?* She shut her eyes to escape their gaze. When she opened them again moments later, it was to find that Dara's elephant had turned and her uncle's back was towards her. She knew she would never see him alive again.

"I must plead his case with the Emperor," she cried desperately.

"Zebo, you cannot. You know his temper."

"I must try. I cannot keep allowing this to happen."

"But you..."

"I am his daughter! I must have some influence over him."

"Even God does not have influence over him."

***

The next morning, Aurengzeb sat in the *Diwan-i-khas* (Hall of Private Audience), to ponder what should be done with Dara Shikoh. Standing beside him, with *mullahs* at her side, was Raushanara. Zebunissa stood behind the screens. The *Diwan-i-khas* was made of white marble, with agate, pearl and other gemstones inlaid in decorative floral motifs, as in the Taj Mahal. Sheets of gold in a threefold pattern decorated the ceiling while shards of glass sent sparks of light bouncing across the hall.

Zafar Khan stepped forward. "Majesty, Prince Dara has sent a letter begging you for clemency." The Prime Mister's voice was grave.

Aurengzeb laughed mirthlessly. "Foolish coward! He cannot even accept death like a man, yet he desired to be Mughal Emperor!"

The *mullahs* and Raushanara laughed aloud in sycophantic chorus, mocking Dara.

"Read the usurper's letter!" commanded Aurengzeb.

*My Brother; My Emperor,*
*I have no further thought of sovereignty. I only wish it may be auspicious for you and your descendants. My execution is an unnecessary preoccupation for your lofty mind. Grant me a house to live in, and a maid to attend to my needs, and I will devote my life in retreat to praying for your good.*
*Your servant and brother,*
*Dara*

Aurengzeb's demeanor changed. The sneer left his face and he no longer mocked his brother. After a moment he said, "Sister Raushanara, what say you?"

"I say death to the usurper!" The *mullahs* began chanting: 'Death to the usurper! Death to the usurper! Death to the usurper!'

Aurengzeb's thin lips curved in a smile. His decision to slay Dara was being vindicated.

Zebunissa spoke from behind the screen, "Majesty, your humble servant seeks permission to speak." When the Emperor briefly raised his hand in permission, she quickly said, "Majesty, Prince Dara Shikoh…"

"Dara-the-Usurper!" hissed Raushanara, challenging Zebunissa's authority to speak.

There was silence. Aurengzeb smiled.

"Forgive me, Majesty," Zebunissa said, "Dara-the-Usurper is your eldest brother. You have always championed morality in this land. What morality is there in killing one's own kin? The war is over. You are the victor. Spare this man's life so his children will not be fatherless."

Raushanara fumed inwardly. "Majesty! This war can never be over as long as an older brother of the Emperor lives. Naysayers and rebellious elements will continue to insist on the laws of primogeniture, arguing the eldest son should be Emperor."

Zebunissa's eyes met the gaze of Aqil Khan, standing at attention, anxiety clear on his face. He shook his head from side to side, imploring her not to argue with her father. But Zebunissa knew that none but she would dare urge the Emperor to turn his decision away from death. "If that is true," she said clearly, "then killing Dara-the-Usurper will not silence those voices for Shuja-the-Usurper, also older than the Emperor, is still at large."

Raushanara looked livid, fearing her articulate niece would influence Aurengzeb towards leniency.

"Great Emperor," Zebunissa pleaded, "forget not that you are both children of the same parents. Years ago, when your father was exiled and your step-grandmother imprisoned you and Dara-the-Usurper, holding you as hostages to prevent your father rebelling against the Emperor, it was your brother, Dara-the-Usurper, who cared for you."

The story silenced the hall. In a rush those horrific memories of their joint imprisonment as children flooded Aurengzeb's mind. He recalled how their step-grandmother had verbally abused them, how traumatized he had felt. It was still vivid in his mind – urinating in bed from fear, the taunts that he was too weak to be a man, the days he was forced to dress like a girl for the amusement of the harem… His heart still pounded when he remembered those days. His escape had been meditating on the *Koran*.

In those crucial years, when Aurengzeb had been too young and small to care for himself, Dara had protected and defended him, even though it was commonly known that Dara was not overly fond of his pious and awkward young brother.

Aurengzeb motioned to Zafar Khan, who stepped forward with head bowed. "Has Dara-the-Usurper said what he would have done with me had he won?"

"Majesty, the Usurper said he would have had you dismembered and each limb sent to a different corner of the empire."

"Fiend!" cried Aurengzeb, rage flooding his heart, obliterating every other feeling. "This but proves the Usurper should receive no mercy! Bring his head to me on a platter."

Zebunissa's heart sank. She knew Dara would be killed.

***

The aroma of roses filled the room as small pots of rose water were placed systematically across the hall where the Makhfi would gather. As the candles were lit, the sweet smell of incense fused with the aroma of flowers to create a mellow atmosphere. Zebunissa had chosen the members of her exclusive poetic society carefully. Apart from her four loyal sisters (wise Zubdat, flamboyant Badrunissa, spinster Zinat, and young Mihir), she had invited Akbar, now six, to attend and recite. There were also court poets, forbidden by the Emperor to compose poetry, who Zebunissa included – Mawlana Abdul Qader Bedil, Kalim Kashani, Saa'eb Tabrizi, Ghani Kashmiri. However, they were not invited to every meeting.

A pervading sense of sorrow filled the chamber. The women of the harem had learnt of Dara Shikoh execution. The news had arrived on winged feet, whispered behind palms which no longer bore any trace of *mehendi*. When his brother's decapitated head had been presented to Aurengzeb, the Emperor had raised his jewelled dagger and stabbed the severed head repeatedly. He then sent it to Shah Jahan as a 'token of love'. Shah Jahan had been pleased to receive a gift from his estranged son, but when the velvet cloth on the platter had been raised, the decapitated and mutilated head of Dara had stared back at him. The Emperor smiled when he heard the feeble Shah Jahan and his once powerful sister, Jahanara, had fallen to the floor, beating their chests in an agony of grief.

"Shall we begin, ladies?" Zebunissa sat reclined on velvet bolsters, a devious smile on her face. "Who wishes to go first?" she enquired, seemingly oblivious to their sadness.

The other women and the eunuchs said nothing, their gazes fixed on the floor, still grieving. Surreptitiously they glanced at each other, wondering how Zebunissa could be so callous about the news.

Zebunissa sipped her *shirazi* and said, "I shall begin if you will not."

*Come my souls arrange the banquet*
*Set the candles on,*
*Drain a cup or two in memory*
*Of the dead and gone.*

The women looked up, staring at Zebunissa's smiling face, surprised that her poem was an ode to the many family members their father had slain. And why was she smiling? Zebunissa jumped up and began acting out her verse.

*Prize the passing hour and ransack*
*All the wealth of life*
*Watch and while the bulbuls slumber*

*Pluck the roses' life.*

She dipped her hand into a pot of rose water and lifted out a handful of petals, placing them before Zinat. The ladies wondered if their leader had secretly imbibed wine and became intoxicated. *Who else would invite them to celebrate life at such a dark hour*? But Zebunissa looked directly at Zinat's tear-stained face and began to quietly recite her next verse:

*Peck not humbly like a captive,*
*At thy dole of grain*
*Boldly snatch the choicest morsels*
*From the fire of pain.*

She placed her hand on Zinat's face, as if imploring her to abandon her sorrow and embrace life.

*Let no phantom frighten thee*
*'Tis a passing gleam*
*Life's severest trials are but*
*Mere ripples in a stream.*

Zebunissa walked over to an image of a lion on a tapestry hanging on the wall, which represented the Emperor. As if addressing Alamgir himself, Zebunissa intoned:

*Fortune ever changes.*
*Dread not fortune's ban and bane*
*All the power of the moment*
*Is simply a mirage in vain.*

The girls wondered if Zebunissa was telling them something; a message meant not for every person in attendance but the core members of the Makhfi.

*With a daring bow encounter*
*One day you too will meet*
*That your own kin is silently planning*
*For your rendezvous with defeat.*

The women stared at their animated leader. Zebunissa had a plan, she knew her sisters would be her soldiers. This was but the beginning of a long collection of poetry, and meetings. Together, they would formulate plots, recruit allies, and eventually overthrow their maniac father. She would harness her sisters' loyalties to deposing her father and rescue the kingdom from his clutches. The Mughal sisters would do what the

Mughal sons had failed to accomplish – win back the throne.

Zebunissa sensed the presence of her ancestors as she announced to the others the formation of the new society. The great Mughals – Babur, Humayun, Akbar, Jahangir – were all there, standing on one side, while their wives and sisters, including her beautiful grandmother Mumtaz, stood on the other. In that moment Zebunissa silently vowed to lead the kingdom out of darkness and restore the family name to its former glory.

PART II

## 6
## The Proposal

*Give me thy tears, O Makhfi, let them rain*
*In quenching torrents on my burning heart;*
*So hot its pain*
*At every sigh I breathe the flames outstart.*

5 December 1660

Staring out of her balcony, heavily veiled, Zebunissa took note of how Delhi had changed in the years since her father's coronation. Churches and temples had been demolished and 'victory' mosques constructed, using rubble from the demolitions; women could no longer walk in public without male escort and covered from head to toe in thick garments; the playing of music led to harsh punishment and anyone caught humming a tune was imprisoned and tortured; all men irrespective of their faith, were required to have long beards. Oddly, this last bit upset Zebunissa the most. *Men's faces should be chiselled and muscular, with an appropriate amount of neatly trimmed facial hair*, she would say to anyone who listened. Now, men had beards longer than a women's hair.

So, when her father announced a marriage proposal for her with the Prince of Persia, Farouk Malik, she was horrified. As with all Persian men, Malik had a clean shaven head and chin, but had a large moustache.

"You will be the Empress of Persia! There the rules are less strict," Zubdat told her enthusiastically.

A half smile crossed Zebunissa's face. "Why would I leave my court and kingdom here in India to be the Persian Empress?" she asked.

Zubdat was about to point out it was a woman's inevitable lot to leave her parental home, but seeing the adamant look on her sister's face, she held her peace. There was no arguing with Zebunissa.

But Badr, as ever, was not so forbearing. "This is not *our* kingdom, but *his*, Zebo," she cried. "We are merely his slaves, to do as he ordains."

Zebunissa cupped Zubdat's face, shaking it from side to side. "My lovely sister," she said, "I told you...we are at war! Every day is a new battle! Aba wants this marriage for me only because he wants the city of Kandahar from the Persians."

Kandahar had been the flashpoint of numerous battles between the Mughals and Persians; its strategic location important to both empires. Merchants from China, Persia, Central Asia and India, all crossed through this silk route city. Controlling it meant controlling trade. Mughal ancestor Babur, first took the city, but it soon fell into Persian hands. Babur's grandson, Akbar, had regained control, only for his son, Jahangir, to lose it. Shah Jahan won it back in 1638. However, eleven years later, Kandahar once again fell to the Persians, and the young Prince Aurengzeb had failed to wrest control of it during his expeditions.

Zebunissa knew that Koranic law obligated the groom to provide a dowry to the bride's family. Aurengzeb could ask for anything, including the precious city.

"I shall help my father achieve his goal," Zebunissa said quietly.

"You will marry Farouk Malik?" Badr shot back, surprised by her sister's sudden docility.

Zebunissa smiled impishly. "I do not marry without knowing the man first. I will ask to meet him as a precondition to marriage."

"Do you think Aba will allow this?" Zinat asked doubtfully.

Zebunissa walked away to look out of her balcony at the destitute city she had been gazing at before. "There is not much Aba allows, but in pursuit of Kandahar, I am sure he will allow this."

Zinat came to stand beside her. "Aba will be most pleased to have Kandahar back from the Persians," she said innocently.

Zebunissa, her mind calculating and scheming, stared at her young sister. "I know," she remarked softly.

***

The royal gardeners with their underlings had begun to clear the ragged gardens after years of neglect, restoring them to their original beauty. While the Head Gardener drew outlines for hedges on parchment, the others trimmed the lawns in the hot arid heat. Flowering shrubs and trees were transplanted from the countryside and under the direction of artisans, planted purposefully to add colour. Roses of different hues were arranged concentrically and surrounded by neatly trimmed shrubs – red roses in the centre followed by pink and mauve. Along the edges of the fountains, yellow and purple flowers had been planted. The gardeners had trimmed two bushes to resemble lifesized elephants with upraised trunks. Colourful birds, peacocks and pigeons were released into the gardens to add to their charm.

Masons replaced the cracked marble in the paving and platforms and repaired the fountains. In the evening, candles were to be placed, their flickering flames reflecting in the water. After months of renovation, the majestic Red Fort was restored to its full glory and stood ready to receive the esteemed Persian guests. The Emperor had permitted the lifting of the prevailing diktat banning music, so melodious *sitar* music was once again heard in the marbled halls.

For the delectation of the visiting Persian royalty, a grand feast had been prepared, featuring twenty dishes of chicken, lamb and goat, artistically decorated with nuts and raisins.

Zebunissa sat next to her father, a thin veil covering her face, her almond-shaped eyes glittering like diamonds through the aperture created in the material. Her turquoise outfit was decorated with large pearls and a red ruby necklace circled her neck.

"My dear, you look beautiful. If God in his glory could create just one creature, it would be you."

Zebunissa smiled at the overly generous compliment, knowing her usually taciturn father wished for her complaisance. The Emperor leaned towards her and asked in a whisper, "Do you find any fault with Farouk?"

Zebunissa bent her head. "If you find no fault in him, how should I?"

Aurengzeb patted her shoulder, pleased. Zebunissa merely smiled.

Prince Farouk sat at a distance, opposite Zebunissa and Aurengzeb. He appeared bored, withdrawn, almost irritated to be at the event. Aurengzeb sent Aqil Khan to entertain him.

"Prince," Aqil Khan said to Farouk, gesturing at the sumptuous feast, "Is the food to your liking?"

Farouk burped loudly, shocking Aqil with his lack of etiquette. "It is adequate," said the Prince, shocking Aqil once again by dipping some bread into the wine and throwing it into his mouth.

"Where are the women?" Prince Farouk enquired.

Aqil raised his brows. "Women?" he asked, surprised.

"Yes. I was informed Indian women are more luscious than Persian ones."

"Prince," responded Aqil, trying to hide his annoyance, "prostitution has long been banned by the Emperor. Here there are no women to have illicit relations with."

The Prince stared at Aqil in astonishment. He was about to reply when a grey haired man in his entourage whispered in his ear, advising restraint. Farouk nodded, waving a hand as if shooing away a fly. "Go," he said to Aqil, "Tell your Emperor I am enjoying the feast."

Aqil Khan walked slowly back to where the Emperor sat, sending a disappointed glance towards Zebunissa. He bowed before Aurengzeb. "Majesty, Prince Farouk wishes to convey his enjoyment of the feast," he said, trying not to divulge his emotions.

"We are delighted!" Aurengzeb replied, raising one hand. Immediately a servant came to stand beside him. "Have a basket of the finest mangoes sent to Prince Farouk's chamber."

"Yes, Majesty."

Aqil was about to turn away when Zebunissa interjected, "Aqil Khan! With his Majesty's permission, I would like the Prince to join the next meeting of my prayer group."

Aurengzeb looked surprised at the request. "Why so, child?" he enquired.

Searching for a response that would be found acceptable by her father, Zebunissa paused and then said, "Majesty, though it is not a prerequisite for marriage, I wish to gauge how much the Prince knows and understands the teaching of the holy *Koran*."

Aurengzeb contemplated the request and then nodded. "But Aqil Khan will also be present," he instructed.

Zebunissa stared at Aqil Khan, willing him to agree. Aqil returned her gaze stone-faced. But no one denied the Emperor his least wish. "It will be my honour," Aqil Khan said rather reluctantly.

"It shall be as you wish," said the Emperor.

***

Prince Farouk appeared at the silver pavilion in the gardens expecting a grand meeting of poets and writers. Instead, he was greeted by an empty lawn with intricately carved bushes and colourful flower beds. Wondering if he had come to the wrong location, he began to turn back.

"Welcome to my prayer society – the *Makhfi*, Prince!" Zebunissa appeared, wearing a black gown so fine in texture that the shapely contours of her body could be clearly seen. She wore no veil. Farouk stared at her fair face in shock. Zebunissa smiled. "Is something wrong, Prince?"

Farouk fell to his knees, as if in worship of her beauty, reciting,

*I am determined never to leave the temple*
*There where I've bent my head*
*There I will serve, there alone is my happiness.*

Zebunissa looked down at the clumsy Prince at her feet, staring up at her, his heavy moustache covering the lower half of his face. 'How awkward it must be to kiss someone with such a large moustache,' she thought with an inward smile.

*How lightly do you deem the game of love, oh infant?*
*What dost thou know about the untold longing?*
*And the heartbreak, and the burning fever of love?*

Unbidden, Sulaimon's handsome face rose before Zebunissa. In a rush, she recalled all of their secret rendezvous in the gardens while the *zenana* slept. The perfumed garden reminded her of their trysts beneath the jasmine trees. But in Sulaimon's place stood the awkward Farouk.

"Pray rise, Prince! It does not become one of such high estate to kneel before a maiden," Zebunissa said, touching his shoulder.

Farouk rose to his feet, unable to take his eyes from her face, bemused by the gentle swaying of thin robes.

"Do you truly wish to marry me, Prince?"

Farouk nodded mutely, incapable of speech, his arousal complete.

"Will you be faithful to me?" Zebunissa knew he would not but felt it necessary to ask anyway. Again he nodded, not uttering a word. She continued to smile seductively at him, interlocking her fingers with his and rubbing her thumb in suggestive circles on his palm. Farouk began to breathe heavily, fighting to control the passion that flooded through his body.

"If you promise to cherish and love me, I will agree to marry you, worship you and share my body with you alone."

Farouk closed his eyes as a shiver ran down his body.

"Do you promise?"

Farouk nodded, beyond speech.

"Then I will tell my father that I agree to this proposal." Zebunissa proceeded to kiss him on the cheek, dreading the thought of kissing his lips. "Go away now before someone sees us," she whispered throatily, completing his downfall.

Farouk began walking away awkwardly. Zebunissa knew that walk; she often had that effect on men, bringing them to shattering climax. Smiling, she turned and walked away, waving a hand towards Aqil Khan, hiding in the bushes. Zebunissa knew that without his help, her plan would never have worked.

***

Aurengzeb had begun preparations to move into Kandahar as soon as the Persians had arrived in Delhi. Confidant of his ability to sway others, he was sure Zebunissa would agree to the proposal. Looking at the map on the table, he imagined what the kingdom would look like when it stretched to Kandahar. 'The empire looks like a headless bird. Kandahar will be the headpiece.' A sudden thought entered his mind. 'What if Malik does not agree to the marriage or the Persian Emperor backs away from giving Kandahar?' Aurengzeb felt his heart clench at the thought. He shook his head violently. 'That cannot happen! Kandahar is all but mine. Allah has ordained me to rule it in his name.'

"Majesty, Empress Raushanara desires audience."

Aurengzeb nodded and rose to greet his sister. "Allah in his greatness has raised us up, showing us mercy. Our enemies are in prison, our kingdom secure, and soon Delhi will be lit with fireworks the like of which has never before been seen, to celebrate the marriage of Zebunissa with Farouk Malik!"

"Has Zebunissa given her approval to the match?" Raushanara enquired as they both sat down and a servant presented red sherbet.

"Not yet!" Aurengzeb said, taking a sip of the cool rose-scented drink. "But she had assured me my will is hers."

"And what is your will, brother?"

Aurengzeb turned to his desk and suddenly brought his clenched fist down on it. "To take back what is rightfully mine – Kandahar!" His ancestors had ruled Kandahar in the past; he believed it was thus his birthright. It haunted him that, as a young Prince, he had failed to take the city from the Persians. But he had received from his father fewer men and less ammunition than he had requested. Yet the Emperor had blamed him for the failure and banished him from court. Aurengzeb dreamed of the day he would ride into Kandahar atop his elephant, demonstrating to his father that he had finally won Kandahar back for the Mughals.

"Do not be in such haste, brother. Securing a dowry takes time. But first, there has to be formal agreement to the marriage, which has still to happen; then there will be a contract with the Persians, when the cost of the wedding and the dowry will be discussed; finally, you will have the opportunity to formally ask for Kandahar."

Aurengzeb looked at his sister as if she was too foolish to understand his brilliance. "You are wrong," he said. "I have already sent an emissary to Persia informing their Emperor of the wedding date and my conditions for the dowry. The preparations have begun."

Raushanara looked at her brother incredulously. "Forgive me Majesty, but to make all these arrangements without first conferring with Zebunissa is taking a great risk. That girl is cunning and devious. If she refuses, the marriage will not happen!"

"Are you suggesting I should fear my own daughter?" Aurengzeb's eyes glittered dangerously.

Raushanara knew she had to tread carefully. It was not inconceivable that her brother's wrath would fall on her head. "No indeed, Majesty. Merely that it is wise to be cautious. Zebunissa is no less evil than Jahanara."

Aurengzeb let out a deep sigh. He had loved Jahanara like a surrogate mother, but he could not forgive her for favouring Dara for the throne. He had imprisoned her along with their father, for he knew she would never support his policies or reign. Raushanara's voice drew him back to the present.

"The reason for my visit today was to inquire when you propose to release Sultan."

"Never!" he shouted, clenching his fists. Aurengzeb was shocked by the question. "Never mention that traitor's name in my presence!" He waved for Raushanara to leave.

Instead of doing so, she placed a hand on her brother's shoulder and said in a more conciliatory tone, "I know he is a traitor, but you need an heir. You have two sons: Mohommad Sultan and Muazzam the coward."

"You seem to have forgotten that I have four sons, not two."

"Yes, but Azam is nine and Akbar six; neither can be the heir."

"I do not need an heir. When Allah calls me to his paradise, there shall be a war and the strongest shall be Emperor; throne or coffin."

"As Empress, I think Azam should be made heir if Mohammad Sultan is to remain in prison. Muazzam is a weak and feeble individual. The empire will disintegrate under him. At least Azam is of noble blood."

Sultan and Muazzam had been both born to Nawab Bai, a Hindu, making them easy targets for orthodox Muslims. Azam and Akbar had been born to Dilras, a Persian, giving them higher status.

Aurengzeb pondered the issue and finally nodded his head. "When the time is right, perhaps Azam can be made heir, but not now. Now I must plan the royal procession to Kandahar."

Raushanara quickly looked up. "Majesty, beware of Zebunissa! She cannot be trusted. Ever since you slayed Sulaimon, she has blood in her eyes. More than Sultan, it is she who should be imprisoned before she causes you harm!"

"Nonsense," said Aurengzeb dismissively. "I trust my daughter. She has assured me she will follow my will."

"Majesty, Princess Zebunissa desires an audience," announced a guard.

Aurengzeb looked at Raushanara as if to say, 'See, did I not tell you so?' He gestured for her to be brought in.

Zebunissa entered, dressed in dark robes, her face covered with a black veil. She walked towards the Emperor and gracefully raised her hand to her bent head in the traditional *adab*.

"What brings you here, child?"

Zebunissa glanced at Raushanara, only her eyes visible through the eye slits in her veil. Turning towards the Emperor she said clearly, "Majesty, I have considered the matter and have decided, for the sake of my Emperor and the kingdom, to marry Prince Malik."

"*Allah ho Akbar*!" Aurengzeb raised his arms in gratitude to the Almighty. He came forward and embraced his daughter. He looked at his sister over Zebunissa's head, saying, "You see Raushanara, my daughter has raised my head, not severed it as you suspected!" He embraced Zebunissa again.

"Majesty, I would never allow your head to be lowered. Who would say such a thing?" Zebunissa questioned, her luminous grey eyes meeting Raushanara's dark brown ones like a clash of swords. Each knew the other was a foe.

***

Prince Farouk spent most of his life galloping horses across the deserts of Persia, where water and lush gardens were found after journeying a full day. So, when Aurengzeb housed him in the *haveli* across from the imperial palace, he felt he was in paradise. Fountains shot sparkling jets of glittering water across his courtyard and jasmine and rose bushes filled the air with perfume. Farouk lamented that this haveli used for guests in Delhi was, in fact, grander than his palace in Persia.

Feeling melancholy, he called for the servant assigned to serve his every command. To his surprise, a slim youth of fourteen entered. "Where is my regular servant?" he asked, surprised.

"He is unwell with a fever. I am his nephew, Karim."

Farouk stared at the boy's slim, hairless body. He was dressed only in baggy trousers and a cummerbund. But the Prince was far from complaining. "Is there anyone else in the *haveli*?"

Karim shook his head, staring at the ground in all humility. "Just the old cook, but she is asleep. I was told you bathe at this time; should I prepare the *hammam*?"

Farouk looked at him, his eyes narrowed. "Who told you that, boy? I bathe in the morning, not at night."

Karim looked up at him with doe-like eyes rimmed with *kohl*. "The heat in Delhi is fierce and dries the skin. I have a special oil to massage into the skin to keep it supple; bathing before sleeping keeps the body cool."

Farouk stared at Karim's lips, mesmerized. He wished the boy would leave him alone and go elsewhere. His head throbbed the way it had when Zebunissa had met him in the gardens. His heart raced as his eyes roved over the beautiful boy, praying for divine intervention. But no power came to save him from himself as Karim bowed and began to undress him for the massage. Farouk shivered as the soft hands began to knead his body.

As he bent over the Prince's muscled back, Karim smiled to himself for he knew Farouk's weakness.

***

When Farouk awoke, Karim was gone. He lay back, dark depression flooding his soul. Despite his promise to his royal parents never to allow the devil to control his mind, he had once again touched a young boy. He prayed no one had been watching.

## 7
## Rendezvous With Defeat

*Here, suffering souls, the solace that you need!*
*Tear not your wounds, no longer make them bleed.*

19 August 1661

Outside, the sky was filled with dark clouds, heralding rain. Inside her chamber, Zebunissa lay in bed, staring at the vaulted ceiling. Sleep had deserted her night after night, though she knew not why. A month had passed since the ill-fated marriage proposal from the Persian Prince. When news of his perversion spread, the alliance was called off. Zebunissa took pleasure in the blanket of regret and disappointment that spread far and wide. Every passing day made her feel more triumphant at having brought the Emperor so close to the prize he sought, only to have it taken away.

During this time, Zebunissa continued to organize the *Makhfi,* taking care to keep their activities subdued. Zebunissa had never intended to marry Prince Farouk. She had initially wondered why a Persian Prince would come all the way to India to wed. Surely, beautiful ladies existed all over Persia, and with Kandahar and several other strategic cities already under their control, what did the Persians hope to gain by the alliance? Aqil Khan had told her of Farouk's request for women during the royal banquet. It planted an idea in Zebunissa's mind – to send women and wine, from her secret collection, to Farouk, saying they came from Aqil Khan. Sharing Zebunissa's disdain for the Emperor's methods, Aqil agreed.

A few days later, an entourage of women, opium and wine arrived at Farouk's *haveli.* The debauchery began immediately and carried long into the night. Oddly enough, though Farouk became inebriated with alcohol and opium, he did not touch the semi-naked Turkish, Persian, Central Asian and Indian women parading before him, allowing his men instead to do the feasting. Finally, one of his entourage divulged his secret to the woman he was with: though the Prince bedded women, he preferred boys.

Though surprised due to the Prince's passionate reaction to herself, Zebunissa ordered a suitable boy found and sent to the Prince. Following the liaison, the boy was instructed to run to the Pearl Mosque and throw himself at the feet of the *mullahs* and beseech them saying, "Forgive me *Imam,* I beg of you!" The *mullahs* had scoffed at him but he had continued to beat his breast declaring, "I have slept with a Prince. I have had a liaison with Prince Farouk!"

The days following the revelation had been pleasing for Zebunissa. Her plan had worked just as she had hoped. Karim had successfully seduced Farouk; the Prince had been humiliated; Karim had informed the *mullahs,* who made loud protest against the proposed wedding, and Aurengzeb, learning of the incident, had no choice but to evict the Persian Prince with his entourage and call off the marriage at the behest of the *mullahs*.

From beginning to end, Zebunissa had controlled the players like pawns in a game of *shatranj,* moving each according to what she envisioned. She wondered if those who had created the game had recognized the reality created by the laws of nature – that each one was created by the maker to behave in a preordained manner – the diagonally-moving pieces could never move straight, while the straight ones could not move diagonally; the horse moved unlike either, and no one else moved like the horse. People were no different. Everyone was born to behave in a certain way. Learning what that way was and then manipulating it to gain the upper hand was the way to gain true power.

Day by day Zebunissa watched her father hang his head in despair, as if someone he loved had died. She observed how her tyrannical father grew weaker, losing weight. He ate poorly and was subject to sudden fevers. He had ceased holding court and remained in his chambers for most of the day. As the Emperor grew weaker, Zebunissa felt some of the strength she had lost after Sulaimon's death, return. Though she presented the appearance of one shocked and grieved by what had transpired, she privately rejoiced, plotting her next move. 'Die, evil one! This waiting is killing me,' she thought.

Rising from her bed, Zebunissa decided to write to her brother:

*Muazzam, my brother*

*I know you take pride in being a member of the Makhfi. I thought to send you a poem I recited at our last mushaira – an event incomplete due to your absence.*

*When hope decays, all pleasures cease to please*
*Useless is power, wealth and ease,*
*When moment arrives and to whom I turn,*
*If he turns away from me, my temples burn.*

*You must race like a river*
*Surges from its might source*
*When the Lion falls asleep*
*And his life has run its course.*

Zebunissa paused. *My temples will burn*. Would Muazzam heed the warning, that if he betrayed her he would face her wrath? Would he understand that *the Lion falls asleep* referred to their father dying; that when he did, Muazzam must rush to Delhi? Zebunissa sealed the scroll and called a eunuch to deliver it. She had learned that Raushanara, too, was secretly hoping Aurengzeb would die so that she could install young Azam, a boy of nine years, in his place. Through him she would wield the real power. So Zebunissa decided to groom Muazzam; a clumsy and cowardly man, but alas the only son left.

Zebunissa clapped her hands. When a slave girl entered the chamber, she said, "Bring me ginger tea. I am too awake to sleep and too drowsy to remain awake."

The girl returned and placed a warm cup of ginger tea in front of Zebunissa, who noticed the girl's calloused hands and inwardly lamented the plight of slaves in the harem, whose sole purpose in life was to serve others. Sipping the warm tea, Zebunissa instantly felt a rush of energy. This was what she needed. She welcomed this simple drink for what it did for her after her sleepless night.

Suddenly, she heard loud crying from the adjacent chamber. The hot tea spilled from her hands and stained her robes, burning her skin. Annoyed, she rose to enquire what the commotion was about. Entering the next chamber, she saw women crying and beating their breasts in agony; some were breaking the glass bangles they wore. Alarmed by such a display of grief, Zebunissa asked urgently, "What has happened?"

One of the concubines ran up to her sobbing, "Princess! The Emperor has fainted and cannot be woken!"

Zebunissa turned and rushed to the Emperor's chambers, the women hurrying behind her like a flock of birds, their black robes flapping. The royal *hakim* was bent over Aurengzeb's gaunt body. But the head eunuch barred the way into the chamber and the women were compelled to remain at a distance, sobbing and calling out.

"What has happened to my father?" Zebunissa cried out. "I demand to know!" She could see the *hakim* holding her father's wrist, feeling for a pulse as the monarch lay seemingly lifeless. Secretly, she prayed this was the moment when the *hakim* would proclaim the Emperor dead. How foolish she had been to delay writing to Muazzam. What harm would it have done to send him a message a week earlier? Now he would receive word of the Emperor's death before her letter and it would be too late. Azam would have been installed as the new Emperor. Apparently distraught, she brought tears to her eyes. "He is my father! Let me go to him and sit by his side," she pleaded.

"Princess!" admonished the head eunuch. "You must permit the *hakim* to do his work. He cannot be disturbed now."

Aqil Khan approached the chamber with hurried steps and was immediately permitted to approach the ailing Emperor.

Zubdat was enraged. "Why is it that he is allowed in and we, his own children, are not?" she cried

"He is the Emperor's trusted advisor; you are not," the head eunuch said, turning away.

Aqil Khan came towards the women gathered in the doorway and said, his voice comforting in its deep tones, "Ladies of the *zenana,* pray be calm while I check on the Emperor's health."

Zebunissa's gaze remained focused on Aqil as he moved towards the figure on the bed, her eyes like those of an archer following a moving target. She saw Aqil bend towards the *hakim* and whisper to him. The *hakim* responded by nodding his head. Aqil then moved towards the Emperor's head and placed a hand on his forehead. His eyes lifted, singling out Zebunissa; he shook his head in the negative. Zebunissa knew Aqil was telling her that her father was not dead. To the others his gesture conveyed the situation to be grievous. Zebunissa wondered if the Emperor would perhaps survive after all.

Aqil approached the huddle of women again. As he stood before them, his eyes on the floor, a hush descended on the women. "Ladies, the Emperor has suffered a stroke. He cannot speak or communicate with anyone. He is breathing but has no faculties left. I do not know if he will recognize anyone."

"Aba!" cried Zebunissa, tears rolling down her face. She fell to the floor, pounding her chest. "This cannot be happening! First my marriage is abandoned and now father is sick! God save my family!"

The other women tried to restrain Zebunissa as she continued to act out her apparent grief. "Aqil Khan, please tell me if the *hakim* thinks he will survive. Tell me he will be well!" Leaning on her sisters, Zebunissa stared straight into Aqil's eyes.

He understood what she wanted to know. "Princess, it is too early to tell. The *hakim* says that is not common for people of the Emperor's age to make a full recovery from such a massive stroke."

Privately ecstatic, Zebunissa knew she had to maintain the public perception of being devastated by the news. "Allah no!" she cried. "Save our Lord! Why have you forsaken my father! Save us! Long live Alamgir!"

Her sisters dragged Zebunissa away, fearing her outburst would disturb the *hakim*. She continued to act distraught, yelling and screaming, tears streaming down her face. "Save my father! Save my father!" she chanted again and again. But in her heart rose the joyful whisper: *Allah ho Akbar* (God is Great)!

***

Her sisters escorted Zebunissa to her own chamber. "Get the opium!" Zubdat ordered one of the maidservants. "She must be made to sleep. She cannot handle this news. She will surely go mad!"

There was the sound of rustling skirts and Zebunissa saw Raushanara approaching. She clutched Zubdat's hand and whispered, "Say it again, louder, so the witch can hear you."

"Get the opium now!" yelled Zubdat. "Zebunissa must sleep! She has gone mad with grief, hearing of her father's illness!"

Zebunissa continued to sob disconsolately for the benefit of those around her as Zubdat and Mihirunissa fanned her face and patted her hands. The slave girls quickly closed the doors. Gradually the crying transitioned into silence and then soft chuckling.

"We did it! We have freed the kingdom from tyranny!" rejoiced

Mihirunissa. "We have won!" The girls grabbed each other in an embrace, chanting, "We have won! We have won!"

Zebunissa broke free to caution her sisters. "Not yet! We still have work to do. We must act quickly. I sent Muazzam instructions to march on Delhi only this morning and I fear the news of Aba's health will reach him before my letter. Zubdat, send one of your eunuchs to Muazzam immediately. Tell him he is now acting Emperor of Delhi and must march on the capital before it is too late." Zubdat nodded.

Zebunissa turned to Mihirunissa. "Send word to our grandfather in Agra that the Emperor is gravely ill and he must resume his role as true Emperor of India. Once he is installed, he will appoint Muazzam his heir and have him proclaimed as such."

Zubdat asked what Zebunissa would be doing in the coming days, when she and the other Makhfi members executed their instructions.

"I am supposed to be sedated and asleep, remember?" The sisters looked at each other in bewilderment. "With me supposedly under the influence of the opium elixir you have administered, no one will suspect me of orchestrating events. While everyone is focused on Aba's health, we will come from behind and march into the fort with Shah Jahan and Muazzam on either side!"

Mihirunissa asked what was to be done with Raushanara. "She is the only one who can foil this plan. We must keep a close eye on her activities."

"Leave that to me!" exclaimed Badrunissa. "I have a long history with that witch. I know who she sleeps with every night. I will make sure I know everything she is doing, sisters."

"Then let us join hands Makhfi!" declared Zebunissa.

The girls joined hands, reciting the verse Zebunissa had composed at the first Makhfi meeting:

*With a daring bow encounter*
*One day you too will meet*
*That your own kin is silently planning*
*For your rendezvous with defeat!*

# 8
# The Parchment

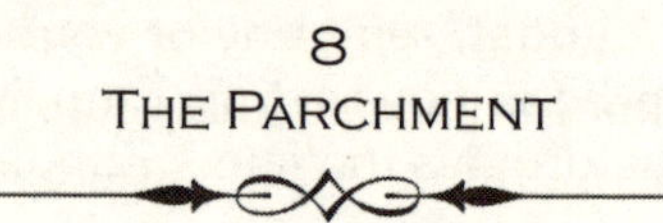

*Here is the path of love—how dark and long*
*Its winding ways, with many snares beset!*

30 September 1661

The *mullahs* stood to the left in the *Diwan-i-Khas* while the ministers, according to rank, stood to the right. Zebunissa stood with her sisters behind the screened windows, as was customary. Zebunissa was infuriated to learn that Raushanara, as current Empress, was permitted to sit on the throne in Aurengzeb's place. She pursed her lips, hatred for her aunt filling her soul.

"The Emperor is gravely ill and struggles for his life," began Raushanara, addressing the court. "May Allah protect him and grant him many more seasons of life. I pledge before you to act as his Regent in all affairs of the realm and execute my duties as he would have desired."

"Empress, we do not accept your rule. A woman cannot rule in place of the Emperor," protested Bairam Khan, Chief of the *mullahs*.

"Why so?" demanded Raushanara imperiously, looking at the offending cleric with dangerously glittering eyes. "My brother anointed me Empress."

"He did, Empress, but he did not appoint you his Regent."

For once Zebunissa was pleased at the bigotry of the *mullahs*.

"To impress the royal seal on official edicts and confer grants on nobles, that is your role. You are not the Emperor's heir."

'The heir! Bring the heir!' the line of *mullahs* chanted in support of their leader.

"Silence!" commanded Raushanara. "The Emperor has appointed no heir."

"Empress, if you would permit me to offer a solution?" the Prime Minister, Zafar Khan, intervened to say. "The Emperor has four sons, and according to Mughal tradition, one of them must be the heir. Let us confer and choose an heir amicably."

Zebunissa had long viewed Zafar Khan with admiration for he had served the kingdom for many years and possessed greater wisdom than anyone else she knew. She also knew Raushanara wanted Azam; that this assembly was nothing but a charade to present him as the heir.

"Then there can be no doubt who should be heir," retorted Raushanara. "Mohommad Sultan is a traitor, unfit to rule. Prince Muazzam is an inept coward who cannot be trusted with such a responsibility. That leaves the two younger ones – Prince Azam and Prince Akbar. Prince Akbar has barely self-awareness; he cannot be considered. That leaves Prince Azam. We should appoint him the heir, and allow the *mullahs* and ministers to groom him to the greatness of his father!"

Zebunissa felt enraged but begrudgingly admired her aunt's cunning wit. By presenting Azam as an impressionable and promising youth, she had managed to prevent anyone labelling him in any other way. By mentioning the *mullahs* and ministers as his guides, she had quelled their dissent. Zebunissa knew she had to speak or all would be lost. "Azam would be a disaster!" she said clearly from behind the screen. "Azam is too young to understand matters of court, and his impressionable age makes him susceptible to all influences, whether of infidel or Koranic origin."

Raushanara turned her head. She knew who had spoken.

There was scattered chatter in the Audience Hall. Zebunissa paused for a moment for the import of her words to register in the minds of the courtiers, then she continued, "We need an Emperor now! If we do not, the Persians could seize the opportunity to mount an attack, and the kingdoms of the Deccan may erupt once again in revolt. It is necessary to show the centre is still strong!"

"What is it that you suggest, Princess?" Zafar Khan enquired.

The voice from behind the screen never wavered as it said, "That we bring Emperor Shah Jahan, back to sit on the Peacock Throne. His return will restore confidence among our allies, especially the non-Muslim, who have been alienated by the policies of my father. It will also send a powerful message to our neighbours that we are strong. My grandfather was a valiant warrior and none have forgotten this!"

"Never!" stated Raushanara harshly. "That man turned the empire into a hell of sin and debauchery. He brought disgrace on the name of the Mughals."

The *mullahs* nodded in agreement. Zebunissa knew this would happen and brought forth her long considered suggestion. "There is another solution," she said. "Appoint Prince Muazzam as interim Emperor. He is of age and, with guidance, can serve till my father recovers."

"Muazzam is weak and ineffectual," responded Raushanara.

"Yes, so we need not fear he will become more powerful than the Emperor. When my father regains his strength, Prince Muazzam can return to his own pursuits and the Emperor shall resume his reign."

"This is twisted logic!" snapped Raushanara.

Zafar Khan once again intervened. "Empress…Princess… I implore you…this is not a time for debate. The important question is what the Emperor himself would wish done if he could communicate."

"He would want Azam," said Raushanara. "I have proof."

Zebunissa looked bewildered at the sudden announcement. Was this yet another scheme by her devious aunt?

"My brother imprinted his finger on a written parchment which clearly mentions that in the event something happens to him, of all his sons, Azam is the most qualified to succeed. He did not publicly declare him his heir for he feared his other sons would slay Azam."

"Then it is settled," *Mullah* Bairam said. "Produce this parchment before us, Empress, and we will accept Prince Azam's right to the throne. Otherwise we summon Prince Muazzam."

Zebunissa was ambivalent at the course of events. She now had no doubt about Raushanara's intention to install Azam as a puppet and rule through him. She herself had failed to convince the *mullahs* to accept Muazzam, as she had hoped. She knew Muazzam needed to be present in court to prove that he could rule on his father's behalf. She also had to ensure the fictitious proof Raushanara claimed to have of Aurengzeb's wishes, never reached the court.

***

"That parchment must be fake!" exclaimed Zubdat, seated amidst her fellow Makhfi members in Zebunissa's chamber. "Aba would never ever entrust the empire to a nine-year-old, expecting a child to take his place!"

Zebunissa listened patiently as she pondered her next move. "I don't think Aba ever planned to name an heir; he truly believed he was immortal." She raised her silver cup and sipped the *shirazi* it contained. "There is no parchment. But…if there is? Badr, you took the responsibility of spying on Raushanara. Find out whether there really is a parchment or not. If it exists, we must get it before she presents it to the court. And if it does not, we must know how she is planning to create one!"

Badr looked at Zebunissa, her eyes calm and confident. "Do not be concerned, sister, I will discover the truth. Aunt Raushanara and I have an old story that needs conclusion."

***

Badrunissa sat alone in her room late that night, a single candle flickering on the low table beside her. Dressed in her thin night clothes, she had covered herself with several shawls. On this particular night she suddenly felt vulnerable. She reached out and placed her hand over the flame, allowed its dancing tip to touch the centre of her palm. Scenes of a young Raushanara, in bed with her lovers, flashed before her eyes. Badr blinked rapidly, trying to escape the images. Another image gleamed before her eyes – a man with a dark beard and moustache, hunched over her as she quivered in the corner. "Open your mouth," he said slowly as she trembled. Again she blinked, willing the image to disappear.

Tears filled Badr's eyes as she heard once again the echo of her father's voice: "Raushanara, watch over Badrunissa in the coming years. Dilras is ill, and I am off to the Deccan for another campaign."

"Do not fear, she will be safe with me, brother," Raushanara responded. "Come, Badr."

As she sat gazing into the flickering flame. Badr felt rage fill her mind. Again she heard the distant echo…"Open your mouth…"

"I beg you Aunt Raushanara, I do not want to watch."

"How will you learn if you do not watch?"

"No…no…"

"Open your mouth."

"No...Aunt Raushanara...please."

Laughter resounded as young Badr choked on her own tears.

"This is survival, Badr. This is how you wield power in the world of men. Now do as you are told."

"No!"

Suddenly, Badr threw out an arm, knocking the nut dishes to the ground. Panting, she tried to catch her breath as tears rolled down her cheeks. Deep in her bosom, in a place she never allowed anyone to enter, Badr knew she was a damaged woman. The years spent with Raushanara had changed her forever. At first she blamed herself, thinking that she had perhaps shown interest in being part of Raushanara's promiscuous world. Before her father had entrusted Raushanara with her care, Badr had naturally gravitated towards Raushanara more than anyone else, fascinated by her jewellery, her kohl-lined eyes and dramatic personality. She was the aunt who showered Badr with affection. 'Was this why Raushanara did this to me? Was it my fault? Did I ask for it? Did she not understand that I did not like touching those men or seeing her performing those carnal acts?' By the time Aurengzeb returned and Badr was reunited with her sisters, she was a changed woman. Thereafter she was often taken to task and disciplined by her mother and older sisters for her boldness and dramatic behaviour. She was no longer the Badr they had known. Now she was promiscuous, flirtatious, and in the words of one concubine, 'free with her sexuality'. She could not help it. This was who she had become.

Badr wondered once again if there had always been something in her that Raushanara had picked up on and thus exposed her to that life, or was it Raushanara's treatment that made her into what she was? Badr wanted lovers, not a husband, for deep within she felt unworthy. She knew not how to show love except in a raunchy manner. She cursed and embraced her broken identity. She existed, but no longer lived. "You made me this way, you witch!" she hissed into the darkness beyond the feeble candlelight. "But my time will come and you will pay!"

***

Badrunissa flitted like a shadow into her aunt's chamber and once again hid in the small alcove that years ago had been her refuge from Raushanara and her lovers. Badr waited patiently and presently heard the Empress's jubilant laughter as she approached her chambers. Badr froze into stillness.

A tall slender man followed Raushanara into her chambers, holding onto her from behind as she flirtatiously laughed at his advances. Roughly, he threw her onto the bed.

"Do you treat the Empress like a common wench?" Raushanara asked, her voice a mixture of hauteur and lust. "Do you forget I am royal?"

The man grinned, ignoring her words. Pulling off the scarf he wore, he slipped it behind Raushanara's neck, using it to pull her closer to him. "I am your Emperor," he whispered.

"Raushanara does not follow anyone's command," she responded giddily.

"But you will respond to mine."

Badr shut her eyes, the spectacle reminded her of the dark days, of memories she wished to suppress. For a fleeting moment she wondered if she had done the right thing by volunteering to spy on Raushanara. Was she ready for what it entailed?

"Is anyone in the royal harem as thirsty for love as you Empress?" Raushanara's lover inquired, licking her neck and drawing her closer into his embrace.

Raushanara's bosom heaved in ecstasy. "No...they are all fools... I tried to teach some of the younger ones...but they are all fools."

Badr eyebrows drew together. She recalled a second Princess entrusted to Raushanara's care – a thin, fair skinned girl of great beauty, born to a junior wife. The fragile girl had wept all the time. 'What happened to her?' Bard wondered. 'Was she still alive? Where did she go?'

"Oh yes!" cried Raushanara as her lover dipped deeper into her. Badr closed her eyes, praying for the end.

"Stay with me, you fiend!" whispered Raushanara hoarsely as the man continued to mount her from behind. "The other Princesses may be younger, but I am better!"

Badr's mind began to wander. Did this tall, good-looking man really enjoy being with an older, heavyset woman? If he could do this to her aunt, what would a young, sensual Badr mean to him? Perhaps this was the man she needed to seduce and use against Raushanara. Badr smiled; she knew where Raushanara's nemesis lay.

For the next hour she sat hidden, enduring the sights and sounds of Raushanara's passionate tryst. It was a small price to pay for the revenge she planned to take.

***

"So why does Raushanara call you Aziz if your name is Fahad?" Badr lay naked next to Raushanara's lover, exhausted from his sensual session with Badr.

"Aziz is my middle name; she prefers it, but I hate it."

Badr smiled up at Fahad, her head on his shoulder. "I bet that isn't all you hate," she said impishly. "It did not look like you enjoyed yourself very much two days ago."

Fahad looked down at her, mildly annoyed. "You were there?"

"Oh yes," she chuckled, "hidden behind the curtains."

"But why?"

"To learn Raushanara's secret."

"What secret?"

"She plans to make Prince Azam the next Emperor, with herself as his Regent. She claims she has proof, a parchment written by the Emperor, that this was his wish."

"What has this to do with you…or me?"

"I must find what proof she has, if indeed she has any. I know she is lying; I need to know how she expects to create a fake parchment. I need your help for this."

Fahad leapt out of bed as if a scorpion had bitten him and ran for his hastily discarded clothes. "No! I do not wish to be involved in this! I am a simple soldier of the guard; if she ever finds out I have plotted against her, she will have my head crushed by elephants!"

Badr knelt on the bed, her bosom covered with a thin sheet. "But if you do not assist me, I will tell Raushanara that you slept with me to spite her. Either way you will be crushed by elephants!"

Fahad lunged at her, about to strike. Badr whipped out a jewelled dagger from under the pillow she had lain on and held it to his throat. "Make your next move cautiously soldier!" she whispered.

Fahad stepped back.

"The only way out for you is to help me. Once Raushanara is deposed, she can no longer harm you. You will be free to do as you please; no longer her servant."

"What do you wish me to do?" Fahad asked, knowing he was trapped.

***

"So your informer told you this parchment has an official seal but no finger imprint?" Zebunissa shook her head in disbelief at the lengths to which her aunt would go to fulfill her designs.

"Yes, the parchment clearly states Azam is Aba's favourite son, and has a seal affixed, but no fingerprint."

"Then she will attempt to get to his bedside and obtain the fingerprint." Zebunissa sipped her *shirazi* thoughtfully.

With the Emperor now gravely ill, the Makhfi felt emboldened to stretch the rigid norms that had bound them. Drinking *shirazi* was now a common practice with the nobility.

"We must keep vigil at Aba's bedside." Zebunissa walked over to a long turquoise divan and descended sideways onto it. She stared at the ceiling, silver cup in hand. "We will take turns to stay at his bedside. With us there, Raushanara will not dare to approach him."

The women gathered around Zebunissa's divan. She looked at them warningly. "Do not discuss this with anyone; not your male companions, slaves, or any of the eunuchs."

"We could enlist mother's help to keep watch," Badr suggested.

Zebunissa paused, wondering if her stepmother, Nawab Bai, was too naïve to be trusted in such a fraught situation.

Zubdat spread her hands. "She has been almost constantly at Aba's bedside since his illness. She has free access to him. It would help to enlist her. The five of us can only do so much."

"You are right," said Zebunissa. "Keeping vigil on Aba will tie us down and prevent us from actively assisting Muazzam in securing the throne. We should enlist her, but do not tell her about the Makhfi or what we are planning. Just say Raushanara cannot be left alone with Aba."

***

Violent thunderstorms shook the capital city for several days. The River Jumna roiled and rose like hissing serpents, only to fall back in frothing fury. Zebunissa had failed to reach Prince Muazzam; he had fled before receiving her note, fearing for his life in a war of succession. Rumour was rife in the empire that the Emperor was dead. Though Prince Muazzam had received word of the Emperor's illness, he had resisted coming to Delhi, fearing capture or death. Zebunissa knew such fears were not unfounded; Raushanara had dispatched her henchmen to escort Muazzam to Aurengzeb's bedside. Accidents happened frequently on the road, and it would not have been beyond the realm of possibility to hear that Prince Muazzam had taken ill and succumbed during the journey. Hence, Muazzam had taken refuge with Raja Jai Singh in the far reaches of the Empire. Jai Singh, though a supporter of the Emperor, still harbored loyalty towards Shah Jahan, whom he considered the true living Emperor. Zebunissa decided to write to him:

*Excellency,*

*As you are aware, the Emperor is gravely ill. He has lost the ability to speak and has high fevers. The court physicians have attempted to bleed him in an effort to control his temperature, but this has had the effect of worsening his condition. I know my brother has arrived as your guest, seeking shelter. Though he possesses the strength of the Mughal soldier, he lacks the experience to execute the duties of a monarch. Hence I ask you to march with your army to Agra to secure the release of my grandfather, Shah Jahan, and escort him, with my brother, Prince Muazzam, to Delhi. Under my grandfather's tutelage, he will learn the duties of a monarch and rule until my father recovers.*

*Princess Zebunissa*

The intent was clear: Muazzam was to be a temporary stand-in ruler till Aurengzeb recovered. Should the letter fall into the wrong hands, Zebunissa could prove her innocence by saying Shah Jahan's release had been sought for the purpose of training a naive youth in his father's absence. She sealed the scroll and handed it to her eunuch, Didar. "See that this is put into Raja Jai Singh's hand," she directed.

***

Raushanara opened her ruby-studded jewel box and stared at the *Muhr Uzak*, the Royal Seal – an object too large for her hand as it had never been meant for a woman's use. Made of solid gold, it had Persian inscriptions on the side and a large diamond on top.

The legendary *Muhr Uzak* had passed through many powerful hands over the centuries before it found its way to Raushanara. This Royal Seal was so important that no one, not even the Emperor, could reverse its authority once stamped. In its grandiosity lay its true purpose.

On hearing her brother had collapsed, Raushanara had rushed to his bedside. Her status as Empress allowed her to rush past the eunuch guarding the door, where many of the harem women still stood sobbing. Aqil Khan stood aside as she, ignoring the protests of the *hakim*, fell sobbing onto the Emperor's chest, burying her face in his robes. She knew the *Muhr Uzak* was always carried on his person, so she moved her hands over his torso, apparently in grief. But to no avail. The Seal was not there. Raushanara raised her head and asked the hakim what was to be done. While he spoke of bleeding the Emperor to bring down his fever, her eyes swept the chamber, looking for the Emperor's official robes.

When the *hakim* motioned her to move away, she reluctantly did so, walking to the divan where lay the robes the Emperor had shed. As Aqil conferred with Hakims, their backs turned, Raushanara gently lifted the robes, knowing the heavy *Muhr Uzak* would weigh down any garment. Like one caressing the carcass of a fallen mother, she lifted his outer *kurta*. Realizing it was empty, she buried her sobbing face in it. She then bent to gently lift his *pajamas* and immediately felt a heavy weight preventing her from lifting them. Her eyes widened. *Could this be it?* Supporting the weight with one hand she felt the contours of the object with the other. There could be no doubt; it was the Royal Seal. Surreptitiously, she slipped it out, her back to the others. No one looked her way, preoccupied with the Emperor. With head bent and hands hidden beneath her robes, she walked away, bowed by grief.

Raushanara knew the others would soon realize the *Muhr Uzak* was missing but this did not concern her. Indeed, the fact that it was lost was to her advantage for it would argue that any document bearing the Royal Seal had been stamped before the Emperor had taken ill, increasing the legitimacy of that document. In the finest calligraphy, Raushanara wrote on pressed parchment:

*Upon my death, I believe no son of mine possesses the qualities of a true Emperor except for my beloved son, Prince Azam. I therefore declare him my favourite son.*

Though there was no signature, the fingerprint and Royal Seal would be sufficient to convince the Prime Minister and the *mullahs* to support

Prince Azam. Lifting the *Muhr Uzak* in both hands, she dipped it in bright red laq and pressed it onto the document. Pushing down the seal she stared at its incontrovertible imprint. As she watched, the laq dried and set. The next step was to get the Emperor's fingerprint, but this would be tricky. At his bedside hovered the women of the harem, like flies over a carcass. Slipping in and out of the Emperor's chamber without anyone noticing was impossible. She knew she would have to create a diversion, but she knew not what.

Raushanara lay on her bed pondering the possibilities – fire, fainting, loud noises, arrival of a dignitary… Every possibility had flaws. She knew there would be no second opportunity without raising suspicion. She remained awake all night, waiting for the right idea to enter her calculating mind. Hour after hour she struggled to find a solution. Then, shortly before dawn, she found her answer. She knew what she had to do. Raushanara could now fall asleep.

# 9
# THE POISONING

*O careless ones, in vain*
*The treasure of your life has passed away.*

5 DECEMBER 1661

Zebunissa sat knitting a shawl as she kept vigil beside her sick father. Aurengzeb opened his eyes, tried to speak, and slipped back into unconsciousness, ignorant of who was beside him. Zebunissa remained with him for most of the day, not trusting even the women of the Makhfi with the arduous task as keeping Raushanara away from the Emperor. Each time he woke, she would attempt to give him water, wipe his mouth, or cradle his head, for the benefit of the slaves who also functioned as spies. Finally, he began moving his head from side to side, making incomprehensible sounds.

"Aba, it is I, Zebunissa!" She moved closer and cradled his head.

'This was the head of the greatest warrior in the empire once,' she thought; this was the mind that decided that slaying his own kin and presenting their severed heads to his father was appropriate and just; this was the face that commanded armies to invade neighbouring lands; this was the mouth that had branded Hindus infidels and dictated that his own perverse version of Islam be followed in every Muslim home in the kingdom. His emaciated body gave her pause, realizing how vulnerable and weak he was, though he remained ruler in name. She gently put her hand under his neck. She pondered for a moment if she should do the unthinkable. Could she, like him, slay her own kin? It would all be over if she did – Shah Jahan would be Emperor again, her beloved aunt Jahanara reinstated as Empress, the masses allowed religious freedom, and bonds with neighbours and allies repaired. Perhaps her lone surviving uncle, Shah Shuja, believed to be hiding in the jungles of Bengal, would return and resume his role as Governor. One stroke…one jolt would reset the entire empire.

Zebunissa looked around at the slaves. They had fallen asleep or abandoned their vigilance; no one was watching her. Taking a deep breath she squeezed the neck she held. "Water!" he cried out feebly. "Water!"

The sound alerted the slaves and Zebunissa knew she was once again being watched. "Majesty, here is some water," she said, holding a gold cup to his lips. He took a few sips and then drifted back into oblivion. "Sleep, my Emperor…" Zebunissa said loudly, glancing at the guards.

Some time later, Zebunissa once again put her fingers on her father's neck, feeling for a pulse. Though she knew how to kill a man by breaking his neck, she had never actually done so. Sulaimon had demonstrated the noiseless technique to her on a beast and she had boasted she would use it on an enemy one day. That the enemy would be her own father she had never imagined. Zebunissa paused, wondering if she was becoming like her father, willing to kill anyone for any reason. 'Surely it is justified,' she told herself. 'Does not every murderer think he is justified? Is there a killer who is not convinced of the justness of his act?' She looked around again at the slaves; they were asleep. She knew she had to find the courage to commit the act. Carefully, she positioned her hands.

There was a sudden outcry and the sound of running feet. A slave girl from the harem appeared in the doorway and cried, "Princess! Allah help us…Prince Akbar is dead!"

A rush of fear went through Zebunissa. Quickly, she pulled her hands from Aurengzeb's neck and rose, rushing out of the imperial chamber towards that of her most beloved brother. "Akbar!" she called as she ran. She could hear other women from the harem hurrying behind her. She entered Akbar's chamber to find blood all over the floor and Didar bending over the motionless body of the young Prince.

Zebunissa fell on top of the small frame, sobbing, "Akbar, wake up! You can't leave me! You cannot leave your sister!" She pulled his small body to her, feeling like her heart was breaking. She wept as she had done only once before in her life, when Sulaimon was killed.

"My Princess!" Didar said urgently, "the Prince is not dead! There is a pulse. Here, you can feel it here."

Zebunissa looked up, her heart pounding in her chest. She placed two fingers in Akbar's groin and pushed deeply. Shutting her eyes, she concentrated, praying for a pulse. She felt a pulsation but could not tell if it was her own. "I do not feel anything," she told Didar in an agonized voice.

"It is there," he replied calmly. "The *hakim* is on his way."

The *hakim* quickly arrived and began examining Akbar. "What has he eaten?" he asked.

"He had his evening meal and milk, then began vomiting blood," Didar replied.

"I feel a pulse."

Zebunissa closed her eyes thanking Allah for saving her precious brother. "Can you cure him?" she asked the *hakim*.

"I do not know yet, Princess. Perhaps there was something in the Prince's meal. I will have to examine his wastes and anything left from the food and milk."

Zebunissa sat next to the almost lifeless body of the young Prince, cradling his head in her bosom and rocking back and forth.

***

Raushanara had remained in her apartment since Akbar's near-fatal poisoning. The commotion that overtook the harem as the young Prince's condition deteriorated left the Mughal household drained and void of any enthusiasm for politics. Raushanara knew she might eventually become implicated in the poisoning, but for now, no one was pointing a finger at her. She had visited the sick Emperor every day and soon realized that Zebunissa and the Makhfi ladies had stopped keeping vigil at his bedside. Though Nawab Bai remained, Raushanara did not view her as an obstacle.

As Raushanara sat in her chamber, she gestured to her eunuch to approach. "Take this *sherbet* to the Princesses," she told him. "They have not eaten. They will need their strength to care for the ailing Prince."

"It will be done," the eunuch replied, bowing. "I will tell them you have sent a tray for their refreshment."

"No!" Raushanara paused. "Tell them Nawab Bai sent it. If they know it comes from me, they will not drink the sherbet. Nawab Bai is with the Emperor so she will know nothing about it."

"And Nawab Bai…should I take her something?"

"Give her the same sherbet but tell her Zebunissa has sent it."

Though reluctant, the eunuch feared the Empresses' wrath, so he bowed and hurried away.

Raushanara knew the sleep potion in the sherbet would lull the Princesses to sleep even as they kept vigil by the ailing Prince. She waited till midnight and then slipped out of her chambers on silent feet. She circled the outer courtyard of Zebunissa's apartment where Akbar and the Makhfi women were. She stood still, listening for any sound of activity within. All she heard was an almost melodious snoring. She could go no further without raising suspicion. Nevertheless she pondered whether to enter; if discovered, she could simple say she had come to check on Akbar. She hesitated, knowing no one would believe her. If anything, it would ignite the already flickering suspicion that the poisoning had been deliberate, and no one had more to gain than Raushanara, who was positioning Azam to be proclaimed heir.

Turning away, Raushanara walked through the *zenana* apartments to Aurengzeb's chambers. Finding the Makhfi deep in slumber induced by her elixir, she hoped to find Nawab Bai asleep as well. She tiptoed into Aurengzeb's chambers and saw Nawab Bai seated on the ground, her head resting on the foot of the Emperor's bed. Raushanara was unsure if she was truly asleep. It was well past midnight. She noticed the golden cup in which her sherbet had been served; it was half empty. Had Nawab Bai drunk enough of it to make her sleep? Raushanara sighed. 'Such a docile woman!' she thought scornfully. 'This is what happens when you spend a lifetime without drinking liquor; half a cup does the work of a full one.'

Raushanara walked over to Aurengzeb's bedside and lifted his hand and felt his wrist. She noticed the fingers were cold, and the pulse thready. He would die soon, she concluded. Pulling the parchment naming Azam as heir from her bosom, and taking a small bottle of black *kajal* from her waist, she laid the parchment on the Emperor's torso. Opening the small bottle of *kajal*, she gently took Aurengzeb's thumb and dipped it in till the thumb was as black as this fateful night. Reaching for the parchment, she pressed his thumb hard on the document. It only remained for the imprint to dry. Dropping the Emperor's hand, Raushanara carefully held up the parchment, blowing on it. Finally, she folded the parchment in thirds and placed it neatly inside her tunic, a smile on her thin lips.

Suddenly she felt a strong hand grip her right wrist. Turning quickly, she saw it was Nawab Bai. She had witnessed the deed! Nawab Bai pulled Raushanara towards her, causing her to lose her balance, stumble and fall. The usually docile Nawab Bai thrust her right hand into Raushanara's tunic to pluck the parchment, but before she could, Raushanara caught Nawab Bai's hand in an iron grip. She slammed her fist into Nawab Bai's chest, causing her to fall back. Raushanara quickly scrambled up and tried to run out of the apartment, but Nawab Bai managed to grab hold of Raushanara's gown and began tugging on it. Desperately, Raushanara caught hold of Nawab Bai's hair and pulled, hoping the pain would cause Nawab Bai to release her.

But Nawab Bai would not relent. Her face contorted in pain, she grabbed Raushanara's *pajamas* with both hands, pulling them down.

"You witch!" she yelled. "You scheme to use this moment of darkness to plunge us further into chaos by installing a puppet? This is your brother who lies here!" Nawab Bai pulled ferociously at Raushanara's *pajamas*. The fine material ripped in her hands, exposing the ageing Empress' private parts.

Raushanara now wore only her tunic. But after a moment of shocked embarrassment, she quickly realized it allowed her to freely move her legs. She kicked Nawab Bai in the stomach, still holding Raushanara's *pajamas*. Gripping Nawab Bai's hair with one hand, she pounced on her, pushing her to the ground. Holding her down with her weight, Raushanara continued to pull Nawab Bai's hair, forcing her head upwards. In agony, Nawab Bai began crying for help.

Raushanara, half-naked on her sister-in-law's back, used her other hand to cover Nawab Bai's mouth. "Hush, you useless mouse!" she hissed into Nawab Bai's ear. "You cannot defeat me! I will install Azam and rule the kingdom! And when I do, you will be my slave. You will clean my *hammam* and prepare water for my bath. I will sell you to the cleaners for their amusement. You cannot stop me, you cripple!" Viciously, he banged Nawab Bai's head on the marble floor.

The last thing Nawab Bai saw before she lost consciousness was the manic light in Raushanara's eyes.

Quickly pulling on her ripped pajamas and holding the garment at her waist with one hand, Raushanara hurried out of Aurengzeb's chamber.

## 10
## The Coronation

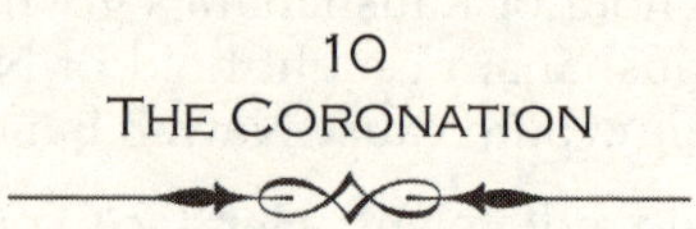

*Within the jungle of this world of woe*
*The lion of desire stalks ravenous.*

6 January 1661

Muazzam trimmed his beard in the same manner his ancestors had –a thick hooked line connected his eyebrows and chin, while a moustache covered his upper lip and fell in two thin lines to merge with his beard. Unlike Aurengzeb, Muazzam was not fair-skinned but dark. When he appeared before Raja Jai Singh in his Mughal robes, a gold-studded dagger in his belt, the Rajput was taken aback. "Hey, Ram! You are the striking image of your grandfather Shah Jahan!" he declared.

Muazzam smiled, having gradually come to terms with the reality that he would be the next Emperor of India. Zebunissa's support had strengthened his resolve and with Raja Jai Singh by his side, he felt emboldened to march on Delhi.

"Majesty, you have been a gracious host but my sister, Princess Zebunissa, insists we do not delay in assembling the army and marching on Agra to release my grandfather, and my aunt, Jahanara. With his re-installation as Emperor, my father's tyranny will cease!"

"Do not worry, Great Prince," responded Jai Singh. "I have already sent the necessary commands to my Generals to prepare the army. We will be in Agra next week!" Jai Singh walked over to Muazzam and placed a hand on his shoulder. "Come with me, Prince," he said with a warm smile, and led Muazzam through the palace to a small room on the far side.

Muazzam could smell incense and *ghee,* which he knew the Hindus used in their prayer rituals. The aroma became stronger as they walked through the corridor. Eventually, they entered a domed room painted in gold. Lamps hung from the ceiling and in the distance stood a blue statue of the Hindu God Krishna, playing a flute. Muazzam knew he was in the presence of a revered deity.

Jai Singh folded his hands in prayer and bowed as Muazzam watched stoically. Jai Singh then dipped his finger in the red vermillion powder that lay in a golden plate before the deity and placed a red dot on Muazzam's forehead. "Victory be yours, Great Prince!" Turning to the deity once again, he bowed low in homage. Rising, he looked at Muazzam and said, "You shall be Emperor!"

Muazzam placed his hands on Jai Singh's folded hands and thanked him for his kind gesture. "Your loyalty will not be forgotten, Maharaja. While I reign, Hindu and Muslim will live in harmony once again."

***

The Peacock Throne sparkled as the rays of the sun reflected from the pearls, rubies and diamonds in its canopy. Shah Jahan had ordered the gem stones placed in a way so that every time the sun shone, the Peacock Throne glittered. The same enchantment greeted anyone entering the Taj Mahal, which Shah Jahan had spent much of his reign building. The entrance of the majestic monument was studded with mirrorwork and gemstones. As one walked through the main gate, the jewels seemed to take turns to sparkle. But all this magnificence and beauty were of little consequence to Shah Jahan, a prisoner of State, nor to Aurengzeb, on the verge of death. The choice of successor to the Peacock Throne hung in limbo. Court was once again convened in the *Diwan-i-Khas* to discuss the future of the monarchy. Raushanara shrewdly avoided the throne, taking a more humble place in the foreground. Zebunissa and Nawab Bai stood behind the screen, opposite her. Behind Raushanara stood the *mullahs* and on the other side of the hall stood the Rajputs and other nobility.

The Prime Minister took his place beside the empty throne and gestured for silence. "We are assembled to discuss the future of the monarchy. It is imperative that we install a caretaker Emperor until Emperor Alamgir has recovered his health. Without an Emperor, I fear our adversaries will sense weakness and attempt to invade."

There was silence. Neither Raushanara nor Zebunissa would admit their choice for Emperor was self-serving.

The Prime Minister turned towards Raushanara. "Empress, you mentioned you had proof that the Emperor wished Prince Azam to be his heir. Are you prepared to present this proof before us?"

Zebunissa stared though the *jali* at her aunt. She noticed that Raushanara was more composed than she had been at previous gatherings. She also saw the half smile that crossed her aunt's face.

Raushanara glanced around the assembly. "Nobles, Ministers and servitors of the Emperor, I declare with pride that even in the most difficult times of my brother's life, I have remained his most trusted companion and advisor. When the infidel Emperor Shah Jahan fell ill, it was I who infiltrated into the home of Dara-the-Usurper, and duped him so that Alamgir would emerge victorious in the war of succession."

Years ago, Shah Jahan had fallen ill and many had believed he was about to die. Thus, Aurengzeb and his brothers had launched a rebellion against Dara, the heir apparent. However, even their combined armies were outnumbered by Dara's men. It was then that Aurengzeb had sent Raushanara to Dara, under the pretext of seeking asylum; claiming Aurengzeb had evicted her and she needed protection. Gullible and naive, Dara had succumbed to Raushanara's pleas and had even sought her counsel on how best to defeat Aurengzeb. Raushanara had used the opportunity to provide Dara with false information about Aurengzeb's military positions. Acting on this information, Dara had found himself outwitted by Aurengzeb, and ultimately lost the battle against his brothers.

Zebunissa had been saddened to learn her father had won the throne through treachery, having always viewed him as a valiant warrior who fought and won. Listening to her aunt's words, she was once again reminded of the sadness that had flooded her soul; her helplessness in doing anything to change the course of events. She felt ashamed of her heritage, where she had once been so proud. But even more, she felt embarrassed to be related to Raushanara, who not only betrayed her brother Dara's trust, but was now bragging about it in court.

"My brother spoke to me many times about his heir," Raushanara continued. "He was devastated by Prince Sultan's betrayal, and thought Muazzam weak and ineffectual. Thus he named Prince Azam as his favourite son!" She pulled out the rolled parchment and held it up. "This scroll has his imprint and the Royal Seal!"

"The document is fake!" Zebunissa's voice rang boldly across the great audience chamber. "The Empress fabricated it and then placed my father's finger on the parchment while he lay unconscious! When my mother, Nawab Bai, tried to stop her, she pulled her by her hair and beat her till she fell unconscious!"

"That is a lie!" shot back Raushanara. "I never forced anyone to sign anything!"

The Head *mullah*, Raushanara's closest ally, held up his hand for silence. He turned towards the grilled window and addressed Zebunissa. "Princess, do you have any witnesses other than Nawab Bai herself, to corroborate such an allegation?"

Zebunissa knew the *mullah* would speak on Raushanara's behalf and had no doubt been tutored beforehand. "There were no other witnesses for it happened in the middle of the night when the palace was asleep and the guards stood outside the closed doors of the Emperor's chamber."

"Since it is your word against that of the Empress, we have no option but to conclude the parchment is real."

"Or that it is fake!" shot back Zebunissa. "The last time this court assembled she had no proof. And now, suddenly, this is produced, complete with fingerprint and Royal Seal! Does not anyone else in this court question how such a document can be so perfect?"

It was Raushanara's turn to speak. "Perhaps Princess Zebunissa can tell the court how, even if I forced the Emperor's fingerprint on the document, how could I have made it with the Royal Seal?"

There was immediate murmuring among those in the hall. Zebunissa herself was taken aback, having anticipated being questioned about the Seal.

"Princess," the Prime Minister said, "the presence of the Royal Seal on the document has to be considered."

Zebunissa paused before declaring with conviction, "She stole it!"

"This discourse leads us into darkness," the *mullah* intervened. "We are accusing the Empress, who has proven her loyalty to the Emperor from the time before he was Emperor, of lying to the court! And yet there is no proof presented. I wish to remind the assembly that what we should be discussing is why Prince Azam cannot be considered as the Emperor's heir, according to his stated wishes?"

"He is but a child," Zebunissa said.

"Then we shall train him," responded the *mullah*. "The great Emperor Akbar was also a child when his father died, but he became a great Mughal ruler!"

Zebunissa felt her position weakening; she had no proof but Nawab Bai's words, and Raushanara had cunningly secured the support of some of the most influential men at court.

The Prime Minister finally spoke. "It is acknowledged by all that we must have an heir to the throne. In view of the document presented here, bearing the Royal Seal and the Emperor's finger impression, we must declare Prince Azam the heir. But we cannot coronate a new Emperor before the previous one has entered the Halls of Paradise. Hence my counsel is to install Prince Azam as caretaker ruler until the Emperor has recovered."

Zebunissa saw Raushanara glittering smile suddenly disappear; she had not anticipated the Prime Minister's caveat. Breathing quickly, Zebunissa felt rage flood her being. She shot a look at Raushanara, only to see her aunt gazing mockingly at her, standing behind the screen. Zebunissa walked away in haste, the Makhfi members following behind.

***

Zebunissa knew she must warn Muazzam, urging him to march on Delhi before the official installation began. Fearing that a letter openly imploring him to march on Delhi would be construed by the *mullahs* and Raushanara as an act of sedition to overturn the wishes of the court, she once again penned a cryptic poem carrying a veiled message:

*My Dear Brother*

*The Makhfi meetings have not been the same without your presence. I am sending you a poem I wrote the other day, thinking about you.*

*O COME, my Love, for I am worn and wasted,*
*I have no longer strength nor will to wait;*
*My heart bears countless wounds and I have tasted*
*The poisonous anguish of the shafts of fate.*

*Breeze of the dawn, come, see the wild confusion*
*The fall sun has wrought in all my bowers;*
*Only my heart's blood with a strange illusion*
*Colours the parterre erst so gay with flowers.*

*Just so Love's flowers are blasted. Other traces*
*Are none but hearts wounded and bleeding sore.*
*All that is fair the surge of time effaces:*
*Father is gone and Zebunissa is no more.*

*Your loving sister Zebunissa*

Zebunissa prayed Muazzam would understand. Should he not, Azam would be installed.

***

Turquoise silk robes stirred in the breeze as Muazzam mounted his horse. The many stringed necklace of rare pearls Raja Jai Singh had gifted him rose and fell on his breast as his horse moved forward. As he gazed at the cavalry of thousands following him on his journey to Agra to free his grandfather, and then march with him to Delhi, he sat straight on his horse, looking more like the warrior commander the empire needed now and less like the feeble prince he was always thought to be. The thousands strong cavalry he commanded were Hindu Rajput soldiers, legendary warriors with a reputation for fighting to the last man and never surrendering. The Rajputs were a key ally of the Mughals, having taken glorious part in every major conquest. Officially, the Rajput kingdoms were part of the Mughal Empire and their soldiers obliged to serve whenever the Mughal Emperor called upon them. Several Rajput Princesses had married into the Mughal royal family, their Rajput Hindu blood intermingling with Muslim blood in their shared offspring.

Muazzam had seen how the Rajput Rajas had grown disenchanted with his father over his racist policies, destruction of Hindu temples, and the enforcement of heavy taxes on Hindu kingdoms. The outlawing of music and the arts was a minor edict compared to the restrictions he placed on non-Muslims. Hence Muazzam and Zebunissa had little trouble in securing their support to free Shah Jahan and overthrow Aurengzeb. Muazzam heard the beating of the taut-skinned kettle drums as the cavalry prepared to march. A fanfare of trumpets sounded as Muazzam and Jai Singh led the army towards the gates of the fort. Along the way they passed the markets and dwellings of the nobility; they bowed, *tikkas* on their foreheads and hands folded, a prayer on their lips as Raja and Prince passed them on their way to battle.

Muazzam caught a glimpse of an old hunchbacked woman with grey hair and missing teeth, standing beside the pathway. As he passed she raised one hand and shouted, "Oh Krishna! Protect these sons of yours!" Emotion engulfed Muazzam as he saw how the very people he had been taught to hate as infidels were treating him like a son, one of their own. In that moment he felt the weight of the hopes, aspirations and dreams of the entire kingdom resting on his shoulders. But the thought of turning back or escaping never entered his mind even as his heart thudded in his chest. The echoes of the townspeople chanting their

Hindu war cry, *Har Har Mahadev*, resonated in his ears. For a moment he too, desired to join the thunderous chanting instead of voicing the Muslim cry of *Allah ho Akbar*! He felt at one with these people who had sheltered and protected him when he sought refuge, and who were now sending him off to battle with accolades and blessings. Staring proudly ahead, he took a deep breath and then let out a slow sigh. He knew what he had to do – race towards Agra, a journey of several hundred *kos*, without stopping to rest, and free his grandfather.

***

Three *kos* from Agra, Muazzam noticed a line of burgundy-robed soldiers barricading the entrance to the city. Uncertain why the road was being thus barricaded, Prince Muazzam rode over to the Mughal Commander of the force on duty.

"Greetings Prince! We did not expect to see you here." The Commander was a plump man in his forties, his manners polished; he appeared to be a long serving soldier from the days of his grandfather's rule.

Despite his reputation for weakness, Muazzam was no fool. He knew he could not trust anyone. "I have been asked to check on my grandfather, the Emperor Shah Jahan. I am told his health is poor."

"Allah is merciful!" responded the Commander. "We have just come from the fort. The old Emperor is in good spirits."

"I must follow my orders, Commander, and visit the Emperor myself. Let me pass." Muazzam maintained a calm demeanor, convinced that an all-out battle this early in the journey would not be to his advantage.

"Certainly Prince, but I too, have my orders and must obey them. I must ask from whom you have orders to enter the fort?"

"Sir, you overstep your bounds! I am the Prince of India and can visit my grandfather when I wish."

"I beg your forgiveness, Prince, but I have been instructed to guard a three *kos* periphery around Agra. No one may enter with a weapon."

"Who dares issue such instructions?"

"The Emperor."

"The Emperor is on his deathbed!"

"Not Emperor Alamgir, but his son, Emperor Azam."

Muazzam instantly became cautious. He had mistaken the Commander as a well-mannered loyalist of his grandfather, but it now appeared that he was an ally of his aunt, Raushanara. Muazzam knew Azam had not yet been installed as interim Emperor, and to call him such was an act of sedition. This man had obviously been sent at Raushanara's behest. The words of Zebunissa's poem flashed through his mind:

*O COME, my Love, for I am worn and wasted,*
*I have no longer strength nor will to wait;*

She had been warning him not to delay coming to Delhi. Perhaps, she was telling him Shah Jahan's release would have to wait until matters in Delhi were brought under control. Muazzam lifted his head and turned his horse. Seeing this, a smile spread across the Commander's face. Muazzam knew he must have orders to engage him in battle and then slay him, under the pretext that freeing Shah Jahan was an act of sedition. Muazzam rode quickly back to where Jai Singh waited with his army. Though the Rajput Raja knew he was outnumbered by the burgundy robed Mughal force guarding the fort, he waited calmly to learn which way the wind blew.

Muazzam halted beside Jai Singh in a cloud of dust. "It's a trap!" he whispered. "My sister was not telling me to hurry to Agra, but get to Delhi before Raushanara overthrows Aba and establishes herself, through my brother Azam, as the defacto ruler of India. She already has sympathizers in the army. We must hurry!"

***

Though Zebunissa scoffed at the changes occurring around her, her heart was sorely troubled. Using soft words, sweet promises, stinging threats, and at times ruthless force, Raushanara was relentlessly increasing the number of her allies. The *mullahs* remained squarely on her side, while the nobles were split between a faction that followed the *mullahs* into Raushanara's camp, and a faction that preferred Prince Muazzam on the throne, and hence supported Zebunissa.

Within days of the installation of the puppet Emperor, Raushanara had him renew her status as *Padishah Begum* and grant her permission to hold the *Muhr Uzak*. She also prompted him to gift her the apartments that belonged to Aurengzeb's senior wives, including Nawab Bai. She sat beside him in the *Diwani-i-Khas*, whispering instructions into his ear.

But as Prince Akbar's condition continued to improve, Zebunissa began to spend less time caring for him and more in forming her strategy. She called meetings of the Makhfi in her chambers at night, knowing Raushanara did not dare outlaw the Society; at least not yet. Aware that Aurengzeb's spies were now working for Raushanara, Zebunissa knew she had to be careful who attended the meetings. The Makhfi, yet again, proved to be the best cover. Zubdat, Zinat, Badr and Mihirunissa attended, along with Mawlana Abdul Qader Bedil, Kalim Kashani, Saa'eb Tabrizi, Ghani Kashmiri and their ad hoc mentor, Aqil Khan. They came, dressed in expensive garments. They drank the lemon juice and wine served and listened with pleasure to the *sitar* being played, now that the enemy of the arts was no longer in power. They had come a long way from the monotonous humming.

Zubdat began her recitation.

*I ask, oh, world that has fallen*
*When will the messiah come*
*In his absence my head has fallen*
*With agony my heart is numb.*

The intent was clear. Zubdat was inquiring about Muazzam's whereabouts. Zebunissa had expected the question. She would recite last, addressing all their concerns. Mihirunissa went next:

*Was I once in paradise*
*Or but a pleasant dream*
*For I awake in agony*
*And none can hear me scream.*

*When in place of a great lion*
*A serpent attempts to roar*
*All in its path will be stung*
*As it races through my corridors.*

*I ask the Lord for mercy*
*For a thousand sins I've done*
*Where can I find his mercy*
*To where should I run?*

Zebunissa understood Mihirunissa's anguish. Raushanara was a serpent worse than Aurengzeb. She had to be stopped, whatever the means. Zebunissa glanced around the chamber, trying to read the emotions of the nobles (spies Raushanara had planted). Men of no poetic talent, they seemed oblivious of what was in fact being said about their leader under their watchful eyes. Zebunissa turned to listen to her other sister, Zinat.

*An old lion sleeps in his lair*
*Shunned by his progeny*
*Return him to his glory*
*Give him back his dignity.*

*Let him turn this jungle*
*Into the paradise it had once been*
*Let him spend his final days*
*Grooming the most deserving of his kin.*

Zebunissa took a deep breath and looked once more at the spies. The poem was not cryptic enough, she feared. The plan to free Shah Jahan and have him groom Muazzam had been discussed in the *Diwan-i-Khas,* in front of the court. Would the buffoons Raushanara had sent to spy on the Makhfi, who seemed more intent on the wine than the poetry, understand the layers of meaning?

One of the men raised his hand. "*Vah vah*!" he said in appreciation. Soon *vah vah* echoed round the chamber, each man calling out loudly, lest he be perceived to be ignorant of finer things. Silently, Zebunissa let out a sigh.

"Zebunissa, any new poems from you today?" asked one of the women seated to one side.

Zebunissa looked up, hoping her composition would contain the answers they craved.

*LOVE, the marauder, ties to his saddle*
*Many a scalp of his slaughtered foes;*
*With the blood of mankind will paint*
*On the earth's forehead a crimson rose.*

*Paradise turned to jungle.*
*Jungle will give way to paradise again.*
*Await the coming of the messiah*
*Who will rid this world of sin.*

She stopped, knowing she could not read out the passages in which she spoke of the *old lion* (Shah Jahan), the *current lion* (Aurengzeb), the *serpent* (Raushanara), and others. Her message was clear enough she thought; Muazzam was on his way. Raushanara's reign of terror would soon come to an end.

***

The thick sandstone walls of the Red Fort glowed like a ripe apple under the winter sun. As Prince Muazzam rode towards the capital, the fort looked a gleaming ruby. Behind him sounded the hoofbeats of a thousand men; the loyal companions who had ridden with him from Jai Singh's palace to Agra, and on to Delhi. Muazzam knew the walled city had eight gates. Even if the main ones, used for commerce and the reception of dignitaries, were closed, there would be at least one gate left open for travellers.

A hundred yards from the city, Muazzam pulled his horse to a stop. He looked around at his soldiers, who stared back at him in bewilderment. "We must not alarm them with so many men," he said to Jai Singh, his face coated with dust. "You stay here with the men while I go ahead with ten of your finest soldiers."

Jai Singh nodded in acquiescence. "But do not rush in, Prince," he cautioned. "Ride in casually, like you know nothing of recent events. Any sign of haste will raise suspicion." He then turned to his Commander, who would lead the small task force. "If you require assistance, wave the yellow flag. We will know you are in danger."

Prince Muazzam and his company of ten Rajput soldiers rode towards the city. As they approached, Muazzam was surprised to see the large Delhi gate being opened. This could be a trap, he thought. Perhaps, he was being welcomed into the city so Raushanara could arrest him and send him to prison, alongside his older brother. But it could also mean he was not perceived as a threat. This would make the job of securing the throne easier.

Muazzam rode into the city, staying close to his company of soldiers. His dagger and sword were secured to his belt. He kept one hand on the bridle while placing the other on his sword. Inside the city, Muazzam was surprised to see how little had changed. No one acted any differently than they had before Aurengzeb's illness. Women still covered their faces; men maintained long beards; music and arts were still outlawed. It was as if the people chose not to believe the Emperor was dying and change approaching. Nothing short of seeing the Emperor's dead body would convince these people their misery has finally come to an end, thought Muazzam as he rode along Chandni Chowk. In the centre of this major avenue flowed a water canal which, on moonlit nights, glittered in reflection of the moon, hence the name Moonlit Avenue.

As he neared the Red Fort, Muazzam noticed the main gate was shut. He continued to ride forward, ready to summon Jai Singh and his thousand troops if necessary. When the guards stationed at the gate approached his horse, Muazzam said imperatively, "Open the gate!"

"I crave forgiveness, Prince, but the gate can only be opened with the permission of *Padishah Begum*. She is Regent till the Emperor recovers."

Muazzam's face tightened. "I am the Emperor's eldest son now that Sultan has been imprisoned. I demand that you open this gate or I will sever your head!" Muazzam pulled his sword from his scabbard, pointing it straight at the soldier's neck.

"For-forgive me," quavered the fearful soldier. "But if I allow you to enter, I will be killed. The court is gathered in the *Diwan-i-Khas*; I can send a messenger informing the court that you wish to enter the fort. It will only cause a short delay but will help us preserve our necks."

***

Zebunissa stood watching from behind the grilled screens as her young brother, Prince Azam, was placed on the Peacock Throne, utterly oblivious of the responsibilities being thrust upon him. Raushanara stood next to him, heavily veiled. There was a thickness in the air. The Makhfi had become ever more anxious with each passing day and Zebunissa had struggled to keep them calm. Gazing into the *Diwan-i-Khas,* she sensed an aura of uneasiness. The taut faces of the nobles and *mullahs* clearly reflected their discomfort. No one was content with the choice, yet felt helpless to do anything about it. Alamgir was on his deathbed; Shah Jahan imprisoned and presumed demented; Prince Sultan imprisoned on charges of high treason; and Prince Muazzam's whereabouts unknown. Even so, permitting Raushanara to assume the throne was unthinkable, even to the *mullahs* whose favour she had effectively secured. Women were not created to rule over men, they declared unequivocally. Though she was an enlightened scholar, the daughter of a living Emperor, and grand-daughter of another, Zebunissa too, found herself powerless to assume the throne and steer the empire through these tumultuous times.

The *Qazi* began reading aloud the proclamation in the Emperor's name: Alamgir. All those in attendance observed the ritual; none dared suggest it be read in Azam's name as he was to be merely an interim Emperor, installed but not crowned.

"Prime Minister, pray begin any business of State." The high piping voice of the nine-year-old was an embarrassment for the court, Zebunissa felt. How could this day have come? She couldn't shake the humiliation in her bosom at watching her father's court answering to a child.

The Prime Minister stepped forward. "Majesty," he began, "we have a man who stole a loaf of bread from the hands of a widow."

"Death to the fiend!" yelled Azam, raising his golden dagger into the air.

Murmuring began to circulate around the court. Zebunissa's heart sank. She noticed Raushanara stepping forward but Bairam Khan, the Head *Mullah,* stopped her with a gesture and stepped forward himself.

"My child..." he began, then coughed and cleared his throat and said again, "Majesty, one cannot simply kill someone who commits an offense. We have laws that deal with various offenses and there are degrees of punishment." The *mullah* spoke as one tutoring a student.

Zebunissa thought how sad and strange it was to see the great Mughal Empire in the hands of an immature child being counseled by a *mullah* of fanatical faith. Her face reddened with anxiety. A sudden commotion at the back of the court drew her attention. All eyes turned to discover the cause of the stir. Had a scuffle broken out, or had someone perhaps fainted in the crush? As she stood on tiptoe among the other women, all craning their necks to see, Zebunissa saw a soldier, dressed in the burgundy that marked him as an imperial guard, making his way hastily through the crowd. Had there been a crime that required the court's immediate attention, she wondered? Why was a guard permitted to disturb the proceedings of the court? Was the kingdom under attack? Zebunissa held her breath. If the kingdom was to be attacked now, the invaders would find little resistance.

The guard whispered urgently into the ear of the Commander of the Guards who was on duty in the hall. Zebunissa grew impatient at not knowing what was being said. Suddenly, she noticed that having listened to his subordinate, the Commander stepped forward, bowed and said, "Majesty, I have just been informed that Prince Muazzam is at the entrance of the fort and seeks permission to enter!"

There was loud cheering and clapping from the harem women behind the screens. Zebunissa grabbed her chest in relief. Many in the audience hall joined in while the *mullahs* and Raushanara stood in stoic silence.

"Brother Muazzam has arrived!" cried Azam in terror, jumping up from the throne in fright, rather like a deer who had spotted a tiger. "Aunt Raushanara! Do not let him kill me!" he pleaded in tears, clutching Raushanara round her waist.

Zebunissa saw Raushanara quickly hide the hysterical lad in an embrace, likely hoping to prevent further humiliation. But it seemed to be too late. The spectacle of the installed Emperor displaying blatant cowardice seemed to astonish everyone, much to Zebunissa's delight. Zebunissa knew that this young lad was no Akbar; he lacked the mental maturity and confidence to be an Emperor. The mere mention of his brother had caused him to run and hide. The Empire would disintegrate. Zebunissa continued to watch the spectacle, her heart filled with elation and sorrow in equal measure.

"Will Muazzam be able to overthrow Raushanara and her pet Emperor?" asked Zubdat as she nudged Zebunissa.

Zebunissa glanced at her sister and then looked ahead. "He won't need to. I think Emperor Azam's reign is already coming to an end with the mere mention of Muazzam's name! Look…" She pointed to the little puddle that had formed around the child Emperor's feet. Holding her hand over her mouth, she began to laugh. Soon the whole hall was laughing to see that young Azam had wet his pajamas.

Raushanara, who had her head bent over the boy, looked up to see what the cause of such hilarity was. Startled to see the puddle at her feet, she quickly moved backwards, pulling the boy with her. Petrified, Azam resisted, rooted to the spot. In the tugging back and forth, Azam slipped on the wet marble floor and lost his balance. The new Emperor elect lay at Raushanara's feet in tears while the crowd roared in laughter. Zebunissa was ecstatic. The day had begun with no news of Muazzam and Azam as the heir apparent; it now seemed that the day would end with Muazzam on the throne and Raushanara humiliated.

"Get up!" hissed Raushanara angrily. "All you had to do was issue a proclamation to have Muazzam arrested!" The public humiliation was more than she could bear. Raushanara shot a scathing look at the crowd who immediately fell silent. She grabbed Azam's shoulder and thrust him towards the screens, away from the sneers and prying eyes of the court.

The courtiers gazed at the empty throne. "In the absence of a royal directive, I hereby decree the gates to be opened and Prince Muazzam be allowed to enter," declared the Prime Minister.

Zebunissa hid a smile. She remained silent, hiding her jubilation. She looked up hearing the sound of horses approaching the *Diwan-i-Khas*, but the ornate pillars hid her view.

*Hail Prince Muazzam!* The crowd began chanting as soon as Muazzam dismounted from his horse. Zebunissa saw him lead a small procession into the heart of the court. The chanting became louder as those chanting marched with him towards the Peacock throne. "Hail Prince Muazzam!" Zebunissa continued to purse her lips and bit her lip so as to not seem too exuberant. The women of the Makhfi pressed their faces against the marble screen behind which they were standing. Then, Muazzam emerged from behind one of the large stone columns, wearing his jeweled turban and a well-groomed beard. Zebunissa reckoned that for the first time, her brother looked like an Emperor.

The dense crowd of dignitaries quickly separated down the middle, akin to a piece of cloth being torn apart by a brute force, as Muazzam and his cadre of soldiers marched down the center. Muazzam finally stood at the front of the hall facing towards the crowd, as if purposely avoiding sitting on the throne.

"Welcome home Prince!" said the Prime Minister, bowing as Muazzam nodded acknowledgement. "A man without a head cannot last long; in the same manner, the House of Timur cannot last without an Emperor!"

Zebunissa bit back a smile at the Prime Minister's remark. It suddenly seemed that everyone was now in favour of making Muazzam Emperor. Timur, the legendary ancestor of the Mughals had attacked India several hundred years ago and looted lavish bounty, which he took back with him to his ancestral home, Samarkand. Several generations later, Timur›s descendant, Babur, once again invaded India, but unlike his ancestor, he remained and established an empire and the Mughal dynasty. The Mughals still took pride in Timur's initial conquest that had paved the way for future invasions. Hence the Mughals proudly referred to themselves as the House of Timur.

"Prime Minister," said Muazzam. "I am here to protect my home and the empire from our enemies. With the accord of all those present here, I wish to ascend the throne and accept proclamation as Emperor in my name."

The Head Mullah stepped forward and bowed. "I would like to utter a few words if the court permits." When the Prime Minister nodded, the *mullah* continued. "Proclamation cannot be done so simply. If the proper prayers are not said, and the proper ceremonies conducted in accordance with Islamic law, then Allah will not bless the kingdom with his mercy. We must be patient."

Muazzam's eyes flashed and his mouth pressed into a thin line. He looked towards the screens where Zebunissa stood. If only Zebunissa's advice could reach Muazzam's ears. But alas, it could not. Zebunissa knew that Muazzam would have to manage on his own.

"It is well said. We will wait for the appropriate prayers to be said. For now Prince, perhaps you would like to rest after your journey," he suggested.

"I have not come to rest!" declared Muazzam. "I have been on the road for many days because we must protect the empire! Forgo these prayers; there is much to do!"

"Every Mughal Emperor has adhered to them," admonished the *mullah*. "Prince Muazzam, you have sworn to protect your father's throne. What is the hurry? Let there be celebration for a few days while we plan the declaration in a manner befitting an Emperor."

Muazzam seemed to have cooled his rage. He decided to use the moment to garner an additional favour. "I shall wait then!" he said, "but I ask that my grandfather, Shah Jahan, and my beloved aunt, Jahanara, be freed from imprisonment in Agra Fort to be present at my declaration as Emperor."

"That is impossible without the royal decree of the Emperor," said the *mullah*, a steadfast opponent of Shah Jahan's secular policies.

Zebunissa's face tightened but Muazzam responded calmly. "*Mullahji*, if you wish me to believe you have accepted my ascension to the throne without reservation, then surely you will see no harm in acceding to my wish."

Zebunissa noticed the *mullahs* look at each other in bewilderment, likely unused to having their diktats questioned.

Muazzam continued, "Either we hear the declaration in my name now, or we wait for the prayers and preparations to be concluded as you desire; in which case you must accept my wish as a decree from your future Emperor."

Zebunissa was astonished. Such clever manipulation was not in Muazzam's nature. Every move he had made till then had been led by the cryptic messages hidden in her poems, but not this; this was Muazzam's own.

The Head *Mullah* bowed. "So be it. Free whomsoever you wish, but be aware that once Emperor Alamgir regains his strength, he will once again sit on the Peacock Throne and he will not be pleased with this decision of yours."

Zebunissa merely smiled. 'If he regains his strength,' she thought.

## 11
## EMPEROR MUAZZAM

*Tell me, O Makhfi, is it I who sin?*
*Is this my sin I bear?*

8 MARCH 1662

And so it began. Muazzam, Alamgir's clumsy son, known to be weak willed, was about to become the seventh Mughal Emperor of the House of Timur. Zebunissa wondered what kind of a ruler her brother would be. Would he adopt the secular policies of his grandfather or the strict fanatical rule of his father? On this day, her most beloved sister and confidante, Zubdat, sat beside her, trying to calm her emotions.

"No one can predict who will be great and who will not," Zubdat remarked, neatly folding the shawls lying in a messy pile on Zebunissa's divan. "Greatness comes at unexpected moments."

Zebunissa recalled her family's history had begun over a century ago, when her ancestor Babur invaded India, advancing from his home in central Asia. After him his son Humayun had inherited the throne but died at an early age. Humayun's toddler son, Akbar, thus became the defacto Mughal Emperor. Zebunissa's face tightened every time she remembered how Raushanara had invoked Akbar's name to make the case for Azam to be Emperor, claiming that child rulers were as effective as adult ones. Did that witch Raushanara really think Azam was to be compared to Akbar, who even as a child understood matters of court?

Zubdat smiled and let out a sigh. "Raushanara did all she could to convince the court to favour her. But we won. You must stay calm."

Zebunissa closed her eyes to calm her nerves. Under Emperor Akbar, the Mughals had indeed enjoyed remarkable power and glory. He broke centuries of tradition by marrying a Hindu bride, bridging the gap between the Muslims and Hindus in his empire. His secular policies expanded the empire's reach and led to him being known as Akbar the Great.

Zubdat carried a pile of folded shawls to the camphor wood chest in which they were stored, safe from insects and moths. "I am sure Emperor Akbar thought every Emperor after him would follow his example. No one could have predicted that Akbar's own son, Jahangir, would be a heroin addict."

Zebunissa smiled mischievously as she sipped her ginger tea. "They say he consumed so much opium that it was rumored that on most days he was too drugged to rule the kingdom."

Zubdat skipped towards Zebunissa and jumped on top of her. "And who ruled in his place, my dear Zebo?"

Zebunissa began to laugh, catching hold of Zubdat's hands in her own. "His virulent Queen, Nur Jahan!" she said.

The two girls laughed, rocking back and forth, holding each other.

"Nur Jahan remains an enigma to a Princess like me," remarked Zubdat. "Let's see, she was temperamental, bossy and vicious. She had strong opinions and considered herself superior to most men! Well, I know no one like that…who can take over if Muazzam proves to be inept!"

Zebunissa playfully punched her sister. "Enough sarcasm!" she admonished, her spirits lifting. "You bring up a good point though. What kind of Emperor will Muazzam be? Will he follow Emperor Akbar, or contribute architectural glory like our grandfather, Shah Jahan did?" Zebunissa had a wistful look on her face. "During grandfather's reign the Red Fort was renovated and beautiful edifices constructed all over India, including the Taj Mahal. Perhaps Muazzam will add to his legacy."

"As long as he is not like Aba, any alternative will do," retorted Zubdat, throwing her pendant into the air and catching it expertly.

Aurengzeb was the sixth Mughal Emperor and he publicly scorned his predecessors' tolerant ways. He viewed non-Muslims as infidels and from a young age, took pleasure in destroying Hindu temples and statues. He abhorred vanity, and viewed the construction of opulent edifices as an affront to God. Thus, even the Taj Mahal was left to the mercy of time and the elements, with no money spent on its upkeep. Incrementally destroying a century of progress, Aurengzeb's reign was a nightmare for most Indians; except for the orthodox *mullahs* who now enjoyed unlimited power.

***

On one pretext or the other, the *mullahs* continued to stall providing a date for the Emperor's declaration. This worried Zebunissa; she knew she could not trust them. After pressure was brought to bear by the Prime Minister, they finally agreed to a date. The ceremony would take place on a Friday, after morning prayers. Zebunissa was well aware that much could happen in the week before the appointed day. She decided to convene yet another meeting of the Makhfi; this one to be held in Muazzam's honour. Copious quantities of *shirazi,* as well as *hookah,* was available for all to enjoy. A feast had been prepared with *mugli masala, mutton saag,* and tray after tray of *seek kebabs, shammi kebabs, do peesah, roghali josh, shahi korma,* and every imaginable fruit the kingdom had to offer – grape, pomegranate, mango, papaya, watermelon, oranges, guava, pear and custard apple. There were over a hundred different dishes, served along with lemon juice, mango juice and various wines.

Zebunissa sat on a floor cushion, leaning on small decorative round pillows. Across the chamber she saw Muazzam, a look of drunken bravado in his eyes. Zebunissa had expected him to sit next to her. Instead, he had led his entourage to the centre of the hall, ignoring Zebunissa altogether. A frown between her eyes, Zebunissa motioned for the recitations to begin. Zubdat took the lead:

*Welcome the wind that has blown into our hearts,*
*Stealing the sorrow that dwelled within*
*Free are we now to open the doors of our lives*
*A new day is about to begin.*

There was general applause for Zubdat's poem. Clearly, it was an ode to her brother, the future Emperor. But Muazzam himself barely acknowledged his sister's lines as he reclined on bolsters, sipping *shirazi* and staring intently at the slave girls serving him. Zebunissa took note of this as Mihirunissa began her poem:

*I awoke and saw the carriage*
*Which was carrying me in the direction of sin*
*I changed not the horse but the direction*
*So a new journey I can begin.*

It seemed that Mihirunissa too, had taken note and was concerned that Muazzam was getting rather too complacent about his new position. He had been handpicked by the Makhfi to change the course of the kingdom, not to replace one tyrant with another.

Just then a light skinned slave girl wearing a fitted *kameez* and flowing *ghaghara* offered Muazzam a cup of wine. As she bent to hand him the cup, Zebunissa noticed Muazzam staring at the deep vale between her breasts. The girl, seeing this, bashfully straightened up and began walking away. Muazzam grabbed her by the wrist and pulled her towards him as she made soft sounds of distress. As a slave, she had no right to resist the Prince. She did not belong to any particular person; anyone of royal blood could have her for she was just a piece of property. Refusing the Emperor-apparent was tantamount to seeking death. So when Muazzam pulled the wretched girl towards him and forced her onto his lap, the harem women merely watched with pitying eyes, unwilling to admonish the future Emperor.

Zebunissa too, stared at Muazzam in marked disapproval but he stared back at her in mocking defiance. Taking another large gulp of his *shirazi*, some of it seeping from the corners of his mouth, he waved a hand in Zebunissa's direction, saying, "Continue Princess!" The slave girl sat uncomfortably on his lap as he fondled her legs. She knew it was not her position to protest, she could only make muted sounds and try to move away move away in seeming bashfulness. She dared not display her rage.

The story of the slave girl who had slapped a Mughal Minister was legendary. Years ago, a slave girl had resisted the advances of one of Aurengzeb's advisors during a feast by slapping the noble. Though Aurengzeb himself was adamantly opposed to debauchery and rape, he was even more set against women degrading men, especially a slave girl angering a nobleman. Hence he had asked the *mullahs,* keepers of the Word, to sentence her for her crime. Their sentence was merciless. She was stripped naked and drenched in oil, then placed in a small arena with wild dogs, who attacked and ripped her to pieces. The spectacle was watched by men and women alike, to serve as a warning to all women. Disrespecting a man in the Mughal dominion was unacceptable.

Zebunissa knew she could not admonish Muazzam in public, lest she lose public support for his bid to be Emperor. She moved her gaze away from Muazzam but looked quickly back when she heard the slave girl scream. Muazzam had pushed his hand into her *kameez* and was fondling the girls' breasts as tears rolled down her face. The Prince's men erupted in drunken laughter. Zebunissa struggled to remain quiet. Closing her eyes, she turned away. Muazzam withdrew his hand from the slave girl's *kameez*. Thrusting his hand between her legs, he pushed his fingers into her as she yelled in agony.

"Muazzam!" Zebunissa said in warning, her face set.

"Do not concern yourself sister," Muazzam retorted, struggling to restrain the slave girl. "See how she likes it!" He withdrew his hand from her and stuck his *wet* fingers in the air for all to behold. "She has been touched by an Emperor!" Once again his cohorts erupted into boisterous laughter as the slave girl tried to curl up to hide her shame and pain.

"No, she has not!" snapped Zebunissa, her light eyes flashing angrily. "You are still a Prince, Muazzam, and I will see you remain just that if debauchery is what you have in mind!"

Unceremoniously Muazzam pushed the girl off of his lap, into the arms of one of his guards, who began to grope and fondle her. Muazzam stood up and walked to the centre of the gathering. "No one here can stop me! I am the Emperor, the only one! Every person must submit to me!"

The Makhfi stared at Muazzam incredulously. He was nothing more than a feeble weed that they had nurtured into a tree in the hope that he would provide them shade. Now he was bearing down on the very ones who had raised him up?

"I do whatever I desire!" Muazzam looked at the slave girl, who was now weeping piteously. Smiling, he looked back at Zebunissa. "I will start with her," he declared. Grabbing the girl he hoisted her over his shoulder as she cried out and struggled in protest. Her struggles caused him to lift his hand and hit her hard. The girl cried out in fear and pain. "Come men, let us have some fun tonight!" Muazzam strode out with the girl. His entourage followed eagerly in his wake.

The women let out a collective sigh, raising trembling hands to their lips. Zebunissa's heart was wrung with pity for the young slave. "What have I done?" she murmured.

***

Zebunissa spent the better part of that night tossing and turning on her pillows, seeking the oblivion of slumber. But sleep, that fleeting companion, had abandoned her the same way she had abandoned the slave girl. Zebunissa knew the girl would never be the same after what Muazzam and his men would do to her. If she was lucky she would die, ensuing her escape from the lifelong shame of being a rape victim in Mughal India. If she was not so lucky, she would live with lifelong injuries, unable to bear children, having difficulty controlling her bladder, finding it painful to walk…as well as suffering a lifetime of emotional and mental trauma. This would be coupled with the most injurious fate of all – being disowned by her family. Starving and ostracized, she would have two options – to become a minor concubine for a minor noble, or suicide.

Zebunissa blamed herself. Lying on her back with an arm over her forehead, she stared at the ceiling. The moonlight from the tall casements reflected on her face. 'Where do I go from here, Lord?' she wondered. If Muazzam was so uncontrollable as an Emperor-apparent, she wondered what he would become as Emperor. What was worse was that he lacked both the intellect and piety of Aurengzeb that had occasionally curbed his fanatical bent of mind, providing a moral compass for his policies. Would Muazzam be worse than her father? Would she be to blame?

There was a knock on the door. "Zebunissa, it is we the Makhfi, who cannot sleep!"

Zebunissa sighed. "Enter! It seems that sleep has deserted us all in punishment for creating Muazzam."

"Did we make a mistake in bringing back Muazzam?" asked Zubdat.

"No, we did the right thing," Zebunissa said, annoyed by her sister's afterthought. "After years of intolerance and fanaticism, what the kingdom lacked was a rapist! We have succeeded in elevating a monster to the throne; who will attack young girls for his pleasure."

The women looked away in embarrassment. Zebunissa's anger cooled as suddenly as it had flared up. "Forgive me, I feel devastated by what happened today."

"So are we!" cried Zinat. "We cannot allow him to be Emperor."

Mihirunissa, a childhood favourite of Muazzam's, interceded to say. "Perhaps brother Muazzam just needs guidance. If we stick to the original plan of releasing grandfather Shah Jahan from prison, he can tutor brother Muazzam in matters of both empire and emperorship."

"It is too late for that now," responded Zebunissa. "I will not ask Muazzam for anything."

"Then we have only one recourse," said Zubdat despondently. "We must go to the *mullahs* and tell them we are withdrawing support for Prince Muazzam."

The other girls nodded silently but Zebunissa stood motionless. "There is one final way," she began, breaking the brittle silence. The Makhfi knew Zebunissa always had some plan in mind, so they waited for her to continue. "Mihirunissa, you are closest to Muazzam. Go to him tomorrow and tell him I am going to the *mullahs* to inform them that we are withdrawing our support for him. If he is wise he will come and meet me."

***

Muazzam hurried into Zebunissa's chamber late the following evening. "My sister, forgive me!" He knelt at Zebunissa's feet as she sat on her divan smoking a *hookah*. "Mihirunissa told me you will withdraw your support and hand me over to the *mullahs*. Forgive me, sister! I was drunk; I did not know what I was saying or doing!"

Zebunissa pulled on her *hookah* and blew the perfumed smoke into Muazzam's face. "Hand me my slippers, you fiend," she said quietly.

Muazzam rose to get the velvet slippers lying some distance away, but Zebunissa stopped him saying, "No! Crawl to them. I have not given you permission to stand!"

Muazzam reluctantly crawled to the corner of the room and picked up the slippers. He rose to walk back but Zebunissa stopped him saying, "Crawl to me!"

"But I cannot crawl and carry the slippers at the same time," Muazzam protested.

"Then carry them in your mouth like the dog you are!" Zebunissa shot back.

Muazzam was taken aback. He sensed her rage and was noticeably shaken. He fell to the floor and slowly crawled to her, humiliated at having to carry her slippers in his mouth.

"Keep your eyes on the floor, dog! I did not give you permission to lift your head."

Muazzam stopped in his tracks, anger flaring in his hazel eyes but then slowly resumed his crawl, staring at the ground, slippers in mouth.

Zebunissa pulled the slippers from him and dropped them on the floor in distaste. Taking another pull at the *hookah,* she instructed him to kneel before her. Muazzam waited in fear.

"Tell me, dear brother," she began, staring at the ceiling, "what became of that poor slave girl you fondled in my chambers?" Muazzam remained silent, eyes on the floor. Zebunissa knew this did not bode well; her brother must have done something unforgiveable to the wretched girl. "Come Great Prince, Greatest of the Great, 7th Mughal ruler, tell me what became of the girl you publicly inserted your fingers into before the Makhfi, before your own sisters, before the court of scholars and poets I brought you into because I thought you were fit to be Emperor. Tell me, what happened to her?"

Muazzam began a muted gibberish.

"Speak up, you dog!" Zebunissa commanded, her lips curled in disdain.

Muazzam began to weep. "She died, sister," he sobbed.

Zebunissa did not move, feeling relieved the girl had been released from her agony.

"Forgive me sister," Muazzam wept. "I was drunk. I didn't know what I was doing. Forgive me!"

"Forgive you?" Zebunissa sneered. "You killed an innocent girl and you expect forgiveness?" She grabbed her slippers and slapped Muazzam across the face with them as hard as she could. Muazzam turned away, shielding herself. Throwing the velvet slippers to one side, Zebunissa rose and began raining blows on her brother's head with her balled fists. "Is this what your mother taught you? Is this what your sisters taught you?" She ran and grabbed the supple stick kept especially to dust her bed each morning and began beating Muazzam as he writhed, begging for mercy.

"Tell me what you did to her…I want to know!" Zebunissa demanded, her mind enflamed. When Muazzam did not respond, merely kneeling at her feet, weeping, she poked him with the stick and shouted, "Tell me! I want to know!"

He raised his bleeding and bruised face and sobbed, "I will tell you, but please do not beat me anymore! After we took her away, we tore her clothes off and took turns with her. I went first, then my men. She begged us to stop, but we did not…could not... Eventually she lost consciousness…still it went on. After we were done, we threw her off the balcony into the road. She died there in the gutter."

Zebunissa could hardly breathe. Rage flooded her very soul. Grabbing her *lathi,* she slashed Muazzam across the face. "You good-for-nothing! We used to make fun of you when we were children! We called you our little pet mouse because you were not even strong enough to be called a dog! I gave you dignity, and you used it to spit in *my* face and kill one of *my* slaves!"

Muazzam shook with sobs, begging for mercy. Zebunissa turned her face away as if she could not bear the sight of such worthlessness at her feet. "You will issue an allowance for her family of two mohurs a month. They will be allowed into the royal kitchen for their household food needs, and be treated for the rest of their lives by the royal *hakims*!" Muazzam nodded his head.

"And you are unfit to be Emperor!" Muazzam looked up in horror and panic. "I will only support you publicly if you issue a proclamation immediately calling for the release of Emperor Shah Jahan. He is the true Mughal Emperor and only he knows how to run the empire." Again, Muazzam nodded in acquiescence.

Zebunissa bent down and looked Muazzam in the face. "And if you ever defy me again, I will make you scream and experience agony you cannot even imagine." She rose, saying harshly, "I will castrate you and your men, so you spend the rest of your days as *hijras*."

Zebunissa knew that for a man to be called a *hijra* was the ultimate affront to his manhood. She hoped Muazzam knew that she was not making an empty threat; she would do as she had said. He simply nodded, his tears mingling with the blood and sweat on his face.

"Now leave my chambers and never return!"

As Muazzam rose and began to walk away, Zebunissa called out, "Stop! Bend over!"

Fearfully, Muazzam bent over as directed. Zebunissa pulled his pajamas down and thrust the sharp end of her stick into Muazzam's behind. Muazzam yelled in agony. Pulling out the bloody, soiled *lathi,* Zebunissa held it to Muazzam's face. "You have now been touched by an Emperor!" she spat.

***

Tuesday was the day of blood, the day justice was administered as directed by the planet Mars. Muazzam donned blood-red robes upon the counsel of his advisors, for on this day the citizenry would be shown the brand of justice their Emperor administered. The *Diwan-i-Am* or Hall of Public Audience, a vast 12,000 square foot hall, seemed inadequate for the large number of people gathered to witness justice being administered by the new Emperor. The *mullah*s stood to one side, the Hindu Rajputs on the other, with the nobility stood in the middle. The women stood behind the screens, hidden from public gaze but able to view the proceedings.

The Prime Minister stepped forward and bowed. "Majesty, we have the matter of the fellow who stole bread from the hands of a widow. Young Prince Azam was unable to render justice; the widow requests that justice be not delayed."

Muazzam had prepared for this day. Zebunissa knew today was a test of his strength and had coached him accordingly. Muazzam lowered his gaze and rubbed his chin as if deliberating on the matter, though he knew exactly what punishment was to be levied. Finally, lifting his head, he ordered the thief to be brought to him.

"On your knees, fiend!" the guards ordered as they dragged in the offender. The man fell to his knees, fearing for his life.

Muazzam stared at the thief as the large gathering looked on. Fearing the Prince would order execution for a crime that did not merit such a harsh sentence, the Prime Minister stepped forward, but Muazzam raised a hand, preventing him from speaking.

"A widow's life is not a complete life," Prince Muazzam said, "She is but half of a whole person. Her husband, who is also her provider and guardian, is no more and she has no one to protect her from a ruffian like you."

"Majesty…"

"Silence! I did not give you permission to speak!" Muazzam harsh command echoed through the hall. There was a long pause. The nobility and *mullahs* stood quietly, their heads bowed. No one dared to stir. Muazzam's words fell into the silence like stones into water. "A widow is not a complete person because her guardian and provider is dead and she has no one to protect her."

The gathering waited, surprised yet mesmerized by what the Prince had said; words taught to him by Zebunissa.

"But who protects a man? A woman is protected by her husband. But who protects the husband? Is it the woman?" With a deviant smile, Muazzam looked at the *mullahs*. "Or is it another man?"

The *mullahs* looked away at the thinly veiled reference to homosexuality. They considered it a blasphemous remark.

Muazzam returned his gaze to the crowd. "The answer is…no one protects a man. A man protects himself. God has ordained man shall protect both himself and his family."

Silence permeated the hall. Those in attendance stood bewildered, wondering what the purpose of the sermon was. The thief lay on the floor, crying and quivering. The hooded executioner waited in the distance for the command to sever the criminal's head.

Muazzam said, "This man's crime, as heinous as it is, does not warrant death. Rather, I wish him to know what it is like to be a helpless widow. I will not slay his family, for it is not their responsibility to protect him. But his right arm, which he used to steal from the widow, shall be severed. From this day forward, he shall have half a life, half an existence. He will have no more power than a widow. And let this be a lesson to my people…" Muazzam raised a finger towards the vaulted arch above his head and his voice grew louder, "…that if anyone attempts to steal from this defenceless man in the future, they too, will meet the same fate!"

The prisoner broke down in sobs, pleading for mercy. But to no avail. The judgement had been rendered and the guards grabbed the prisoner by his armpits and carried him over to the marble slab that was routinely used for decapitations and amputations. The prisoner resisted desperately, flailing and kicking, but the guards pushed him remorselessly forward.

The marble slab was two feet high and the guards positioned the prisoner so that his right arm lay on it. Muazzam looked on, neither smiling nor frowning. The guards held the prisoner still as the executioner raised his axe. Everyone's eyes turned to Muazzam for the final nod, even the executioner. Muazzam's gaze fell on the nobles; every eye was fixed on him, not the prisoner. Not wishing to look towards the screen behind which the women stood and appear weak, Muazzam simply sat in silence, a look of fear and bewilderment on his face.

"You must give the final order, Prince," prompted the Prime Minister, hoping to avert embarrassment.

Muazzam's face lightened. Was he expected to repeat the sentence? But the executioner already held the axe poised in the air. He had never been the priveledged son of his father, brought to watch the proceeding of the court; it had always been Sultan. In a voice lacking conviction, he said, "The order is final!"

The nobles and mullahs raised their brows in surprise. The proper form was to decree, "Let justice be rendered!" But the moment of confusion was short-lived as all eyes turned once again to the executioner and his helpless victim. The axe descended with a thud and a wild shriek from the prisoner, who lost consciousness as blood gushed from his body.

A chant began, growing louder and yet louder…

*Long live Emperor Muazzam!*
*Long live Emperor Muazzam!*

The citizens seemed to have forgotten he was not the Emperor yet for the ceremonial had yet to be done and the proclamation still to be read in his name. But to the common people and the court, it seemed that, for the first time in many months, there was a leader at the helm who would protect the law. The spectacle, despite Muazzam's hesitation over the final decree, cemented his image as the Mughal standard bearer, heir to his father's throne. The time for doubting had passed.

Muazzam listened to the chanting as it echoed around him, his heart beating in triumph. The throne was but a step away.

***

The Maratha army marched north towards Delhi, ravaging everything in its path. They had taken control of the Deccan, destroying hundreds of mosques and butchering thousands of Mughals. The long march from the southern tip of the Deccan to the northern boundary of the empire left Mughal fortresses in ruins, inhabitants slayed, and riches looted. The Marathas were a rebel Hindu clan who found their place in Aurengzeb's intolerant India threatened. Since Aurengzeb's ascension, they had grown in number, controlling vast territories within the Mughal domain. Surprisingly, they had no alliances with the Hindu Rajputs, though they shared the same religion. For their part, the Rajputs continued to maintain their allegiance to the Mughals, in the faint hope that Aurengzeb would be overthrown and a more just and tolerant monarch sit on the throne.

While Shivaji Maharaj, leader of the Marathas, felt increasingly emboldened to extend his control over western and southern India, pushing back Mughal boundaries, in Delhi, Muazzam received word of his depredations, fearing what lay ahead. Convening a council of Aurengzeb's military generals in the *Diwan-i-khas*, he hastened to lay the blame for the Maratha advance squarely on their shoulders. Seated beside his father's bejewelled, gold-encrusted throne, he stared at the generals. "How have you permitted the upstart Maratha to seize control of our forts in the Deccan?" he asked harshly.

His words were unforgiving but the Commander-in-Chief reminded him that he had resisted all their requests to send more troops to the Deccan, preferring to keep them in Delhi to protect his fragile grip on the capital.

"A hundred Mughals are equivalent to a thousand Hindu Marathas!" blustered Muazzam. The generals heard him in shocked anger, remembering the thousands of Mughal soldiers who had been ruthlessly annihilated by the advancing Maratha.

A clear voice spoke from behind the screen. "General," Zebunissa interjected, "we must descend upon the Marathas in equal numbers immediately. Taking the Deccan will serve the enemy as a gateway to the rest of the Empire. We must close the door."

Muazzam did not dare contradict the order. He knew it was the Princess who wielded the real power.

Zebunissa looked toward Muazzam and said, "Prince Muazzam, as interim Emperor, will personally travel with your reinforcements, to show the enemy he is indeed in charge of the Empire." Her stern tone served as a warning to the fearful Mughal Prince.

***

The wind was cold and dry, creeping insidiously into the bones of the young Prince. Muazzam ordered his bodyguards to remain on duty outside his chambers; no one was permitted a break. Inside, Muazzam was finally alone with his thoughts. He closed his eyes, imagining his life before Aurengzeb's illness – the carefree hunting expeditions; the boisterous but secret parties with wine and opium. He had never coveted the throne, knowing his elder brother Sultan was too strong to be defeated in battle. He had never imagined, even in fantasy, the notion of being Emperor one day. That he had been thrust into the role was entirely Zebunissa's doing. Like a bird following the flock, Muazzam too, followed the Makhfi, allowing them to dictate his every move. He was their prop, their tool, their instrument to use as they pleased. What had he received in return – unrelenting threats to his life from the *mullahs* and Raushanara. He was the prime target. There was to be no deviation from instructions, he had been admonished. If he followed the Makhfi's wishes, the *mullahs* would try to kill him, but if he acted against the Makhfi, Zebunissa would kill him as surely as night follows day. Either way he was a dead man.

The attack from the south by the Marathas was a manifestation of this paradigm. If he did not quell the uprising the *mullahs* would prevail, arguing he was unfit to rule, and the Makhfi would threaten him, gladly feeding him to the Marathas. If he did quell the Marathas, the Makhfi would be triumphant. He would be their puppet Emperor, unable to ever exercise his own will; always looking back to see if one of the mullahs' men was trying to assassinate him. Without the strength to say yes or no, he simply wept in his bed.

Muazzam sighed and looked up at the starry night sky which appeared like a cloth of blue velvet, strewn with diamonds. He recalled what his mother had once said to him: "Everything you wish to know about the future and the past is written up there in the sky, if only one knows how to interpret it." What was it saying about him, he wondered? Would he be the next monarch, remembered for his justness and valour? Or would he simply be a puppet for the real power players of the kingdom?

Suddenly, he noticed a star fall from the sky, so rapidly that it did not even leave a pale residue behind. Muazzam quickly sat up in horror. Would that be him? Would he too, fall from grace so rapidly that no one would remember he had existed? Would his time as Emperor be so irrelevant that history would judge him as nothing more than a puppet manipulated by all? Muazzam rose from his bed and dropped to his knees, facing west towards Mecca. "Oh Allah the Almighty, save me! I do not want to die! Release me from these trials. May your divine intervention cause Shivaji to remove his troops from my kingdom without war. I vow to give up opium and women for the rest of my life, and dress in white robes as homage to your greatness!"

Muazzam knew he was lying but in his fearful mind, he sought to make deals with the Lord himself, thinking that his weak lies would be overlooked by the Almighty. "Oh Allah save me…" he wept.

***

"Your job, you son of an owl, is merely to put on your armour and remain in your tent." Zebunissa was scornful of her brother's whimpering. Was this coward the next Emperor of India? She thought in disgust. This feeble-minded man, who would soon have to win the hearts of his people, was cowering with fear at the mere mention of battle. Was this the best Mughal India had to offer?

"I have instructed the generals to draw up the battle plans and the terms for a truce," Zebunissa told Muazzam. "We may need to offer the Marathas some concessions once we have gained some victories, otherwise the war will drag on and the treasury bankrupted. It is already depleted with military excursions elsewhere in the empire. The last thing we need is a costly drawn out war with the Marathas." Zebunissa cast a look of scorn at her brother, seated in fearful trepidation, gazing out at the blue sky beyond the casement. "Aqil Khan will travel south with you to ensure that my instructions are followed and no harm comes to you from any traitors in the army."

***

A month had passed since Muazzam's army had departed Delhi for the Deccan. Special imperial messengers brought Zebunissa word that her instructions had been followed. The Mughals had been triumphant in battle after battle, pushing the Marathas further south and building a strong position for a truce. Zebunissa finally received direct word from Aqil Khan; a source far more valuable than the official despatches, for his message told her what Muazzam's role had been.

*Princess*

*I pray this letter finds you in good health. The Marathas have accepted our offer of truce and will be returning to their lands. We have reclaimed vast territories in the Deccan and almost all our forts. According to your instructions, Prince Muazzam remained in safety during his time in the Deccan. When he arrived, he contracted severe dysentery and remained bedridden, attended by an elder maid. The generals would joke, much to my chagrin, that while the Prince slept in his mother's lap, they risked their lives for the Empire. On one occasion, one of the soldiers pretended to be a Maratha who had infiltrated the camp; he ran into the Prince's tent. The Prince fled, leaving the maid serving him to fend for herself.*

*I write to inform you of this because I believe the Prince, by his behaviour, has lost the respect of the military. When we return to the capital, much will have to be done to restore his honour. It is possible the military will support a coup if this estrangement continues.*

*I humbly await audience with you.*

*Aqil*

Zebunissa sighed despondently. She was aware Muazzam lacked the ability to lead an army, but that he would act in so feeble and cowardly a manner was something she had not thought possible in a Mughal

Prince. 'He will always be a mere puppet,' she thought. 'I must lead until…until someone of valour presents himself to take control.' For now, she would have to protect Muazzam at any cost.

***

Trumpets sounded over the buzz from the crowd of humanity gathered around the *Diwan-i-Am* to witness the declaration of the next Emperor as the mid-day sun bleached the domes and minarets of Delhi outside the red wall of the fort. Elegant Persian tapestries hung from the ceiling. The beautiful hall was crowded with row upon row of dignitaries, arranged according to rank. Behind them were the merchants and lesser nobles. In the third tier stood the commoners, with a row of cavalry officers on horseback behind them. At the very rear stood the line of war elephants, decorated in azure and gold.

Zebunissa had hoped her grandfather and aunt would be present to validate the occasion, but she knew she could not wait. Muazzam had to be installed before Raushanara and her allies had the chance to delay his accession. Nevertheless, she had, through Muazzam, given orders to have Shah Jahan and Jahanara released from Agra Fort and escorted back to Delhi – a journey that would take the frail Shah Jahan several days to accomplish. The empire Muazzam would rule stretched from Persia in the west to Bengal in the east, and from the northern Himalayas to the Deccan in the south. It took a camel sixty days to travel from one border to another – and now it all lay in the hands of the Makhfi.

Muazzam sat beside the Peacock Throne he would occupy after the declaration had been read in his name. With each drumbeat his heart raced faster, fearing one of his own guards was an assassin who would plunge a sword into his heart.

The Qazi stood ready to read from the *Koran* before the official declaration. Raushanara sat to one side of the marble platform, aloof and silent, Azam by her side. The long-bearded *mullahs* stood near her, their faces reflecting jealousy and contempt.

"Where is *Mullah* Omar?" asked Zebunissa from behind the screens that shielded the women of the *zenana*. Omar was the Head *Mullah* and Raushanara's close confidante. Though he was not an ally of Muazzam or the Makhfi, his presence was considered crucial at official state events.

"I do not know, Princess," replied the Prime Minister from his place to one side of the platform below the screened window.

"We cannot begin without him." Zebunissa motioned to Didar. "Find the *Mullah*! We have come too far to lose now."

As the eunuch nodded and left, Zebunissa sighed. The women of the Makhfi stared anxiously down at the scene below them. "If he does not present himself in the next half hour, we will proceed without him!" Zebunissa said in a strong voice to the Prime minister, himself bewildered by the absence of the *Mullah*.

The *Qazi* began the proclamation saying, "In the name of Allah the Almighty, peace be upon him, I hereby ask all those present to lower their heads." Row upon row, every man present bowed his head, looking like a deck of cards suddenly tilted forward. *"Allah ho Akbar!* Grant the Emperor wisdom to underst...."

"The Emperor lives!"

The *Qazi* stopped in mid-sentence as the crowd, heads still lowered, looked in the direction of the agitation. A young *mullah* had appeared beside the Qazi, out of breath from running, his face flushed with excitement. "He lives! Emperor Aurengzeb has regained consciousness! He is alive and wishes to see his son."

Chattering broke out among the crowd, who had been told the Emperor lay on his deathbed. Zebunissa's face froze. Muazzam turned pale. Both had not visited the Emperor for many days, certain he would not recover. Had they made an error of judgement?

"*Mullah* Omar is with the Emperor," the young *mullah* continued, still gasping for air. "He sent me to stop the declaration. Emperor Alamgir will return to his rightful place."

Muazzam looked towards the screened windows, hoping Zebunissa would have an answer. She looked back at him with pity, keenly aware that her plan had failed and Muazzam would incur the full wrath of the Emperor and the *mullahs*.

The *mullahs* lost no time in chanting, *Allah ho Akbar! Long live the Emperor!* The crowd soon joined in: *Allah ho Akbar! Long live the Emperor! Allah ho Akbar! Long live the Emperor!*

'How quickly they turn their colours,' thought Zebunissa, sorrow, anger and frustration mingling in her heart. She looked at the Makhfi, staring back at her with tears of despair in their eyes. Zebunissa knew she had failed them, failed the cause. But she was helpless to do anything about it. As the crowd continued to chant *Allah ho Akbar! Long live the Emperor!* Zebunissa noticed Raushanara staring in her direction. As their eyes met, the marble screen between them, Raushanara smiled.

# PART III

## 12
## A Final Fracticide

*How many hearts, O Love, thy sword hath slain,*
*And yet will slay!*

4 January 1663

A cold wind from the north blew equally on noble and commoner as Delhi lay in its chilly grip. The women in the *harem* moved about with Kashmiri shawls draped over themselves. The muslins of summer were discarded, packed away with dried rose leaves for the arrival of summer. Months had passed since Prince Muazzam's ill-fated day of Declaration. Zebunissa had hoped that when spring came, she would be Empress and effectively the ruler of Mughal India. Instead, her father Aurengzeb was once again on the throne, and she behind the harem windows, while Muazzam sat in prison; another failed rebellion; another of the Emperor's sons in jail.

Aurengzeb himself was not the same man he had once been, his illness having placed a heavy mark on him. His speech was slurred and he spoke with deliberation. All his nobles took note of how he no longer engaged in long discourses with them, opting instead to dictate long letters to his scribe if detailed discussion was needed on some matter. He had grown weak; his high cheek bones were prominently defined; his hair grey; he walked with a stoop.

But Zebunissa did not make the mistake of supposing these physical debilities spoke of an equal weakness of mind, for Aurengzeb remained invincible. The royal *hakims* had told her repeatedly that no one had ever recovered from such a massive stroke, and if the Emperor did, he would be permanently bedridden. But they had been wrong, for here was Aurengzeb, sitting on his throne with his bejewelled turban glistening, issuing proclamations and edicts.

On learning how the family had intrigued against him during his illness, Aurengzeb quickly moved to quell the forces seeking to undermine him. The proclamation to free Shah Jahan and Jahanara was rescinded before ever it reached Agra and part of Raja Jai Singh's kingdom was taken away. Strangely, Zebunissa and the Makhfi were left unscathed, due to the lack of evidence incriminating them and their role in the rebellion. His illness also had a profound effect on Aurengzeb's attitude and policies. The powerlessness of the royal *hakims* to truly cure him had a humbling effect on his psyche. He believed that a Divine hand had delivered him from death and he became more benevolent in his policies: taxes were lowered for all citizens, even Hindus, and salaries of court official were lowered. To help those with large debts, he doubled the value of the silver rupee, much to the chagrin of money lenders. He even eliminated, though temporarily, the taxes on pagodas and temples. Zebunissa feared that her father, once he regained his strength, would incrementally reverse all these changes and continue his reign of terror.

On learning of the plot to install his young son Azam, and the fake document that bore the Royal Seal and his fingerprint, Aurengzeb turned livid with anger. Raushanara's actions were revealed to him by both nobles and commoners. He summoned the court to the *Diwan-i-Khas* to ponder what her punishment should be. Raushanara pleaded with the nobles to remain silent, assuring them that once Aurengzeb died, she would reward them with large estates. But it was too late. No one had confidence in Raushanara anymore and few believed she would outlive Aurengzeb.

"Begum Raushanara asked me for the strong *kajal* the ladies know I make," one of the concubines told Aurengzeb when she was summoned to his presence. "She told me it was required for an official proclamation; it had to have a strong colour, dry easily and never fade. When I asked her who could make such a proclamation since the Emperor was ill, she told me to be silent and mind my tongue if I wished to live."

The concubine was barely twenty years of age, but for Aurengzeb, now fifty-five, age did not matter; she was a beautiful Turkish girl and he wanted her in his harem for his satisfaction. She stood before him draped in black, her beautiful face veiled.

Shiasta Khan, the Emperor's Advisor, standing beside the still feeble monarch asked on his behalf, "Did she cause you physical harm?"

"She did not," the concubine instantly responded, "but she threatened to imprison and kill me if I ever told anyone."

The assembled courtiers in the *Diwan-i-Khas* looked towards Raushanara, seated to one side of the royal platform and draped in black from head to toe. She remained defiant, though fear glimmered in her eyes as Nawab Bai came forward, her face veiled, her form cloaked under layers of dark brocade.

"Begum," Aurengzeb said almost inaudibly, "tell me of your encounter with the Empress." He nodded, encouraging her to speak, wondering to himself how his own sister could have dared insult one of his wives.

"My Emperor, I was keeping vigil by your bedside. The other harem women were attending to Prince Akbar, who had been mysteriously poisoned." She paused, looking at Raushanara though the veil. "Late at night, I heard the sound of soft footsteps. The guards stood outside your door, which was always kept closed. Fearing it was an ill-wisher wishing to slay you in your sleep, I pretended to be asleep so I could catch the fiend. As the person approached your bedside, I noticed it was Begum Raushanara! Immediately, I grabbed her hand to restrain her, even pulling on her *ghaghara*, but she was too strong. Her *ghaghara* and *pajama* were torn in the struggle. Pulling me by my hair, she slapped and kicked me repeatedly, telling me I would wash her *hammam* when she was the ruler." Nawab Bai began to weep. There was shocked silence in the hall. Finally she said, "Forgive me, my Emperor, but I was not able to stop her from stealing your fingerprint."

Aurengzeb's face and demeanour showed nothing of the fury that filled his heart. He turned to Zafar Khan, "Why was Begum Raushanara's document believed to be authentic when Nawab Bai claimed to have witnessed the deception?"

Zafar Khan's eyes widened in fear. "Majesty, it was unclear who was to be believed. I therefore relied on proof, not emotions, to make a decision. Begum Nawab Bai could offer the court no proof apart from her own word, the scales of justice demanded Begum Raushanara's document, which carried the Royal Seal and the royal fingerprint, be considered authentic."

Aurengzeb nodded, knowing his hand-chosen Prime Minister was unbiased in these matters. It was his adherence to the law that had catapulted him to the role of Prime Minister.

Next, Zafar Khan summoned Raushanara's eunuch. "Were you in the harem on the night of Begum Raushanara and Nawab Bai's altercation?" The eunuch nodded. "Tell us, on fear of death, if the drink was laced with any toxins."

The eunuch hung his head, glancing sideways at his mistress and then at the Prime Minister. "The sherbets I was ordered to give the Princesses and Begum Sahiba, had been mixed with a sleep potion, meant to send them into deep slumber so they would be asleep when she attempted to obtain the Emperor's fingerprint."

Aurengzeb waved his hand in silent dismissal. But the eunuch looked up at the imperial platform and said, "Majesty, I humbly beg to present more information." Raushanara shot her eunuch a sharp look, fearing what he might reveal, but the eunuch said, his eyes fixed on the Emperor's feet, "Before Prince Akbar fell ill, Begum visited the neighbourhood *hakims,* known for making poisonous toxins. I saw her feeding an elixir to Prince Akbar before he fell ill."

All eyes turned to look at Raushanara, who rose up as if stung and shouted, "This is a lie! I never poisoned or attacked anyone! This is a conspiracy to blame me for everything that happened! Zebunissa..."

"Silence!" Aurengzeb's harsh command was an echo of the voice that had once held the Mughal Empire in thrall. "I have heard enough! You, who call yourself my sister, who swore to be loyal; in whom I placed my trust, took advantage of my ill health to try to overthrow me. When Nawab Bai, my Begum, attempted to stop you, you caused her bodily harm. You stand guilty of treason; of stealing and misusing the Royal Seal; of using my *nishan* on a fake document while I slept. You are also guilty of attempting to murder a Royal Prince, my son Akbar."

There was absolute silence in the *Diwani-i-Khas.* A sitting Emperor had never before compelled a *Padishah Begum* to be judged in open court. Every person present feared for the Empress' life.

"I hereby sentence you to be trampled on by an elephant till death claims you."

Aurengzeb rose with Shiasta Khan's help and retreated to his apartments as the imperial guard surrounded Raushanara, taking her into custody.

Zebunissa stood behind the screens, shocked by the Emperor's pronouncement. The *Padishah Begum* was to be executed in the most painful and public way possible! Nevertheless, intense relief coursed through her being, knowing her secret was safe. But the relief soon gave way to raging fear as Zebunissa realized that Aurengzeb, ill and weak, was no less brutal, no less ruthless, than he had been when healthy and strong.

## 13
## Illegitimate Child

*Here is the path of love—how dark and long*
*Its winding ways, with many snares beset!*

2 January 1664

As spring approached, Aurengzeb set out with his court for the Kashmir valley. The past year had witnessed a benevolent ruler. But as he gradually regained strength, his benevolence dissipated, almost as if his physical strength came at the expense of morality and virtue. Fearing the hot Delhi summer would impair his recovery, he set out for the pleasant vales of Kashmir.

The centre of the Empire was the Emperor, so wherever he went became the heart. Thus, as he travelled north, the burdens as well as the luxuries of Empire followed him. Eighty camels, thirty elephants and twenty carts were devoted just to carrying the royal records. An additional 100 camels carried 200 trunks of the Emperor's clothes; fifty elephants carried jewels to be distributed to those individuals who had pleased the Emperor with their words and deeds; 100 camels carried cases loaded with silver and gold rupees; another 100 carried water for drinking and bathing; and several large carts carried the *hammam* the Emperor and his wives used for bathing.

At a distance of one *kos* in front of the royal procession rode a horseman carrying lengths of the finest white linen. His job was to cover the carcass of any animal lying on the ground so the Emperor's eyes would not be defiled by the sight. Two tent cities travelled as part of the entourage, one set up in advance of the other so the Emperor would never have to wait if he wished to stop and relax. Anticipating the Emperor, the Grand Master of the Royal Household picked scenic locations to set up the city for overnight halts. The temporary city featured red imperial two-storied tents lined with gold, silk and velvet, each complete with its own *Diwan-i-Am* and *Diwan-i-Khas,* as well as *harem* apartments in the rear. A ring guard of nobles surrounded the area. One tent was filled with sweetmeats, fruit, betel leaf and water. There were separate tents for the kitchen, the officers, the eunuchs, and the animals.

Zebunissa had been given the title of *Padishah Begum* by Aurengzeb following Raushanara's execution. The blood and torture of the previous months still lingered in her mind, so she requested the Emperor's permission to remain in Lahore while the Emperor was in Kashmir. Aurengzeb agreed to his favourite daughter's request.

Raushanara's execution continued to haunt those who had the misfortune to witness it. After imprisonment in a small nine by nine foot cell in a dungeon, Raushanara was beaten and starved for almost a month before her execution, the day of which was chosen as Tuesday, the day of blood for the Mughals, when commoners and nobles alike gathered to witness animal fights, which were infamous in the Mughal court. Elephants, lions and leopards fought while huge crowds watched. The execution of criminals by placing them in the ring with the fierce animals was also watched by the people. But Aurengzeb was the first Mughal monarch to place his own sister in the ring of death.

Zebunissa pitied Raushanara and had pleaded on her behalf to her father, but to no avail. Labelling her a rebel who had tried to overthrow him, he said her deed was far worse than Dara's, a declared rebel, hence the punishment was to be more severe. Beaten and bloodied, the once imperious Empress was pulled into the ring in a cage by imperial soldiers. Silence descended like a blanket on the arena. Ferocious tigers and leopards, starved for two days, were brought in as Raushanara lay inside her cage, her face a mask of horror as the famished animals lunged towards her cage, unable to reach her. The *harem* women began to weep seeing one of their own being thus brutally punished by Emperor.

The cage began to shake from the collision with the felines. Raushanara yelled out, begging her brother for mercy but her words were lost in the sudden roaring of the vengeful crowd, crying for blood. This was the best entertainment they could have hoped for. They would not be satisfied until the prisoner was dead.

The imperial guards entered the arena again, much to the surprise of those watching, excepting the Emperor, who had already determined the manner of her death. The beasts were rounded up by the guards and sent out of the arena as the crowd yelled in disappointment. Had Alamgir decided to spare his sister's life after all?

One of the guards unlocked the door of the cage and pulled the traumatized Mughal out of her confinement as she cried and wept. She was made to stand in chains in the centre of the arena as commoners threw rotten produce at her. A massive elephant was then brought in through a side entrance and the crowd once again erupted in jubilation. Raushanara turned her head, her eyes growing wide in terror as she saw the beast lumbering in. "NO! NO!" she shouted, shaking her head from side to side, but to no avail. Her chains prevented her from running away. And even if she had, where would she run to? Ignoring her pathetic pleas, the guards grabbed her by the chains and led her to the elephant as she struggled to break free. She was laid on the ground and her chains tied to stakes several feet away. Thus she lay, pinned to the ground, the only movement the tears streaming from her eyes. One of the *harem* women quickly turned away and ran to the spittoon in the corner, vomiting till her stomach ached. There were audible cries from the others, some of whom closed their eyes and begun reciting from the *Koran*. Zebunissa looked on, heart and mind frozen by her father's merciless actions.

The elephant lumbered towards the prisoner, trumpeting as it went, its trunk raised high in the air. The huge beast was a terrifying sight. Aurengzeb nodded and the *mahout* directed the elephant to raise both front feet into the air. Raushanara screamed; her eyes wide with horror. With a loud thud, the elephant landed its front feet on the chest of the ill-fated royal. Blood and tissue emerged from every orifice of her body as the beast flattened her body. The crowd whimpered into silence.

Zebunissa felt suffocated, her heart was heavy with sorrow. In the moment of triumph there was no joy. Raushanara had been a thorn in the flesh of her and her siblings; her death had finally released them from her abuse. In many ways she had been far worse than her brother for she did not have his redeeming qualities as a leader, nor had she utilised her own gifts for the betterment of those around her. Aurengzeb had always attacked from the front, but Raushanara believed in attacking from behind. She had deceived her brother, Prince Dara, during the war of succession; poisoned Prince Akbar; stolen the Imperial Seal and placed the Emperor's *nishan* on an official edict while he lay unconscious. She was an evil force and finally she was no more. And yet the fruits of victory tasted bitter to Zebunissa as she watched the highest brought low into the dust. She raised a hand to wipe away the unbidden tears that wet her face.

***

In Lahore, Zebunissa was accompanied by her seven-year-old beloved brother, Akbar, and her friend and confidante, Aqil Khan, whom Aurengzeb had assigned to protect her. On a moonlit night that illuminated her chamber with silver, Zebunissa gazed at Akbar as he slept, a sad smile on her face. Aqil Khan entered the chamber quietly.

Zebunissa's sensed his presence, her nostrils filling with the distinctive *attar* he used. Without turning away from the young Prince, she said softly, smiling, "He has your eyes, Aqil."

Aqil put a hand on her shoulder and looked at their son with pride. "And his grandfather's rage," he remarked wryly. Akbar often threw tantrums that neither Aqil nor Zebunissa could control. He had thrown one earlier that day when he was told to stop playing and wash up for dinner. It took several hours to calm him down but he had refused to eat his dinner, just as he had threatened. Now he was asleep, presumably exhausted by his tantrum.

"There are so many secrets in the kingdom," Zebunissa said, her head turned away from Aqil, "but this one none must ever learn."

"Do you regret bringing Akbar into the world?"

"Never!" Zebunissa turned, looking up at Aqil, then her gaze fell back to her son. "He is the greatest joy of my life. But if a man can imprison two of his own sons, as well as his father, only Allah knows what he would do to you or Akbar, his illegitimate grandchild, if he ever learnt the truth."

Aqil and Zebunissa stared down at the illegitimate son they shared. The candle by his bed illuminated his face with a warm glow while the moonlight bathed the rest of the chamber in shimmering silver. Aqil caressed Zebunissa's head, drawing her into an embrace. Zebunissa allowed her head to rest on his chest, comforted by the warmth and his presence.

It had begun as an innocent bond between a mentor and his student. Aqil Khan tutored all the harem women on poetic composition, as per the wishes of the erstwhile Emperor, Shah Jahan. But unlike her sisters, Zebunissa had a deep love and interest in poetry, inherited from her Persian mother. Her abilities far exceeded those of the other women. Hence Zebunissa and Aqil began spending more time together, honing her skills. When the war of succession had broken out, Aurengzeb left Aurangabad to fight for the throne. Zebunissa and the other harem women were entrusted to Aqil Khan's care as a trusted confidante.

One night, while practicing her poetry, Zebunissa's eyes met Aqil's. After months of tutoring, she had spontaneously created a verse without needing to alter it. Excited by her achievement, she rushed into Aqil's arms to thank him for his patience, pushing herself deep into his muscular frame. Aqil knew he was old enough to be Zebunissa's father. Despite himself, he put his arms around her, his fingers touching the bare skin behind her neck. Feeling a man's hands on her soft, young skin set butterflies fluttering in Zebunissa's stomach and her heart began to race. Aqil tried to move away but she clung to his side, looking up at him with luminous grey eyes. Aqil leaned into her and kissed her on the lips. Zebunissa lips parted and she felt his tongue move over hers. His hands fondled her breasts. Kneeling before her, he tugged at her *ghaghara* and *pajama*, placing his head between her thighs. Zebunissa moaned as an uncontrollable floodtide of sensuality coursed through her body. She reached down, tangling her fingers in Aqil's thick hair. He pulled her down and moved on top of her, and thrust deeply into her. She did not resist, unable to think of anything but him. She welcomed him into her body, glorying in passionate ecstasy.

During that night of passion, when Zebunissa and Aqil took turns dominating one another, Akbar had been conceived. As the days passed and the truth could no longer be denied, Zebunissa knew she could tell no one but Aqil. It was he who suggested they tell Zebunissa's mild mannered and wise mother. Dilras was grieved to hear of her daughter's affair with an older man, especially as she was engaged to marry Prince Sulaimon. She knew with complete certainty that her husband would execute both Zebunissa and Aqil Khan if he found out. As mothers have done from time immemorial, she concocted a scheme to protect her child. She retreated to a summer palace on the outskirts of the city with Zebunissa, declaring she herself was pregnant with Aurengzeb's child and wished to give birth away from Aurangabad, fearing the war of succession would spill into the city. The mullahs agreed this was a wise precaution. So Dilras and Zebunissa left the main harem to give birth in seclusion. In due time Akbar was born and messengers were sent posthaste to inform Aurengzeb of the birth of his son. Mother and daughter returned to Aurangabad after the rituals of childbirth had been completed.

"Your mother was a saint," murmured Aqil Khan.

Zebunissa smiled. Dilras had starved herself during the last month of her daughter's pregnancy so that when they returned to Aurangabad, it would appear that it was she who had just given birth. Though

Dilras ensured that no suspicion attached to her daughter, she never again spoke to Aqil for the rest of her life.

Aqil accepted her silence, his own heart filled with deep respect for a great lady. Now he looked at Zebunissa and said, "I swear on the Holy Book to protect you both to my dying day."

Zebunissa smiled again. "I thank you for your kindness, Sir, but who will protect you?"

"Almighty Allah will."

Zebunissa looked away, gazing out at the night sky. "May Allah protect us all," she said softly.

# 14
# End Of An Era

*Think of the memory of their disgrace,*
*How dark humiliation stains their face.*

31 January 1666

The tidings pierced Aurengzeb's cold heart like a flame-tipped arrow. For years he had exchanged caustic letters with his ailing father, who would call him a 'serpent' and 'wretch', with Aurengzeb responding that he had learned such tactics from his father. The previous week Aurengzeb had been informed that Shah Jahan's health had deteriorated, but he remained unmoved since his father had often recovered from such turns before.

In fact, Aurengzeb owed his accession to the throne to such an episode of illness. Nine years ago, in the year 1657, Shah Jahan had been deathly ill from an infection in his male organs. A lifetime of debauchery with female slaves and concubines had caused the problem. The ageing Emperor could no longer pass urine. The royal hakims lost hope he would survive. Fearing that his brother Dara, with the help of his sister Jahanara, would usurp the throne should Shah Jahan die, Aurengzeb marched on Agra to fight for the succession and declare himself Emperor. To his chagrin, Shah Jahan recovered. But Aurengzeb did not relent in his quest to wrest the throne. Fearing punishment, Aurengzeb continued his march, enlisting the help of Raushanara to spy on Dara and mislead him on Aurengzeb's war strategy.

Aurengzeb was vastly outnumbered by the Mughal imperial army, his campaign poorly funded. But he used his military prowess to defeat Dara and pronounce himself Emperor. Shah Jahan was sent to Agra as a prisoner of state. Jahanara accompanied her father into captivity at Agra Fort, refusing to remain free if he was imprisoned.

When news arrived that Shah Jahan had indeed died, Aurengzeb's advisors assumed there would be rejoicing at court; that Aurengzeb would host a feast; alms given to the poor; prisoners set free, and the harem ladies given new clothing. But, to everyone's astonishment, Aurengzeb was devastated. He ordered official mourning throughout the empire, and donned the traditional mourning attire – plain white robes.

Still recovering from his stroke, Aurengzeb became more dejected and withdrawn, holding court for only a few hours every week. As everyone sat in the *Diwan-i-Khas,* wearing white robes, no one uttered a word. None dared show grief for fear it would be viewed as an act of sedition. The courtiers remained bewildered what to say or do.

"Someone must go to Agra to escort Aba's remains to the gravesite." It was the first time since his accession that Aurengzeb referred to the deposed Emperor as *Aba* (father).

Zebunissa, her eyes full of unshed tears, felt heartened to see a sensitive side to her stone-hearted father.

"Who do you suggest, Prime Minister?"

"Majesty, you are his only surviving son. It must be you."

Aurengzeb pondered the Prime Minister's words; silence permeated the hall. "I cannot go," he finally said, shaking his greying head from side to side. "There is much to do here. Nor can I look upon my sister's grief."

Mullah Omar interjected. "Perhaps one of your children?"

Zebunissa looked up, amused despite her sorrow. Daughters were not allowed to go and of Aurengzeb's adult sons, both were state prisoners.

"My sons are either unworthy of such a distinction or too young. There is no one." Aurengzeb hung his head, shaking it in helpless frustration.

Zebunissa spoke. "Majesty, the time during your illness was confusing for many people. I know Prince Muazzam is a state prisoner, but he did not wilfully revolt against you as Prince Sultan did. Perhaps, for this one event, you can free him? Grandfather would have been pleased to have his grandson lay him to rest when so many of his sons and grandsons have been executed."

Aurengzeb sat in silence, his head turned towards the screen, as if pondering the implication of her words. He had murdered all three of his brothers and his sister, Raushanara. Releasing his own son from prison to attend his grandfather's burial, would be seen by the people as penance for these sins.

"Very well," he muttered, "free Muazzam. Instruct him to travel to Agra and escort the cortege to the gravesite."

"There is one other matter, Majesty," the Prime Minister said. "The former Emperor requested he be buried alongside his wife, Begum Mumtaz, in the Taj Mahal. Do you sanction this?"

After a short pause Aurengzeb nodded, feeling obligated to honour the last wish of his deceased father.

***

Aurengzeb visited the Taj Mahal two weeks later to offer homage to his parents, interred in the mausoleum Shah Jahan had built for his favourite wife. Dressed like a *fakir,* he walked the dusty road to the Agra Fort to visit his sister, Jahanara, whom he had neither seen nor spoken to for many long years. As he walked slowly along the public thoroughfare, he was astonished to see the grief displayed by the common people. All India seemed to weep for the deceased Emperor; a monarch who had brought in a golden age, despite his personal faults. Aurengzeb was taken aback to see how much the people had loved the man he had so hated.

Entering the fort on foot, he walked past the *Diwan–I–Khas* with its empty throne and went straight to the *Summan Burj,* where Jahanara sat, composed and silent on a gilded *divan,* waiting for her only surviving brother.

"Greetings, *Emperor* Alamgir," she said in a mildly mocking tone.

Words forsook Aurengzeb as he gazed at the woman who had given up her Empress status to join her father in captivity. This was the first time they were face to face after he had killed all three of their brothers, and numerous nephews, including Dara's eldest son, Sulaimon. Bent and grey, reviled and alone, he stood before her.

"How have you been Jahanara?" he said slowly.

"It was hard, but Jani and I managed somehow. I wished to distribute 1000 gold coins to the poor in Aba's name, but your eunuch, Itibar Khan, took them from me, saying I cannot do so without your approval."

"It will be done, sister," Aurengzeb said immediately, lifting his eyes to Jahanara's face. "And I will add another 12,000 rupees. You will be glad to know that I have given Muazzam specific orders to inter Aba's body next to Ami's."

Aurengzeb and Jahanara stared past each other, neither knowing what needed to be said or how to move past the bloodshed that divided them. Suddenly, Aurengzeb fell at Jahanara's feet, sobbing like a child. It was as if his secret lifelong hope had also died with Shah Jahan, that one day his father would grow to love him.

Jahanara stared straight ahead, not looking down at her weeping brother, but unable to hold back her own tears.

"I killed Aba!" cried Aurengzeb, his face distorted in sorrow. "Allah will never forgive me. Ami will never look on my face!"

Instinctively, Jahanara placed her hand on Aurengzeb's head, to comfort him. Aurengzeb slowly gained control over his emotions but remained seated at her feet, feeling more at peace than he had in many years.

At last Jahanara said, "Rise, brother. Before he died, Aba gave me something for you." She reached into her bosom and pulled out a folded parchment – the letter she had written at her father's request, to which he had placed his *nishan*. It had given the dying man solace.

*My Son Aurengzeb*

*You and I are both sons of Allah. He has chosen our paths, so who are we to judge each other? As a young man I committed a great sin: I rebelled against my father, killing my brothers. Perhaps that is why Allah took Begum Mumtaz from me but kept me alive for so long – so one day I too would know the pain of a son rebelling against his father; of one child killing another.*

*I do not fault you for anything, my son. You only did what I taught you, and for that I feel shame in my soul. I must answer for it to Allah when I die. But do not think I die wishing you ill, for I forgive you for all the offenses you have committed against me. I ask that Allah will open the doors of Paradise to you, and that you will be a better father to your children than I was to you.*

*Aba*

Aurengzeb looked up at Jahanara, his eyes red. "Aba forgave me?"

"Yes brother. It is over; our long nightmare is over. It is time to begin again. Aba is with Allah, praying for you."

Aurengzeb shook with silent sobs, giving vent to a lifetime of sadness. Ashamed, he felt humbled by his Aba words. He did not know the words had been Jahanara's; that it was she who had known that salvation for both her brother and father rested in reconciliation. The nightmare had to end; the future of India depended on it. She was the only one left who could do it.

Aurengzeb wiped away his tears. Rising, he went to sit in a low chair, holding both Jahanara's hands in his. "I wish all my brothers' surviving children to live with me as my children," he told her. "Jani shall marry my son, Azam, and you will preside over the wedding. Will you agree to give her in marriage to my son?"

Surprised, Jahanara said, "It shall be so, but only if you permit all of your daughters to marry freely. I ask you to end this tradition that denies marriage to royal princesses."

Aurengzeb looked out of the embrasure his father had once gazed at in his dying moments. Outside, dusk had fallen but flaming torches lit the fort for the Emperor was in residence.

"It will be done," he said. "In fact, I think Dara's younger son, Siphr, will be a good match for my daughter, Zubdatunissa. And I have one more request. I ask that you return with me to *Shahjahanabad*, and assume your role as Empress."

It was Jahanara's turn to look away in silent thought. She had witnessed so much grief, so much bloodshed…all for this right to rule this land. Perhaps it had been ordained so. Reluctantly, she looked back at her gaunt-faced brother. "On one condition: I will always be allowed to question you, regardless of what the issue may be."

Aurengzeb nodded. "I agree."

"And you will never harm any member of our family again, least of all the children of your deceased brothers."

"I swear it on the *Koran*."

## 15
## Jahanara Returns

*The festival of love is holden here,*
*The goblet passes; drink thou of this wine.*

15 February 1666

Zebunissa watched in awe as the gold painted elephant carrying her father and aunt ambled through Chandni Chowk on its way to the Red Fort. Years ago, her uncle, Prince Dara, had been paraded as a state prisoner on the same avenue. Now, for the first time, her father was showing love and respect for a sibling; he was bringing home the former Empress, Jahanara Begum.

Of Shah Jahan's seven children, Jahanara was the eldest, four years older than Aurengzeb. After Mumtaz Begum's death, she became a surrogate mother to all of the royal children. As a child, Aurengzeb had been sentenced to fifty lashes on the back for the crime of poisoning his stepmother, Manbhavati, a Hindu. Jahanara had nursed Aurengzeb back to health, protecting him during that time of turmoil. Aurengzeb had developed a bond with Jahanara that was unlike any other. Years later, when Jahanara had been severely burnt in an accidental fire, Aurengzeb had rushed to her bedside and wept. But the sore point of their relationship stemmed from Jahanara's equal love for Dara, and her decision to support him for the throne. Aurengzeb viewed this as a betrayal, though Jahanara's choice stemmed from her concern over Aurengzeb's religious intolerance and his closeness to the *mullahs*, who Jahanara viewed as Mughal India's nemesis.

Crowds of wellwishers thronged both sides of route as the procession carrying the Emperor and former Empress made its way to the fort. Mughal guards pointed their spears at the crowd, hoping to push them back, but it was a futile effort. The public adored Jahanara and her arrival was cheered by the crowds in the same way as an Emperor returning victorious from battle.

Zebunissa watched amazed as the blanket of humanity coalesced around the elephant legs. She had never witnessed such devotion for her father or any of his nobles. Indeed, she had not known the people of Delhi were capable of such love. What did this outpouring of public affection say about Aurengzeb, Zebunissa wondered?

Zubdat walked up behind Zebunissa and gazed over her shoulder at the procession. "I have never seen the former Empress," she remarked. "What does she look like?"

"She is beautiful," responded Zebunissa, a contented smile on her face. "She is fair, tall, with long black hair and a slim physique. You would hardly know she is older than Aba."

Zubdat smiled. "There are rumors she may be reinstated as Empress."

Zebunissa turned to looked at her. "Is it true? Empress Jahanara will reign again?" She paused. "Perhaps she can join the Makhfi."

"Join the Makhfi? If she joins us, she will BE the Makhfi," stated Zubdat, chuckling. "You will no longer head the resistance."

Zebunissa smiled. "I do not wish to be the head, my dear sister," she responded. She turned to gaze out the window towards the teeming world outside. "I just want the empire back and for Aba to see the errors of his ways. If my aunt can change him, then we may not even need the Makhfi. We can just be the poetic society everyone thinks we are. After all, this is not the time for us to be organizing rebellions..." she said, her voice breaking, "...it is the time for us to marry and bear children and watch them grow. We have been robbed of our innocence and youth."

Her own eyes filled with unshed tears, Zubdat nodded. "Perhaps the Empress can return our youth to us."

Zebunissa smiled, her lips trembling. "Perhaps…"

***

A grand feast was organized in the harem to welcome Jahanara back to the capital. The royal chefs had prepared authentic Mughal dishes specially for the occasion: lamb in yogurt sauce, grilled kebab, lamb pulav garnished with raisins, chicken korma, grilled fish in lemon sauce… For the vegetarian Hindus like Nawab Bai, there was vegetable pilaf, moong dal, yogurt with vegetables, tandoori bread and the like. The entire harem was repainted and lavish Persian tapestries hung to add elegance to the chambers.

Aurengzeb's wives, among them Nawab Bai, were seated at one end, with Zebunissa, Badr, Zubdat, Zinat and Mihir on the opposite end. The concubines and slaves sat behind. The smell of rose-scented incense permeated the room and the lamps lent warmth that was welcome on this cold winter day. Aurengzeb arrived dressed in a robe of gold cloth with a silver border; a necklace of pearls and rubies hung around his neck and his diamond-studded dagger was tucked into his cummerbund. His bejewelled figure made Zebunissa wonder if he had discarded some of his earlier convictions. Aurengzeb had always scoffed at rich raiment and jewels as expressions of vanity, and the harem women had perforce followed his spartan lead.

Standing beside him was a woman with grey hair, her fair-skinned face wrinkled and lined. She appeared frail but held her head high, as if born to it. Unlike the women of Aurengzeb's harem, she wore no veil over her face, though her head was covered. Her *ghaghara-kurta* was even more decorative than the Emperor's outfit. Zebunissa looked around for Jahanara, wondering who the elderly woman was. Perhaps another who had shared Shah Jahan's captivity?

A tall Tatar guard announced, "Abul Muzaffar Muhi-ud-Din Muhammad Aurengzeb Alamgir *hazir hai*!" Horns sounded and a light *dhudhumbi* drum began to beat. A few moments later the guard announced Her Imperial Majesty, Begum Jahanara.

Zebunissa gasped in shock, her hand flying up to her mouth. The gaunt elderly woman was her once beautiful, beloved aunt! Jahanara's nine years in captivity had aged her beyond recognition. She no longer looked youthful and energetic, but feeble and tired. A hesitant smile had replaced the dazzling one which had once made all those who saw it, her willing slaves. As the royals walked to the centre of the vast chamber and sat down, Nawab Bai could be seen weeping behind her veil.

Aurengzeb seemed oblivious of the shocked response of the women. He smiled and raised his hand in acknowledgement. Still recovering from his stroke, he spoke with some deliberation. "We...we have witnessed great sadness. The Mughal Empire mourns the loss of a great Emperor, and I, a loving father."

No emotion crossed Jahanara's face as she sat stoically, listening to her brother's words.

"But a new era now begins. I wish to inform you, ladies of the imperial harem, that I have appointed my sister, Begum Jahanara, once more, as Empress."

"*Suban Allah*!" The gathering cried in jubilation. Eunuchs, tatars, slaves, and concubines, all lauded the announcement. The smile on Jahanara's face was once again reminiscent of her earlier days. Though she had aged, her smile had remained the same. 'That is the smile I use to love,' Zebunissa thought to herself.

"From this day," Aurengzeb continued, turning towards Jahanara, "you will carry the *Muhr Uzak* as the *Padishah Begum* of my kingdom."

Jahanara's smile disappeared as she took note of the word *my*. Though it was understood that the kingdom belonged to none but the Emperor, it was considered polite for an Emperor to use the term *our*. By failing to do so, he reminded everyone that he believed the empire belonged to him alone; his family and the women of his harem, existed merely to sustain his wishes.

Aurengzeb placed the heavy seal into Jahanara's hands. She ran her fingers over it gently, as if caressing an old lover's face. There was clapping of hands all around and once again the drums sounded, marking the transfer of the Royal Seal.

When there was silence once again, Aurengzeb said, "I have one other announcement I wish to make. I have decided to give my beloved daughter, Zubdat in marriage to Siphr, son of my deceased brother, Dara. They shall be married this year and the nuptials will be overseen by the *Padishah Begum*."

Once again the crowd rejoiced. What an evening it was turning out to be, Zebunissa thought as she spun round to look at Zubdat in astonishment. Smiling in disbelief, the sisters hugged each other. Zubdat was overcome with delight. She knew she had no say in who her husband would be, or even if she would ever be married. But here she was being bequeathed to someone she had known her whole life, who was royalty, and she could remain in Delhi.

"This is wonderful..." Zebunissa whispered into Zubdat's ear. "Now you will have a family of your own while still remaining close to me."

The other ladies of the harem nodded their heads and smiled at Zubdat, who felt overwhelmed by both the news and the attention.

"Zebo, who is that beautiful girl sitting next to the Empress? She keeps nodding her head at me but I don't know who she is," Zubdat whispered.

"That is Uncle Dara's daughter, Jani. He named her after Aunt Jahanara. She was his most beloved child and was cared for by our grandfather and Aunt Jahanara, during their captivity. She is indeed beautiful!"

"I must make her acquaintance," remarked Zubdat.

"Yes, we must all make her acquaintance. She is as amazing as the aunt who cared for her." Zebunissa felt tears spring to her eyes as she saw Aurengzeb smiling benevolently at Jahanara and Jani. Despite her long festering animosity towards the father she had actively worked to overthrow, she felt a grudging appreciation in that moment, for reuniting her long divided family. "Abu *salaam*," she whispered under her breath.

***

Jani began spending her days with Zebunissa and the Makhfi. The true mission of the Makhfi had not been disclosed to her, at least not yet. Jani was feted as the most beautiful Mughal Princess, and did not lack for suitors among the sons of the nobility. But Aurengzeb refused them all, keeping her for his inept son, Prince Azam. Jani, now twenty-three, had not been made privy to the alliance because Jahanara herself felt uneasy about it. One evening, in her chambers, she spoke to her brother about it.

"I cannot agree to an alliance between Azam and Jani," she told him directly.

Aurengzeb was taken aback but said nothing, merely raising his brows in surprised hauteur.

"In fact, none of your sons are worthy. Two are in prison and the other two are too young!"

"Azam is of rightful age," Aurengzeb responded calmly.

"Azam is just sixteen; Jani is twenty-three."

"Azam does not mind. He adores Jani and wishes to make her his wife." Aurengzeb walked over to Jahanara. "Sister, Azam has grown into a tall, well built warrior. He is likely to be my heir. Do you not wish to see Jani sit beside him one day as Empress?"

Jahanara pondered over what he had said. She had often wondered if the old saying that a Mughal women had to forge a strong alliance with a Mughal man to ensure her survival, was indeed true.

"What guarantee do I have that you will not imprison Azam like you have imprisoned two of your sons? He is coming of age and it is usually the time when Mughal men develop a roar in their throats. We all know what happens when they roar at the great Alamgir!"

Aurengzeb's face turned sour. "If I promise never to imprison Azam, no matter what his offense, will you agree to marry Jani to him?"

Jahanara paused for a moment, considering, then nodded her head.

***

Preparing Jahanara chambers, which Jani was to share, had taken longer than anticipated, so Nawab Bai had graciously offered her private chambers to the Empress and her protégé.

One day, sitting beside a window giving onto the structured gardens below, with their soothing waterways, Jani recognized Aqil Khan's voice coming from behind the curtain that fell over the entrance. "The walls were to be painted green…why are they blue? And the tapestries were to be hung on the wall facing east, not west!"

Jani jumped up joyfully and ran to the curtain, pulling it aside to reveal her enchanting, uncovered face.

"Princess…" said Aqil taken aback, looking away.

"You can look at me, Mirza Khan," retorted Jani grinning impishly. "Rest assured, I have looked upon you and your kindness ever since arriving in Delhi."

"Princess," said Aqil, bowing. "The Emperor will not be pleased to know I have looked upon your uncovered face."

"But why not? You look upon the faces of his daughters."

"I have the Emperor's permission; they are in my charge when he is away."

"Well, I give you permission to look upon me as you please," she replied haughtily.

Aqil Khan, noticeably uncomfortable, said, his eyes still averted, "What can I do for you, Princess?"

Jani looked around at the work being done. "Do you think these chambers will be ready soon?"

"Not soon. It will take a few more weeks."

"A few weeks…" Jani let out a sigh. "I hate living in Begum Nawab Bai's chambers. The women are so loud and there are mosquitos everywhere."

"I will relay your concerns to the Emperor."

Jani paused for a moment and then looked up at him sideways. "Where do you sleep?" she enquired.

Aqil felt a cold chill go down his spine. A lifetime spent as a debonair, chiselled man had given him sufficient insight into when a female was interested in him. "I should be getting back to work," he said turning away.

Jani scanned the room and noticed a small *charpoy* with a *razai*. "Is that for you?" she asked.

Aqil stood in silence, unwilling to comment. Jani put her hand on his upper arm and squeezed gently. "A man of your stature should not lie thus. Come to my chamber when all the lights have dimmed. I will light three candles as a signal that all is clear." With a grin, she turned and walked away. Aqil stood still, his face a mixture of anger and disapproval.

***

Aqil lay on his *charpoy*, haunted by the fact that he had fathered a child with the daughter of a sitting Emperor. Entrusted to watch over them, Aqil knew he betrayed his Emperor's trust by allowing his lust to overcome his duty. 'But am I the only one to blame?' he wondered. Aqil had been married to the daughter of a Persian commoner when they were both teenagers. She had been unable to bear him any children but he had never berated her for this though he longed for a son. As the years passed the relationship between them turned platonic but the trust and bond between them remained deep and strong. Thus, when his wife suddenly died of dysentery, Aqil felt his heart had been ripped out of his chest and thrown to the four winds. His melancholy was so great he barely appeared in court and he began to drink heavily.

Aurengzeb was dismayed at his friend's deterioration. He summoned Aqil and intrusted him with the care of his daughters and Begums while he set out to fight for the throne of India. Uncertain how to entertain the ladies, Aqil began teaching them poetic composition and recitation; delving into his own love for the art. Zebunissa entered his life as a pupil, but her beauty and personality made her irresistible to him from the beginning. Though he often said she was the daughter he had wanted, in actuality she was the wife he dreamt of. But he was strongly aware of the differences between them in age, position and stages of life. She was a Princess, born into royalty; he was a minor noble, living on grace and favour. Thus he never divulged his feelings to anyone, not even himself. When he learned Zebunissa was engaged to Prince Sulaimon, he experienced both jealousy and relief. But as Zebunissa far surpassed the other women in her poetic ability, he found himself devoting more and more time to her individually. Then came the fateful night when Zebunissa recited a poem so beautiful as to make even the angels weep. Aqil was overcome, touched to his core, defenceless against what happened next. 'I was so utterly attracted to her in that moment,' he recalled. As Zebunissa flung herself into his embrace, he was unable to resist. Now, half asleep, he could still feel her warmth, the gentle caress of her hand on his torso, her lips on his. It had their first and last liaison, but he remembered it as if it had just happened. He tossed restlessly as he imagined kissing Zebunissa. Suddenly he was shaken awake by someone slipping onto the *charpoy* next to him.

"Jani!" Aqil leapt off the *charpoy,* wearing only his pajamas. He staring down in horror at Jani, who sat covering her bare breasts with the *razai,* a mischievous grin on her face.

"Mirza Aqil, I came to keep you warm."

Aqil ran his hand through his hair in frustration and anger. "Go to your chamber now!" he commanded.

"But why? Do you not find me attractive?"

Aqil felt guilt fill his soul as he stared at the young girl. Her olive, hairless skin, her long black hair and big beautiful eyes reminded him of Zebunissa. Worse, it reminded him of his own weak mindedness. He felt torn by what he had done to Zebunissa, blaming himself for robbing her of her innocence, though it had been she who had initiated the liaison. Now, years later, a bastard child ran the halls of the Mughal court and would perhaps one day pay for the sins of his lustful father if the truth was ever discovered. Aqil continued to stare at Jani's naked back and then looked away, feeling like a defiler who robbed young girls of their virginity. As tears sprang to Jani's eyes at supposed rejection, he said harshly, "Go from here! I do not find girls like you attractive! Cover yourself and have some self-respect."

Jani looked upon him in horror and grief, sobbing with eyes wide open in astonishment at his rejection. Hurriedly, she clutched at her discarded robe on the floor and pulled it over herself. She threw off the *razai* and fled the chamber, as if from a bed of scorpions. Aqil stood in stoic silence, stunned by what had transpired. Though he turned his anger on Jani, he knew that the words he had spoken were not for so much for her as for him. He was the sinner who had failed to have self-respect.

***

Jani stood in front of her mirror, naked, her face drenched with tears. *Was she really still just a girl?* Was she not attractive? She had never before been rejected. The years she had spent in captivity had taught Jani how to attract men. She had been only eleven when she had seen carnal acts performed in front of her by her aunt. Jani had wept and pleaded, but Raushanara had not relented. Jani began having trouble sleeping; she could not concentrate on anything for long, and she became hypersensitive to noise. She was petrified of dark rooms, preferring to sleep with lanterns lit. Anger, guilt and fear were her unsavoury companions during this time. She often felt suffocated.

For months she tried to repress the memories and forget the acts she had seen. Soon, however, she found herself wanting to engage in the very behaviour that had once repelled her. A raw sexuality had been ignited within her. Any man who attracted her fell prey to her lust. They were powerless to resist her glorious beauty and rampant sexuality. Shamelessly, she began to have liaisons with the Mughal soldiers who guarded them. With each act she felt more dirty and stained, yet she could not resist. Secretly, she prayed for the day her grandfather would die and she would be free to court handsome men and satisfy her urges with them. She deemed herself unfit for the true love of a soulmate.

When she met Aqil and heard rumors of a secret liaison between him and Zebunissa, she gleefully assumed he found younger women attractive. His ferocious rejection made her feel cheap and unworthy, even of older men. 'Is it that I am ugly? Are all those who say I am beautiful simply being polite,' she wondered? But soon her sorrow was dwarfed by another emotion – jealousy. She hated Zebunissa for having what she could not and was determined to prove she was superior to Zebunissa by making Aqil Khan hers.

***

"But he is just a young boy, Aunt, hardly a man! How could you bequeath me to him?" Jani was noticeably upset, tears filling her lovely eyes. She stared directly into her aunt's face, something she had never done before.

"Marriage is not about love, my girl; it is about power and security!" Jahanara replied sternly.

"What security?" responded Jani petulantly. "Azam is a joke at court. He is said to have wet his pants in the *Diwan-i-Khas* while everyone watched and laughed. What power or security will I have married to a worm like that?"

"Jani, you are speaking of your future husband!" Jahanara warned. "Mughal Princesses were not even allowed to marry in my time. Now you have that privilege you are complaining?"

Seated on a floor cushion at Jahanara's feet, Jani buried her head in her hands and sobbed.

Jahanara placed a hand on Jani's shoulder, saying, "Listen to me Jani. I was once madly in love with a young British physician. His name was Gabriel Boughton. We became close, and then intimate. No one other than your father knew of this, else I would have been imprisoned or killed. I eventually broke off relations with Gabriel because I knew there was no way I could live with a *firangi* as his wife in the Mughal dominion. I also knew I could never leave India and settle with him in his land, far away in the West."

Jahanara paused as her voice broke. Regaining her composure, she said, "You are the only person alive who knows about this now. I am telling you this so you know that in my time Mughal Princesses could not marry, so we ended up finding lovers we knew we could never be with, and then living with broken hearts for the rest of our lives. Other women would simply sneak men in and out of the harem, becoming whores. But the Mughal daughters were the royal whores. I had cousins who became pregnant by soldiers, having behaved like animals hungry for food. It all stemmed from the fact that we were forbidden to marry."

Jani listen in astonished silence. Her aunt had never spoken of her secretive past.

"Azam is not perfect, I know. I am unhappy that he is younger than you. But he loves you and it is a good match. As his primary wife, you will enjoy a large allowance and one day, you will be Empress. Your father, my brother Dara, would have been so proud! I have also obtained an assurance from the Emperor that he will never imprison Azam, no matter what the offense. I know my brother will never break his word to me." Jahanara took Jani's hand in her own. "Do you trust me?"

Jani nodded slowly, her eyes still moist. Jahanara kissed her on the forehead. "You know I love you. You are the daughter I never had," she said softly.

# 16
# Riches Beyond Compare

*Safely the Emperors had kept their regal seat,*
*Nor ever known the poison of defeat,*
*So were we not, O Master, led by thee*
*Vain were our struggles, scant our victory!*

3 January 1669

Dressed in a blood-red outfit, Jani was married to Azam in nuptials befitting the Emperor's son. The *Padishah Begum* oversaw every detail herself, just as she had a generation earlier, for Jani's father, Dara. However, Aurengzeb did not permit the wine, *bhang*, music, opium, and nautch girls that had made Dara's wedding memorable. The participants had to be satisfied with Chinese rockets and firecrackers that painted the sky and drumbeats that sounded more like a rallying call to battle than a wedding procession. Of course, this did not stop the women of the harem sneaking in *shirazi* and arak, and intoxicating themselves in the privacy of their chambers.

After the night of celebration had ended, Zebunissa, strolling in the harem gardens as dawn lit the sky, saw a thin figure in the distance. It was Jahanara.

"You are up early, my child."

"As are you, Aunt. You must be exhausted!" Zebunissa remarked, sitting down on the marble floor beside Jahanara's chair.

"Why do you sit there, child? Have the guard bring a chair." Jahanara waved a hand towards a young tatar woman standing some distance away; too far to be privy to the conversation between the two royals but close enough to protect them.

Zebunissa quickly waved the guard away. "Oh let me sit like this, just as I did when you recited poetry to me as a child, remember?"

Jahanara smiled but turned away, unwilling to recall the painful past.

"We have a poetic society, the Makhfi, and we…"

"Poetic society?" inquired Jahanara. "I heard it was a prayer meeting group?"

Zebunissa frowned. "After Sulaimon's death, Aba's heart was perhaps softened by my plight. I dreamt that Ami was telling me to use the opportunity to gain a favour that would empower me. So I chose the Makhfi."

"Empower you?"

"Yes. I must tell you something in confidence. The Makhfi is not what it seems; it is not a prayer group, but instead a poetic society. It is a rebellion." Zebunissa reached into her bosom and brought out a handful of poems she and other Makhfi members had recited at their meetings, as they sought ways to overthrow Aurengzeb's reign.

Jahanara read the poems with increasing incredulity, recognizing the hidden messages of sedition and plots in the poetic verse. She read each one to see if they were all in the same genre – sedition. Quickly, she looked down into Zebunissa's upturned face, her brows raised in horrified astonishment. There were specific instructions and commands encrypted into the poems; through them Jahanara was able to determine just how vast and detailed the operations of the Makhfi had been. Finally, she placed the poems neatly in her lap and stared at Zebunissa, her face showing no emotion. Zebunissa stared back, waiting for her aunt to speak, a veil of fearful optimism covering her face.

"You know you could go to jail if your father ever found out!"

Zebunissa smiled, unconcerned. Covering Jahanara's hands with her own, she said, "We are all going to hell, Empress. If I halt in jail on my way, would it really be so much worse?"

Jahanara freed herself from Zebunissa's grasp and asked quietly, "Who are involved in this?"

"I, Zubdat, Zinat, Badrunissa, and Mihirunissa are the core members. Muazzam, Aqil Khan and Akbar, are also involved."

"Aqil Khan? But he is a close confidante of the Emperor! He trusts him more than anyone."

"Which is why we need him. To the world he is someone who serves the Emperor. In actuality, he seeks to overthrow him, just like the rest of us." Zebunissa paused as Jahanara shook her head in disbelief, before saying softly, "We have come very close in the past to our goal. We almost had Muazzam declared interim Emperor, and even ordered you and grandfather to be freed. But Aba recovered from his illness, miraculously, and everything changed."

Jahanara looked at her niece, upset to learn of the dangerous path Zebunissa and her sisters had taken, and now sought to take her on.

"We wish you to head the Makhfi, Aunt. Please take this weight off my shoulders and guide us like you always did," Zebunissa pleaded, anguish in her voice.

But Jahanara only stared at her with incredulity, shaking her head.

Finally she said, "I am too old for such intrigues, my child. I have neither the physical nor mental strength to deal with more setbacks and failures. I will only serve to drag you back, preventing the wheels of your rebellion from moving forward." Jahanara smiled. "But I support your mission, and will do so to my dying day. That much I promise you."

"Aunt, I have one question. Is it true you married Jani to Azam because you wanted her to be Empress after you?"

Jahanara touched Zebunissa's cheek. "My child, there will be no Empress after me because there will be no empire after your father. I told Jani what I am telling you now. After your father's death, whatever remains of this great kingdom, will be inherited by one of his sons. With Mohammad Sultan and Muazzam out of favour, it will be either Azam or Akbar. Link yourself to one of them; create an alliance. I say this because if you do not, you will end in penury after your father's death. No one will ask anything of you, nor provide for you. Your father killed your fiancé, and could kill anyone else you seek to marry, but he will not slay his own sons. He has promised me he will not even imprison them. Your cousin Jani is linked to Azam. You must do the same, perhaps with Akbar."

"Our efforts have failed in part because none of my brothers have the charisma or character of a true Emperor," Zebunissa lamented, saddened by her aunt's words. "I wish I could raise a Prince to be Emperor; to groom him to take over and keep the Empire alive!"

"You have Akbar. Raise him to be the Emperor your other brothers cannot be." Jahanara rose and pulled Zebunissa's hand till she rose as well. "Come with me; I want to show you something," she said, walking slowly out of the garden and into the palace.

Jahanara led Zebunissa down a dark corridor deep inside the fort. As they walked, Zebunissa noticed the passage was guarded by strong, seasoned soldiers. She had never been to this part of the fort before. Jahanara nodded to one of the guards, who stepped back, allowing them entry. The air had become thick, reminding Zebunissa of the time she had visited Sulaimon in a similar, mouldy dungeon, where she had felt suffocated.

As the two Royals passed from one passageway into another, Jahanara paused to enter their names into a ledger. Zebunissa looked at her in surprise, thinking it strange. Finally, they arrived before a huge door, where they removed all the jewellery they wore.

"Before you enter, let me warn you that what you are about to see is the devil; the cause of our family's ruin." Jahanara's eyes were two deep dark wells of sadness.

When the two women entered the chamber lit with tapers, before them lay riches beyond compare. Zebunissa was dazzled.

Taking a deep breath, Jahanara said, "Feast your eyes on Mughal poison, my child. My whole life I have watched men lose their souls to obtain this – son against father, brother against brother."

Zebunissa stood frozen, staring at the riches before her: 182 kilograms of diamonds, 136 kilograms of emeralds, 300 kilograms of pearls; barrels of precious stones – moonstone, agate, opal – trunks filled with diamond encrusted gold daggers, gold coins, silver swords, gold plate, golden statues, and in the distance, a jewel encrusted golden throne.

"My grandfather, Emperor Jahangir, sat on that throne," said Jahanara. "It fell into disuse when my father built the Peacock Throne. Yet it remains here, a forgotten relic of Emperors long gone."

Zebunissa began to cough, feeling breathless and overwhelmed. Jahanara looked at her in amusement. "I know…it can be suffocating. What value can you or I possibly have when compared to such wealth? One cannot but feel insignificant." Jahanara walked to a smaller chest and lifted its lid. "These are blood rubies." She placed some of the glowing gems in Zebunissa's hands. "They are red with the blood of our loved ones. Legend says that every time a Mughal slays another, these rubies deepen in colour and increase in value." Zebunissa quickly put the gemstones back; holding her hand to her chest, feeling nauseous.

"I was there when my father brought his four sons into this chamber and filled their minds with greed," Jahanara said. "After that there was a palpable difference in them all; they became distant from one another, self-absorbed. Never allow Akbar to enter this chamber Zebunissa, for it will blind him too. No measure of motherly love or sisterly affection will undo the spell. Come, let us leave."

Zebunissa turned to walk out with Jahanara, but the Empress stopped her with a gesture, saying harshly, "Never come here again! You are lucky if you have not already fallen under the spell. If you return, it will never let you go."

## 17
## Jiziya

*No Muslim I,*
*But an idolater,*
*I bow before the image of my Love,*
*And worship her.*

### 2 April 1679

The sun struggled through the hazy fog that blanketed Delhi, sending beams over the sandstone walls of the Red Fort. Alamgir sat proudly on the Peacock Throne, the jewels embedded in it dim in the mist that had permeated the air. By then several marriages had taken place with much fanfare: Jani with Azam, Zubdat with Siphr, and Mihirunissa with Izad Baksh, Aurengzeb's nephew. Jahanara, had presided over them all, even convincing Aurengzeb to release Prince Muazzam on the grounds that he had been *thoroughly tamed*. As Empress, she stood as beside the Peacock Throne, opposite the *mullahs,* who still enjoyed unprecedented power.

After an initial display of benevolence towards non-Muslims, Aurengzeb had incrementally reversed his policies and once again demolished Hindu temples and Christian churches all over India. The Hindu Rajputs stopped attending court in protest. Aurengzeb responded by annexing several of their kingdoms. Zebunissa became increasingly impatient with her tyrannical father, but could not find an opportunity to overthrow him. Instead, she focused her energies on training Akbar in military skills as her Aunt had advised. He was sent away to the jungles for several years, to be trained in the art of war and military tactics by the finest commanders.

"What news from the Deccan?" Aurengzeb asked now, a hint of hesitation in his voice; news from the Deccan was never good. A Hindu rebel from the Maratha tribe, Shivaji Bhonsle, had been at war with Aurengzeb over his intolerant policies since the days Aurengzeb had been Governor of the Deccan. Since then Shivaji had expanded the Maratha holdings considerably, taking several forts and cities at the southern edges of the Empire. Aurengzeb loathed Shivaji and had channelled his rage by destroying more Hindu temples and torturing Hindus. On this day, the news he heard in the *Diwan-i-Am* was especially disturbing.

The Prime Minister stepped forward hesitantly, fear apparent in his mien and eyes.

The Emperor was no fool. "Prime Minister, I sense trouble in your eyes. Speak without fear; I trust your loyalty. What calamity has befallen our kingdom?"

Zafar Khan looked up at the now frail figure on the glittering throne. "The news from the Deccan is not good, Majesty. The rebels have coronated Shivaji as *Chhatrapati*, their Emperor."

Aurengzeb slapped a hand on his knee in anger. "It is only I who may bestow titles on those I feel are worthy! How dare that infidel declare himself Emperor while I still live!"

There was silence in the hall. Jahanara did not speak. She knew Shivaji, the son of a *jagidar* in one of the southern sultanates, had become a hero among the Hindu Marathas due to the stand he had taken against the bigoted policies of her brother.

Aurengzeb took a deep breath. The man had been a thorn in his flesh and had to be removed from the face of the earth. His eyes searched the hall for answers, but no one dared to speak. Finally, he said, "The Hindus think they can insult their Emperor by not attending court, by supporting an illiterate savage as their Emperor, within my domain? Do they not fear the might of the Great Mughal?"

The Head *mullah* responded, "Majesty, kindness has been perceived as weakness by these infidels."

Jahanara looked at the man in displeasure. She detested hearing Hindus referred to as infidels. Mughal tradition was a blending of Hindu and Muslim ways, and every Mughal Emperor in the last four generations, including Aurengzeb himself, had married Hindu wives. Hence every Mughal Royal carried Hindu blood. To suggest the Hindus were infidels implied that the Mughals had infidel blood.

"Send two regiments to Aurangabad, as reinforcement against the Maratha! I do not doubt there will be raids into our holdings now that they have a self-proclaimed Emperor."

"Majesty," began Zafar Khan, "there is little left in the treasury for two whole regiments. Our efforts against the Maratha have come at a significant cost. In the past few years we have had to rebuild three forts and send a constant supply of reinforcements to the Deccan to fight off these rebels."

"Perhaps it is time to impose the *jiziya*?" the *mullah* suggested in humble tones.

"Majesty!" Zebunissa's voice came urgently from behind the marble screen. "*Jiziya* is a tax on Hindus. None of your subjects should have to pay a tax to visit their places of worship!"

"Silence!" Aurengzeb raised his hand. "I will not have my court turned into a market place. I am the Emperor, yet the Hindus resist!"

Jahanara sought permission to speak and Aurengzeb heard her in silence. "Majesty, Hindus are the ocean on which our ship sails. I beg of you, do not tax the waters that keep the ship of our empire afloat!"

Aurengzeb's turned towards Jahanara, his eyes on her veiled face. There was silence in the hall as the court wondered whether the Empress' words would move the Emperor. His next words would decide the victor once and for all.

"Hindus are *not* the sea on which we sail! We sail on the sea of our faith in Allah, His goodness and mercy!"

Immediately here was a loud chorus from the *mullahs*, hailing his piety: *Allah ho Akbar! Allah ho Akbar! Allah ho Akbar!*

Jahanara closed her eyes in defeat. Behind the marble screen, Zebunissa clenched her fists.

Raising his voice above the chants and cheers, Aurengzeb declared, "Our faith will take us forward to defeat the enemies of Islam!"

There were more cheers of *Allah ho Akbar!* They resonated in Jahanara's ears, penetrating her closed lids, filling her mind.

"The sea of our faith shall drown the infidels and engulfed our enemies, for we are Keepers of the Faith!"

The nobles too, joined in the cheering, knowing the Emperor had made his decision. Failing to support him could only bring trouble.

"I hereby decree that from this day forward, every non-Muslim will pay a tax to visit his place of worship. The *jiziya* is hereby reinstated at 48 *dirhams* on the rich, 24 on the middle class, and 12 on the poor. The rich will constitute those earning 10,000 *dirhams* or more a year, the middle class those earning over 1000, and the poor those earning less than 200. Furthermore, non-believers shall travel on foot and pay the *jiziya* with his own hand; he shall stand before the *jiziya*-collector, who shall be seated. The non-believer's hand shall remain below that of the collector, who will take the tax with the words, 'Pay the *jiziya*, O infidel!'"

# 18
# Rebellion

*The wine of my delight has lost its taste;*
*The earth of my existence turns a waste.*

4 April 1679

On the following Friday, Aurengzeb set out in an imperial procession to the Jama Masjid for *namaaz*. Chosen ladies of the imperial harem accompanied him on elephants bearing curtained *howdahs* and in palanquins. Dark rain clouds hung above the Chandni Chowk. A violent thunderstorm seemed to be approaching but Aurengzeb was determined to perform his prayers as planned at the grand mosque.

Zebunissa and Jahanara travelled on the same imperial elephant, listening to the drums beating to announce the Emperor's procession. Zebunissa was shocked to see the entire Hindu citizenry of Delhi and its neighboring villages had gathered in the wide Chandni Chowk to block the procession. The elephants trumpeted and horses moved restlessly, rising up into the air with forehoofs lifted as the townspeople poked them with homemade spears.

Zebunissa looked at Jahanara in astonishment. The Empress' hand covered her mouth in disbelief. "Have you ever seen anything like this, Aunt?" Jahanara merely shook her head.

The protesters began chanting: *No jiziya! No jiziya!*

The citizenry, usually subdued even at the public torture of dissenters, seemed to have broken free of their bondage of fear. They seemed infuriated. Zebunissa began to tremble, fearing for their safety. She saw the General of the Guard motion to the crowd to make way for the imperial elephants, but no one heeded his gesture. An endless sea of angry Hindu protestors stared at the royal procession in defiance with rage-filled eyes. Zebunissa saw some youths throwing stones at Aurengzeb's elephant. She also noticed that the women had left their face uncovered, in direct defiance of the Emperor's edict. The horror was amplified by the little children atop their father's shoulders, screaming and chanting along with their elders. The burgundy-robed imperial guards rode into the crowd with iron spikes and whips, desperately trying to control the unruly mob but to no avail. The crowd set afire effigies and hurled them towards the soldiers. Some flaming fragments landed on the protesters instead, setting them on fire.

The sky began to thunder as Jahanara gazed at the horrific scene. Was this the apocalypse soothsayers spoke of? The great Emperor Akbar had banned the *jiziya,* winning the hearts of an entire generation. Now, a century later, his great-grandson had reversed the policy, bringing doom on his family and kingdom. Zebunissa shivered as the clouds broke and cold rain began to pour down on the crowd. She noticed her father still seated motionless in the rain atop his trumpeting elephant. She knew he was seething with fury at the inability of his Guards to control the crowd.

The spectacle continued for an hour. Aurengzeb's simple robes of prayer became drenched as he took over direct command of the guard, shouting orders and calling for the rearguard to come up. Zebunissa noticed the protestors avoided attacking the Emperor in person; no rocks were hurled directly at him though he was at the mercy of the mob. The protest appeared to be calculated and organized, thought Zebunissa. Did it indicate a widening chasm between the Emperor and his Hindu subjects? When the time was right, she could harness this discontent to overthrow him.

Jahanara began to feel unwell. She motioned to turn the elephant and return to the fort. Zebunissa did not protest, but she saw her father staring at the retreating elephants and palanquins in displeasure. She knew he would consider it a display of cowardice. Looking over her shoulder, she saw him raise both hands towards the crowd, gesturing for them to move back. Zebunissa could not hear what he said but she feared his words bore an ominous message for the protestors.

***

Aurengzeb, his stern face lashed by rain, his humble prayer robes soaked and clinging to his ageing body, his frailty visible to all, felt shame and rage burn through his body. He wiped his dripping face with his sleeve, but to little effect as the ceaseless rain continued to beat down on his head. He quivered like a fish plucked from the river, feeling vulnerable and defenceless. 'Why am I, the Great Mughal, standing wet and helpless, quivering in the cold like a homeless fakir!' His soldiers had failed to tame the crowd, merely killing a few of the more raucous leaders. The crowd kept growing as more people came running from alleyways to join the throng. Aurengzeb knew the imposition of the *jiziya* would be unwelcome to the Hindu citizenry, but he had never expected such a show of united resistance. His head throbbing with anger, he wished only to seek them all slaughtered before his eyes. But he knew he could not retreat to regroup. An Emperor could not retreat before his own people, or there would be mutiny in the kingdom

Seeing Jahanara's elephant slowly turn and make its way towards the fort, he felt further enraged. 'Who told her she could retreat? When I am here to protect her, why is she displaying such weakness before the people!' He shouted to the *mahout* to stop but his voice was lost in the thunder. The Emperor sat motionless on his elephant. Though the noise became louder, his senses dulled to their roar and for a moment he heard nothing. He saw the angry faces of men and women yelling at him. He felt their rage but looked on stoically. Suddenly, in the distance, he saw the face of his father, Shah Jahan. Gradually, every man in the crowd began to look the same. A sudden sickness filled Aurengzeb's bosom just as it had whenever, as a child, his father had scolded him. To Aurengzeb, the scoldings had always seemed to stem from his father's preference for Dara. In those moments Aurengzeb had wanted to lunge at his father and tear his eyes out, but could do nothing. As he looked at the crowd filled with his father's faces, shouting at him, he felt vulnerable and embattled, exposed and humiliated, yet again. He closed his eyes and took a deep breath, reciting a prayer.

Opening his eyes, he let out a roar: "Crush these infidels! Crush them, by the will of Allah!"

All eyes turned to the enraged Emperor as he motioned for his elephant and the procession to march forward. The Guards hurried to do his bidding.

***

Zebunissa, still looking back as the elephant lumbered towards the fort, watched in despair as her father's elephant ploughed into the crowd. Blood and guts spilt onto the streets as protestors ran hither and dither to avoid being trampled. A young boy jumped off his father's shoulders and began running. There were shouts of 'Save the boy!' as he ran towards the imperial elephant, not realizing the beast was enraged. He ran right up to the elephant's mighty leg. His mother tearfully ran after him, screaming for him to stop, but she was too far away. The beast let out a mighty roar and brought down his front leg with a deadly thud.

Zebunissa shut her eyes to obliterate the traumatic spectacle. Tears ran from her eyes onto her nose. She had not wept so since hearing of Sulaimon's death, but now she felt traumatized by someone else's pain. All around people were yelling and crying as Mughal soldiers with spears fended off attacks from the unarmed citizens. The shouts of men, women and children echoed in Zebunissa's ears as she buried her face in her hands, unwilling to believe what was occurring around her. How many would die today, she wondered? How many cremations…and for what…to tax innocent people in order to fund a war of intolerance?

Jahanara leaned her head against one side of the howdah, her eyes closed. Zebunissa heard her murmur, "Take me away from here."

As they moved into the shelter of the fort walls, the sounds of strife faded away, submerged in the drumming of the rain. Zebunissa no longer cared; all she wanted was for the torment to cease.

## 19
## The Last Hope

*Though on the path of love thy feet may tire,*
*New strength shall come to thee, and new desire.*

30 June 1680

Summer seemed to fade early that year. Usually, the month of August was unbearably hot in Delhi, but now a mild chill meandered through the city. The *sadhus* bathing in the Jamuna said the city was haunted by the tormented souls of the vanquished, bringing the unseasonal chill.

Zebunissa had received word that Prince Akbar's training was being conducted in the jungles of the Punjab rather than in the Kashmir valley, already witnessing its first snowfall. She pulled her exquisitely embroidered Kashmiri shawl across her bosom and walked out into the courtyard.

The Empire had been shaken and weakened by the enactment of the *jiziya,* two years before. Jahanara, the Empress, had moved out of the Red Fort in protest, preferring to live in solitude at the mansion of Ali Mardan, who had been one of the architects of the Taj Mahal. She had had a long lasting friendship with Ali Mardan, first in her role as overseer of the Taj Mahal and then when she had designed various monuments and gardens in Delhi. Ali had died many years ago and his mansion remained vacant. Jahanara chose this home of her father's friend as an alternative to the palace. There, she frequently refused audience to those who came to pay their respects or ask for favours, but she always welcomed Zebunissa and Jani Begum, her favourite nieces.

Dissent and mutiny had reared their ugly heads throughout the Empire. The Jats from Punjab in the northwest, the Rajputs from Rajasthan in the west, and the Marathas in the west and in the Deccan, had all launched separate rebellions. The royal treasury emptied as rebellion needed to be quelled in every corner of the Empire. Zebunissa knew the only hope for India was now her son, Akbar. Over a century ago, her ancestor Akbar-the-Great had united India under the Mughal banner. It seemed oddly fitting that in these dark hours a young Prince with the same name would rise to release India from tyranny.

"Princess," Aqil Khan said, arriving before Zebunissa and bowing, "you must not wander about in public like this. The Emperor will be most upset."

Zebunissa grinned. "When is the Emperor not upset?"

Aqil's lips tightened. "You must be careful. Ignoring the *Padishah Begum*'s advice, the Emperor has granted the *mullahs* extraordinary powers. He will use them to quell any voice of dissent."

"Not while you stand by my side to protect me..."

They began walking slowly around the periphery of the courtyard, seemingly lost in a conversation between student and teacher.

"The Emperor is preparing to go to the Deccan," Aqil said.

"I know. There is news that the Maratha, Shivaji, has died and it is rumoured that his ruthless son, Shambuji, is now the new *Chhatrapati*."

"It is true what they say of him. I met Shambuji years ago."

"You!" exclaimed Zebunissa, surpised. "How did a strong and debonair man like you make the acquaintance of a bandit?"

Aqil smiled. He knew Zebunissa could never resist flirting with him whenever they were alone. "He accompanied his father to a *durbar* in Delhi. You ladies were in Lahore at the time."

"Father invited his mortal enemy to a *durbar* in Delhi?"

Aqil nodded slowly. "To put him in his place the Emperor insulted Shambuji by awarding him a cavalry of just 5,000 horses in return for his homage."

"What was Shambuji's response?"

"What could he say? Shambuji is a bandit. I don't know why he even came to Delhi. But in return for a solemn pledge, he was given only 5,000 horses. He stormed out of the *durbar* vowing to fight the Mughals in every corner of the Empire."

Zebunissa shook her head sadly. "The gift of turning enemies into friends is not a gift my father possesses. Instead, he turns friends into foes! He would probably fight Allah if he were a man!"

Aqil chuckled under his breath. Zebunissa paused for a moment and then asked, "When is he leaving?"

"In two days, I believe. Why?"

Zebunissa took a deep breath and smiled. "Because, my Lord, our son will be returning in the next few weeks to take what is rightfully his. This is it, our last chance. If this does not work, nothing will."

"Akbar is returning?"

"Yes. After so many years of intense military training in the jungles and forests of India, he is returning."

Aqil's eyes filled with tears. "*Allah ho Akbar*…God is Great!"

***

Aurengzeb placed his silver helmet on his head with shaking hands. He had worn it since he had been a young Prince. It had protected him from javelins, swords, daggers and arrows; from Hindus, Jats, Sikhs, Uzbeks, Mongols, and *firangis*. When he became Emperor, it had been suggested that he use the traditional helmet worn by Mughal Emperors before him, but he had chosen instead to keep his old helmet. Like him, it too, bore the scars of many military campaigns; though dented, it remained intact. As he donned it now, chain metal covered his face, obstructing his view.

The Prime Minister cleared his throat and said, "Majesty, the *Padishah Begum* has sent a message to inform you that she is not in good health but wishing you victory in your campaign. She also sent this letter."

Aurengzeb sighed, disappointed. He knew he could not command Jahanara to do anything against her wishes. He broke the seal.

*My Brother*

*You are, alas, returning to the cursed home of our childhood, the Deccan. I remember playing there with you and our other siblings as a child, when our whole family, with Aba and Ami, lived in tents in Nizamshahi. Those were simpler times. Today, all that remains of the family are you and I. Everyone else – Aba, Ami, Dara, Raushanara, the others…are gone.*

*I often wonder if anything good comes from the Deccan. Ami died there and her grave was there for many years before Aba built the Taj Mahal. The Deccan was where Aba sent you as punishment when he was upset with you after a military misadventure. That godforsaken land has never brought our family or the kingdom, any happiness.*

*Yet you are returning there to quell rebellions and win riches. You have taken the name and legacy of our forefathers and ruined them. Your bigotry has destroyed alliances and we are in a perpetual state of war as a result. The citizens pay for your intolerance. You will reap the wind, my brother. You will die alone, despised by your own people.*

*Hence I ask you again, repeal the Jiziya. Do not create the cause of your own ruin. I have tried time and again to save you but no one can help a man who is his own enemy. As always, I wish you victory in your campaigns but must warn you that I will not be in this world to greet you on your return. I am tired. I am weak. I can no longer serve the throne. I take solace in knowing I have served the throne with loyalty for as many days as I have lived. Now I am ready to meet Aba and Ami in the Hall of Paradise. I leave this kingdom, this land which was once paradise on earth, in your hands.*

*Jahanara*

Aurengzeb stared down at the letter, re-reading certain passages. Was Jahanara about to end her own life? If she did, it was her choice. He would not grovel at her feet to stop her. He was the Emperor and could not be held hostage to threats, even from the Empress. He crushed the letter and threw it onto the floor, his eyes shining with unshed tears. Holding up his head, he walked towards the door, never looking back.

## 20
## One Comes One Goes

*Fragrant flowers are springing from my blood,*
*And every thorn*
*Wherewith my weary wandering feet are torn*
*Turns to a rose.*

16 September 1681

The harem had been decorated as if the Emperor himself was expected. The walls were repainted, new tapestries hung, the fountains cleaned and refilled with rose scented water, and beautiful oil lamps taken from storage to decorate the halls. Zebunissa had commissioned the entire Red Fort to be cleaned and lit so its vast contours would be visible to onlookers from afar. Using her allowance, Zebunissa provided new clothes to all the harem women and had the royal cooks prepare a grand feast the like of which had not been seen since the days of Shah Jahan.

"I want 200 stuffed chickens, but for the Prince, there must be the Pearl chicken!" Zebunissa ordered. The delicacy required tissue thin strands of pure gold and silver leaf to be beaten into the yolk of an egg. The yolk was then mixed with rice and stuffed into the chicken, which was then trussed and cooked slowly in a clay oven. Once ready, the chicken was cut open and the glistening rice released, like gleaming pearls. Zebunissa had seen this dish prepared during her own ill-fated wedding with the Persian Prince, and had secretly sworn to have it made one day for Akbar.

For her ladies, Zebunissa had the cooks prepare their favourite dish – Murgh Keema Mumtaz Mahal, named after her long deceased grandmother, who had loved this dish. Not surprisingly, it was a savoury chicken dish flavored with poppy seeds and other hallucinogens, on a bed of minced lamb. The delicacy not only tingled the taste buds, but also induced intense euphoria from the poppy seeds. *Shirazi* and *Arak* were poured into giant vats by the nobility, now that the Emperor was no longer in the capital. Aqil Khan had the royal gardeners trim the hedges and groom the lawns. Flowering fountains were scrubbed clean and polished; exotic birds and peacocks were released into the garden.

While she hurried about supervising every small detail, Zebunissa suddenly saw a slave running towards her panting, "Princess! There is dire news from the Empress."

Zebunissa froze. Was Akbar in danger? She could not speak.

Zubdat interjected, "What is it girl?"

The slave hung her head low, unwilling to continue. Zebunissa and Zubdat looked at one another, their faces stoic, pondering the possibilities.

Zubdat walked over to the slave and asked again, "What is it? Speak!" The girl began to weep. "What has happened?" Zubdat demanded fiercely.

The slave looked up, her eyes awash with tears. "The Empress is no more!" she cried as she fell at Zubdat's feet. "The Empress drank a special tonic and took her own life! She was found sleeping in her finest robes."

Zebunissa closed her eyes and began reciting the prayers for the dead from the Koran.

"She is finally at peace, with Uncle Dara, her Ami and Aba, in the Halls of Paradise," Zubdat said softly.

***

As the palace glittered with decorations, Zebunissa and the Makhfi stood on a balcony as the body of the Empress was brought to the Red Fort for the final rites before burial. Runners had been sent to the Emperor to inform him of Jahanara's demise. The Prime Minister had proclaimed an official period of mourning and everyone changed from their colourful clothing into the white robes of mourning.

The chill in the air on this September day seemed to enter Zebunissa's bones. She had seen death before, but Jahanara's demise seemed different from the others; she felt she was witnessing her own funeral, staring at her own remains; the same hips, the long neck, the imperfectly rounded skull, the same height and petite feet. Zebunissa wished she could cry but the tears refused to be shed. She felt suffocated by emotion and grabbed Zinat and Mihirunissa's hands, gasping for air.

A short distance away, Jani stood devastated in her grief, barely able to stand. Between her and Zebunissa there still ran an undercurrent of mutual resentment; both had fought for Jahanara's love. Their parentage worked against Zebunissa: Jani was the progeny of the beloved Dara while she the offspring of the despised Aurengzeb. 'How could I overcome this flaw in my being,' wondered Zebunissa. Aurengzeb's dark shadow haunted her existence like a permanent, disfigured birthmark from which there was no escape. Conversely, Jani was a striking image of her father, the fallen Prince, Dara. In Jani lived the shadow of the now deceased Dara. Spending time with Jani reminded Jahanara of her deceased, beloved brother. Not surprisingly, on her death, Jahanara had bequeathed all her jewels to Jani, causing Zebunissa to feel both pain and betrayal. In the crucible of their lifelong rivalry, Zebunissa began to view Jani with resentment and suspicion.

"Zebunissa! What is it?" The women around her were shocked by Zebunissa's condition. As Zebunissa continued to gasp for air, someone shouted, "Water…give her water!" Others desperately began fanning her face and sprinkling rose water over her. Zebunissa collapsed onto the ground, retching dryly.

The men below looked up at the commotion on the balcony but could not see what was happening. Gradually, Zebunissa quietened and began to breathe deeply, her expression changing from discomfort to grief. Letting out an animal wail, she threw herself into Zubdat's arms crying, "How could she leave us? Everyone keeps leaving us! We lost Ami, our uncles, grandfather, and now she is gone too."

The other women began to weep and wail. "She was more than an Empress; she was the soul of the kingdom," cried Henna, one of Shah Jahan's concubines, who had been with them in captivity. She had returned to Delhi with Jahanara.

"Everyone dies except the one who brings despair to his realm," said Zubdat, stony faced. "Allah, please send us someone who can deliver us from his grasp."

Zebunissa wiped away her tears and gazed down at the crowd standing stoically around the coffin of the Empress, dressed in the white robes of mourning. Beyond them, the streets and alleys were filled with mourners wearing white, like a sea of milk. Such a spectacle had not been seen even when Shah Jahan had died. Zebunissa closed her eyes, raising her palms in prayer. "*Allah ho Akbar*! Accept your child into the Halls of Paradise."

With eyes still closed, she heard a commotion from afar. The crowd separated as if an arrow had pierced it. Riding a chestnut mare with a shining coat, Prince Akbar rode forward like a victorious warrior, his back upright, his head held high. A cadre of soldiers followed him on horseback. Zebunissa smiled. Akbar had grown into a tall, well built young man; he looked like his father had in his younger days, dashing and debonair. But he was fair-skinned like his mother, Zebunissa, though people assumed instead it was from his presumed father, Aurengzeb. She prayed her secret would never be revealed.

"There is our answer," remarked Zubdat with a smile.

"One comes, one goes. Allah took the Empress but delivered Akbar," Mihirunissa said softly.

The Makhfi watched the advancing procession. Their eyes, red with weeping, lifted from Jahanara's coffin to Akbar's advancing horse.

"Will you not say something, Zebunissa?" Zubdat asked.

Zebunissa smiled. "Long live Emperor Akbar!"

# PART IV

## 21
## Jodhpur

*O bulbul, glad within the garden sing,*
*'Tis Makhfi who has won for thee the spring.*

20 September 1681

On an arid Sunday morning, Aurengzeb sat cross-legged before a low table covered with a linen cloth. As Emperor, he had outlawed the use of gold and silver for dining, deeming them instruments of the devil. As he sat alone, the ageing Emperor found breathing difficult in the hot and dry air of the peninsula. The Deccan was an unruly region. Located in the south, it had been merged into the Empire much later than the other regions and had remained largely underdeveloped. Decades of warfare with neighbouring kingdoms and the Marathas, had driven the farmers from their land, turning what had once been lush ground into jungle, infested with rodents and reptiles.

Despite the aridity and heat, Aurengzeb found the Deccan a refuge from the burdens of court. Here, he lived in relative solitude with only his servants and favourite Generals by his side. The pomp and majesty of Delhi was far away. In this humble tent, Aurengzeb felt at home. He took a deep breath and closed his eyes, thinking back nostalgically to his days as Governor of the Deccan when he had built his city, Aurangabad, and destroyed idol-worshipping Hindu temples wherever he had found them. He had felt relief flood his soul whenever he had smashed those heathen idols, using the stones to build mosques in their place. The riches of the temples had been used to build Aurangabad and develop farms.

On this day, Aurengzeb was content to know he would be joined for his mid-day meal by his friend, Shiasta Khan, for he had important matters of war to discuss. He had asked his personal cook to present his favorite dish – a stew of young goat in a thick gravy. For a moment he forgot that, though he was now Emperor, he sat in a tent in a desolate region of the Empire, utterly alone. The servants had already placed a large bowl of rice *pilaf,* buttered rice with raisins and pistachios, in the centre of the table. Cool water from the nearby river was placed in two large flasks, one for each of the diners.

As Shiasta Khan entered, Aurengzeb smiled and motioned for him to sit. He clapped twice and four attendants entered. Each placed a dish before the two men. As they lifted the cloths covering each platter, the room filled with the aroma of spices. The succulent dishes were a welcome change for Shiasta, who had spent the past few days eating modest meals in his tent. The two men began to eat.

"The Rana of Jodhpur, Jaswant Singh, has been taken ill," Aurengzeb observed, raising a handful of aromatic *pulao* to his mouth. "That man is no ally of mine. He has been usurping my authority in Rajasthan for some time now. If he should die, would we be justified in annexing Jodhpur as part of the Mughal dominion?"

"Jodhpur *is* part of the Mughal dominion!" Shiasta replied staunchly. "And we can annex whatever we wish."

Aurengzeb smiled but shook his head. "If only statecraft was that simple, Shiasta. My benevolent ancestors gave these Hindu Rajputs free rein for over a century, and they now see themselves as rightful rulers of those lands. Simply taking Jodhpur will incur the wrath of all the Rajputs."

Shiasta nodded, collecting his thoughts. "If we control Jodhpur, we divide Rajasthan in half; the north will no longer be able to communicate with the south without going through our controls. I have been wanting to do this for a long time, but perhaps now is the best moment to accomplish this."

An attendant arrived with fresh, steaming rice. Immediately the two men fell silent, ever aware of spies in their midst. When the attendant had departed, Aurengzeb leaned towards Shiasta and said in a low voice, "Jaswant Singh has no heir to follow him. The absence of a legitimate heir places the line of succession in doubt. In such circumstances, we have justifiable reason to move in without alienating the other Rajputs."

"Ahh!" Shiasta paused in his eating to register the implications.

"But the key thing is," Aurengzeb added, raising a finger in the air, "that we must be prepared to fight all the Rajputs in the area if it should come to that."

Shiasta gazed at the Emperor in perplexity. "Then why have you come here to the Deccan, Majesty?"

"It is a diversion. The Marathas are always causing trouble in the Deccan, so no one will wonder at my presence here. Now that I am here, I can focus my attention on Jodhpur, without the distractions of imperial life in Delhi."

"Majesty," said Shiasta, leaning forward, "am I the only person who knows of this plan of yours?"

Aurengzeb continued to consume his meal, cooked to perfection. Taking a large gulp of water, he smiled at his ageing companion. "Are you not always the first person I tell such things to?" he remarked.

***

Akbar woke from a dream-filled sleep, still somewhat exhausted from the rigours of the previous day. A warm breeze stirred the muslin curtains of his chamber, reminding him that he was no longer in the jungle, but back in the capital city. He heard soft footsteps and immediately looked up, alert.

"No need to get up, my child," Zebunissa said gently. "You must be exhausted, for I'm told you rode almost nonstop to Delhi."

"I am awake, sister," responded Akbar yawning as he sat up on his bed. "I am a soldier, used to exertion."

"Well, here is some ginger tea and some fresh mangoes for you before you begin the day."

Akbar took a sip of the tea and let out a gentle sigh. The sharp taste of the ginger infused tea was a stark contrast to the cold mountain water he had consumed for the past few years.

"Your hair is too long for a Prince. I will have someone trim it for you and tell the slaves to prepare the hammam. Once you have bathed and finished your prayers, come to me in my chambers. There is much we must discuss."

Akbar merely smiled and watched Zebunissa hurry away, calling out to the slaves. He enjoyed the hot bath they prepared for him, soaking long in the unaccustomed luxury. When he was dressed once again in the silken garments that denoted his status, he walked over to the harem quarters and requested an audience with Zebunissa.

"Come child, sit." Zebunissa gestured to a low divan as Akbar entered. Aqil Khan and the Makhfi were also in attendance, beaming with joy to see the young Prince home at last. "Akbar," began Zebunissa, "we have just heard that the Rana of Jodhpur, Jaswant Singh, has died." Akbar listened attentively, his brow furrowed in concentration. "As per Rajput tradition, his wives committed *suttee*." Zebunissa frowned. She detested the Hindu Rajput tradition of widows, dressed as brides, being taken to the funeral pyre of their husbands and cremated alive.

"Allah have mercy!" exclaimed Badrunissa. "It is a barbaric tradition!" The others nodded in acquiescence.

"It is a terrible tradition but you see it more among the Rajputs than other Hindus," Aqil noted. "They seem to think it honourable to burn women alive!"

"Never mind that," said Zebunissa, annoyed, "what is worrying is that he has left no heirs, making his kingdom ripe for annexation."

"By whom?" inquired Badrunissa.

"By us, the all powerful Mughals!"

There was silence for a moment before Aqil asked quietly, "How do you know this?"

"I have an informant with Aba in the Deccan, his cook. I once caught him jumping over the garden wall to meet with one of the royal concubines for a midnight affair. When I threatened to turn him in, he fell at my feet, begging for mercy. I agreed to keep his affair secret if he became my informant."

Aqil shook his head. "If we attack Jodhpur at a time like this, all Rajasthan will turn against us." The women looked at him with sombre faces. "Without an alliance with the Rajputs, the Empire will disintegrate."

"Let us stop Aba," proclaimed Akbar impulsively, standing up. "We must tell him we do not approve of any military action against Jodhpur."

Zebunissa chuckled. "My innocent brother! You have much to learn about our father and the kingdom! No one can tell Aba what to do!"

"So we simply allow it to happen?"

"Not necessarily," Zebunissa responded, pouring a glass of *shirazi* for herself. "Akbar, you are now part of our secret society, the Makhfi. Officially, you come to enjoy poetry and exchange poetic compositions. However, all our poems are encrypted messages that allow us to coordinate efforts to overthrow the Emperor without anyone else figuring it out. I want you to go to Jodhpur and meet with the two remaining wives of Jaswant Singh, secretly."

"But you said they committed *suttee*."

"Not all his wives. The two youngest ones remain."

"What would you have me say to them?"

"That you support the next Rajput Emperor of Jodhpur. That is all, but tell them in confidence."

Akbar looked down, confused. "How can I support the next Emperor of Jodhpur when Jaswant Singh leaves no progeny?"

Zebunissa grinned. "Therein lies the big secret our Aba has not yet learned." There was a pause, then Zebunissa smiled. "Both Jaswant Singh's wives are pregnant!"

## 22
## The Rose

*Come, O ye weak in faith, for help is here.*

30 September 1681

Aurengzeb warmed his hands over a small fire outside his tent as he set camp with his army in the deserts of Rajasthan. The biting cold stiffened his back and his body ached, but only the lines etched into his face spoke of his pain. He stared straight ahead through the flames at Shiasta Khan, seated directly across.

"Warm your hands, Shiasta Khan. They will soon be drenched in the cold blood of the Rajputs."

News had permeated across Rajasthan that the Emperor was about to annex Jodhpur. In response, the Queens of Jodhpur had evicted the Mughal envoy, effectively declaring independence from Mughal rule.

Shiasta shivered as he looked at the Emperor, not uttering a word.

"I sense fear in your eyes, my friend."

"No, Majesty, it is merely the cold that numbs all feeling." Nevertheless, he quivered at the thought. War with the Rajputs was always a fearful prospect. Valiant warriors, the Rajputs learned from an early age to fight to the death. In defeat their wives committed *jauhar*, to avoid dishonour.

"Majesty, my informants tell me the Queens have left Jodhpur, claiming to be in poor health."

"Pshaw!" uttered Aurengzeb disdainfully. "There is some treachery. They must be conspiring with their other Rajputs."

"Is Prince Akbar still in Rajasthan?" Shiasta enquired.

"I believe so."

"Did he receive Imperial sanction for the visit?"

"I told him he could go." Aurengzeb felt compelled to lie. When he had learned of Akbar's trip to Rajasthan, he had written to Zebunissa to inquire why he had been allowed to go without seeking his permission. Zebunissa had assured her father that the Prince had gone to honour an invitation by the Rana of Mewar; this was merely a pleasure trip. Aurengzeb could not find it in him to admonish either his favourite daughter or beloved son, and lied to cover their indiscretion.

In the silence that followed, Shiasta Khan moved his warm hands over his face and onto his shoulders. "Majesty, I have known you since you were a young lad," he began. "You are as passionate in love as in battle. But sometimes, we forget to guard against those who are most beloved to us. Prince Akbar..."

Aurengzeb raised a hand, admonishing his friend to observe the boundaries which his words were encroaching. Shiasta looked away, knowing that upsetting the temperamental Emperor could have dire consequences. A few moments later, he began anew. "My informants tell me the two Queens are now in Ajmer."

Aurengzeb blew on his chilled hands. "If that is the case, then Ajmer will be burned to ashes! I will destroy all their infidel temples and make whores of their daughters!"

Shiasta Khan smiled. A military man himself, he enjoyed his Emperor's belligerence. "The Rajputs have no idea what wrath they have brought upon themselves," Aurengzeb continued as he brought his face closer to the flame.

***

Zebunissa paced anxiously back and forth in her chambers. She put a hand over her heart, racing with anxiety. "Slave!" she called. A young girl of ten entered. "Bring me some *sherbet*," said Zebunissa, fanning her face. Why had Akbar not written yet? Fear of the unknown began to consume her. Was he hurt? Had he been captured? Had the Rajputs decided to revenge themselves on Aurengzeb's son?

Sweat beaded her forehead as she tried desperately to fend off such ill thoughts. Briefly, the most devastating thought of all entered her mind: Had he betrayed her to join the Emperor? Having been betrayed by Mughal men her whole life, trusting even her beloved son had not been easy.

As Mihirunissa entered, Zebunissa asked her in a strangled voice, "Why has he not written yet? I am told Aba has burned Ajmer to the ground and smashed all their temples into piles of rubble!"

"Be calm, Zebunissa," Mihirunissa said, resting her hands on her sister's shoulders.

"You don't understand," replied Zebunissa, sobbing. "Aba slayed all the priests in the temples and mounted their heads on sticks around the rubbles of the temples. He is intentionally provoking the Rajputs. He instructed his men to ravage the women and then the soldiers urinated on the Hindu statues. I fear for Akbar!"

The slave girl returned with the *sherbet.* Mihirunissa took a sip and then handed the goblet to Zebunissa. "We must be patient. Right now, sending any message is dangerous. We have no choice but to wait for Akbar to write. You cannot help him now."

***

The Makhfi spent the next few days displaying indifference to what was occurring in Rajasthan. In secret, they attempted to use their network of loyalists to learn what the situation in the troubled region truly was. The Jodhpur Queens had escaped Ajmer but their whereabouts were unknown, much to Aurengzeb's chagrin. Worse, the Emperor had sent a message inquiring about Akbar's whereabouts. Rumors began circulating that Akbar had been imprisoned by the Rajputs.

"Zebunissa!" called Zubdat, running into her sister's chamber one morning. "A message from Akbar!" She handed her the sealed letter.

Zebunissa hastily broke the seal and began reading:

*Beloved Sister*

*I have read the poem you sent me with great interest. The words you used in the following stanzas especially moved me:*

*Duly in season comes the spring,*
*Where is the soul-awaking wine?*
*Roses around their perfumes fling,*
*Where is the bulbul's song divine?*

*Roses bestrew the plain, and blue*
*Heaven outspreads its canopy;*

*The flowers have filled their cups with dew,*
*Where is the wine-cup filled for me?*

*I thus decided to compose this poem based on these words:*

*Dewy and fresh the ambient air*
*Summons us out from cell and shrine*
*In the spring roses have bloomed*
*A miraculous gift from the divine*

*At first there were two such roses*
*Whose aromas filled the air?*
*But then one withered in the wind*
*Now only one remains for the mali to care*

*I roam the garden every morning*
*To gaze upon the miracle of beauty*
*Protecting it from the harm of storms*
*I feel is now my moral duty.*

"Praise Allah!" exclaimed Zebunissa, covering her trembling mouth with one hand. "The Queens have delivered!"

Zubdat looked bewildered. "How can you tell?"

"Look, my silly sister. The roses, meaning children….two roses... two Queens gave birth, but one rose died and only one remains for the *mali* to care for!"

"And Akbar is the *mali*." Zubdat sighed, a warm smile crossing her face. "The rose is the son of deceased Rana Jaswant Singh."

"And the ruler of Jodhpur, not Aba!"

"Do you think Aba knows?" Zubdat asked.

There was a pause, then Zebunissa said, "I don't know. But now that the child is born, the Rajputs will flaunt him as the new Rana." She placed a finger on her lips, pondering what was happening in Rajasthan. "There will be no war. Aba is far too astute to declare war on all the Rajputs. No, he will devise some other scheme."

"What other scheme, Zebo?"

Zebunissa stared at her sister. "I'm afraid to know."

***

The burgundy tents of the Mughals blanketed the now devastated, once majestic city of Ajmer. From the tents, some of which were two stories high, flew flags with the Mughal lion. From afar it looked like a bloody wound in the heart of Rajasthan, still fresh and bleeding.

"An imposter!" shouted Aurengzeb angrily, hunched over a map in his tent. Dressed in military uniform, he pointed his aging finger east towards the interior of Rajasthan. "The Rajput Queen is a whore. She carried the seed of some lover in her belly. To save herself she is trying to pass him off as the Rana's son! Jaswant Singh died eight months ago. He was ill, unable to fulfill his manly obligations to his wives for many months before that. Thus I proclaim this child to be an imposter!"

The Generals gathered in the tent stood in silence, their gazes on the ground. It was known that Jaswant Singh had died suddenly and there had been no protracted illness preventing him from impregnating his wives.

But Aurengzeb was adamant. "Where is Akbar?" he asked abruptly.

"Majesty," responded one of the Generals, "his whereabouts are unknown. We fear the Rajputs are holding him hostage."

"Which Rajput dares to imprison my son?"

"We believe the Rana of Mewar, Raj Singh, is behind this treachery."

"Then he shall be warned of the consequences of such treason!"

The plan was thus cemented in Aurengzeb's mind: Declare the Queen's child an imposter and attack any Rajput ruler who dared to object. Nevertheless, the fear of a united Rajput attack remained in Aurengzeb's mind. He would then be left fighting a costly war with troops he needed to fight the Marathas in the Deccan. Nevertheless, he continued to prod his Generals to reach out to the various Rajput rulers to inform them of the 'imposter's' birth.

## 23
## 100 Soldiers

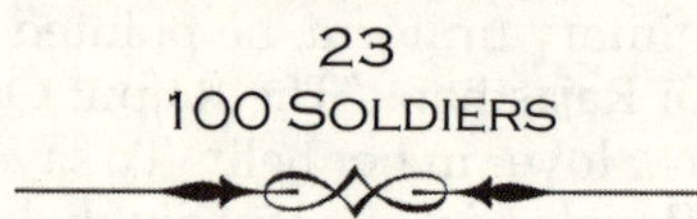

*Behold the fire renewed within my heart,*
*My sighs have lashed it with their breath until*
*the flames outstart.*

10 October 1681

Akbar sat on the balcony that Rana Raj Singh had ordered prepared for him. The mornings were cold in this desert kingdom and Raj Singh had provided his guest with shawls from his own collection; they were embroidered with the Hindu motifs of lotus and sun. As Akbar sipped the *chai* brought to him at dawn, he pressed his growling stomach. The Rajputs ate lamb and chicken sparingly, and Akbar found himself having to satisfy his appetite with the Rajput concoction of *Maas ka Soola,* meat cooked in a ginger lemon paste with yogurt and butter. He yearned for the aromatic dishes of the Mughal court he had grown up on. But the magnificent spectacle of the rising sun made him forget such trivial matters.

"His Highness approaches," announced a guard.

Akbar hastily rose to greet his host. "Highness, why did you trouble yourself? You could have sent for me."

"Pray be seated, Prince. I did not wish to disturb you so early but I received a letter late last night from your father. You may read it." The Rana handed the missive over and turned to gaze out at the orange sun rising over the distant dusty hills. He put his palms together and closed his eyes in prayer, seeking benediction. Akbar quickly unrolled the scroll bearing the broken imperial seal, reading eagerly, his heart thumping in his chest.

*Rana Raj Singh*

*I convey my pleasure that you have administered my dominion of Mewar with a firm hand. For this I commend you. I am informed that my son,*

*Prince Akbar, is residing with you as your guest, but now desires to return to Delhi. It is time he resumed his duties as a Prince and soldier. Please have him escorted to my encampment at Jodhpur at once. He will march with the army to Delhi when the time is right.*

*May Allah's grace be with you.*

*Alamgir*

"My father thinks I am your hostage?"

A servant placed a warm cup of *chai* in front of Raj Singh, who raised his hand to command the servant to leave. Once the man had withdrawn, he said, "My chambers are infested with your father's spies, hence I considered it more prudent to come to you. There are few I can trust."

As Akbar squinted his eyes in thought, a characteristic he had inherited, unknowing, from his father.

Raj Singh took a sip of the tea, enjoying the warmth in his throat. "I propose to write to your father that I imprisoned you in retaliation for his razing of Ajmer; that I will return you in exchange for the 100 Rajput soldiers imprisoned during that siege."

Akbar smiled. "I am worth only 100 soldiers?" he remarked.

"Prince, this is the language of diplomacy. I must ask for something. Once you return, you can serve as my informant and help to expel the Mughal army from Rajasthan. We will chase your father all the way to Delhi, defeated. In return, you will be Emperor."

"You are too kind. I am a soldier, unversed in the ways of diplomacy. I feel honoured by the trust you have reposed in me."

Raj Singh leaned back and gazed out over the horizon. "Dear Prince, your ancestor, the legendary Emperor Akbar, began the tradition of marrying our Rajput Princesses. Ever since, every Mughal Emperor has married our daughters. The blood in your veins is the same that runs in ours. But your father has chosen to shatter all the goodwill and ignore the ties of blood. He has killed so many of his own family members there is no longer anyone who can stop him. You are all that is left; our last hope."

Akbar felt humbled yet frustrated by the incessant comparisons to his illustrious forebear whose name he bore. The very name gave rise to unreasonable expectations to restore the lost glory of the Empire; a task he felt was impossible.

"Highness, I am nothing like my father. Nor am I am a reincarnation of Emperor Akbar. Those days now belong to the ages." Akbar looked out from the balcony at the expansive fields below. There was silence between the two men.

"Prince," said Raj Singh leaning forward, "we Hindus believe in reincarnation, but I personally do not. You and I are made of dust and will return to dust. What we do for our people is all that remains. I have no doubt you will be a just Emperor in your own right."

Akbar sighed, his gaze returning to his companion. "I pray I will one day repay your loyalty and trust."

Raj Singh leaned back in his gilded chair, the look in his eyes difficult to read. "You will, young Prince," he said, "you will."

***

Aurengzeb sat cross-legged facing west towards Mecca when Shiasta Khan entered with an urgent missive from Raj Singh. Aurengzeb dislike being disturbed during his prayers but he knew Shiasta Khan would not have done so without reason and so bent his forehead to the ground and then rose, gesturing for Shiasta to read the letter aloud to him.

*Greetings Alamgir, Emperor of the Mughals*

*As you have requested, preparations have been made for Prince Akbar to travel to your camp in what was once Ajmer. I recall spending summers in this once-great city that you have reduced to rubble. My mother made offerings in the temples you have desecrated and we lived in the palaces you have destroyed. I have invited Prince Akbar to be my guest and so he shall remain till the 100 Rajput soldiers, whose sole crime was defending their homes against your attack, be returned; to be reunited with their families.*

*Raj Singh*

*Rana of Mewar*

"Does this fiend think he can bargain with me?"

Shiasta Khan moved forward with a conciliatory gesture. "Majesty, it would be unwise to rush to judgement. He may be asking for the 100 soldiers merely to save his reputation with his people, who are undoubtedly upset at hearing about Ajmer. In the interests of diplomacy, 100 soldiers are nothing. It is merely a face saving gesture before his people."

Aurengzeb's anger cooled. "Make the switch at once. I wish my son returned to me immediately. If even one hair on his head is hurt, I will destroy all of Rajasthan!"

## 24
## Start Of War

*Think not that with joy and with ease I pursue my desire;*
*With heart that is weary, with footsteps that lag and that tire.*

29 October 1681

Zebunissa placed a warm wax seal on the scroll containing the lines she had composed for Azam. "Jani, this prayer is for your husband."

Jani grinned. "You know my husband is not as pious as you and your sisters."

"Sadly, you are right. But still my pious heart commands me to reach out to all my brothers in the language of the Holy Book." Zebunissa knew Azam would mock the prayer she had sent but it helped to keep the myth of her society being a prayer group alive. Zebunissa had been declared Empress and *Padishah Begum* by her father, taking the exalted place of her deceased aunt, Jahanara. She was now the first woman at court, superceding even the Emperor's living wives. Eyes followed her everywhere.

"Prince Azam is tense following the Emperor's rebuke for taking so long to arrive from Bengal," Jani said softly, hanging her head, expecting a comforting response from the Empress.

"The Emperor is upset with everyone," responded Zebunissa curtly. She placed a hand under Jani's chin and lifted her face, forcing her to raise her eyes. "Travel from Bengal, in the east, to Rajasthan in the west, is a gruelling journey. I am glad Azam and you have chosen to rest for a night in Delhi before moving towards Rajasthan."

Jani smiled as she grabbed Zebunissa's hand, gently lowering it. "I feel the Emperor's anger is not so much at us but at Prince Akbar failing to invade Udaipur, as the Emperor commanded."

The calculated remark stung Zebunissa. Any negative mention of her son was always ill received. She knew Jani's words were not completely unjustified. Having procured his return from the Rajputs, Aurengzeb had high hopes that his soldier son would lead his armies to a triumphant victory over the Rajputs by wrestling the strategic city of Udaipur from them. Instead, Akbar seemed to be stalling and seeking excuses to justify his slow march. Zebunissa also knew that rumours were rife that Akbar had forged a secret pact with the Rajputs, a seditious act; an allegation Aurengzeb seemed to disbelieve for now.

"Akbar is waiting for the most opportune time to attack. The Emperor must be patient." Zebunissa's tone was harsh, warning Jani about forming hasty conclusions.

"Zebunissa, you know the Emperor has no patience," Jani remarked, walking over to Zebunissa's desk and glancing over the scattered papers there. "Who wrote all these poems?" she asked, surprised. "They look like they have travelled a long distance. Do they not know that poetry has been banned in the kingdom? And why is Akbar's name on some of them?"

Zebunissa hurried past Jani and grabbed the papers. "They are old poems. The Emperor knows I possess them." She went to a small cupboard and, taking a key from the bunch that hung at her waist, opened it and thrust some of the papers in, quickly locking it again.

"May I not see the compositions?" Jani asked, wondering what Zebunissa was trying to hide.

Zebunissa knew she had raised suspicions. Turning, she chuckled apologetically. "I promised the Emperor I would not circulate them."

Jani frowned. "I feel you are hiding something from me. Those papers are not poems from the past are they? And why is Akbar's name on them?"

Zebunissa was startled but tried to hide her emotions using a commanding tone. "Watch your tongue! Remember you speak to the Empress! I can have you imprisoned for false accusations."

"Do not threaten me," retorted Jani. "Imprisonment will lead to a trial, especially if the prisoner is the daughter-in-law of the Emperor. At the trial these papers will be presented. Then what will you do?"

Jani noticed some papers remained on the desk that Zebunissa seemed to be trying to block from her vision. Jani reached around Zebunissa and grabbed a hold of the papers with her right hand. Zebunissa grabbed her wrist and tried to wrestle the papers from her. Jani pushed Zebunissa with her hips, but she was no match for Zebunissa's strength;

pushing Zebunissa was like trying to hit a stone wall, and Jani bounced back. Zebunissa moved herself in front of Jani and lunged her elbow into Jani's abdomen, causing her to bend forward in excruciating pain. Zebunissa then grabbed the papers out of Jani's hand and pushed her away towards the entrance. Jani coughed, gasping for air. Zebunissa, out of breath herself, yelled, "Do not interfere in my personal matters ever again or else I will have you executed before the Emperor even learns of my decree!"

Jani trembled with rage. She scanned the room for a weapon, anything to strike Zebunissa with. 'How dare she touch me?' She noticed a silver hookah near Zebunissa's feet. Should she try to grab it and swirl it at Zebunissa? What if she missed? Zebunissa looked murderous, ready to spill blood. Jani decided not to fight, for now. She stared back at Zebunissa with scorn and contempt. "This is not over yet. You will regret ever crossing me!"

From that moment on Jani would detest Zebunissa to her dying day; there would be no forgiveness. *Groom a man to be Emperor,* her aunt Jahanara had said. Zebunissa had clearly been posturing for Akbar, Jani concluded. Well, she would in turn prop up Azam, much as she despised her incompetent husband. The stakes were too high. If Zebunissa won, Jani knew she would end up like her father, Dara. Zebunissa would parade her in dirty rags on a filthy elephant in Chandni Chowk, making her beg for mercy before denying it. Then she would sever Jani's head and place it on a platter. 'No…never!' Jani thought. 'I will be Empress and Azam, Emperor.' Zebunissa would not win.

Holding her abdomen, Jani limped out of the room without making further commotion. Today was not the day to hit back. The war of succession had begun, not between the sons of Aurengzeb, but two of the royal women of the Mughal court.

***

Sandstorms had prevented Aurengzeb from accurately surveying the Aravalli Hills where the Rajputs were positioned. But on this morning, the wind had fallen across the desert and the dark silhouette of a plateau rose from uneven ground. The calmness of the scene contrasted sharply with the violent battle Aurengzeb hoped to wage here with the help of his sons.

"Father, you wished to see me?" Akbar, dressed in dark metal armour with a bullet shaped helmet on his head, reminded Aurengzeb of his younger days. Like him, Akbar too was fair-skinned, had a muscular physique, and excelled in the art of war and military tactics. "Those hills you see over there, my child," he began as he and Akbar rotated their waists in the direction of the *Aravilli* hills, "are where the enemy has positioned himself. I have sent your brothers Azam and Muazzam to the hills with their cavalry to assess the strength of the enemy. Based on what they find, we will plan our attack."

Akbar grinned. "Why not just hit the enemy with a full scale invasion, Father?"

"No! You must never do that. If you attack your enemy head on with the arrogance of overpowering them, you risk losing a great many of your men if your assessment of their strength is flawed. Besides, this is Rajasthan - land of the Rajputs. I suspect they chose those hills for a certain reason. They must possess some strategic advantage for them. Never under estimate these enemies, my son."

Akbar sighed. He knew his ruthless father had no qualms about sending soldiers on a suicide mission if it led him to have a better assessment of the enemy's strength. Reports of Aurengzeb's brutality had been circulating ever since he attacked Rajasthan. After leveling Jodhpur, Aurengzeb had the sacred Hindu idols carried to Delhi so they could be interred in the steps of the Jama Masjid so that the faithful can trample on the infidel idols as they entered the mosque. His soldiers had been given full permission to commit atrocities, including raping women, burning homes, looting treasure and worse of all, forcing Hindu citizens to eat beef, an act that Hindus believed was sinful and punishable in the afterlife. Aurengzeb's men further demeaned the Hindus by splashing beef fat on their idols and forcing many of them to consume it before killing them.

Akbar scoffed at the notion of being linked to this army, but he had already received instructions from Zebunissa on how best to dupe Aurengzeb into thinking of him as an ally until the right moment. He scanned the hills that he was being asked to overtake. With small nooks in every area, it would be very easy to mount a surprise attack on the Mughal army by an army of Rajputs that are familiar with the terrain. For a moment, he hoped his men would be slain as retribution for the atrocities they committed. These fiends should be slayed like cattle just the way they slayed those helpless townspeople. But he questioned the morality of his thoughts. *Can a Commander watch his men being slain simply because he does not agree with them?* He knew he had to protect the soldiers, though their Emperor held their lives cheap. He could not lead them on a suicide mission.

"I cannot wait to reach those hills," he told his father. "I yearn to burn Rajputana to the ground!"

Aurengzeb smiled at his son's words. Akbar did not smile.

***

The following week Zebunissa received a letter from Akbar.

*Respected Sister*

*I pray this letter finds you in good health. We are camped before the Aravalli Hills, waiting for an opportunity to mount an attack on the Rajputs positioned in the hills. Azam and Muazzam were sent with their regiments to stage an assault, with the intent of learning how many soldiers the enemy has, and their positions. Both lost their entire regiments, returning bloodied on a donkey, in humiliation. Father has instructed me to march into the hills with the entire might of the army at my command, currently 70,000 soldiers. This will leave him with only a few thousand to protect him and the camp. Once entrenched in the hills I can declare myself Emperor and imprison father. I did not wish to take any steps without consulting you.*

*Akbar*

"Why would this idiot not use cryptic poetry like I told him to?" Zebunissa was speechless. "What if this letter was to fall into the wrong hands? We would be ruined!"

Zubdat poured her some *sherbet* from a silver flask. "Drink this. You must stay calm."

"I cannot be calm, Zubdat! We are so close to our goal! Aqil, we cannot afford for something to go wrong like it always has before."

"Yes, but yelling will not solve the problem," Aqil replied. He took the silver glass from Zubdat and held it out to Zebunissa. "Zubdat is right…drink this. It will cool you and give me a chance to think what the next step should be."

Zebunissa took the glass and sipped the cool rose scented drink "What do you mean deciding what the next step should be? We must write to him...a poem."

"There is no time for poems," interjected Zubdat. "We cannot afford something going wrong again. If our instructions are misunderstood by Akbar, we will all be in trouble."

"But if the letter falls into the Emperor's hands?" shot back Zebunissa. "Would that not be worse?"

"Not if the messenger is someone we trust," remarked Aqil from where he sat pensively staring at the ground.

Zebunissa and Zubdat turned to gaze at him. "This is the Mughal Empire," said Zebunissa. "Here, no one can be trusted."

"Not even me?" Aqil asked quietly, offended.

"What are you saying?"

"I will take your letter to Akbar myself. Ostensibly concerned about the Emperor's health, you will direct me to travel to the imperial camp to ascertain the truth. While there, I will deliver this letter to Akbar, without speaking to him."

"Why put it in writing?" Zubdat asked. It seemed the height of foolishness.

"The camp is full of spies," said Aqil. "It would be best to have no discussion with Akbar. I will instruct him to burn the letter."

Zebunissa closed her eyes, breathing deeply. It was a risk...but one she had to take. There was no time to lose. "Very well, I will write the letter and seal it. Akbar must be told he cannot declare himself before Aba has been imprisoned. If he suspects sedition, capturing and imprisoning Aba will be more difficult. Akbar must remain in his good graces. This must be understood."

"Write a letter, not a poem," responded Aqil. "I will personally ensure it reaches Akbar safely."

***

Shortly before sunrise the next dawn, Aqil scanned the outstretched horizon as he patted his horse on the neck. He drank deeply from the flask of water he carried and then took a deep breath. Behind him rode a small cadre of loyal soldiers, men he had hand picked in his many journeys with Aurengzeb across the Empire. He now turned his horse to face them.

"We journey to battle yet again, my comrades. My hair has gone white, and my hands are less steady, so I count on your protection and loyalty now more than ever."

His men lowered their gaze in deference to their beloved leader, showing the first signs of frailty and age. Riza Khan, himself elderly but larger in size and strength than Aqil, raised his head. He possessed the heart of a loyal soldier who is loyal unto death, though he lacked the qualities of a leader.

"Mirza Khan, your hands are still flexible for you know combat well. Your greying hair speaks not of weakness but wisdom gained from a lifetime spent as a soldier." The men nodded their heads in silent acquiescence.

"And before any sword touches you, Commander, our bodies will have fallen in your defence."

Aqil smiled at Riza's words. He gazed at his men, knowing them to be his brothers. They had marched and fought side by side for many long years. Aqil turned his gaze eastwards across the wide plateau that led to Rajasthan. He thought of his young son Akbar, fighting under the Mughal standard. 'I dragged you into the middle of this madness, and now you ride a wild tiger. You are paying the price of my lust, my weakness, my child.' Aqil felt shame and sadness. He recalled that night Jani had come to him and he had rejected her overtures. Why could he not have done the same with Zebunissa? This would never have happened.

Riza Khan broke into Aqil's reverie: "Aqil Khan *jai ho*!" The men took up the chant and soon many voices filled the air: 'Aqil Khan *jai ho*!' 'Aqil Khan *jai ho*!'

Aqil looked at his men, shame in his heart. If these loyal men knew what their leader had done, the role he had played in this game of chess, would they still hail him as their leader? Taking a deep breath he kicked his horse into a trot, leading his men east to their destiny.

***

The *hakim* picked up a sharp dagger and expertly pushed it into the elbow crease of his patient. "We place the dagger into hot water first to remove impurities," he explained to his apprentice, a young lad of fifteen, who had dreams of being a royal *hakim* himself one day. The *hakim* pushed gently until a bright red flow of blood gathered around the edges of the dagger. He then removed the dagger and looked at his apprentice. "Bring the water basin."

Placing the bloodied dagger into the basin, he began bleeding the arm into another basin to his left, once again explaining to his apprentice why it was important. "This will remove the impurities in his blood. It will also weaken him, but with time his body will make more blood, not contaminated by impurities."

"Who is this nobleman, sir?" asked the apprentice, nervous about watching a bloodletting for the first time.

"Aqil Khan, one of the Emperor's most trusted advisors. He came here to inquire about the Emperor's health, at the behest of Empress Zebunissa begum. But he has acquired an infection from the dirty waters of this arid land."

"Sir, may I enter?" Riza's deep voice could intimidate the most valiant of warriors, but he lowered it for the royal *hakim* whose healing abilities were respected even by the enemy.

Continuing to bleed his patient, the *hakim* murmured, "Soldier, do you not know better than to come in when a patient is being treated?"

"I beg your forgiveness, but my commander wished me to deliver a letter he carries in his pocket, to Prince Akbar."

"Why would he entrust you, a foot soldier, with such a task?"

"Sir, I have raced to more battles than I can now remember, with Mirza Aqil. He and I have saved each other's lives on the battlefield. Such is the relationship between us. He trusts me like a son."

"Like a son!" the *hakim* exclaimed, brows raised. "Soldiers have many sons from what I am told. Your battles make you thirsty for flesh and your seed is littered across the grounds you fight over."

Riza looked away in dismay; he knew not how to answer. Finally, he said, "Sir, if you will permit, may I look for my Commander's letter while you are attending to his other needs? I assure you I will not disturb you."

"Not now!" The *hakim* shot Riza a sharp look, causing him to step back. Fearing to offend the Emperor by upsetting the *hakim*, Riza withdrew and retreated to the soldiers' quarters.

A few hours later, the *hakim* washed his hands in a basin of warm water. He had placed a tight bandage on Aqil's arm, from which copious amounts of blood had been drained. Wiping his wet hands on a linen cloth, the *hakim* casually searched for the letter Riza had mentioned. Holding it in his hand, he turned to his apprentice. "These soldiers only think of war. But the health of the patient should supersede all war plans. Alas, they are born of war, fed on war, and will one day die in war."

Jani Begum entered the tent. She and Prince Azam had been at the imperial camp for several weeks. She had heard of Aqil's illness and had come to enquire after his health.

"How is Mirza Khan, *hakim*?"

"Princess, why did you trouble yourself? I would have come to your quarters to give you an update," said the *hakim*, bowing low.

"It matters not, *hakim*. But all the women are concerned about Mirza Khan. He has been our mentor for many years."

The *hakim* stood upright. "I have bled him but the heat of the desert is not good for him. I have thus instructed the slave girls to fan him and sprinkle cold water throughout the night. This, more than anything, will help him."

Jani looked at Aqil's ailing body and felt tears spring to her eyes. His eyes were only partially open so Jani could see only the whites. His skin was pale and sweaty, his hair covered with dust and perspiration. He was breathing through his mouth in a scratchy hum, like a horse about to die. Jani began to fear the worst. She still carried lust in her heart for this man though she was embarrassed she made advances to him even after being bequeathed to Prince Azam. She too, had heard the rumors that he had room in his heart for only Zebunissa, but he consistently denied this, and Aurengzeb had never doubted Aqil's sincerity. Two women, whose fathers had fought for the throne of India a generation before, were now embroiled in battle for just about everything else.

Jani casually glanced at the letter the *hakim* held and noticed the royal seal. "What is it you hold in your hand, *hakim*?"

"It is a sealed letter, Princess, carried by Mirza Khan for Prince Akbar, I believe."

Jani's eyes widened. Why was Aqil carrying a letter for Akbar, and why was it sealed? Sealed letters were either from the Emperor or Empress. Since the Emperor was present in the camp, the letter had to be from Zebunissa.

"One of Mirza Khan's soldiers had come for it but I turned him away because I was in the midst of my treatment. I was about to..."

"Give me that!"

The *hakim* and his apprentice both froze at the violence of her tone. Jani struggled to regain her composure and said, "I mean, if it is a royal communication for Prince Akbar, it should not be given into the hands of a minor soldier. Who knows what he might do with it?" She stretched out her hand for the letter.

The *hakim* and his apprentice looked reluctantly at one another.

"Now!" Jani ordered, raising her voice.

Royalty was not to be denied by such as he, the *hakim* thought dourly as he handed over the letter. Jani glanced at it and hid a smile. This was no ordinary letter. Perhaps it was connected to the papers Zebunissa had been trying to hide from her. Casually, Jani tucked the letter into her blouse and walked out of the tent. She began walking hastily past the smoky campfires lit throughout the imperial camp as the hot sun began to set, leaving a chilly mist. Her heart raced as she pondered the possibilities of what the royal letter contained. She quickly entered her tent, directing her maids to leave. Pulling the letter from between her breasts, she broke the seal and quickly perused the letter.

*Akbar*

*I am sending you this letter through our trusted friend, Aqil. You must not declare yourself Emperor during your attack in the Aravalli Hills. If you reveal you are conspiring with the enemy to overthrow Aba, he will sever ties with you and declare you an enemy. In that capacity your ability to control his actions will diminish. It is better that you attack the Aravalli as you have been planning, claim victory by having our Rajput allies accept defeat, allowing you to imprison them, and then summon Aba to for a presentation of the captives.*

*Upon Aba's arrival, your soldiers will surround and imprison him. At that time you shall be declared Emperor of Mughal India! Follow these instructions and do not veer from them!*

*Zebunissa*

Jani raised her hand to her mouth in silent horror. "Allah, have mercy!" she whispered. Her eyes widened. "Sedition!" Slowly, she folded the letter and sat down, pondering what her next move should be. Should she go to the Emperor? No! Zebunissa would simply deny having written the letter and could even, using her skills of manipulation, convince the Emperor it was written by her, Jani, daughter of his arch enemy, Dara Shikoh, to incriminate Zebunissa. 'Blood is blood,' she thought. 'The Emperor will never forsake his beloved Zebunissa for me.'

Jani continued to ponder. This was her moment; she could not squander it. The first shot had to come from Zebunissa, but the next one would be hers. Only fools attacked from the front. It was best to hit the enemy from behind a thick veil. She would not follow in her father's footsteps and be outwitted. This time, victory would be hers. She decided what to do and smiled, murmuring, "I said you would regret crossing me, Zebunissa!"

***

Jani moved Azam's sweaty arms away from her naked torso. She knew he needed the pleasure of her flesh in the midst of the chaotic military campaigns in which he was a mere pawn. Thus, she had lured him to her chamber and offered him *shirazi* that her eunuchs had smuggled into the camp for the pleasure of the wives of nobles, accompanying their husbands. Extreme care had been taken to hide this from the Emperor. With the morale of the camp low, it had not been difficult to secure the silence of the guards in exchange for a skin of the sweet wine.

Azam had become inebriated; ripe for seduction. Still slim and attractive to her husband, Jani did not need to work very hard to convince the Prince to disrobe and make passionate love to her. She made sure she tired him out, knowing the combination of *shirazi* and rough sex would send Azam into deep slumber, from which he would not awake till morning prayers, if then.

Jani carefully extricated herself from Azam's embrace and grabbed a shawl to cover herself. Tip-toeing around the tent, she slipped into a gown and walked over to her dresser and sat down to write a letter. She felt exhausted. Her skin was as pale as the moon and deep dark shadows had formed under her dark luminous eyes. She paused for a moment and looked at her dishevelled self in the mirror. Was it merely a reflection of the churn inside her? 'Is this how we all end?' she wondered. 'Is there such a thing as a gracious Mughal woman or are we all just dark creatures inside?' There were so many stories of debauchery and betrayal, of lovers and incest; a lineage of vultures and whores that outwardly pretended to be gracious royalty. 'I wonder if my grandmother Mumtaz Begum, was different? There are no rumors about her. Perhaps she was all that is good in us.'

Indeed, the love story of Mumtaz Begum and Shah Jahan had never been spoiled with the suspicion of affairs and lies. Yet every Mughal Princess and Queen seemed to harbour dark secrets. 'Were we born this way or does the life at court make us what we are?' Jani's gaze shifted from the mirror to the objects on her table – a small peacock figurine, a hair clip, and a small golden vessel with ink. She looked up again at her reflection in the mirror and whispered, "I'm sorry Aunt Jahanara. I could not be the Princess you wanted me to be."

She wrote a letter to Akbar, forging Zebunissa's signature.

***

A parchment drawing of the Aravalli Hills lay spread on the low table. Aurengzeb looked at his Commanders. "According to our estimates, the enemy has 50,000 men concentrated in this valley." He circled the area of interest with a stick. "When Azam attacked from the east, the Rajputs led him into this valley and massacred his men. Similarly, when Muazzam attacked from the south, the enemy led them into the same valley. There, the enemy has the advantage."

Akbar stood listening intently as Aurengzeb, his shoulders dropping with age, mapped out his battle plan. "Akbar's regiment will go north and secure positions behind this valley. That will leave us 5,000 soldiers, who will attack from the east. They will be the decoy. The Rajputs will once again lead them into the valley, exposing their positions while attacking our men. At that time, Akbar, you will take your forces into the valley from the north and massacre the enemy!"

"Brilliant!" exclaimed one of the Generals. "Your strategy is imaginative and brilliant!"

"The Emperor is the greatest soldier Mughal India has ever known," declared another Commander sycophantically. "These Rajputs will regret crossing swords with us."

"But what of the 5,000 soldiers being sent to certain death?" enquired Akbar.

"They are soldiers!" exclaimed Aurengzeb irritably. "They are born to die in war!"

Akbar's lips clipped together, knowing his father's cold heart had no room for anyone else's suffering. Though nervous he had still not heard from Zebunissa, he tried to remain calm to avoid raising suspicion.

There was a slight commotion as a dishevelled Azam entered the tent, helmet in hand.

"I summoned a council an hour ago, Azam!" the Emperor snapped. As the years went by, he found it harder to control his temper. It flared up in a moment, like a flame leaping to the sky.

"I crave your forgiveness, Majesty," Azam replied, trying to catch his breath.

"And this is not a place for women," admonished Aurengzeb sternly as he directed his gaze to the veiled figure of Jani, standing behind Azam.

Jani bowed her head saying, "Majesty, the Empress Zebunissa has sent a letter for Prince Akbar, which Aqil Khan asked me to deliver."

Aurengzeb's tone softened. Still shaken by Aqil's illness, he waved a hand for Jani to hand Akbar the letter.

"Princess, I thank you," said Akbar, bending his head.

"Is it anything important Akbar?" questioned Aurengzeb as all the Commanders, including Azam, stared at Akbar and the letter.

Akbar chuckled. "Probably just my sister reminding me to watch my health and serve you loyally, father." Quickly, he tucked away the folded letter and held up the flap of the tent for Jani to leave.

Once the council had broken up, Akbar quickly walked to his own tent and opened the letter. To his surprise, it was not sealed.

*My Beloved Brother Akbar*

*Do as you suggest. Declare yourself Emperor once you are safely in the Aravalli Hills. Do not wait to capture the Emperor before declaring yourself. I am confidant your forces will overpower Aba once you have your Rajput allies with you. Burn this letter once you have read it.*

*Zebunissa*

The writing looked authentic to him but there was no royal seal. The letter had been folded as if it had been carried in someone's clothing. Could it be that Aqil had given it to Jani as she too, may be a member of the Makhfi? He had never been told Jani was an ally. He wondered if he ought to go and question her.

Just then a voice cried out, "Prince! Your horse is ready. The Emperor wants the cavalry to gather at the north side of the camp."

Akbar stood for a moment, uncertain. He turned his head towards Jani's tent, wanting to ask her why there was no royal seal, but there was no time; the Emperor did not suffer laggards. And if someone overheard their conversation, the whole plan could fail. No, it could not be done in such haste. He would just have to trust Jani. Putting on his helmet, he raced towards his horse.

## 25
## The Proclamation

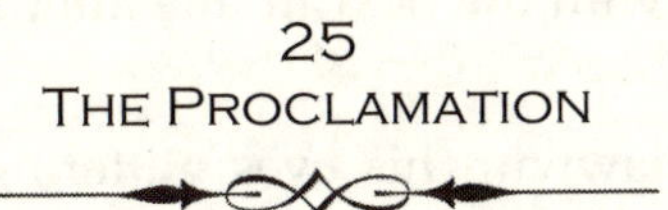

*"May there still shine*
*The torch of hope that Thou to us didst give!"*

1 November 1681

"Instruct your men to move slowly." Akbar knew his nervousness could be heard in his quavering voice. Nevertheless, he fixed his gaze on Tahawwur Khan, his confidante and childhood friend, and close ally during his rugged years of training. Apart from the Makhfi, Tahawwur was the only one who knew of Akbar's plan. Both men stared intently into the narrow passage that led to the northern Aravalli. Akbar squinted, wondering if this narrow passage would lead to wealth and power, or depravity as another State prisoner.

"Hail the Emperor! Hail Alamgir!" chanted one of the men, causing Akbar and Tahawwur to turn towards him. Akbar stared straight at the soldier, contempt in his eyes, but Tahawwur gently shook his head, sending his friend and Commander a silent warning. Wryly, Akbar nodded. Turning back to the soldier, a smile flitted across Akbar's face. The soldier, emboldened, raised his arm into the air and shouted again, "Hail Emperor Alamgir!" The words seem to echo endlessly in the rugged mountain terrain. After a brief pause, many voices took up the chant: 'Hail, Emperor Alamgir! Hail, Emperor Alamgir!'

"No!" yelled Akbar, punching the air with his fist. Silence fell over the men as Akbar's voice rose over their chants. "Today we hail no man, only Hindustan!"

The men focused on their young Commander as he told them, "My comrades, we hail Hindustan, we hail the House of Timur! We hail the Great Mughals who have ruled before, who spent months and years in rugged terrain, building the Empire. Hail Babur!"

Babur had been the first Mughal to invade India over a century ago, becoming the first Mughal Emperor of India. Akbar wanted to remind his men that Babur's blood flowed in his veins.

'Hail Emperor Babur!' his men chanted.

Akbar continued with the next in line after Babur. "Hail Emperor Humayun!"

Akbar looked at Tahawwur, his eyes glittering like those of a man drunk on wine. Tahawwur picked up on Akbar's hints and shouted, "Hail, Emperor Akbar!" The legendary Akbar ascended the throne after Humayun. Again the men roared, 'Hail, Emperor Akbar! Hail, Emperor Akbar! Hail, Emperor Akbar!'

Akbar felt a thrill course through his body as he heard his name resound around the hills, even though he knew the men were chanting not for him but instead for his revered ancestor. Taking a deep breath he let out a jubilant roar. Deliberately, Akbar drew his sword and turned his horse towards the narrow path that just moments ago had made him fearful. Pointing his sword forward, he called his men to battle. There was no turning back.

***

The runner, exhausted from the swift uphill run from Akbar's camp, confirmed the news.

"So this Mughal contingent is a decoy?" Raj Singh asked, seated on the golden chair brought especially for him from his palace.

"Highness, this is a ploy often used by the Emperor Aurengzeb," warned one of Raj Singh's generals. "He used it against the Persians in Kandahar, when he sent some soldiers ahead while he attacked from the rear. He does not hesitate to sacrifice his men."

Raj Singh ran his hand over his long greying beard, pondering the situation. He had not had any direct contact with Akbar in months and cryptic messages through runners brought only snippets of information; it was not enough to devise a war plan. What was Akbar up to? "How did the Persians then defeat Aurengzeb?" he asked.

His General chuckled. "Highness, Aurengzeb is not as crafty as he imagines. The Persians guarded their fort on all fronts, so when the rear assault began, they were prepared. We too, should prepare for a rear assault."

"Yes," agreed Raj Singh, "but not with canons or artillery, only infantry." He had not confided in any of his Generals, fearing one of them could be in the pay of the Mughals.

"No artillery or canons? But our soldiers will pay the price with their lives if we rely only on hand-to-hand combat."

Raj Singh looked disapprovingly at his General, displeased to have his authority questioned. "It is a narrow space. What if our canons and artillery cause boulders to rain down on our own men? It would be unthinkable!" shot back Raj Singh. He was worried that stray gunfire could mortally wound Akbar, and destroy all hopes of overthrowing Aurengzeb. He was adamant about taking no risks.

"As you wish, Highness," the General responded reluctantly.

As his Commanders filed out of the tent, an uneasy feeling rose in Raj Singh's belly. He knew his fate was inextricably tied to Akbar's.

***

Akbar instructed Tahawwur to plant his men along the ridges overlooking the Rajput camp and lie low. Much to the surprise of his men, the Rajputs had already secured their position facing north, as if they had known a northern assault had been planned. Both camps stood less than a mile apart the rugged terrain, separated by a stretch of flat land that would be the battlefield once battle began. In the distance, gunsmoke could be seen and the sound of canons heard, presumably from the south assault by the 5,000 Mughal soldiers who had been sent to their deaths to create a diversion. Akbar's face tightened every time a cannon was fired.

*Boom!* Akbar clenched his fists and bowed his head. "Forgive me, my comrades," he whispered. "Forgive me for not coming to your aid. But I must take this path if I am to prevent more bloodshed."

The faint sound of chanting began in the distance. Akbar listened carefully as the sound grew into the Rajput war cry, *Har Har Mahadev!* The Mughal soldiers stood tense and anxious as the Rajput chant swelled. They knew the Rajputs were fearless warriors and bloodshed was nigh. *Har Har Mahadev! Har Har Mahadev!*

Akbar rose up in his stirrup and gestured to his soldiers to respond with the Mughal's own war cry: *Allah ho Akbar! Allah ho Akbar! Allah ho Akbar*!

The conflicting war cries resounded round the gorge, a precursor to battle. One of the armies would soon release a shot, artillery fire or even a spear thrown in the direction of the enemy. Retreat meant surrender of the position and a white flag meant complete surrender.

Akbar knew he had to act quickly. He did not want a soldier or Commander unaware of his alliance with Raj Singh to inadvertently signal the commencement of hostilities. "Tahawwur!" he called to his friend. "How do I declare myself Emperor with everyone chanting war cries?"

"Prince," Tahawwur said in his deep calm voice, "you were the one who rallied the troops and called for the chanting."

"It was in response to the Rajput's war cry. I had to do something or it would have implied weakness or surrender! Who is in heading the enemy forces?"

***

He had meant to alert Akbar that his soldiers were ready to engage him and his army for whatever plan he had in mind – pretend capture or by declaring himself Emperor outright. But it seemed that Akbar had misunderstood, for the Mughal war cry rose in response. The battle must not be allowed to begin, Raj Singh thought to himself. He instructed his Generals to stop the chanting. Accordingly, the Rajputs ceased chanting but the Mughal soldiers continued.

"Highness," one of Raj Singh's generals said urgently, "If we wait for them to launch an attack, we will be at a disadvantage. The enemy knows we are here. I suggest a frontal assault."

Raj Singh, pacing back and forth, worried and uncertain, lost his temper. "I suggest you keep your mouth shut!" The other Generals froze in shocked surprise. Raj Singh turned his gaze towards the enemy lines murmuring, "Tell me what you want me to do, Prince."

As if in answer to his prayers, from a distance, a towering man emerged with his hands raised. *Was it Akbar?* Raj Singh squinted, trying to see more clearly. *No, the man was far too tall.* "Tell the soldiers to hold fire," he instructed quickly. The man was walking quickly but the distance was vast. 'The man's safety is of paramount importance,' thought Raj Singh. Should someone harm him, a battle would commence and all hopes of overthrowing Aurengzeb would be dashed forever.

***

Tahawwur Khan knew that sending Akbar was too dangerous and no foot soldier could be trusted. Thus he had suggested the Prince send him to the Rajput camp to inform them of his intention to declare himself Emperor; there would then be no need for either army to surrender. Akbar had sighed in relief and enthusiastically embraced Tahawwur's plan.

"If they harm even one hair of your head, I will launch a full scale attack!" he had told Tahawwur. Fearing that such an action would destroy the plan, Tahawwur walked as coolly as he could towards the enemy, his arms raised to show he carried no weapons and came in peace. Weather in the hills was erratic. The mornings and evening were extremely cold, but the days were exceptionally hot. As Tahawwur walked through the vast plain that lay between the two armies, the shadow of the surrounding mountains disappeared as the sun rose over his head and sweat poured down his face. He wanted to lower his hands to wipe away the sweat, but feared someone would mistake his gesture. The ploy of sending an unarmed man to the enemy with peace overtures, only to have him draw hidden weapons and slay the front line, had been used by Aurengzeb. Tahawwur feared his mission would be construed by the Rajputs as another such ploy.

As he approached the Rajput camp, one of Raj Singh's generals yelled, "Soldier! Stop where you are!"

Tahawwur halted. "I come bearing greetings from Emperor Akbar."

"Emperor Akbar? Emperor Akbar rests with his ancestors!"

"The rule of Aurengzeb the Usurper has ended, and I come to announce the ascension of Emperor Akbar, who wishes to meet with his brother, Rana Raj Singh."

The General chuckled. "Emperor Akbar! Is this some new ploy by the Mughals to enter our camp?"

"Please inform the Rana of my arrival. He is aware of this."

"Remain here," said the General. Warily, he turned and walked off towards the rear of the camp to inform Raj Singh.

***

Akbar's heart had been racing ever since Tahawwur began his long walk to the enemy camp. He felt exhausted. 'No shot has been fired and I feel ready to collapse,' he thought. His soldiers remained alert in their positions, ready to charge if anything untoward happened.

Tahawwur could no longer be seen. He had been escorted into the camp, presumably to meet Raj Singh. 'But would he actually get there?' Akbar wondered. Following months of Mughals pillaging their temples, raping their women, and burning their homes, would the Rajputs extract revenge on this unarmed messenger before he even reached Raj Singh? A prolonged silence fell on the camp. His helplessness began choking Akbar but he could not make a hasty decision that would compromise his plan, Tahawwur, or his men. He kept up a strong front while trembling with fear and anxiety.

Then, in the distance, he noticed a pink dust cloud on the plains, as if hoofs and legs were marching towards him. *Were they on the attack? But there were no war cries. Was Raj Singh marching himself or had he sent one of his Commanders?* Unblinking, Akbar continued to stare. "Lay down your arms!" he yelled to his men. "General Tahawwur Khan is with them. He has secured their surrender!" One by one the men laid down their swords and shields.

The procession halted at a distance. As the dust settled, Akbar could see soldiers on foot with long spears, with others on horseback. In the centre, behind these men, came a decorated elephant with a canopy. Seated on this enormous beast were Raj Singh and Tahawwur. Akbar let out a sigh of relief. Tahawwur's plan had worked! There would be no misunderstanding, no battle.

Suddenly, drumbeats resounded as the front ranks separated as if by a mighty force. Raj Singh and Tahawwur dismounted and walked towards Akbar. Jasmine flowers were strewn before them so their feet would never touch barren ground. Akbar felt his heart begin to thud, knowing this was the formal acceptance of him as Emperor. Horns sounded as Akbar eyes met those of Raj Singh. As Raj Singh and Tahawwur reached him, they bowed their heads in homage.

"Majesty, I hereby recognize you as Emperor of all Hindustan and offer you my allegiance and service."

"Hail Emperor Akbar!" shouted Tahawwur, looking towards his men, standing unarmed in the distance, unsure what was occurring. Would they be committing treason by recognizing the new Emperor? They looked at one another for answers. Sensing their indecisiveness, Tahawwur addressed them saying, "Aurengzeb the Usurper illegally seized the throne of the great Shah Jahan! His activities have forced our Rajput subjects to turn and fight against us. We now give our loyalty to the true Mughal heir – a man who will restore the Empire to its former greatness by uniting Hindu and Muslim! Hail Emperor Akbar!"

The men looked at one another in bewilderment, unsure how to react. Then, from the last ranks in the distance, a soldier yelled, "Hail Emperor Akbar!" Silence followed. Tahawwur, sensing an opportunity to support the lone soldier repeated, "Hail Emperor Akbar!" After a few moments, some of the men of Akbar's regiment began chanting, 'Hail, Emperor Akbar! Hail, Emperor Akbar! Hail, Emperor Akbar!' The crescendo of voices built until the very heavens rang with the chant: Hail Emperor Akbar!

A jubilant smile crossed Akbar's face hearing the men chanting his name. Looking skywards, he thanked Allah. He looked around at the Aravilli Hills, his new kingdom. Though rugged and barren, it was more than he had when the day had begun. He had awoken as a Prince, but tonight he would sleep as Emperor. Zebunissa's dream had finally come to pass.

***

Akbar traversed the intervening plain to where the Rajputs had set up camp. Jubilant music accompanied him. Smiling, he advanced towards the large golden chair adorned with precious metals, offered to him in homage by Raj Singh to the new Emperor. As Akbar walked, glorious marigold garlands were placed around his neck by the Rajput Generals. Finally, he sat down on his throne and looked upon the congregation, a mingling of Rajputs and Mughals. Akbar knew the proclamation as Emperor could only be done following rites and rituals and consultations with astrologers and theologists. He needed to be in Delhi before he could formally sit on the Peacock Throne. However, in order to assert his authority in Rajasthan, he had to participate in the festivities the Rajputs deemed worthy of the occasion.

"Majesty," began Raj Singh, "a grand feast has been prepared to celebrate your ascension to the throne and the end of Aurengzeb's, reign of terror." He clapped twice and a succession of men entered, bearing silver platters of food: rice with split peas, hot breads, moong dal, fried potatoes in gravy, mutton in lemon-ginger paste, roasted chicken, and fruits.

But the festivities were not prolonged as battle resumed on the southern front. It came to a gory end with all 5,000 Mughal soldiers being slaughtered, as Aurengzeb had anticipated. He waited to hear his son Akbar, leading the northern contingent, had launched a surprise attack and overwhelmed the unsuspecting Rajput enemy. The news that his son had declared himself Emperor and joined the enemy; that there would be no attack; remained unknown to Aurengzeb.

Seated in the tent prepared for him, the pomp and pageantry passed, Akbar listened as Raj Singh assumed the lead in planning further action. The Rana asked the question that had been niggling in his mind the whole day: "Why would Empress Zebunissa tell you to declare yourself Emperor without providing further instructions?"

Akbar turned away, misgivings filling his heart. "I do not know. I was merely instructed to declare myself but nothing further."

Raj Singh looked at Akbar thoughtfully. "Hmmm, then we must plan the next move. We must go to Ajmer."

"Ajmer?"

"Yes. It is where your father has stationed the bulk of his army. We must reach there before he does and bring them under our command." Raj Singh sat down and explained his plan in detail. "You must issue a proclamation immediately, deposing your father and proclaiming your rightful claim to the throne. I will instruct my men to begin minting coins in your name and start distributing them in all Rajputana. Creating the aura of inevitability is key!"

Akbar stared at the Rana, pleased yet nervous about taking such a giant leap against his implacable father. Unable to speak, he merely nodded and sipped some *shirazi* to calm his nerves.

***

Akbar woke to a chilly morning the following day. He noticed a beautiful cashmere shawl neatly folded on a chair placed next to his bed. No doubt it was for him. Since declaring himself Emperor, Raj Singh and the other Rajputs had bestowed lavish luxuries on him, befitting a Mughal monarch. Even the tent provided was no ordinary enclosure but two stories high, with servants to do his bidding, and even concubines for his pleasure, though his thoughts were far removed from carnal pleasure. Wrapping the shawl around himself, he walked over to the entrance and stared out at the surrounding hills. Though no snow fell here, the peaks nevertheless looked white, probably from water that had frozen in the night. During the day the ice would thaw, only to freeze again at night. He noticed a young Rajput woman, probably the wife or concubine of one of Raj Singh's Commanders, chasing a little boy along the dusty track. The boy could not have been more than two years old. Akbar immediately thought of his own son, Nikusiyar, born a year ago. Akbar had not been able to spend much time with his newborn following Jaswant Singh's untimely death and his own expedition to Rajasthan. Nikusiyar was being raised in the harem under the watchful eye of the Empress Zebunissa, his grandmother.

Akbar had wanted to write to Zebunissa to tell her what he had done and what Raj Singh and he had planned as the next steps. He knew she would be proud of him, thrilled to know she had finally won against Aba. He yearned to see the look on her face when she learned the news, but knew that both his travelling to Delhi and her coming to Rajasthan were far too risky. No, she would have to wait to learn about the success of their revolt from the imperial messengers who would be sent across the Empire. No one would suspect she was the chief architect of what had happened.

"Rana Raj Singh wishes audience, Majesty," announced a slave. Akbar nodded, still suffering from the fatigue of the previous day's dramatic events.

"Greetings Majesty!" said Raj Singh, entering and bowing.

"Rana, do not bow to me. Of all my father's rules, this is one I agree with: Bow before God, the maker of all men; not to me." Akbar gestured for him to be seated. "Has the news of my rebellion reached my father?" he enquired.

"I would assume so."

"Then why no news…no threats…no impending battle?"

"Your father must be shocked; plotting his next move. But we must not wait. We must launch a mid-day attack, and in the fury, escape via the northern route. We have 18,000 troops; 12,000 of your men and 6,000 of mine. On the way to Ajmer, we will pick up more troops from some of the minor Chiefs in our jurisdiction and gain another 12,000 men or so. With a 30,000 strong army, we will be in a strong position to wage war if our plan does not work. If it does, we can double our ranks with Mughal soldiers in Ajmer. We will then be unbeatable!" Raj Singh began naming the minor Chiefs who would readily offer their troops and those who would need convincing.

Akbar looked up, annoyed. The plan seemed to keep changing. Till then, Zebunissa had plotted the strategy, knowing the Emperor's thoughts. Now, this Rajput Rana was devising the strategy without even consulting him. "Why must we keep changing plans?" he enquired. "Why not stick to what we have already discussed?"

Raj Singh dismissed Akbar's concerns, mentioning the names of the small chieftains he was hoping to absorb into the rebel army. "There may be need for some pay-offs," he said, leaning forward. "Has the Emperor provided you with funds we can use to buy off the more greedy Chiefs?"

Before Akbar could respond, Raj Singh had reverted to his monologue, cursing the smaller chieftains whom he knew would have to be bribed. He began a discourse on the role of Kings; how they were required to decide in the best interests of their people, not what filled the coffers.

Akbar grew restless listening to these meanderings but knew he could not alienate Raj Singh, his only ally now that he had declared himself Emperor. Raj Singh's protection was worth the annoyance. Akbar walked to the window from where he had seen the young boy and his mother earlier. As he stared at the unforgiving landscape, he murmured to himself, "Allah, guide my hand..."

## 26
## Loyalty And Betrayal

*Friends had I, many friends, who shared with me*
*Days glad and sad,*
*But mine they are no more, I am cut free*
*From all I had.*

10 November 1681

"Akbar has proclaimed himself Emperor!" exclaimed Zebunissa, horrified. "But my specific instructions were to pretend to be taken captive by the Rajputs, so Aba would not suspect anything until it was too late!"

"What difference does it make?" asked Zubdat in a low voice. "The point is he is Emperor and the might of the Rajputs is with him!" She raised a tight fist into the air.

Zebunissa buried her face in her hands, frustrated by her sister's lack of understanding. "Akbar, you fool!" she whispered. "It is too early to declare yourself!" She looked up at Zubdat, her face lined with torment. "All he needed to do was pretend to be taken prisoner and win allies. He would have been taken to Ajmer, where he could have rallied the 30,000 strong Mughal troops already there, with the help of the Rajputs. Together, they could have formed an army of 60,000 men and marched to Delhi. By the time Aba learned what had happened, we would have closed the gates to Delhi, proclaimed Akbar Emperor, and seized the treasury." Zebunissa shook her head from side to side in despair. "How could this have happened?"

"I do not know," responded Zubdat, sitting down beside Zebunissa. "Aqil Khan was supposed to deliver the message straight into Akbar's hands. Do you think he betrayed us?"

"I have to assume, based on what I am hearing, that he did not give Akbar my letter. Something must have prevented him, or perhaps he was always working with Aba…"

"But if he was, Aba would have known the truth about the Makhfi long since; he would have imprisoned us all."

"Perhaps Aqil did not wish us to be imprisoned; maybe all he wanted was for us to fail. That way he could protect Aba while not letting us know he had double-crossed and misled his own pupils." In her usual way, Zebunissa began putting together the facts she knew, to ascertain the truth.

"We thought we were the hidden ones but it seems it was Aqil who was the hidden one!"

"Damn the wretch!" cried Zebunissa, tears filling her eyes.

***

As Raj Singh had planned, Akbar and his men, with the Rajputs, began their march towards Ajmer. They were greeted by small Chiefs and Rajas along the way. The number of men under their command began to swell, but not by as much as Raj Singh had hoped. The combined forces now numbered 25,000 men. The rebel army set up camp outside the Ajmer and a city of tents, alleys and lanes quickly sprang up. The makeshift city was organized by hierarchy, with Akbar and the Rajput nobles housed in the grandest tents at the centre of the encampment. Once again Akbar issued a proclamation declaring himself Emperor of Mughal India.

Hours turned into days but no word of surrender came from Aurengzeb's camp to the young, self-proclaimed Emperor. Finally, on the third day, a runner delivered a letter to Akbar. It was not from Aurengzeb but the Mughal army: *Prince Akbar, you are not our Commander. We follow the true monarch of Hindustan, Emperor Aurengzeb. Prepare to surrender to us or prepare for battle.*

There was a sense of shock in the rebel camp. "Wretches! Who do they think they are talking to?" cried Akbar, infuriated. He refused to back down. "Tell the Commander of the Mughal army that he and his men will be slaughtered and fed to the dogs for crossing their Emperor! They are traitors!"

Raj Singh offered wise council, saying, "You father must have instigated them. No General on his own, would feel so emboldened to send such a message."

Akbar stared ahead pensively. "Or perhaps they are indeed loyal to my father?" he murmured. "After all, he has marched and fought with them since he was a young Prince. My father is nothing if not a warrior, and they respect that."

"Akbar...Majesty, I have been a King longer than you have been alive. Generals switch sides all the time, depending on which way the wind blows. In the end, people just want to live and prosper. No one chooses the losing side. Your father must be near, if not here already. We must be vigilant! He will no doubt send in spies."

Akbar's blustering demeanour abruptly changed to one of fear. Raj Singh's plan had not worked. If his father knew of his proclamation, his life would be in serious jeopardy. Not knowing who to trust, he had no choice but to go along with whatever Raj Singh decided. Akbar slowly sank back in his chair and stared straight ahead at the entrance of the tent.

As night fell on the rebel camp, Raj Singh's Generals posted twice as many guards as usual, fearing that a night assault by the Mughal army was imminent. Tossing restlessly on his bed, fearful thoughts besieged Akbar's mind. He wondered whether he could trust Raj Singh and the Rajputs. He had spent time with them and even become their ally, but did they really trust him enough to continue supporting him if he lost the coming battle? Or would they abandon him as quickly as they had hailed him Emperor? His uncertainty suffocated him.

Suddenly he heard stealthy footsteps outside his tent. Grabbing his sword, Akbar ran out of the tent, shouting, "Who goes there?"

"Majesty, it is I," said the tall dark figure.

"Tahawwur? Where are you going at this time of night?"

"Nowhere… I could not sleep so I decided to walk around the camp to make sure everything was secure."

"It is cold and we have men to attend to that."

Tahawwur gave a chuckle, unsure what to say. "Do not be concerned, I will be fine. Get some rest."

Tahawwur's hesitant demeanor made Akbar feel uneasy. It was unlike his friend. "God protects those who honour him," he said.

Tahawwur nodded slowly. "You are my heart, dear friend." He bowed and walked away.

***

Akbar woke late the next morning. Surprised at the advanced hour, he sprang up and looked around. His meagre possessions were neatly placed on top of boxes as makeshift dressers. Bending before the bowl placed beside his armour, he washed his face. In the background he could hear birds chirping. Closing his eyes, he thought how, at this time of year, blossoms perfumed the air in Delhi, and many different bird sang in imperfect harmony.

Suddenly, a thought occurred to him: How was it that all he could hear in a military camp were birds? Where were the sounds of clinking armour, soldiers running, horses neighing? Quickly, he went to the opening of the tent and looked out. The camp was deserted! While the tents remained, the soldiers had all gone, Rajput and Mughal. Akbar ran out shouting, "Where is everybody?"

A small band of Mughal soldiers appeared, their eyes glittering dangerously. The group was led by a stocky man of heavy girth, carrying a mace. "You betrayed us, Prince!" he shouted.

Akbar was taken aback. He gazed into the bloodshot eyes of his accuser, who looked ready to slaughter him and said, "No...never! I would never betray you."

The men came closer, spears and javelins in hand. Akbar noticed they wore armour, ready for battle. "Where…where is Tahawwur?" he asked.

"Where?" yelled the same soldier who had accused Akbar of betrayal. "Where is Tahawwur? You tell us!"

"I saw him late last night; I don't know where he went."

"We think you sent General Tahawwur to Aurengzeb, with a secret message detailing our battle plan. You and Tahawwur were spies of Aurengzeb! That is why he sent you a letter congratulating you on duping the Rajputs! It was a plot!" spat out another soldier with scars on his face; badges of a life spent in combat.

Akbar froze. So Tahawwur had not been walking around to ensure the security of the camp; he had been on his way to Aurengzeb! 'How could Tahawwur betray me?' The very idea was unthinkable! This was the man who had helped him reach the Rajputs when the two armies had stood facing each other in the Aravalli Hills. 'Did he do that just to betray me when it mattered most?' Akbar shook his head in denial. Looking up, he saw the soldiers staring at him, weapons in hand. He knew this was not the moment to allow melancholy to consume him.

"Fortunately our men intercepted the letter before it could reach you, before you could bring disaster on us all!"

"What plot?" asked Akbar, bewildered. "There is no plot! I have been betrayed by my most trusted General. He and my father are trying to malign me so our alliance breaks apart!"

"The alliance is finished!" yelled another soldier. "The Rajputs have fled and the Mughal soldiers have scattered. No one has faith in you or your alliance anymore, Prince Akbar!"

"Then why are you still here?"

The men began inching closer, gripping their weapons. His heart pounding, Akbar began walking backwards, hoping to maintain some distance between him and the blood thirsty men. He regretted coming out of his tent unarmed and looked around for a stick or even a pot, anything that could be used in defense. But there was nothing.

Suddenly, there was a loud explosion. *Boom!* Catapulted suddenly into the air, Akbar fell a few feet away on the dirt road. Writhing in agony, he rose slowly and looked around, but all he could see was thick acrid smoke, as if a cannon had been fired. He noticed the men who had confronted him lying on the ground, eyes staring sightlessly at the heavens in shocked surprise. One of them suddenly shrieked in agony, and Akbar turned in his direction. He cringed in horror as he saw the nature of the man's injuries – both legs had been blown off and blood was pouring like a river from both limbs.

Without warning, there was another explosion, this one further away, so that Akbar felt the tremor but was not directly impacted. He hobbled to the bleeding man and pulled him into his tent for cover. "Soldier, you must tell me where the Rajputs went!" he yelled.

"Nev…never! You are a traitor! We betrayed our true Emperor for you and this is how you repay us. You set a trap for the Rajputs." The man struggled to speak. Akbar desperately shook his head from side to side, denying the allegations but the man did not see it as his lifeblood drenched the ground. "We were sent with you to the hills to fight the Rajputs," he said hoarsely. "You….you told us to accept you as our new Emperor, only to be called traitors by the Rajputs. I…I…" The soldier began to weep, whether from pain or shame, it was hard to know. "I…faced the humiliation of being called traitor after a lifetime in the service of the Mughals."

Akbar reached for the soldier's hand and interlocked the man's bloody fingers with his own. Pressing hard, he said, "Comrade, you have served with courage. Your children will be proud. Blessed are those who call you father, brother, husband, and friend. I swear to you before Allah that I did not betray you. I swear on the life of my one-year-old son, Nikusiyar, that my heart is pure; that I have not lied to my men. It is true I saw Tahawwur last night, but he assured me he was merely securing the camp. That he was leaving to join the enemy I did not know, and still cannot believe."

The soldier continued to moan and struggle as Akbar looked deep into his pain-filled eyes, cradling his mutilated body. "This letter from my father that you speak of must be a ploy to turn you men against me. Soldier, when was the last time an imperial letter fell into enemy hands so easily? Tahawwur leaves and a letter incriminating me is intercepted…the whole thing has been planned by my father! May Allah forgive him for I cannot. Tell me soldier, where have the Rajput's gone?"

"You swear on your dead mother's grave that you speak the truth?" gasped the soldier.

Not knowing that his real mother was not the deceased Dilras, but the very-much-alive Zebunissa, Akbar replied, "I swear it!"

"The Rajputs have gone to Jodhpur. Jaswant Singh's newborn son, Ajit Singh, is there. They have gone to secure his safety. Go! They left only an hour ago."

***

"I cannot remain here when Akbar needs help!" Zebunissa said, fretting at her own helplessness.

"He has help," Zinat reminded her. "Raj Singh is with him."

"He cannot be trusted. None of them can! I must go to Akbar! He will not know what to do."

"You will do no such thing!" exclaimed Zinat, annoyed. "Any sign of you will immediately raise suspicion on all of us. Just write a letter to him in your usual encrypted poetry."

"No more poetry!" Zebunissa said firmly, shaking her head. "I cannot take a chance on Akbar not understanding me. I will write in clear language and send my most trusted tatar guard to Rajasthan."

"And where in all Rajasthan will you send your tatar guard?"

"To Jodhpur. I have already learned the Rajputs are congregating there. If Akbar has declared himself, it is where he will be."

Zinat looked at her sister, her eyes wide with surprise. "How do you know this Zebunissa? Are you guessing or has someone told you?"

Zebunissa returned her sister's gaze disdainfully. "This is why none of you could ever overthrow Aba, you don't think like him the way I do. Everyone will be in Jodhpur because that is where the newborn heir to the Rajput throne is. His security is paramount for the Rajputs. Everyone will be in Jodhpur, eventually…" Zebunissa looked away, engrossed in deep thought.

***

"Listen to me…I am not the enemy!" Akbar pleaded.

The soldier kicked him in the abdomen, causing him to curl into a ball in pain. "We will teach you what happens to people who cross us Rajputs!" the man yelled, looking down at the helpless unkempt royal, now reduced to ripped clothing and no weapons. Pulling Akbar up, he hurled him against the wall, causing Akbar to moan in agony as his beaten body collided with the stone wall before falling back to the ground.

Before the soldier could move, a stern voice commanded, "Leave him! I will speak to him alone." It was Raj Singh. He entered the prison cell and gestured for a chair. Hastily the soldier left and returned with a stool, which he wiped with his own shirt. "Leave us!" Raj Singh said.

Hearing the familiar voice, Akbar opened his eyes and looked at the Rana with guarded anxiety. Painfully, he pulled himself to a sitting position, leaning against the wall.

"Have you eaten today?"

"Oh I was just about to have my morning *maas ka soola* when I discovered my entire army had deserted me, and then a cannon ball exploded in front of my tent. It quite put me off my food."

"Your sarcasm has no place here. We were just as shocked as you to learn of your father's plan."

"You have no idea!" exclaimed Akbar, clutching his belly. "You did not learn of any plan…you fell into his trap!"

"What trap?"

"To turn you against me! Don't you see, you fool?" Akbar grit his teeth as pain shot through his body. "My father laid a trap for you, Rana, and you walked straight into it! He ensured that Tahawwur, who was working for him all along, spoke to me before he left, so people would think the two of us were in cahoots. Then my father sent an incriminating letter addressed to me, but meant for you, so you would suspect me of double-crossing you. And you did exactly as he thought you would. Instead of talking to me, you fled with your men, destroying our alliance. All 12,000 of my men either fled or rejoined my father. The few thousands we had picked up en route returned to their liege Lords. All that remains is your 6,000 troops!"

Raj Singh stared at the Prince in disbelief. Though Akbar's words made sense, he was reluctant to pass off Aurengzeb's letter as a trap. Rolling it out, he read it once again.

*My Son Akbar*

*You have made your father and the Empire proud! By infiltrating the enemy ranks and pretending to overthrow me, you have allowed those Rajput fools to remain camped at Ajmer while I march on Jodhpur. All of Rajputana will soon be ours!*

*Alamgir*

"You mean this letter is fake?"

"As fake as the piety my father uses to justify burning your temples!" Akbar wiped his bloodied lip with his sleeve. "Here, look at this." He handed Raj Singh the letter Jani had given him, instructing him to declare himself Emperor.

"But there is no royal seal," observed Raj Singh once he had perused the contents.

Akbar nodded, trying to rise. "I do not know if this really comes from the Empress, but it contained the only instructions I received. I had no time to verify the letter's authenticity, but now, seeing how events have transpired, I would not be surprised to know someone purposely handed me a fake letter to mislead me. Zebunissa always seals her letters to me."

"Majesty!" exclaimed Raj Singh, his posture one of abject apology.

Akbar only shook his head, disgusted by the man's perfidity. "Here... help me up," he said, knowing he did not have the strength to rise alone.

Raj Singh bent and helped the beaten Prince to his feet, propping him up against the wall.

"So what next, Rana?" Akbar asked wearily.

"We must protect the heir!" replied Raj Singh, straightening up.

"The heir! What about protecting me?"

Raj Singh nodded quickly. "We must remain in Jodhpur so that we can use our limited resources to protect you both."

"So be it."

***

Akbar spent the next weeks in growing anxiety. He heard muted chatter from the nobles and princes at the court of the Jodhpur about the Mughal army closing in; he spent his nights pondering what his father was thinking. Was Aurengzeb enraged by Akbar's actions or had his heart thawed towards his favourite son? Would he be willing to forgive if Akbar bent before him in humility? Akbar shook his head…it was out of the question…he had tasted from the front and now considered himself the seventh Mughal Emperor.

There had been no correspondence from Zebunissa in Delhi. The monsoon season had begun and letters from Delhi took longer to arrive. So Akbar spent his days eating, hunting, sipping fine wine and enjoying the pleasures of the harem, graciously offered to him.

Finally, a letter arrived from Delhi.

*Beloved Akbar*

*I do not know why you did not follow my instructions to pretend to be taken captive by the Rajputs. By declaring yourself Emperor prematurely, you gave Aba the chance to regroup his army and plan his next move.*

*If this message reaches you it will mean my intuition was correct and you are fortified in Jodhpur. But you cannot stay there long. Make plans to escape to the Deccan. There, you can meet with the Maratha Chhatrapati, Sambaji, son of Aba's nemesis, Shivaji. He has the men and the will to oppose the Mughal army and install you as Emperor. I have arranged for him to accept you as his guest. Meanwhile, I will court the nobles here in Delhi to support your claim.*

*Zebunissa*

"Summon Raj Singh!" Akbar instructed his attendant, placing the letter on the low table before him. His mind wandered back to the days of his childhood, when Zebunissa had smothered him with love, protecting his every waking hour.

Raj Singh entered, his Generals behind him.

"I have finally received a letter from Delhi," Akbar said, walking over to where his sword and armour lay. "I must go to the Deccan. You will provide me with cover and soldiers to secure my safe passage there."

Raj Singh looked at Akbar in bewilderment. "Soldiers will be provided, Majesty, but what is there in the Deccan?"

"Sambaji."

"Sambaji? Ah yes, the son of Shivaji, who remained a thorn in the Mughal flesh to his last day."

"And now his son commands an army larger than the Mughals. I will go and seek his help."

"Very well; it will be arranged. Since you are leaving Jodhpur, perhaps we should also make arrangements to sneak infant Ajit Singh out as well," Raj Singh said, looking from Akbar to his Generals, who nodded in agreement.

"Do as you think best, Rana." Akbar hastily donned his armour, his mind focused on his own safe passage. "I am leaving. I suggest you all do the same, so when my father burns Jodhpur to the ground you are not caught in the flames. But it is your decision to make."

With these words, Akbar left the chamber, taking only his weapons and armour. His meager personal belongings no longer mattered to him, not even the self-incriminating letter from Zebunissa.

The Rana and his Generals followed.

***

As planned, Akbar disappeared into the vast Deccan, where he spent several weeks slowly making his way to Sambaji in the hope of resurrecting his rebellion. Ajit Singh left Jodhpur under cover of night, hidden in a caravan of cooks, maids and labourers, with his own mother dressed as a maid. A small contingent of Rajput soldiers remained behind so the Mughals would not assume the whole town was deserted. But it was a doomed defence. Yet again, another Rajput town was destroyed; its temples turned to rubble; its riches looted; its people ravaged.

***

"Majesty!" The man was panting so hard he found it difficult to breathe. "These are Prince Akbar's belongings. I retrieved them before they were lost in the fire!" He held up a makeshift cloth bag filled with what seemed to be clothes, jewels and papers.

"I wish to see nothing belonging to that usurper!" exclaimed Aurengzeb, his voice trembling. "You should have burned them with the rest of the fort. I will skin him alive!"

Aurengzeb's trusted ally, Sadullah Khan, intervened to instruct the soldier to have one of the harem women sort through the belongings. This was a common practice. Following Prince Sultan's rebellion, a generation ago, the harem ladies had the responsibility of sorting through his belongings. This allowed the royal family to maintain secrecy and keep untrustworthy nobles from using any information gained to spread rumours and gossip in the court.

When the soldier asked who in the harem should be entrusted with this sensitive task, Sadullah was unsure. Should he have the belongings sent to Delhi, to Zebunissa the Empress? But the journey would take several days and no doubt the contents would be scrutinized and any information relayed back to the army camp. No, there was no time. Someone in the camp had to do the sorting, but who? Sadullah considered the women present. He knew no concubine or slave girl could be entrusted with this. Then he remembered Prince Azam's late arrival at the war council, much to Aurengzeb's chagrin. Accompanying the Prince had been his wife, Jani Begun. She was the highest ranking lady in the camp. Furthermore, now that Akbar was out of favour, surely Azam would be the heir apparent, and Jani the next Empress. If Aurengzeb challenged him, he could use this logic to defend his decision. And so the soldier was instructed to make his way to Jani Begum's tent.

# 27
# Exposed

*Give me thy tears, O Makhfi, let them rain*
*In quenching torrents on my burning heart;*
*So hot its pain*
*At every sigh I breathe the flames outstart.*

1 December 1681

That evening, Jani undertook the lone task of sorting through Akbar's belongings, cataloguing everything – jewels, clothing, papers, and personal items. She already knew what she would do with them. The jewels would be given to her favourite servants; those who had served her diligently and endured the hardships of battle after battle in the deserts of Rajasthan; the clothing would be distributed to slaves who had nothing but the loin cloths they wore. For them, Jani thought, silk muslin or a thick robe would be riches of a lifetime. The personal items she would either discard or deliver to his wife in Delhi, according to their value.

As she began sorting through Akbar's possessions, she deduced the worth of each item as far greater than anything she or her husband possessed. A bracelet of solid gold, encrusted with rubies and emeralds, had been given to Akbar by his father on his return from military training; a silver dagger with rubies had been presented to him on his twentieth birthday by the Emperor; a necklace of pearls the size of a women's toes, also lay in the bundle. No such gift had ever graced her husband's neck. And yet, Akbar had discarded such priceless ornaments without a thought.

Jani was folding some beautifully thick blue pajamas when she heard a crunching sound, like paper. She held up the garment and shook it. A folded note slipped out. Jani quickly opened it and read it. It was the letter from Zebunissa. Wondering if it was authentic, Jani went to her dresser to find the original letter Zebunissa had sent through Aqil

Khan for Akbar. She placed both letters side by side, comparing the handwriting. It was an exact match. Both had the royal seal.

Jani felt her heart thudding in her chest. What should she do? Was there enough in this letter to convince the Emperor that Zebunissa was behind the rebellion, or would she incur the wrath of the raging Emperor? 'I will tell him that I found the letter. He will read it and discover for himself that his daughter has been plotting with his rebel son. I am innocent; I merely stumbled upon the letter while sorting Akbar's belongings as requested. There is nothing to incriminate me.'

Jani rehearsed what she would say over and over again, refining her words to ensure perfection. Finally, she took a deep breath. Hiding the letter beneath her shawl, she set out for Aurengzeb's tent.

***

"Majesty! Pardon my intrusion at this time of day, but your humble servant brings you grave news!" Jani said, head bowed.

Aurengzeb was displeased. Upset at not having found Akbar, he was ready to unleash his temper on anyone who crossed his path. But Jani's carefully framed words stopped him and his anger turned to curiosity. "What news do you bring?" he demanded harshly.

Jani peered at the ageing monarch through her still lustrous lashes. His shoulders drooped from a lifetime of war and bloodshed, betrayal and murder. Composing herself, Jani cleared her throat and said, "I know where Prince Akbar went."

Sadullah Khan, standing beside Aurengzeb, quickly looked up.

"I found this letter in the Prince's belongings that Mirza Sadullah Khan asked me to go through. It is best that Majesty reads it himself." Taking her hand from beneath her shawl, she held out the rolled missive.

A servant took it from her and handed it to Aurengzeb, who continued to stare at Jani with suspicious eyes. He lowered his gaze to the letter and began reading. In silence, the Emperor looked up, his eyes wide with astonishment, glittering with rage. His breathing became heavy. "I am betrayed!" he whispered Aurengzeb. "I have been betrayed by my own kin! The two children on whom I bestowed my love, have forsaken me and joined forces to overthrow me!"

"Majesty, what does the letter state?" asked Sadullah, hoping to diffuse the Emperor's anger. He feared that Aurengzeb, in a rage, could attack anyone.

"That traitor Akbar is in the Deccan, with the infidel Sambaji! His rebellion and safe passage was organized by none other than the daughter I have loved and trusted the most – Zebunissa!"

"Majesty!" Sadullah Khan gasped in horror.

Jani hung her head low. Aurengzeb threw his hands into the air and turned away, unwilling to face anyone. He leaned his head on his balled fist. Silence hung like a thick fog within the tent.

Finally, Aurengzeb said calmly, "Inform my daughter I am returning to Delhi and wish to see her in the *Diwan-i-Khas* to discuss military matters. There is to be no word spoken of this letter or that I know of her involvement in the rebellion. Is that clear!"

"It will be as you wish, Majesty," Sadullah Khan said.

Jani nodded her head in silence.

"Leave me! I wish to be alone with my thoughts."

## 28
## Last Gathering

*I searched for joy, but never found the end;*
*My empty hands, outstretched, can greet no friend.*

10 January 1682

Zebunissa called a final meet of the Makhfi. The usual dignitaries gathered: Mawlana Abdul Qader Bedil, Kalim Kashani, Saa'eb Tabrizi, Ghani Kashmiri; and the royal women, Zubdat, Badr, Zinat and Mihirunissa. Soft music played, rose scented water and *shirazi* were served to the guests.

Reclining against her satin bolsters, Zebunissa looked around the chamber. "Who would like to begin?" she enquired, knowing no one would.

News had already reached Delhi that Akbar had fled to the Deccan, and rather than chasing him, Aurengzeb was returning to Delhi. The Makhfi wondered how, in the midst of such major events, the Empress appeared mellow and ready to recite poetry.

"Then let me begin," she said calmly, a smile tugging at her lips.

*No flower, no nightingale am I,*
*So from the garden mournfully*
*I go. O breezes, free to stray,*
*Back to her garden find your way,*
*And greeting to my Love convey.*

*Exiled and driven from thee I pass*
*Upon my journey; like the grass*
*And patient reeds I bend and shake,*
*As my despairing road I take,*
*Leaving the body for thy sake.*

*Before the soul who understands*
*Be silent: in the desert sands*
*He learnt his lore. Break not the rest*
*Of the afflicted and oppressed*
*With poisoned arrows in his breast.*

"Enjoy this night, Makhfi! Let this chamber resound to your words, so they may echo for centuries. You and I will blend with the earth, but the words we write and recite will live on."

They looked at each other in bewilderment. Where was Zebunissa going? Was she preparing for a night departure to the Deccan? What was she up to? Zubdat and Badrunissa looked at her, tears in their eyes, unsure what to make of her madness.

Ghani Kashmiri was first to speak. "If the Empress will indulge this servant, I would like to recite a verse." Zebunissa nodded.

*He who plunged into difficulties is free from difficulties*
*How can the house of a bubble be smashed by a wave?*

Others began reciting their verses, each on the subject of freedom and release, having been told this was to be the theme of the night.

Mirza Bedil recited in his sonorous voice:

*The wave and the foam cannot see in to the depth of the ocean:*
*A whole world is restless for the knowledge of reality,*
*Yet, does not possess the necessary qualification.*

"Mirza Bedil, your words are wise. They shall outlive you and me." Zebunissa smiled, a triumphant look on her place.

A grand feast followed with numerous dishes of chicken, lamb, goat and fish, fried potatoes and eggplant. Finally, the men and women of the Makhfi bid each other farewell, as if recognizing this was their last meeting. Some wept, others smiled. Zebunissa looked on, dry-eyed and calm.

When they were all gone, only the sisters remained. "Are they declaring you the next Emperor, Zebunissa?" inquired Zubdat facetiously. "Everyone was emotional tonight, but not you."

Zebunissa smiled. "My emotions are in my poems." She looked around to ensure they were alone and then said quietly, "Badr, Zinat, Zubdat, Mihirunissa, meet me in my chambers at eleven tonight."

***

As Zebunissa had requested, her sisters walked to Zebunissa's chamber at the appointed hour. The night was chilly and windy. The high-pitched howl of a stray dog could be heard as the women waited to be announced. Zubdat hugged herself as the cold caused her to shiver.

"Why did you not bring a shawl like us, Zubdat?"

"I did not think we would be waiting outside for so long," Zubdat responded, her teeth chattering. "What's taking so long?"

A maid suddenly rushed out from the Empress' chamber, saying frantically, "Princesses, the Empress has gone!"

"Gone? What do you mean gone?" asked Mihirunissa sharply.

"She is no longer in her chambers. She left a note for each of you."

The four Princesses quickly opened their letters and began reading. Zubdat finished first and looked up, astonished. She looked at her sisters, who were beginning to weep as they read.

"What does your letter say, Zubdat?" Mihirunissa asked, her voice trembling.

Still bewildered, Zubdat said, "It thanks me for a lifetime of friendship and service. She tells me to always serve Siphr well and never let him strike me. She is leaving me one-fourth of her jewels, and her favourite pendant."

"What about yours, Badr?"

Badr shook her head, weeping. "She thanks me for a lifetime of friendship and service too!"

"That fool...thanking me for a lifetime of friendship, as if thanks was ever necessary," Mihirunissa sobbed. "She gives me one-fourth of her jewels, and warns me never to let my husband abuse me; to continue writing poetry till I die. She entrusts her writings to me."

As the women wept openly, Zubdat ran into Zebunissa's chambers. Her belongings were placed in four neat piles for her sisters, but everything else was gone. Had she fled to the Deccan?

"Zubdat," said Mihirunissa, "with Zebunissa gone, will we be held responsible for her actions by Aba?"

"I do not know, nor do I care. I am tired of living in fear. If I am held responsible for her actions, it will be my honour."

"And I," said Badrunissa.

"Do not worry," admonished Zubdat. "Zebunissa would never let us take the blame for her. She has a plan." Zubdat wiped away her tears. "She always has a plan."

***

It was chilly but the morning glow of the sun painted the wide marble pillars so they looked as if they were made not of white marble but gold. Aurengzeb sat on his Peacock Throne while the nobles stood at the foot of the marble platform that elevated him. Rajputs were no longer present at court; their attendance no longer required by Aurengzeb. The harem women watched the proceedings from behind the marble screens behind the Emperor.

The *mullahs* were aware something important was to occur, that someone was to face punishment. Rumours had begun circulating that the Emperor had found the culprit behind the recent rebellion; that it was someone within the royal household. Though expecting to see the imprisonment or execution of one of the royal Princesses, neither the *mullahs* nor the nobility knew the identity of the wretched soul facing Aurengzeb's impending wrath.

The official court announcer announced, "Empress Zebunissa Begum is summoned to appear before the Emperor!"

The Makhfi looked at one another, uncertain what to do. Should they tell the Emperor Zebunissa had fled and left her belongings to them? Would it implicate them in the plan, bringing their father's wrath upon them in place of Zebunissa? Frightened, they stood in silence.

The call was made again: "Empress Zebunissa Begum is summoned to appear before the Emperor!"

Silence shrouded the *Diwani-i-Khas*, followed by muted chatter as the gathering wondered where the Empress was.

Aurengzeb's eyes surveyed the pillared hall, wondering where his daughter could have gone. No one ever disobeyed a summons from the Emperor. Had someone warned her of what awaited her? "Zubdat, Mihirunissa, Zinat, Badrunissa…I command you to appear before me!" Aurengzeb's voice was stern, though a shadow of its former thunder.

The four Princesses began to weep as the Tatar guards motioned them to move away from the screen and go down to stand before the Emperor. They knew they had no choice; it was an imperial command. Hanging their heads low, they stood huddled together before the Emperor, veiled and fearful.

"Where is your sister?"

Eyes riveted to the marble floor, the sisters shook their heads from side to side in wretched misery.

"Look at me when I speak to you!" The women raised their heads and lifted their eyes, trembling with fear.

"Your faces and your silence betray you! I know you have answers! Tell me or I will have you all executed!"

"Majesty, we do not know," pleaded Zubdat. "We had our evening meal together and found out later that she had gone, leaving us some of her belongings. We know no more…"

"You lie!"

"Majesty!" interjected Badrunissa. "We have no knowledge of where she went and when. She hid her secrets from us."

"But you knew she was working with that traitor Akbar!"

The women froze for a moment, each pondering whether to lie and uphold the Makhfi pact, or tell the truth and incur their father's wrath.

Mihirunissa stepped forward. "Majesty, we knew nothing! We discovered she had been helping Prince Akbar very recently. We tried to stop her but she threatened to have us all killed!"

The other three sisters stared at Mihirunissa, their eyes filled with disgust and rage.

But Mihirunissa did not look at them. She knew there was only one way to save herself; to deny all knowledge and betray Zebunissa's trust. "We tried to send word to you but she had spies everywhere, even with you in Rajasthan. We feared her wrath in your absence."

Zubdat, Badrunissa and Zinat stopped weeping, enflamed by their sister's betrayal. They stare at her with anger and loathing.

Aurengzeb's hooded gaze saw it all; Mihirunissa pleading for understanding and his other three daughters staring at her in speechless rage. He felt sadness stir in his heart; an emotion he had long forgotten. Raising his head he said, "Mihirunissa, when we find Zebunissa Begum, what is the punishment you deem fit?"

Mihirunissa took one step back. "Majesty…I…" she stammered looking towards her sisters for support. On their faces she saw the shame of her betrayal. Quickly she raised her face towards her father and said, "I…I do not know."

"You do, Mihirunissa. Listen to the voice that speaks within you. You are a Mughal Princess; your whole life has been spent in court. You have seen and heard judgements passed. Now tell me what punishment befits your sister's actions." For a moment Aurengzeb smiled, enjoying pitting one sister against another. "Should I perhaps show mercy?"

Mihirunissa cowered as the Emperor spoke, knowing his words were rooted in sarcasm. She nodded her head.

"Or should I have her executed like that wretch Dara, so many years ago? I could present her head at your next Makhfi meeting."

The four women looked at the Emperor in horror. How did he know about the Makhfi, and how much did he know? Did he know of the cryptic messages in the poems, that they were all involved in not one but several Makhfi plots, as were Prince Muazzam, Prince Akbar, and Aqil Khan? How much did he know?

"Zubdat, you were closest to Zebunissa of all of her sisters. You tell me what I should do. Should I grant her mercy, imprison her for life, or execute her?"

Zubdat swallowed and composed herself. Taking a step forward, she said confidently on Zebunissa's behalf, "Majesty, you should…"

"Execute her!" declared a woman's voice.

The crowd turned in the direction of the voice. It was Zebunissa, dressed all in white, adorned only with a single necklace of glowing pearls. The crowd looked on in hushed silence as Aurengzeb stared at his favourite child, bereft of speech.

Zebunissa bowed. "Majesty, all you have said is true. There was a secret poetic society to which I and my sisters, as well as certain distinguished poets, nobles and scholars, belonged. We met secretly for many years. We recited poetry and celebrated our love for the arts. But we never discussed politics. The Makhfi's realm was poetry, not politics. I decided many years ago to overthrow you and instate my brother Akbar as Emperor. But I acted alone. I knew I could trust only myself in such an undertaking." Zebunissa looked at Mihirunissa, who turned away, sobbing.

"Prince Akbar and I are the rebels you seek; there are no others. I have cleared my chambers and am ready to become your prisoner. I accept whatever punishment you wish to impose."

Aurengzeb looked at Zebunissa as she stared up at him fearlessly. He had not expected her to appear in court and admit to everything she had done. None of his many foes had ever, so courageously, accepted their role against him. Yet here she was, his most beloved child, admitting everything she had done, preparing to become his prisoner. For long moments he sat in silence, remembering the child he had loved for her sharp wit, her ready intelligence, her gift of grace. How had he failed to see the hatred in her eyes?

Zebunissa spoke again. "Majesty, there is one last matter. Here is the *Muhr Uzak*, the Royal Seal. I no longer have use for it. Give it to Mihirunissa. She is a loyal daughter and will always do as you say."

Sadullah Khan stepped forward and took the heavy seal in his hands.

Aurengzeb raised his head, his eyes glittering as of old. Nothing and no one was above the Throne. "I hereby pronounce that Zebunissa Begum is convicted of treason and sedition, of plotting to overthrow the Emperor. She is hereby sentenced to imprisonment for life!" He nodded to the guards to arrest the daughter he had loved above all.

The women of the harem and Zebunissa's beloved sisters began to weep inconsolably. Even the nobles in attendance wiped away their tears as the proud Empress was escorted to prison.

## 29
## SALIMGARH

*Long is thine exile, Makhfi, long thy yearning,*
*Long shalt thou wait, thy heart within thee burning.*

6 JUNE 1684

Zebunissa was sentenced to life imprisonment at Salimgarh Fort. Her new home had once been a palace before the Mughals invaded India. When her ancestors had begun to build more lavish palaces for themselves, this one had fallen into neglect and ruin. Aurengzeb had converted it into a prison. Here he had held his brothers Dara and Murad, before executing them.

No such fate awaited Zebunissa; her life had been spared. Her cell was more elegant than most people's homes. She had beautiful tapestries on her walls, golden cushioned furniture, and amenities such as mirrors and make-up. She also had her own servants and a *hammam* for bathing. However, she was not permitted to go out and correspondence to and from the cell was regulated. Thus, she could never write to Akbar nor was it safe for him to write to her.

As she sat at her low table, trying to complete the poem she was composing, she heard a familiar voice call her name: "Zebunissa!"

Putting her inked quill down on the table, she rose and quickly walked to the prison door. "Zubdat!" she cried joyfully.

"How are you, sister?" Zinat asked as Badrunissa and Zinat stood beside her, tears in their eyes.

Zebunissa merely smiled and asked, "What are you doing here?"

"We asked the Emperor for permission to see you several months ago, but you know how Aba is." The Tartar guard accompanying them threw them a look of warning. In Salimgarh the wall had eyes and ears. "We were told yesterday that we had been permitted to visit you, just this once."

The guard moved away, disinterested in the sister's idle chatter. The prison door remained shut.

"Where is Mihirunissa?" Zebunissa asked. "She did not come?"

It was Zubdat who said, "We asked her to come but the truth is she feels too ashamed. Aba has made her the Empress."

"And how is she handling her new role?"

Badrunissa smiled. "Like a loyal soldier!"

There was a moment's silence, then Zubdat said, "Zebunissa, I do not know if we will ever meet again. I feel compelled to ask you, before it is too late, one final question: How did you know Aba was coming for you?"

Zebunissa smiled in resignation, as if the answer no longer mattered. "I told you, I have spies everywhere. I *had* spies everywhere… Now my world is reduced to this small cell."

"What do you do all day?" asked Badrunissa, sadly.

Zebunissa smiled, dark circles shadowing her grey eyes. "I write."

"Write? They permit you to write?"

"Yes, my sisters, I write to keep the Makhfi alive. One day, long after we are all gone, our writings will remain and tell the ages that even in this time, when all forms of art was banned, there were a few who dared to write and promote the arts, even though it meant risking our lives to do it."

The women clasped hands through the bars that separated them for eternity. Zubdat began to weep, tears rolling down her face.

"Why are you crying, silly one?" inquired Zebunissa.

"I...I just wish we had not lost! All that work...a lifetime of planning... all gone to waste."

"No!" corrected Zebunissa. "Nothing went to waste! We fought, and we won! We showed our father that even though he forced his will on us, he could not change who we were. We...his children…all turned on him. We filled his zealot home with music and laughter, poetry and song. We showed him no army could stop us. If he imprisoned one, another would rise against him. He knows that now. He knows he will die alone, never having conquered our hearts."

"And what of Akbar?"

Zebunissa paused, looking away. "Akbar has to chart his own course. I can no longer guide him." She smiled sadly. "Tell Mihirunissa not to soil her heart with shame and regret. I harbour no ill feelings towards her. I have nothing but the fondest memories."

"Has Aba written or spoken to you since the imprisonment?"

"No, he refuses to write or speak to me. I too, have not reached out to him. I know my betrayal pierced him more surely than any sword or spear." Zebunissa looked at her sisters, chin held high. "I am glad about that."

1686

Zebunissa had been in prison for five years, filling her time with writing poetry, never wasting a minute. It was as if she kept pouring ingredients into a boiling pot, watching it bubble to life.

"Mirza Khan is here to see you, Princess." The guards had been instructed not to refer to her as Empress, only as a State prisoner. Nevertheless, the guards and her servants called her Princess, so as not to rob her entirely of her royal identity.

"My love," Zebunissa whispered as a sunken, lined face of Aqil Khan appeared beyond the bars of her door. He had long recovered from his illness though he looked much more frail now.

"Forgive me..." she said, tears filling her eyes.

"No!" he said sharply, shaking his head. "Forgive *me*, my love. I failed you."

Zebunissa wept as if letting go of a lifetime of sorrow. Was it the sorrow of losing Aqil, of never being able to hold him, of never being able to acknowledge him and Akbar as her family? Perhaps it was the sorrow of knowing their companionship had not triumphed against a ruthless despot bent on imposing his narrow world view on others.

"Had I not become ill on my journey, taken greater care to see Akbar, your note would have been delivered directly to him and our plan would have succeeded."

"I know. But you could not foretell your illness. It was because of you that I found out what had happened in time to settle my personal matters. It was you who told me my father had learnt the truth and was marching on Delhi to imprison me."

"When my health improved, Akbar had fled with the Rajputs. It was too late for me to help our son."

"You did the right thing. By staying with my father, you were able to see what he was seeing."

"I wanted to break that wretch Jani's neck when she took your letter to your father, but I was helpless. If I had protested, he would have known I was with you and killed me instantly. I would never have been able to tell you that your father knows the truth."

"And if I had not learned the truth from you, I would not have been able to sort out my affairs in time."

There was a pause as the two stared and one another, tears in their eyes, smiles on their lips.

"Why did you not run?" Aqil's voice shook with emotion.

"That is not who I am," she admonished. "Besides, where would I have gone? My own son is on the run, seeking refuge with the Marathas, the Rajputs, anyone who will take him in. Where would I have taken refuge? As a woman, who would have protected me?"

"I would have," Aqil responded, his mouth stern.

"I know…" She caressed his face through the bars that forever separated them. "But who would have protected you? Akbar needs at least one parent he can go to if the need arises."

"But this..." Aqil looked around him. "You expect me to accept you living like this?"

"Not accept, but I ask you to be patient." Aqil stared at Zebunissa as her voice took on its usual firm tone. "One day he will die, and when he does, our son will be Emperor, and I will be free. I will fill this kingdom with art and poetry. My books will be printed in every realm of the dominion and the present will be but a minor stain in the greater history of our people. The Makhfi will live again, Aqil! Just be patient."

Aqil put two fingers to his mouth and then placed them gently on Zebunissa's lips. She closed her eyes, recalling their union years ago.

"Go, my love. Do not visit me again. You will weaken my resolve with your tenderness. Help our son to fight."

Aqil nodded, tears flowing down his gaunt face. Turning, he walked away. Zebunissa wept silently, her eyes closed in agony. She covered her mouth with a trembling hand, fighting the overpowering urge to call his name…to see him return.

She went to bed early that night, feeling sad but relieved. It was as if a tremendous burden had been lifted from her shoulders. She slept peacefully. She knew Aqil would never disobey her wishes that he stay away from her. His presence weakened her resolve and she needed to stay strong as long as she was in captivity. Zebunissa knew she would never see Aqil again.

1701

"Princess, you have a visitor."

Zebunissa's old guard had died the previous year and the new one was more sympathetic to the ageing Princess. Perhaps fearing the wrath of Aurengzeb if he mistreated her, or a reconciliation between father and daughter, the young guard spoke kindly to his prisoner. Zebunissa now limped when she walked and her hair was as white as her clothing.

"My child, bring forward anyone who wishes to see this old lady. I have no say in the matter." As she limped to the prison door, she continued, "I told you, just allow anyone who wishes to see this poor old lady to come forward." Zebunissa limped to the door and grabbed hold of the bars with wrinkled, arthritic hands, peering down the corridor as far as her limited vision would allow. Much to her surprise, a short, hunchbacked shadow appeared.

The shadow too, walked with a limp, with the assistance of a cane. Emerging from the shadows, Zebunissa saw it was an old lady, her once lovely face now wrinkled and drawn. She appeared frail. Zebunissa wondered if it was one of her old maids who had come to visit her one final time before the end came.

"Empress," the old lady said in a familiar voice, bowing her head.

It had been a long time since anyone had addressed her so and Zebunissa looked at her visitor curiously. "Who are you? I do not recognize you though I have heard your voice before."

The woman, head bowed, murmured, "I have not been able to recognize myself for many years now, Empress."

"Raise your head," Zebunissa said gently. "And I am not the Empress. Calling me such may land you in the prison next to mine."

"No prison can be worse than the prison of my body," the women lamented, slowly raising her head and looking into Zebunissa's eyes.

Zebunissa's brows drew together. Who was this emaciated, seemingly ill woman? There was something about her that was strangely haunting, like a forgotten line of a poem… Zebunissa could see she had once had great beauty.

The woman said, "I am your culprit, Empress. I am the reason you are here. I am the cause of this kingdom's endless sorrows."

"Hush! Do not speak of such inauspicious things! You are delusional and will incur the Emperor's wrath for such words..."

"No punishment can be worse than what Allah has given me. Empress, it is I...Jani."

Zebunissa moved back in astonishment. She stared at the face before her, trying to find remnants of the fair skinned, chiseled beauty she remembered. Jani stared back, aware that Zebunissa was studying her face to confirm her identity.

"Jani! Why are you here?"

Jani rested her head wearily on the prison bars. "To beg for your forgiveness."

"Forgiveness for what?" Although Zebunissa knew of Jani's role in misleading Akbar, she feigned ignorance.

"It was I who intercepted the letter you sent for Akbar and then gave him wrong instructions, hoping to foil your plan. Later, after Akbar fled, it was I who went to the Emperor and handed him your letter. Were it not for me, Akbar would be Emperor today and you reclining in your palace rather than wasting away here!"

Zebunissa smiled. Aqil had learned of Jani's role long since and told Zebunissa, warning her and urging her to flee. But she had decided to face her father's judgement instead, knowing the wheel would inevitably turn. Looking at Jani now, she said, "Only Allah decides who will succeed and who will fail. Do not blame yourself."

"But I destroyed the Empire!"

"No, it was my father who destroyed the Empire. You merely fought against your rival, as harem women do. Jani, you and I were Aunt Jahanara's most loved nieces. Her love spoiled us. When she left you all of her wealth, I felt jealous because I thought she had loved you more than me. It was childish. I did not realize that she left you more because, unlike me, you had no father and needed more than I did. It was only much later that I understood that she wanted you taken care of as well as I was. But I never understood why you resented me."

Jani stared at Zebunissa helplessly. "Because of Aqil!"

"Aqil?"

"I loved Aqil, and I knew he loved you. He rejected me for you. I married Azam because the Emperor instructed me to, but my heart always belonged to Aqil."

"Look at us," said Zebunissa wryly. "We spent our lives hating each other; feeling rejected by those whom we thought cared for the other one more!" Zebunissa covered Jani's hands with her own. She leaned forward and said, "I forgive you, Jani. Do not carry any burden in your heart."

Jani gave a convulsive sob. "Empress, I thank you. I can die now..."

"Die?"

"A few years ago I found a growth in my right breast. A *firangi* doctor in Delhi, Dr. Martin, asked if he could examine me. I did not allow it as he ate pork and drank wine. I did not want to be touched by him. But the growth grew bigger and has spread to my other breast. I am told all my energy goes to feed this growth and there is no cure. I wanted to see you before I die, to atone for my sins."

Zebunissa sighed. Had there ever been love and laughter in this life? All she could remember was pain. "Go in peace, Jani. There is no need for atonement. Only Allah decides who has sinned. Do not punish yourself."

As Jani slowly left the prison, Zebunissa looked away, shedding tears and lamenting the plight of a woman she had hated. She knew she would never truly forgive Jani, but she did not wish to deny a dying woman some peace.

1702

Zebunissa died quietly in her sleep on 26 May 1702. As if knowing the end was near, she told her guard, whom she affectionately called 'My Child', to sleep well, for there was no fear she would escape the next morning. Akbar was in Persia when the news of her death reached him; Aurengzeb was in the Deccan. No State funeral was organized, nor was a day of mourning observed. The few remaining members of the Makhfi mourned in private. Zebunissa, Mughal Princess and

Empress, was buried in a modest tomb, with none but the gravesmen to see her make her final journey.

Empress Mihirunissa ordered Zebunissa's cell be sealed and left undisturbed. Aurengzeb, away in the Deccan, did not care to overturn her order. He continued to wither away in the years that followed and, as Zebunissa had predicted, died a frail and lonely man, convinced he had been a failure. He begged his sons not to quarrel over the throne, but to no avail. With Akbar having died in 1705, in Persia, the contenders were the three Princes, Muazzam, Azam and Kam Baksh, Aurengzeb's son from a concubine.

Muazzam defeated Azam, who was too demoralized to fight after the death of his wife, Jani. Kam Baksh too, was slain. Muazzam thus became the next Mughal Emperor of India, adopting the name Bahadur Shah. In the spirit of the Makhfi, he attempted to repair the strained ties with the Rajputs, but it was too late. With Aurengzeb's death, the long period of cultural and political decline culminated in the disintegration of the Empire. And in 1739, the Emperor of Persia, Nadir Shah, invaded Delhi, slaying thousands of its residents and looting the riches of the Mughals.

The once vast Mughal Empire was now reduced to the city of Delhi, with the Mughal Emperor but a figurehead. With its riches gone and glory lost, the later Mughals were a patchwork of minor rulers whose reigns sometimes lasted years and sometimes just months. But it no longer mattered. They had no power to execute any of their wishes.

1752

Two soldiers walked cautiously down the dark damp corridor, torches in hand. Moisture dripped from cracks in the stone ceiling. One of the men ran his hand along the wall, feeling for any indentations that would indicate a hidden treasure room.

Suddenly he halted. "Look at this!" He called to his companion, raising his torch. "There is stone everywhere else but this area has bricks. I bet there is hidden treasure behind this wall!" The soldier's voice was rough with excitement.

The two men looked at one another with glowing eyes, intoxicated by the possibility of untold wealth on the other side of the brick wall. Pulling short axes from their belts, they began chipping away at the brickwork. Bit by bit, the stones began coming loose, strengthening the soldiers' resolve. Eventually the wall collapsed to reveal a rusted metal barred door. The men looked at each other in bewilderment. Together, they pushed at the door, using their combined weight. Again and again they threw themselves at the door. Eventually, with a weary sigh, the door collapsed.

The men stood up and walked gingerly into the dusty chamber. Looking around, they noticed a dusty but beautifully carved low bed in one corner, and a grimy, gem encrusted mirror with a handle of gold. One of the soldiers picked up the mirror, wiping it with his hand. Crystal clear glass appeared under the thick grime and he saw his own disheveled and exhausted image.

"It seems to me that someone powerful lived here even though this place looks like a damp prison. Look at this!"

The other soldier nodded, disappointed that the chamber seemed to have nothing else of value. "But where are the jewels? They must have tried to hide something! Must be why they sealed it off."

"Come here!" The first soldier called, bent over a low wooden desk, beautifully carved with leaves and vines. Lifting the lid, he saw sheaves of old parchment.

"What is it?" asked his companion, hoping for coins.

"It's a note from the former Empress Mihirunissa. It says: *Behold, here is the Diwan-i-Makhfi, composed by the Empress Zebunissa from the years 1658-1702.*"

"1658 to 1702? But for the Mughals, those were the dark years. Poetry and the arts were outlawed."

The soldiers began rummaging through the pile, reading poem after poem, composed by Zebunissa. The papers included work from before her imprisonment as well as compositions during her captivity. It seemed to the soldiers that Mihirunissa had gathered them into a book, left to be found long after her father had passed from this earth.

"So during those years, poetry was flourishing in Hindustan?"

"It seems so. Perhaps Aurengzeb was not as successful in eradicating the arts as he imagined. Despite his ban, there were obviously poets and writers. This proves it."

"Let's take this to the Commander. He is a lover of the arts. Maybe he will reward us with gold coins!"

"Splendid idea!" It was not the wealth they had hoped for but perhaps the Commander would give them enough for a round of drinks at the tavern.

The soldier carefully picked up the pile of parchment, tied together with string. The pages had hardened and become brittle; any attempt to fold them would have resulted in them falling apart. Carrying their dubious treasure, the soldiers walked out of the chamber where the writings had been interred for over half a century. "Come on, Makhfi!" said one of the men light-heartedly. "Let's get you out of this dungeon. You've been imprisoned long enough!"

## Reader-Author Q&A

- WHAT MADE YOU WRITE THIS BOOK?

After *Mistress of the Throne* was published, I was inundated with emails requesting a second edition. Having already covered most of Jahanara's life, I chose to write a sequel that revolved around another Mughal Princess, who, like Jahanara, was her father's favourite, and who, at one point, bore the title of Empress. The chief difference between the two was that while Jahanara fought for her father's survival and for his reign, Zebunissa plotted to overthrow hers. That she started her own secret poetic society with her sisters intrigued me because the existence of the Makhfi is rarely mentioned in Mughal history. But the role Aurengzeb's own children played in resisting his authoritarian policies and fomenting rebellion, was worth learning and writing about. Thus, I made the focus of this sequel Aurengzeb and his children, specifically his most beloved child, Zebunissa.

- HOW MUCH OF THE HIDDEN ONE IS FACT AND HOW MUCH FICTION?

There is more fiction in this book than there was in *Mistress of the Throne*, because very little has been written about Zebunissa and the Makhfi. In constructing this book, I used the same methodology I used in my other book: First I made an outline of what is known and then I filled the gaps with my own conjecture of what might have happened between two different points of fact, to cause the course of history to go from one point to the other. Thus, we know Zebunissa was Aurengzeb's most beloved child, so we start the book with her being his most ardent defender. We also know that she was engaged to Sulaimon, who was executed, and shortly thereafter Zebunissa turned on her father. Thus, I created a narrative in which Sulaimon is tortured in the most inhumane manner and Zebunissa visits him in prison shortly before his execution, using this fictionalized account to explain her metamorphosis from loyal daughter to the rebel Princess. We also know she was betrothed to Prince Farouk of Persia, and that he tried to compose poetry to impress her. We also know Aurengzeb sought a liaison with the Persian Empire to wrest control of Kandahar from the Persians. Shortly after the engagement collapsed, he suffered a stroke and was on the verge of death for some time. Did the failed engagement have something to do with the stroke? Here, I exercised poetic license to show these events were linked and Zebunissa orchestrated events to accomplish her larger goal of overthrowing her father.

In another instance, Raushanara's ascendency as Empress after Aurengzeb gained the throne, is a well documented fact. She also engineered a plot to have Azam sit on the throne when Aurengzeb fell ill, and was ultimately executed for this. How did Zebunissa feel about Raushanara? Here there is a gap in the facts, but assuming she began to detest her father, it is likely she also detested Raushanara as well, since both possessed similar qualities of intolerance and greed. Thus, the chapters focusing on Aurengzeb's illness were devoted to the infighting between Zebunissa and Raushanara.

The rebellions of Muazzam, and later Akbar, are well documented in history, but the role Zebunissa and the Makhfi played are not. Could individual brothers and sisters have been fomenting their own independent rebellions without any knowledge or collusion with one another? I took the liberty of showing that the historical record of small independent revolts against Aurengzeb, be it by Muazzam or Akbar, were linked through central coordination by the Makhfi.

It is believed that Zebunissa had had a brief affair with a man named Aqil Khan, but how long such a liaison lasted or whether there were any progeny born of it, remains unclear. Thus, I opted to expand on this little known fact and use it to give more depth to the rebellion being fomented by the Makhfi.

Lastly, we know Zebunissa was eventually exposed and imprisoned for the rest of her days. Rather than present this episode as a defeat, I have tried to show Zebunissa as strong and resilient through her final years. I also had some of the major characters visit Zebunissa in prison (not recorded in history), to bring closure to different story lines presented in the book – her feud with Jani, her relationship with Aqil, her final moments with her sisters.

That her writings were discovered years after her death is a fact but how they were discovered remains unclear. Thus, I tried to merge the decline of the Empire by showing soldiers searching for riches, presumably after an invasion that ran deep into the capital city of Delhi, which is where Zebunissa was imprisoned. These men find the collection of poems and take them back to their leader, thus setting Zebunissa free and fulfilling her own prophecy that the writings would live on after all others had perished. The discovery allowed her work to become widely available to all.

- WHY HAVE YOU PORTRAYED JANI BEGUM IN A NEGATIVE LIGHT?

There is not much written about Jani Begum. Here is what we know: She was the beloved daughter of Dara. After his death, Jani accompanied Jahanara and Shah Jahan into captivity in the Red Fort, presumably sent there by Aurengzeb, to escape 'abuse' from Raushanara. After Shah Jahan's death, Aurengzeb had Jani marry his son Azam, with whom she had a long marriage. Jahanara openly stated Jani was her most beloved niece and left her all of her jewels. Jani herself died in old age, presumably from breast cancer. This is where the historical record ceases. Constructing an entire life story of a person from such limited information was daunting. Additionally, it is well chronicled by travellers and historians that the Mughal harem was a hotbed of jealousy and infighting. Thus, rather than construct Zebunissa and Jani into two dimensional 'good/bad' roles, I tried to give them both the very human emotion of jealousy – Zebunissa because Jani was Jahanara's favourite, and Jani's about Aqil. In doing so, I hoped to avoid creating the Dara-Jani lineage as 'good', relegating the Aurengzeb-Zebunissa lineage to 'evil'. Both women were products of their circumstances and this was reflected in their attitudes. I wrote a final scene in which the two come together to bring closure to their disputes so the reader walks away with a sense of sympathy for both women, who, through no fault of their own, found themselves caught in difficult circumstances.

- HOW DID YOU RESEARCH THE MAIN PROTAGONIST, ZEBUNISSA?

There isn't much written about Zebunissa. For reference, two books were used to obtain the bulk of the information: *The Peacock Throne* by Waldemar Hansen and *Captive Princess: Zebunissa, Daughter of Aurengzeb* by Annie Krieger Krynicki. Both books give non-fictional accounts of Zebunissa and the Mughal Empire during the time period covered in this book. I also used English translations of the *Diwan-i-Makhfi* to find and quote certain poems of the Makhfi.

- SEVERAL CHARACTERS FROM MISTRESS OF THE THRONE MAKE A SHORT APPEARANCE IN THIS BOOK AS WELL. WHY DID YOU BRING THEM BACK?

*The Hidden One* purposely doesn't begin precisely at the point where *Mistress of the Throne* left off because by the time Shah Jahan died (the ending of *Mistress of the Throne*), the rebellion against Aurengzeb was well underway, with some key characters such as Raushanara already executed. To begin the book from this point would have required a massive flashback during which many scenes and conflicts would have to be told retrospectively, with the ending already known to the reader (an unfortunate element of any flashback). Thus, I chose to begin the book from when Aurengzeb wins the war of succession and also show the gradual evolution of Zebunissa from beloved daughter to vengeful rebel. Additionally, I still wanted to show what effect the execution of Dara had on Zebunissa, and the role Jahanara played up to her very end in protesting Aurengzeb's policies. Thus, I opted to bring both characters back to bring closure to their lives and also give them their due in the story of the Makhfi rebellion.

## Acknowledgements

There are countless people responsible for writing this book. While the first book in this series, *Mistress of the Throne*, was made possible by the unwavering support of my family, this sequel was also made possible by the collective support of the readers themselves. Had it not been for the countless emails asking for a sequel, it may have been left unwritten. The readers were the driving force behind this book.

I also want to thank again the members of the Long Island Writer's Guild, for their helpful comments with different parts of the book.

Finally, I thank the one person who, in the midst of her own hectic schedule, took the time to read the manuscript cover-to-cover, and edit it heavily – my wife Supurna.

## Wish To Publish With Us?

We are always keen to look at interesting content across genres. Please email your submission to: **submissions@leadstartcorp.com**

The submission should include the following:

1. **Synopsis**
   A summary of the book in 500 - 1000 words. Please mention the word count of the manuscript.

2. **Sample chapters / Poetry**
   A couple of chapters from the book; these need not be in order, just send the best two chapters of the book. Or a few poems if the same is a collection of poetry.

3. **A Note About The Author**
   An interesting note about yourself (about 200 words).

4. **Additional Information**
   - Target audience
   - Unique selling proposition
   - List of illustrative content (if any)
   - Other comparative titles
   - Your thoughts on marketing the book